THE
RIG

Also by John Collee

Kingsley's Touch
A Paper Mask

THE
RIG

John Collee

WILLIAM MORROW AND COMPANY, INC.
New York

Library of Congress Cataloging-in-Publication Data

Collee, John.
   The rig / John Collee.
      p.   cm.
   ISBN 0-688-11482-2
   I. Title.
PR6053.0423R54   1992
823'.914—dc20   91-40664
                                                                        CIP

Pringed in the United States of America

First U.S. Edition

1 2 3 4 5 6 7 8 9 10

BOOK DESIGN BY LISA STOKES

*To the men of Rig 2 and Rig 55,
especially* GENE HOUSE, *who, one
evening near Besisike, in Madagascar,
gave me the idea for this story*

PART
ONE

Chapter 1

A crowd had gathered along one edge of the airstrip, grouped by the side of the open, palm-thatched hut that was intended, though never used, as a waiting room. Farther back, on the edge of the forest, stood a group of nomads, on whom the significance of the event was lost. Their naked children had never seen a plane before and were mesmerized by the tiny diamond that suddenly appeared far to the east.

The diamond grew and sparkled, remaining indeterminate in form even when its engines became audible over the cicadas. Then another noise distracted them, and the children scuttled for cover. Two GMC pickups were approaching through the stunted citrus trees, sun glinting off the smoked-glass windows. They drew up on the edge of the laterite strip and disgorged their cargo of fair-skinned men—huge, confident men in jeans and high-heeled boots. One by one they jumped to the ground, swinging their suitcases easily over the tailgate.

The African teenager called Martine shaded her eyes against the sun. She was trying to recognize her lover, Ben, but in their caps and sunglasses the Canadians often looked the same to her. Above them the plane came roaring over the treetops, wriggling into the line of approach to land, splay-footed on the baked runway. When she looked back, Ben had taken off his trucking cap and was coming toward her, striding through the crowds of well-wishers with his leather carryall in his hand.

She had put on lipstick specially and washed herself with peanut soap. She was wearing the tortoiseshell earrings he liked. It worried her that he didn't smile. As she reached up to kiss him, he put an arm around her shoulders and steered her away. "Martine. I have to give you something."

They walked to the edge of the airstrip, then beyond it. Twice he glanced over his shoulder. She had a thorn in her foot and was beginning to find his anxiety infectious. When she stopped to adjust her sarong, he kept plowing on. Behind them the plane had already taxied back. The few incoming passengers had disembarked. Suitcases were being loaded. The Canadians were saying their last farewells.

"Quickly, honey."

She turned again and followed him, ducking under the branches, until, satisfied that they were out of sight, he stopped and rummaged in his carryall.

"Ben!" someone shouted in the distance.

In the depths of his bag, Ben Lowers had found what he was looking for. "See this, Martine?"

She was still hoping for a good-bye present and was disappointed when he handed her a bulky package. "I want you to send it to me."

"Send it to you?" she repeated. It seemed an unusual request. He was flying straight home, and the post was notoriously unreliable. Around them the cicadas fizzed and rattled.

"Take it down the post office and post it to me when I've gone, okay? It's got my address on it."

"You can't take it with you?"

"I can't take it with me. All it needs is stamps."

"Ben!" The voice in the distance was more urgent this time. *"Malak, malak!"* It was Malagasy for "hurry up," part of the argot of the rig workers.

"I hear you!" he yelled back. His voice sounded tight and

strange to her. Martine weighed the package in her hands.

"It's just paper," he said. "Just some documents, okay?" He pressed a Canadian banknote in her hand. "For your family," he said. "I'll send more. You're beautiful. I'll write."

She let him kiss her.

"Plane's going, Ben!"

He ran off. Martine sat down on a stone to attend to the thorn in her toe.

As she emerged from the trees, they had already closed the passenger door. The townsfolk stood, waving and shouting, as they had waved and shouted to the Israeli citrus planters, to the Swiss Forestiers and the German eye doctors. The West came and went. Africa remained.

The Twin Otter taxied to the end of the runway, turned, then raced back, lifted, settled, lifted again, then roared over their heads, already banking back toward the capital.

Martine watched in silence as the wings settled and the plane turned its rear on them. She was already turning away when a shout brought her attention back to the plane, now waving and rolling in the sky like a bird hooked on a fishing line. Something separated and fell flashing toward the treetops. The plane was tumbling out of the sky. Now it cartwheeled onto its back and disappeared into the trees.

Almost as the first shock wave came bowling toward them, Martine began to rethink her future. There seemed little chance now that Ben would be sending her any more money. Neither would he have any need for his parcel. It was a very heavy parcel—a kilogram at least. She didn't know how much it would cost to send it to Canada—ten thousand francs Malgache, maybe more. Her family could live for two months on that much. Amid wailing and lamenting, the noise of whistles and car engines, she stood, hugging it to her chest. The Canadian banknote was still crumpled in her palm. Under the circumstances it seemed a shame to waste it on postage stamps.

★ ★ ★

The plane crashed at two-fifteen. Perpetude Peyrame was later able to attest to this with some confidence, because at two o'clock she had resumed a long-neglected habit—her afternoon date with Father Mitchell.

They had both resisted the general exodus in the direction of the airstrip, choosing instead to enjoy the unfamiliar tranquillity on the veranda of the Grand Hotel. In the two years since their first arrival, the Canadian oilmen had never learned to respect the siesta.

"The end of an era," said Father Mitchell.

Perpetude knocked her glass of grenadine against his and said, "The return to normal." She had spent the morning settling bar bills and clearing the detritus from their last-night party: empty bottles of Three Horse beer, Marlboro packets, cassettes and broken glass in the dance hall, loose change and used condoms in the bedrooms. On the street beyond the veranda, the hotel's rubbish stood uncollected. Those nylon sacks had once held grain and still bore the misleading stenciled logo A GIFT FROM THE PEOPLE OF AMERICA.

"You're not expecting anyone off the plane?"

"Just one."

"Who's that?"

"No idea—he'll get a lift from someone."

Father Mitchell shook his head. He had always admired her casual attitude. Perpetude was métisse: half African and half French. She was thirty when he first arrived at the mission, but in the ten years since then she didn't seem to have aged. He watched her wipe the bloom of sweat off her throat and wondered guiltily if the pleasure he had long derived from her company was due to some vestige of the sex urge.

"What are you looking at?"

"At you. I've never understood why you stay on here."

Perpetude shrugged. "You think I'd rather live in 'Tana?"

She was joking. Antananarivo, the capital, was starved of rice these days, and news came back now of students demonstrating in the streets.

"Actually . . . " Father Mitchell laid his hand on hers. His own hand was a relief map of veins and sunspots. He seemed on the point of a minor confession, when he closed his mouth abruptly. Simultaneously she felt the same thing: the odd impression that a ghost had boxed his ears and shoved him in the chest.

"What was that?" As he spoke, she was interrupted again by a roll of thunder from the far end of the street.

Magically the dusty white street acquired people. It happened like this each year at the beginning of the rains, as though the water had somehow fertilized the dormant seeds of the town's inhabitants. They emerged from the houses and Indian stores, from the mosque and the school and the shuttered gendarmerie. Policemen in their underwear, storekeepers' wives, bleary from sleep, gathering sarongs about their waists. They looked at the cloudless sky and then to the end of the main street, where now, above the ragged fringe of palms that bordered the town, there appeared a spiral of black smoke.

"The plane."

As they left the veranda, another blast, louder than the first, made Perpetude clutch at the railings. An egret rose squawking from the roof of the PTT. Father Mitchell was looking for his hat. Perpetude got into the jeep and fumbled with the broken end of the ignition key.

"Get in," she said.

As they negotiated the potholes in front of the courthouse, pedestrians waved frantically for them to stop. Perpetude slowed to a crawl, and in an instant the backseat was crammed with passengers. Everyone had a relative at the airstrip. Everyone had a question. Dust rose, filling the vehicle, swamping her lungs and sticking to her skin. Perpetude edged forward, shouting out of the window for children to keep clear of the wheels. Farther down the street the lieutenant of police began to flag her down also, then, abruptly self-conscious, ran inside instead to put on his trousers.

In the wet season the river would overflow its banks, and Morondava would be surrounded by a crescent of floodwater. Now, in the arid heat before the rains, the road crossed brilliant salt flats. The causeway, with its frayed pelt of tarmacadam, ran parallel with the sewage pipe. Beyond the salt flats, the shantytown started, mud and thatch dwellings clustered under the palms.

Tracks joined the road on either side. From each of these an impromptu cavalcade was already embarking in the direction of the airstrip. Barefoot children tried to keep pace with bicycles, *moto-vélos,* and overladen *taxis-brousses.* A dog ran, barking, onto the road. Perpetude swerved to avoid it, and the passengers in the back tumbled into each other. She found herself hating the Canadians. Ever since their arrival, they had been nothing but trouble. The first massive truck off the supply boat had pulled down the telegraph wires, leaving Morondava without telephone communications for a week. Finally this.

As the airstrip drew nearer, they passed a taxi coming back. The cars stopped opposite each other, and everyone started talking again. Two or three people changed vehicles. There had been a terrible accident. The plane had crashed. The Canadians were all dead.

"All?"

"Dear God," said Father Mitchell.

"*Vita.* Finish. All dead."

Suddenly embarrassed by her own meanness of spirit, Perpetude tried to reconjure the faces of some of the men. The blond Ukrainian with the moustache; the short, talkative one with glasses. Men with names of one syllable: Ron, Jack, Don, Mel. Every night for the past month they had taken over the bar in the hotel, buying bottles of Johnny Walker as fast as she could import them, drunkenly making passes at her and swapping photographs of children, wives, and ranch-style bungalows.

Villagers were catching up and trying to get in the jeep.

Perpetude told them there was no room, pulled away again, stalled, lurched forward.

They turned up the dirt track that led to the airstrip. In the sky up ahead the pall of smoke had grown and thickened, spreading at the top like an anvil.

This wasn't real, she told herself. This wasn't happening.

Smuts of soot gathered like insects on the windscreen. People were running toward them through the blighted citrus plantation. The passengers in the back craned forward in order to shout through the open window to their friends outside the car.

"*Qu'est-ce qui se passe? Qu'est-ce qui se passe?*"

People milled around the car. Perpetude pulled on the hand-brake. Everyone had an opinion. The plane was overloaded. It was not overloaded. The pilot had been drunk, the pilot had not been drunk, don't listen to this man, he wasn't even there. I tell you the plane was overloaded, there was an explosion, then it fell from the sky, there was no explosion.

In the center of the airstrip the commandant of police had gathered a large group around him and was offering a lengthy and unwarranted explanation of why the tragedy was not his fault. Father Mitchell interrupted him. Some decisions had to be taken. Where was Dr. Finartsoa? Someone should bring the ambulance. They would need to cut a path to the plane. They would need the army. There would be survivors. There would be no survivors.

Losing patience with this new round of debate, Perpetude set off across the airstrip. At the forest's edge a group of nomads in blankets and spears looked on in bewildered silence. She turned to the African boys around her and shouted for machetes. A few men ran back to their vehicles, but the majority plunged on regardless into the forest.

Father Mitchell and the chief of police were still locked in debate. Perpetude hitched up her cotton dress and pushed into the trees.

★   ★   ★

It was farther to the crash then she had anticipated. In the few seconds between taking off and falling out of the sky, the plane had traveled five or six kilometers, and here, under the canopy of trees, it was easy to lose one's direction. The boys ran ahead, barefoot over the flint and spear grass, crashing through the desiccated undergrowth. All the while the cicadas kept up their perpetual din.

Perpetude emerged, panting, into a tiny clearing, where an ancient baobab tree had disintegrated, creating a perfect circle of fallen branches. She brushed a twig from her hair. She was drenched in sweat, and her cotton dress was ripped. She could hear the others veering off course, bounding away to her right. She called to them and got no reply.

Reaching another clearing, she realigned herself on the pall of black smoke and headed back into the woodland. She crossed the dry bed of a river tributary, studded with bleached eucalyptus logs. She could hear wood exploding and trees falling. Smoke seeped through the trees from every direction. In the smoke and flying ashes above her head, the buzzards swooped and hovered, looking for lizards escaping the flames.

She called again, and one of the boys answered off to her right. She headed toward his voice and saw flames.

The plane had blasted a clearing for itself, the far side of which was still alight. Smoke wound between the trees, finding a route to the windless sky above. She could make out a wingtip, a piece of crumpled fuselage. With the smell of burning metal came long-forgotten memories of Paris, men in crash helmets with clubs. The barricades on the Avenue Foch.

The body of the plane lay like a crushed cigar tube among the splintered trees. If anyone had, by some miracle, survived the fall, they would surely have been consumed in that holocaust. Another tree toppled and crashed. The fuselage creaked and settled.

There were people around the outskirts of the clearing now.

Hanssen, from the sugar factory, was there, untypically silent. There was another European a few yards away, whom she didn't recognize. For a moment she assumed absurdly that this was one of the Canadians who had somehow survived the crash. Then she realized he wasn't one of the oilmen—this jaunty blond-haired man in football shorts, nipping in and out of the tree trunks for a better view. He was a tourist. He was her tourist.

He was taking photographs.

The heat from the burning forest kept them back until dusk, by which time the fire had burned itself out. One by one the watchers left the side of the waterhole and waded warily across its oily waters. The plane was a bent and blackened hulk. A door had burst open. They gathered around it—a grubby deputation, brushing away flies and slapping at mosquitoes. Those who saw into the tangled innards of the plane immediately regretted having looked. The tortured black shapes inside bore no resemblance to humans, except for the gashes of red where a charred limb or torso had split open.

At the airstrip bonfires were being built to guide in the army helicopters. Perpetude walked slowly back to her jeep. A smudge of black still hung in the windless air, above the forest, blotting out the sunset.

The tourist was standing by her jeep, waiting for her to return. He had already loaded his carryall into the back.

"You run the hotel here?"

She nodded.

"The name's Kirk," he said cheerfully.

He got in the jeep, and she drove him to the hotel in silence.

Alone in her room, she shampooed her hair twice, convinced, even after the soot and ash had been rinsed away, that the evil smell of carrion remained. She stood naked in the shower, trying to wash away the memory itself, until a voice outside told her the army were arriving. Five hours earlier she had raised her glass of grenadine to the end of an era. Now, stained, drained, and exhausted, she suddenly had the chilling premonition that this was only the beginning.

Chapter 2

Monsieur Velo-André Bakoutou-son, minister for mineral resources of the People's Republic of Madagascar, stood on the runway of Ivato International Airport and wished he were dead. The temperature had hit forty that morning, and the only cloud he could see was a tiny white scuff mark on the metallic rim of the sky.

Sweat was pouring out of him like warm water from a sponge, gathering under his suit in the cleft between his buttocks, trickling down the backs of his knees, and leaking through the laceholes of his black patent-leather shoes. He fingered the knot of his tie and eased the sweaty wristband of his watch, discreetly angling the dial so he could read it. Sunlight thundered off the stainless-steel coffins and the regimental brassware. A horsefly settled on his ear, then his eyebrow, then his nose. He slapped at it, and it moved along the line to torment the minister for culture.

The cortege continued, crawling at a snail's pace toward the waiting Hercules. Velo-André leaned forward in his waterlogged shoes and squinted along the line of sweating dignitaries—church leaders, cabinet ministers, generals, and ambassadors. Forty-three men and women shoulder to shoulder on the tarmac. At the end of the line a small canvas awning had been arranged to shelter the president of the republic and the

Canadian ambassador. The rest of them stood and suffered under the full weight of the heat.

The first of the coffins had still not reached the aircraft. Velo-André turned to see if the last had left the airport yet and noticed that the crowd behind him had grown. Half the population of Antananarivo seemed to be there, standing on the terminal's balcony or pressed against the wire-mesh perimeter fence. Happy, inquisitive people in sensible African clothes, crowding in to witness his final humiliation.

After all those months and years of meetings, planning, bargaining, and expenditure, the great oil exploration of the east coast had proved fruitless. He had planned for the last drilling crew to slip away quietly on a scheduled flight. But the crash of the charter plane had turned Velo-André's personal disappointment into an international spectacle. This tuneless Western funeral march was not just a lament for sixteen dead Canadians, it was a lament for five years of futile planning. And to many ears it was a death march for Rakoutouson's government.

Velo-André mopped sweat out of his eyes. The final coffin was loaded. The plane's huge maw closed like the mouth of a coral fish. The rotors began to turn, blowing hot air back across the runway, tugging like a critical fashion adviser at Velo-André's turn-ups and overlarge lapels. He watched until the plane was a speck on the horizon, then plodded back to the waiting cars.

The black leather upholstery inside the presidential Mercedes was crazed and cracked like the surface of an old painting. Velo-André eased himself across it, his shirt sticking uncomfortably to his back. The driver closed the door for him, then they nosed off through the departing crowds.

As soon as they were clear, they rolled down the tinted windows, let some air circulate through the car. It was dusty, overheated air, but it was air nonetheless. The president loosened his tie and mopped his face with his handkerchief.

"Do you have to do that, Velo?"

Velo-André had taken off his socks and was wringing them out through the open window. "I'm sorry," he said. "I know it's unpleasant."

"I'll tell you something more unpleasant." The president had switched from dialect into French, which the driver couldn't follow so easily. "I spoke to Istasse. He's calling an election in the spring."

"This spring?"

"Yes."

Claude Istasse, the head of the air force, had recently formed his own party within the Front National pour la Défence de la Révolution. They had been expecting a challenge from him, but not quite so soon.

"He told you that this morning?"

"Just before I left."

"He has a fine sense of timing."

"He's got a talent for publicity as well. His picture's on the front of next month's *Jeune Afrique*."

They passed a bullock cart with car tires, houses made of red mud and cow dung, peasants living in boxes on the dusty shoulders of the road.

"Well," Velo-André said, venturing a joke, "your picture's on the front of *Ici Madagascar*." *Ici Madagascar* was the official tourist brochure.

The president didn't smile. His short hair was turning gray, and there were thick creases at the corners of his mouth. He had aged over the years in office. Maybe they both had. Velo-André recognized then that he had reached one of those crucial moments when one has to grasp fate firmly by the neck or live in its shadow for the rest of one's life. "I've had an idea," he said.

In downtown Edmonton there were cars backed up 105th Street on both sides of Jasper Avenue. In front of the First Presbyterian

Church an outside broadcast van from CITV was blocking the inside lane. Spence drove on two blocks to the multistory carpark and came back on foot. He wasn't looking forward to the memorial service. The thing was a damned circus. It had taken him half a bottle of Jim Beam to decide to come at all. He could just about drive in a straight line, but walking was more difficult. He hadn't worn the suit since he got out of the hospital, and, unlike his working pants, it had not been adjusted to accommodate the shortening of his left leg. He tripped as he reached the curb, lost his walking stick, and grabbed, cursing, at a newspaper box for support. He could see the church another block away.

Steps were the worst. He'd found over the last three weeks that the quickest way to climb them was to lever himself up in reverse. The steps to the church were laced with camera cables. Most of them now converged on a man in his mid-forties—a couple of years older than Spence—confidently fielding questions from the crescent of lights and cameras below him. His straight blond hair would often blow across his face, and, between statements, he would sweep it back with an automatic gesture that probably looked good on TV. Spence assumed him to be a member of the administration. It seemed since the Madagascar crash that every politician in Edmonton had been freeloading on the publicity bandwagon.

Inside the church, people nodded to him and clasped his hand as he passed. Spence found a seat and squeezed in on the end of the pew, lifting his stiff leg with both hands to get it out of the aisle. The rows immediately in front of them were reserved for the bereaved wives and families: Bob Leoppky's widow, Tom Connolly's widow, Al Parachuik's brother and the twins.

Sitting, Spence half turned to steal a look around the rest of the congregation: thick-set, uncomfortable men drawn largely from Edmonton's drilling fraternity. Through McCabe Drilling, the Madagascar project had once employed two full-

time crews. Most of them were less familiar with the interior
of a church than they were with Chez Pierre's strip bar across
the road.

The organist struck a chord. As he stood, Spence glanced
at the opposite aisles and suddenly found himself looking directly at his ex-wife, Nancy. Her coat collar was pulled up to
her neck. She still had the heartbreaking freshness of a high
school cheerleader. She looked up briefly, met his eyes, and
immediately became preoccupied with the black silk handbag
she was carrying. Whenever she was excited or embarrassed, a
circle of color appeared in the center of each cheek, like a child's
doll or the mannequins in Eaton's.

She must have whispered something to the man beside her,
because he leaned forward, then back again, out of sight. She'd
come here with Clyde. They'd come here together.

The minister had arrived in the pulpit.

"Dearly beloved," he was saying, "we are gathered here
together to pay tribute to the many fine men, husbands, and
fathers, who perished so tragically . . . "

There was more—some poetic baloney about foreign
fields—but Spence heard almost none of it. He could hear nothing but his own breathing. Nancy and Clyde. Clyde and Nancy.
Their presence was a constant distraction, like a bright light just
outside his range of vision.

" . . . lives cruelly ended in their prime, families torn asun-
der . . . "

Were they holding hands over there? Spence could no
longer hear the service. When the others got up again to sing,
he couldn't follow the words, and when they all bowed their
heads in a semblance of prayer, he couldn't concentrate on the
dead men. He was thinking of Nancy. This everyday nightmare, this familiar madness.

The preacher stopped talking, and now the soloist in the
choir started singing—the kind of song that made everyone
blow their noses. Spence leaned forward and groped for his

stick. He snared it with a finger and managed to push himself
onto his feet. He hopped and hobbled down the aisle and pushed
through the glass doors into the lobby. He was suffocating. He
was drowning.

He shouldered aside the heavy church door and stepped
out into the glare and noise of 105th Street. A posse of reporters
was waiting at the foot of the steps. They looked up at him,
wondering if he were important enough to interview. Spence
headed off around the side of the church. Anywhere to get
away.

It was cold here, out of the sunlight. Spence stopped and leaned
back against the wall of the church. He could feel the freezing
brickwork through his coat and jacket. On the Baker Center
opposite, the temperature said minus ten. Workmen the size of
ants were bolting reindeers to the metal structure above it.

Spence closed his eyes and took a lungful of cold air.

"Spence?"

When he opened them, Cora Skipton was standing in front
of him.

"You okay?"

"Cora."

She was watching him with her hands in the pockets of
her black skirt. She wore a black jacket, and her eyes were
hidden with dark glasses.

"I couldn't face it either," she said. "You want to walk?"

He didn't, but she slipped her hand through his arm and
led him down 105th. She was a bright, athletic woman. At
school at the University of Alberta she'd been a pretty good
sprinter. They walked together past the Canadian Utilities
tower-block.

"I hear Dennis offered you a job," she said.

"Is that what he called it?"

"What do you call it?"

"I call it a piece of BS," Spence said. "Some sorry-ass rig
inventory back there in Madagascar."

"What's wrong with that?"

Spence didn't answer. Rig inventory was the job given to time-expired assistant drillers who were good for nothing else. You started taking rig inventory jobs and next thing you knew you were out on the back-lease, cleaning pipe threads with a rag soaked in paraffin.

"You got something better to do?" Cora asked.

"Sure, chores and stuff," he said vaguely.

"Because I just thought if you were to go out there—"

"I'm not."

Cora tidied up a strand of auburn hair. "That if you did, you could check up a couple of things."

"Check what?"

"The plane crash."

Spence smiled and shook his head. He'd heard this bullshit a week ago from Roy Duigid's widow. "The local air force looked it all over, and then those Norco guys went through all the findings and—"

"And they said stuff had been tampered with."

"They said things could have been better, but they pretty well proved what caused it."

"No, they didn't."

They had reached Jasper Avenue. Spence leaned against the fire hydrant outside Standard Life Mall, waiting for the lights to change.

"Forget it, Cora. What's past is past. You said that to me yourself enough times."

"This is different, Spence. Right until the accident no one here knew what the heck was going on over there. And then they laid everyone off. It just seems—"

"Seems what, Cora?"

The lights said WALK. They crossed the road. "It seems phony, that's all. I mean even before the crash. All this secrecy and then just suddenly dismantling the whole operation. I don't think Norco cared what happened to those guys. I don't know, maybe they weren't looking into safety too much. I just think if a guy's got the chance to go out there. Just to see what happened, huh?"

There was music playing from the outdoor speakers as they walked under the canvas awning of Beaver Hills House Park. Mirrored tower-blocks loomed above the trees: Royal Lepage, the Metropolitan Tower, the Ramada Renaissance Hotel.

Cora took off her sunglasses, blew her nose, and turned her clear blue eyes on him. "I'd go out there myself if it wasn't for the boys," she said.

"You would?"

"Sure I would."

He looked for a laugh, but she didn't respond.

"Listen, Cora," he said. "I know what you're doing, and I appreciate it."

"What am I doing?"

"Cora." He tried to put his arm through hers again, but she pulled away. "You don't have to bullshit me, we've known each other too long. You're either trying to get me out of Nancy's hair or you're scared I'm going to slit my wrists. Either way you have to come up with a better play than this one."

"You think I'm doing that?" She had a delicate face. Now, in the glare of the autumn sun, it looked thinner. "You really think that's important to me?"

"Sorry, Cora. I just figured—"

"Let me tell you something, Spence." Suddenly, to his surprise, he saw that she was furious. "I lost a husband on that two-bit operation, and you lost a damn fine friend. I'm up there at Slave Lake trying to work the hog farm on my own, trying to keep it together. I don't mind that you haven't been up to see me since you got out of the hospital. You've had problems of your own."

"Cora—"

"But you could have picked up the phone, couldn't you? You could have done that, huh? The number of times I sat beside your hospital bed. The number of times Skippy came last time he was on leave. And what do I get from you?"

"Cora—"

"Not a peep. And then the one time I ask for—sure maybe it's foolishness, but that still doesn't stop me thinking—the one time I ask for your help . . . " She was raising her voice. Some kids sharing a cigarette in the park entrance turned to look at her. "You think I'm worried about *you,* for Christsakes, about YOU."

"Cora, I didn't think you were serious."

"I don't mind you getting drunk, Spence. I don't mind you wallowing in self-pity. I can kinda understand how you got that way. What I don't understand . . . " She was walking back through the birch trees, Spence hobbling along the brickwork paths, trying to catch up to her. "What I don't understand is why you had to become so damned selfish."

Out on Nisku Industrial Estate they were holding an auction of Caterpillar tractors. Men climbed through the heavy machinery, slapping the metal panels and revving engines. Smoke belched from the big D9's into the cold, prairie sky. Spence drove on past Pipeline Alley Café and the derrick service companies to the sign that said MC CABE DRILLING.

There was a new girl in reception. Through the blinds behind her Spence could see an open-plan office where phones were ringing and people passed pieces of paper around. So this was the real world. Spence compared it with the inertia of his own domestic existence and suddenly felt ashamed. As a rig superintendent he never had a moment to himself: morning reports, construction, requisitioning, logging, the host of conflicts and comedies that made up a working day. But during the long weeks in the hospital and the longer weeks recuperating at home, he had somehow lost touch with the pace of normal life. Out at his little acreage the less he did, the less he felt like doing—chopping firewood, shopping, and feeding the chickens somehow took up the whole morning now.

He was sitting in the waiting area, gloomily pondering this, when Dennis came out of his office. After thirty years in the business Dennis had a complexion as rutted and pitted as any rig site. He smiled and said. "Spence, what d'ya say?" But Spence had noted the fleeting expression that immediately preceded that. It was the expression he saw increasingly in the faces of his friends, the expression that down-and-outs elicited from the shoppers in West Edmonton Mall. Fear of embarrassment. Fear of being made to feel guilty. Fear of being asked to reach into their pockets for a dollar.

"I've been thinking about our talk." Spence began.

"Hang on, I've just got to hand this over."

He led Spence through the maze of room dividers. Spence waited, while Dennis went through the documents with one of his employees. They were pitching for an exploration program in Belize now. Business was booming.

He guided Spence back into his office and closed the door behind him. "So what talk was that?"

A plate-glass window made up one wall of Dennis's office, screened by strip blinds and overlooking an artificial lake. There was a photo of Myra on his desk, standing outside the double-wide trailer they owned down in Reno.

"About Madagascar."

"Aw, that. No, sorry, we got someone. Anyway, that's all changed."

"What's changed?"

"What hasn't changed." Dennis smoothed his hair with one hand. He'd been doing this for as long as Spence had known him, but he still never got it to lie flat. "I tell you," he said, "dealing with that place is like taking porcupine quills out of a dog's mouth. Soon as you get rid of one problem, you find another."

"So what's changed, Dennis?"

"They decided they want to buy the rig for themselves."

"Who did?"

"The government of Madagascar."

"Can they afford it?"

"Who the hell knows, probably just jerking me around."

"Well, I can deal with that," Spence said.

"No, you can't."

"Why not?"

"'Cause, I told you, we already got someone. If you'd taken it two days ago, it would have been yours, Spence. How come you got so keen all of a sudden?"

"Cora asked me to go," he said.

That got Dennis's attention. "You believe that bullshit?"

"Some," Spence lied.

"In that case there's no way I'd send you."

"'Course I don't believe it," Spence said, but Dennis was already off on a tangent of his own. "What is it with these people? They think I don't have enough problems. They think this job isn't difficult enough without some damn-fool conspiracy theory. What do you think Standard Life have been harping on about? How am I supposed to sort out this compensation if no one—"

"Forget I said that, Dennis. I don't believe it any more than you do. I told her that myself. I just want the job."

"A week ago you told me you were busy."

"You know that was bullshit. Truth is, I'm all fucked up, Dennis. I wake up and spend half an hour just staring at the ceiling. I spend most of the rest of the time either drinking or feeling sorry for myself. If I don't do something soon, I'm scared I'm going to end up like the natives down on 96th Street. That's the real reason I'm here."

Dennis came around the desk and held him by the shoulders. "Spence. Spence. You know I love you. If you'd have said yes the first time . . ."

"Yeah, I know." Spence disengaged himself, reaching for his stick.

"Next time we get something suitable—"

"Sure, Dennis. I hear you."

Spence's house at Fort Saskatchewan was built of aspen, now silvered with age and crusted with lichen, the kind of traditional prairie house they liked to paint on Thanksgiving cards. It had once stood completely remote in a lazy bend of the North Saskatchewan River, but more recently the neighboring sections had been bought up by the owners of car dealerships and insurance franchises. Their modern bungalows remained out of sight for most of the year, though in the summer the air sang with the sound of these play farmers clearing the scrub with their dinky little chainsaws, and on Sundays the single-lane blacktop was clogged with Corvettes and Chevvy saloons.

Spence walked into the front room. He stood for a moment looking at his reflection in the window: a lean, tanned face and thinning, sandy hair. Outside it was starting to snow.

The phone rang.

"Hello."

"Okay. I phoned the other guy. How would you feel about four and a half grand?"

"I'd feel better about five."

"I offered him a grand to pull out. Say yes before I change my mind."

Spence smiled. "I appreciate it, Dennis. I'll remember you in my will."

"Keep beating yourself up and I might just get to collect."

"When do I leave?"

"Beginning of next week. Mandy'll get you a ticket."

"Tell her my leg gets cramped in Economy."

"Cut the son of a bitch off, then. It's no good to you anyway."

"Thanks, Dennis, I appreciate it. You take care now."

"I've got to be off my head."

"Hey, while I think of it, have you had someone rig watching?"

"Yeah, there's some old Danish guy over there. Runs the sugar factory. His name's Manson . . . Hanson? It's on a bit of paper here. I think that's an *h* . . . Hanson."

"Is he reliable?"

"If he's as good as this typist, he's not worth shit."

Chapter 3

"More *jus de grenadine*, Father?"

"Thank you." Father Mitchell pushed his tumbler across the bleached wood table. To their left, beyond the palm trees, the sea washed, hissing over the white-hot sand. They were seated as usual in the south side of the Grand Hotel's L-shaped veranda, which allowed him a view down Morondava's main street. Its surface was too bright to contemplate for long, and he turned back to Perpetude.

"I believe," he said, "that you are expecting another Canadian guest."

"Am I?" The telephones were not reliable, and news often came via the mission.

"Next week. Morgan Hanssen's supposed to be looking after him. You don't look very pleased."

"Do you know if he's staying long?"

"I imagine he'll be up at the rig most of the time. He's coming to do an inventory—an inventory for the government. For our government." Father Mitchell laughed, and dabbed his watery blue eyes. "Apparently they want to buy it."

"Why do you laugh?"

"Because Velo-André is so naïve—elections in four months and his great oil exploration has fallen through. He obviously thinks he can succeed where Norco has failed."

"Is that impossible?"

"Pshaw." Father Mitchell swatted a fly and cleaned it off his finger with a handkerchief. "It's not very likely, Perpetude, you have to be logical."

"Do you?"

He knew when she was teasing him. Father Mitchell took off his Panama and rubbed the permanent red mark that it left on his forehead. "Anyway they've got more than that to worry about."

He was referring to the spring elections. In the Indian shops down the street they were already selling cloth printed with the photograph of the opposition leader.

"You mean Claude Istasse?" she said. "Now there's a logical man."

"You talk as if you know him."

"Actually I know him quite well. He was educated at the Sorbonne."

"You were at university with him?"

She said yes, but her expression told him more.

"You had a relationship with him."

"We were very young," she told him, wondering as she did so why it made her feel awkward. Like a daughter confessing to her father. Like a wife to her husband. "In a way he was the reason I got married," she said. "It didn't last long."

Father Mitchell fanned himself with his hat. "Perpetude. I must say. I must say, you're full of surprises . . . " He cleared his throat. "Anyway, what's wrong with him being logical?"

"Because I think politics is too complicated for logic. This Ten-Year Plan he talks about. As though the world made sense. As though the future could be controlled, while we all know it can't—even on the simplest level it can't. That's what I don't like about Claude Istasse," she said.

"And the Canadians?"

"As a group—yes."

"And me?"

She laughed but didn't contradict him. Yes, he was pomp-
ous, and authoritarian, but down here on the coast Christian
morality was such a lost cause that there was something insanely
heroic about his mission. Across the road from them a group
of girls loitered in the shade outside the covered market. Two
of them still wore faded McCabe Drilling hats and Western T-
shirts. In the short term, Christ the Savior had proved no match
for Michael Jackson.

Father Mitchell was still waiting for her reply.

"You think I'm wasting my time here," he said. "Don't
you?"

"Of course not."

"I do," he said.

"You're not thinking of leaving us?"

He had been on the point of retiring three years previously,
when the oil exploration was announced, but the expansion of
the town had given a new lease on life to the mission. Ironically,
the rampant immorality provided him with a new sense of
purpose. Father Mitchell had been as sorry as anyone to see the
oilmen leave.

"I was going to tell you a while back," he said. "I've been
offered a job."

"Where?"

"In the capital."

"Will you take it?"

"That depends."

He sipped his grenadine and looked down the street again.
Beyond the peeling walls of the Banque de Madagascar, the
street sellers were laying out their wares for the afternoon: herbal
medicines and amulets, pick-and-shovel blades, oil lamps sol-
dered together from dried milk tins, and erotic wooden carvings
of the type featured on tribal gravestones.

"Depends on what?" she asked.

Father Mitchell saw something and stood up. "I'll tell you
some other time." He finished his drink and reached for his hat.

Turning, she saw the reason for his haste—Morgan Hanssen, the stocky foreman from the sugar factory, was making his way up the street toward them with his bobbing, clod-footed gait, elbows flapping like the wings of a muscular, flightless bird. His khaki shirt was decorated with an abstract pattern of machine oil, syrup, and grease. Father Mitchell patted her bare shoulder and hurried down the veranda steps.

She watched them meet under the tamarind trees in front of the gas station, watched Hanssen mime some hearty greeting and Father Mitchell sidle past, his hand held in front of his mouth as though worried he might inhale some infectious particle of the Scandinavian's black soul. Perpetude took the grenadine back to the fridge and returned with two bottles of beer.

Spence left Edmonton at night. Below him the prairies stretched on forever, studded with the lights of farms and villages and tiny branch lines.

He reached in his bag and took out the accident report from the Madagascar crash. There was a compliment slip inside it from the National Transportation Safety Board, addressed to Cora and signed by Clyde.

The report itself was a sheaf of fourteen closely typed pages. It was prefaced by a brief synopsis:

About 14.15 local time on August the 15th, Howies Aviation Inc. DHC (Twin Otter), operating as Norco flight 056, crashed immediately after takeoff at Morondava, Madagascar, in excellent weather conditions.

The airplane was completely destroyed when it fell from approx. 600 feet into dense forest. Both pilots and all fourteen passengers were killed in the crash and subsequent fire. On the basis of the evidence available the National Transportation Safety Board determines that the probable cause of this accident was a combination of pilot error and failure to secure the rear luggage door.

The more detailed history of the flight covered two pages, starting with the airplane's original departure from Ivato International Airport in Antananarivo. Spence scanned through it till
he reached the moment when the crash occurred:

> Witnesses on the ground stated that the airplane took off
> in a southwesterly direction, against the prevailing wind.
> It climbed for three or four seconds and was beginning to
> bank to the right, when the nose abruptly turned down-
> ward. Opinion is divided as to the exact sequence of events.
> But most are agreed that the luggage door separated in
> flight and fell down independent of the aircraft.

Spence turned to "Wreckage and Impact Information."

> The major part of the wreckage was confined to an area
> about 68 feet long and 45 feet wide. The airplane crashed
> into thick deciduous forest, an area of which was burned
> in the ensuing fire. The fuselage was nose-down 60 degrees
> to the horizontal and pointing southeast. Both wings were
> sheared, with torn sections of fuselage sidewall attached.
> The rear section behind the wings was bent forward at 90
> degrees to the rest of the fuselage in the same southeast
> alignment. All the wreckage was severely charred and
> melted in places. Searchers combed an area of approx. 4
> square miles for the missing luggage compartment door,
> which was not recovered.

Spence crumpled up the compliment slip and closed his
eyes. Outside, a protective covering of pink cotton wool enveloped the globe.

From 25,000 feet the Nile was a strip of silver foil discarded
on a dun-brown wilderness. Spence slept again through the brief
refueling stop in Nairobi. He awoke with a searing pain in his
leg as the air expanded behind the artificial hip. His headphones

had fallen off and were now buzzing like a trapped insect in the palm of his hand. Below them lay a desert of red and gray mountains. Somehow he had imagined Madagascar to be green.

The Renault taxi that drove him to the capital seemed held together by some flexible material designed to absorb the huge potholes in the road. They drove through the smaller ones, swerving to avoid anything more than a foot deep. Children and chickens gamboled by the roadside.

The shanties gathered and pulled themselves together into a town, which wrapped itself around the crescent-shaped escarpment bordering the lake. Around the water's edge ran an avenue of jacaranda trees, cascades of blue flowers in their upper branches. The lower trunks served as barbershops and lottery stalls. Street hawkers sold peanuts and newspapers and patent medicines. Towering about them stood the unlikely fifteen-story tower-block of the Antananarivo Hilton.

They had put a Christmas tree in the hotel lobby. The desk clerk gave him a room on the fourth floor at the back of the hotel and a message on headed notepaper from Velo-André, minister for mineral resources, asking to meet him the next morning at the Centre Culturel et Sportif. An African man in a black shirt looked up as he crossed the lobby.

Now, from his bedroom window, he looked down over the roof of the restaurant to the turquoise swimming pool below. Someone was rhythmically swimming lengths, cutting a pattern of intersecting diagonals in the water of the pool. The town's expatriate community had bagged the best loungers and were sleeping off their lunches. A group of Korean engineers, who'd come in on the same plane as Spence, walked around the pool in their suits with their hands folded behind their backs.

Spence slung his bags below the bed, closed the blinds, and lay back on his bed, reaching automatically for the bottle of duty-free in his carryall.

★   ★   ★

Nancy skated through his dreams, her legs scissoring, skirt blowing backward over her hips, her skates tracing perfect curves on the snowy surface of the lake. He was running after her, falling, laughing, trying to run and falling again. His breath condensing. The cold air nipping his lungs.

Nancy drifting effortlessly away from him, toward the snow-laden pines and the mountains beyond.

He had met her six years ago while he was working four and four for Exxon as rig superintendent in Venezuela. He'd been home with Skippy and some other friends, knocking a hockey puck around, when he'd noticed her farther out on the lake—an angel off a Christmas tree, skating perfect circles. Backward, one leg up, then the other, completely absorbed.

The guys had bawled him out for not concentrating on the game, until finally, frustrated, he threw down his stick and skated over to talk to her.

Round and round she skated. Short dark hair, dazzling green eyes, a wide, delicate mouth. His friends' catcalls faded behind him.

She stopped when Spence approached her. She had a way of putting her head to one side like a woodchuck if there was something she didn't understand. And there she stood: gems of ice sparkling in her hair, her breath crystalizing, and Spence speechless, hypnotized, unmanned, sweating in his hockey gear, and finally resorting to, "Look, I don't suppose . . . I'd really like to take you out for a meal."

"You would, huh?" She skated away from him, laughing.

"So, what do you say?"

"What do you expect me to say? I never met you in my life."

"I expect you to say yes."

She said no.

Nancy always skating, teasing, elusive, weaving circles around him, drifting away from him, soft as snow, bright as metal. Steel on ice.

He saw her on the lake a couple of times afterward and finally persuaded her to go out with him. They met quite regularly after that, but there were always other men around her. They were never exactly dating.

Once she came out to see his house. When she said goodbye, she reached out and trailed a fingernail across his lip.

One weekend they drove up north to Skippy and Cora's place and slept in separate beds, then drove home past Slave Lake, listening to music, talking and talking as if there were no tomorrow.

Two weeks went by. His shift in Boca del Pao was approaching. They still hadn't slept together, and each time they met, he felt ill with the pressure of desire for her.

He called by at her apartment without any particular plan for the evening, and she offered to fix him some food.

Nancy strolling around the apartment in jeans and a pink cashmere sweater, putting together a salad. Spence sitting at her kitchen table, feeling strangely out of breath when she looked at him. When she passed him a beer, their fingers touched.

He remembered her saying, "Are you all right, Spence?"

"Sure, I'm fine."

She said, "If you'd rather we didn't stay in, we could go out."

"I'm fine staying in," he said.

"Well, if there's anything you want to do, just tell me."

She held his eyes for a second, and he wondered what she meant by that. Speckled green eyes. She had a way of looking at him as though she'd never had a carnal thought in her life. He never learned to read her.

"You know what I'd like to do, Nancy?"

"What?"

"I'd like to take all your clothes off and drink Scotch out of your belly button."

"Too bad, buster." A smile. Then she put her hand on his

shoulder, consoling. Then she said, "I don't have any Scotch."

He managed to laugh.

She said, "Can you wait, Spence?"

"Sure I can wait."

She leaned closer and kissed him. She bit her lower lip lightly as she withdrew. He saw the center of it turn pale, then red. "Because if you can't . . ."

"What?"

Her hand moved to his hip. His stomach contracted.

She said, "I could probably find a thimbleful of rye."

Chapter 4

By a quarter to nine the heat had already come into the morning. Spence climbed, two at a time, the crumbling steps that led up through the capital. To either side peasant farmers crouched in the dust, with small pyramids of onions or tomatoes arranged like votive offerings on sack cloth in front of them. Behind them, clinging to the gradient, rose the houses of the old town.

The native domestic architecture consisted of a two-story clay hut built on a framework of timber, but here in the city center the French had modernized the design. They had faced the houses with cement, substituted bricks and mortar for mud and wattle, zinc roofs for straw. They had enlarged the windows and embellished whole new stories with verandas and balconies. It reminded Spence of the small hill towns in Quebec. Except that now, ten years after independence, these houses had reverted once more to their African origins. The rough wooden outhouses had returned, cluttering the cul-de-sacs and courtyards. The paint had peeled, revealing first plaster, then cement, then mud. The windows had been narrowed with boarding, the shutters jettisoned, the balconies condemned. The legacy of ten centuries of Western architecture had been dismantled and used to build shanty dwellings or to repair potholes in the road. Spence stopped to rest his leg.

When he looked back, he saw a man in a black silk shirt bending over one of the stalls.

Farther along the escarpment the town seemed to stretch and straighten, dust herself down, and regain some of her former civic dignity. He found the Centre Culturel et Sportif behind the tall hedge that separated the Ministry for Economic Development from the Hôtel de France. The path to the clubhouse led past a swimming pool and fell away on his right to a group of red gravel tennis courts. Beyond the farthest wall a glacier of tin roofs tumbled off down the hill toward the football stadium.

Spence took off his sunglasses and squinted in the glare from the walls. A man in tennis whites rose to meet him. It was a moment before Spence recognized him as Velo-André, because the man conformed so little to his mental image of a politician. Small, benign, and two sizes wider than his Aertex shirt, he had a round, dark face and a comedian's moustache, which refused to follow the contours of his face.

"Mr. Spence. Pardon my informality," said Velo-André. "Saturday mornings I play tennis. My doctor insists on it— not for reasons of health but because it is with him that I play." He chuckled at this little pleasantry and waved energetically to the waiter. "What will you have?" he asked.

Spence propped his stick against a chair. "What are you drinking yourself?"

"*Coca désinfecté*—disinfected with rum. The coca is made here under license, but one cannot be too careful about the water they use."

"I'll have the same."

"*Deux coca désinfecté*," said Velo-André, winking broadly to the waiter, who had obviously heard the joke many times before but smiled dutifully nonetheless. Velo-André sat back, hitching the legs of his shorts over his thighs.

"So," he said, "at last we meet."

"At last?"

"Oh, yes. Before you are arriving here, I am able to do a small research about you."

"Dennis sent you my work record."

"Dennis McCabe, yes, exactly. It seems you are a man with very much experience of oil exploration."

"I guess."

"You have oil in the blood!" said Velo-André victoriously, as though he'd been storing the expression for some time, awaiting an opportunity to use it. "My own blood," he continued, "flows with official tampons." Then he realized he had overextended the figure of speech and quickly mimed stamping documents with a rubber stamp. "Ah, drinks."

The waiter placed them on the table, as the minister for mineral resources made fussy guiding gestures with his hands. From below them came the regular tok-tok of practice balls being expertly returned across the nets. Velo-André took a sip and smacked his lips appreciatively.

"So why did you want us to meet?" Spence asked.

"Because from two leafs of paper one cannot tell if one will like a man."

"Is that important?"

"It may be . . . in the longer term."

"I get a feeling you're fixing to ask me something."

"We shall see. If it is possible for us to purchase the rig, it hit me that a man like yourself might be looking for a challenge. A new beginning, perhaps. In a developing country."

"Where? Here?" Spence asked, trying to erase the skepticism from his voice.

"Indeed."

"What? Drilling?"

Velo-André held up his hand, sensing Spence's unease and fearing for the fragile proposal he was constructing.

"In time. In time, maybe. As you know, Norco has been prospecting on the coastal plain around Morondava for almost two years. They didn't wish to renew the concession. The operation cost my country nothing, but we have nothing to show for it."

Spence said, "You must have gotten a fair bit of foreign investment along the way."

Velo-André gave a hollow laugh. "Foreign investment? Two hundred million dollars' worth of holes in the ground. The only benefit that presents itself is the chance to buy a drilling rig of our own relatively cheaply."

"Cheap?"

"I said relatively cheap."

"I thought that's what you said. I know it's the reason I'm out here, sir, but do you have any idea how much a rig would end up costing you?"

Velo-André made a balancing movement with one hand. "We estimated twelve million dollars new, ten million, nine maybe, considering the location. It is only an idea of course but—"

"That's just for the hardware. You'd spend half as much again each year just to keep it racked. And once you start running the thing, you're talking about big money. You know how much mud costs? Do you know how much drill pipe costs? A bit? One drill bit would set you back twenty-five thousand dollars, and you need one every week. They drilled five holes on your west coast for forty million dollars apiece. Can your country raise that kind of money?"

Velo-André shrugged.

"Well, I'm telling you they can't. I mean, I'm no politician, but I do know how much beans is. There's women on the street out there selling six tomatoes, six tomatoes for God's sake—"

"Government is not quite so simple as . . . beans and tomatoes."

"I know, I'm sorry."

Velo-André looked away, over the ramshackle city. You couldn't see the lake from here, but the top of the Hilton was just visible and, beyond it, the reticulated pattern of rice fields and waterways. "I can see you think I am being unrealistic, but the seismic work was so promising. There are plenty of ways to raise capital for a project like this: World Bank incentives, diplomatic accords. One must look to the future. All the evidence suggests that the oil is there. I believe we can find it. A few expatriate advisers. A training program for our own people. A small operation to start with, but . . . " Velo-André smiled and made a hopeful gesture.

"What I'm trying to tell you, sir," Spence said, "is there's no longer any such thing as a small drilling operation. Thirty years ago you could throw up a rig and make a hole in the ground with some chance of success, but things don't work like that anymore. All the easy oil's been found. The French punched your coastline full of holes twenty years ago—if it was anywhere near the surface, they'd have found it then. Norco did three years of seismic work on this place and spent God knows how much computer time processing the data. What they don't know about the geology of this region isn't worth knowing, and they pulled out."

"You sound as though you are trying to talk your company out of a sale."

"No. I'm just making sure that you know what you're embarking on. Maybe it doesn't bother you. Maybe you don't believe me."

"On the contrary, Mr. Spence. I believe everything you say. I have had dealings with oil executives for some time now, but precisely because you are not an executive I trust you more than any of them."

"Well, I'm flattered, Mr. Velo, and I'll do that evaluation for you, but, to be honest, if you think you can run your own oil industry, I think you're pissing into the wind."

Velo-André frowned, then grasped the metaphor and chuckled. "Pissing into the wind," he said, "is our national pastime. You will remark during your visit to this country that we are a very religious people. We have Protestants, Catholics, animists, ancestor worshipers, sorcerers . . . you will have seen such people in the streets. And below us . . . you see how many churches? It is the same everywhere. Even the smallest village has its church. You see over there how many spires there are? And I assure you that they are all in use. In a country like this, one has need of hope—illogical hope but hope nonetheless. Unfortunately I do not believe in God. But I do believe in technology. If you like, the rig is my church."

"It's an expensive church."

"All churches are expensive."

"Sure, and most of them are a waste of money, hey?"

Velo-André laughed good-naturedly. It seemed an apt moment to leave, so Spence rose to his feet. As they shook hands, the African looked past Spence and called, *"Ah. Dr. David—à l'heure comme d'habitude."*

A thin, dark man was coming up the driveway, carrying two tennis racquets. In the gateway just beyond him Spence fancied he saw the African in the black shirt. When he looked again, there was no one there. Maybe he was getting paranoid.

"So long," said Spence. "Think about what I've said."

"Enjoy Morondava," said Velo-André. "It was once a very popular resort."

"I'll do that."

Popular with whom, he wondered—from the air, Madagascar didn't look like a place for tourists. Only three minutes out of the capital, he had already left the fertile plateau far behind. Now, and for the next half hour, the Dakota hung over a dun-colored wasteland. To the limits of Spence's vision, the country had the appearance of a crumpled sheet of brown paper. The only signs of habitation on these eroded mountains were the few spidery paths, scratched in white as if by a child, and the small collections of houses that appeared, inexplicably, on remote hilltops.

Even the rivers seemed unable to bring life to this desolation. They meandered through it, burdened by sediment, sometimes red, sometimes brown, supporting only fragile margins of foliage. It was not until, two hundred miles later, they broke through the crumbling hills that some color came back to the landscape. It began as thin fingers of greenery that ate like locust grubs into the barren mountains, then opened onto a landscape as flat and as vast as the prairies. This diluvial plain had been flooded and reflooded by the sinuous rivers, colonized by trees, swamped by the sea, baked dry by the sun, and drenched by the rains, till it had the appearance not of dry land but of a crazy archipelago. Fifty miles inland from the coast they were flying over islands—islands of forest in clay, islands of grass in forest, islands of swamp in grassland, and islands of nascent rice in the vast, shallow lakes.

Etched into this bizarre landscape, Spence now saw, were the marks of oil exploration: seismic lines—the axes along which an area's geology is divined—straight as a razor and no wider than a single vehicle, cutting through heath and swamp and paddy and lake. As the forest thickened toward the coast, the lines gave out, the forest gave way to brilliant mangrove, the plane began to wheel, and there, in a corona of sand, Morondava.

As they flashed over the town, Spence saw glinting tin roofs, a breeze-block church, a mosque, a school, and a cluster of civic buildings. Along the beach, bamboo fishermen's huts were crammed into the shade of the palm trees. The river opened out at the town's southernmost margin, staining a wedge of sea brown, but half a mile offshore one could plot in crystal water the point where the reef began.

They turned toward the runway, and Spence glimpsed, far to the west, the black hole in the forest where the Norco plane had exploded. The Dakota leveled, tipped, and choked back, and the strip opened to receive them.

★   ★   ★

There were no taxis. One by one, the old Renaults and Peugeots belonging to the foresters, the hospital, the leper colony, loaded up and headed off through the trees. Spence flagged down the mail van, and they rattled off down the approach road, trailing a pennant of dust.

At the end of the main street the Grand Hotel stared out to sea with the wistful charm of an abandoned French dowager. As Spence climbed the steps, his boots resounded on the hollow boards. The venetian blinds that once shaded the veranda had been replaced by a makeshift bamboo screen, which offered some protection from the smelting heat outside. He stopped inside the tiled ground-floor hallway, pulling his shirt away from his back. Beyond the hallway was a small, shaded courtyard with creepers planted in pots made from the hollow root balls of palms. Out of this greenery there now emerged a woman in a printed cotton dress.

"Monsieur Spence? Je suis Madame Peyrame."

Spence still found himself comparing every attractive woman he met with his ex-wife, Nancy. Perpetude Peyrame could not have been less similar: Her skin was very dark and her long hair thick and unruly. Nancy's eyes had been green. Madame Peyrame's were black. Nancy used to wear slinky designer dresses, but the French woman's had not been fashionable since the sixties; stretched across her deep cleavage and flaring at the waist, its floral pattern had faded from repeated washing. Now she dried her hands on it and said, *"Je vous donne chambre douze."*

"I don't speak French," Spence told her, but she continued to talk at him regardless. *"C'est pas le Hilton, mais il y a une douche et un ventilateur qui marchent. Si vous avez besoin de quelque chose, Amin Bahera s'occupera de vous."* He understood from the keys she was giving him that she'd allocated him a room. Now she turned away again and began to shout into the gloom at the back of the hotel. *"Amin Bahera. Viens ici."*

There was no reply. She made an irritated noise with her teeth. *"Encore endormi, c'est toujours la même chose. Allez, je vous montrerai la chambre moi-même."*

She took the key out of his hand and led him up the broad, wooden stairs. There was a gallery surrounding the courtyard with numbered doors leading off it. She opened one of these and walked in. Spence's limp had slowed him down on the stairs, so he was just entering the room when she threw open the shutters. A breeze came in off the sea, blowing the husks of dead insects across the floor. There was no lampshade, but the linen was clean. The walls had once been pale blue. Spence had stayed in worse places before.

The French windows led out onto a broad balcony that ran along the front of the hotel. Madame Peyrame had seen some African boys on the street. Now they exchanged words in shouted French, and she laughed—a rich, liquid laugh to match her voice. Turning back to Spence, she said, *"Voilà la douche au coin. Il y a du savon et une serviette."*

She walked back into the room, switched on the fan, and waited till it creaked into life.

"C'est tout. Le dîner est servi à huit heures."

She turned and left. Spence shut the door. Why this sudden desolation? Madame Peyrame's insistence on addressing him in a language he didn't understand was merely irritating. French Canadians had elevated that particular snub to an art form. What cut him was the carefree exchange with the boys outside and the instant resumption of formality. It had reminded him of Nancy, flirting and giggling on the phone with Clyde, then hanging up all affection, all sensuality along with the receiver. Spence flung his bag on the dresser and undid his shirt. Most depressing of all was the realization that his ego had become so puny and sensitive. As with the wasted leg, the slightest knock sent it skittering off balance. He closed the shutters, took the bottle out of his carryall, then sat on the bed, listening to the surf and the sawing of the palms. He drank and thought about

Nancy. He drank and thought about the good times with Cora and Skippy. He drank some more and thought about the men who had once been his friends and workmates, blasted into oblivion in this bleached fragment of the French empire. Spence no longer feared death. Death was only darkness. What he feared most was this: the slatted twilight in which one could perceive the futility of all endeavor.

He drank until his eyes began to close. Presently he fell asleep.

Chapter 5

In London they had begun stringing hexagons across the road all the way down Regent Street. Illuminated, they had the appearance of snowflakes, but by day they reminded Charles Hunter of the drilling-site markers on his world map at Norco House.

A policewoman in Day-Glo sleeves waved him across Oxford Street, holding back the tide of pedestrians. They had commandeered the bus lane with orange bollards to make room for the press of Christmas shoppers. It wasn't raining, but there was water in the air. The Mercedes had a single windscreen wiper, which, even at its lowest speed, squeaked and screeched on the glass. He turned up the CD: a selection of Pavarotti arias. For the past two years, working with the Canadian drillers as operations manager in Madagascar, he'd listened mostly to country and western music. But since his promotion to vice president, UK, he'd been obliged to entertain more lavishly, and a working knowledge of opera occasionally came in handy.

He turned around the bend of Regent Street toward Trafalgar Square, and the traffic stopped again. He'd be at the pool in ten minutes. Hunter had always kept fit. Now he found swimming relieved his innate tension. He drummed his fingers on the steering wheel, waiting for the lights to change. He would never describe himself as a worrier, but he liked to feel in control, and in the last couple of weeks Madagascar had been knocked disconcertingly out of his grip.

The item of most interest was confirmation that Velo-André wanted to buy the oil rig. Velo-André was the worst kind of politician; instinctive, vague, and tolerant of chaos. The chances were, as Claude Istasse's office implied, that Velo-André was just following a whim, but Hunter still didn't feel confident of this. Sometimes he despised Velo-André for apparent naïveté, but sometimes, as now, he wondered if it was just a sophisticated front.

The recruiting of an independent assessor was something Hunter had anticipated. It was inevitable at some point that the rig would need to be evaluated and sold on. But now, as he drove through Piccadilly Circus, Hunter wondered if there had been any significance in Velo-André's decision to recruit a man through McCabe's. Inventory men were ten a penny. Why go back to the Canadian drilling company, when there were plenty of companies closer to Madagascar in Europe? There were wives of the McCabe employees who, on purely emotional grounds, held Norco responsible for the crash. Hunter wondered now if, in going to McCabe's, Velo-André had been looking for someone who might take his side against Norco. Or was it purely a matter of convenience, of going back to a familiar address?

Pavarotti moved on to another aria, and, simultaneously, Hunter abandoned that particular train of thought. Before heading up the exploration program in Madagascar, he'd run operations in Africa for seven years and had long since given up trying to understand the minds of African politicians.

He parked in St. James's Square and walked across Pall Mall to the RAC Club. Inside, some city bankers were making their way up the lyre-shaped staircase. On the first floor a vast, baroque dining room looked out onto the gardens at the rear of the club. Hunter headed downstairs, checking in at the locker room to pick up his trunks.

The clock on the changing-room wall said ten minutes past one. He'd left the office at five minutes to. Ten minutes to reach the club. Five to get changed. Half an hour in the pool and back in the office by two o'clock sharp. When he stood on the scales, they said thirteen stones. For a man of his sturdy physique, it wasn't bad, but he could lose that half. He'd get Nicola to put him on fifteen hundred calories for the next couple of weeks. Hunter examined his profile in the mirror and banished Velo-André from his mind. He'd get someone to double-check the rig site, but otherwise there was nothing to be done. He'd already seen a job résumé on the McCabe man and had been gratified to learn that he was a burnt-out case. He had nothing to fear from Spence.

Spence woke, it was half past nine at night. He walked through the swooping palms and hobbled down to the beach. Here the oilmen had thrown up a makeshift jetty by scuttling and welding together two seagoing barges. Even by moonlight he could see that the metal skin was already corroding, and the sand with which the barges had been loaded down was washing out through the seams.

Looking up the coast from here, he could see, between the trees, the fires and lanterns of the fishermen's village. Their outrigger canoes were drawn up above the waterline. Farther along the beach an open wooden building jutted out on stilts over the sand. Spence could see lights and hear the faint strains of music.

As he approached, the music became clearer: high-pitched, frenetic music that sounded as though it was played on bottles and scrap metal. By the light of a single neon tube Spence could see children clinging to the wire mesh of the discothèque windows and clustering like moths around its open doorway. Spence waded through them and ducked inside.

At its far end the wooden dance hall was half open to the sea, but the heat inside was still stifling. At first Spence could make out little more than a galaxy of eyes and teeth, but as his own eyes grew accustomed to the light, the faces took shape, laughing and shouting above the music. If a couple left the dance floor, another took their place, as if some monumental communal endeavor would fail should they lapse for a moment. They danced on their way to the dance floor, and they still danced as they returned. The barmen were dancing, the band was dancing. The single men who stood in the shadows were beating out the rhythm on the wooden walls, and the African girls who hung around waiting to be offered a beer were swaying in time to the music.

There was one other European in the bar, a stocky, balding man with Victorian side-whiskers and a face that was all one smile.

"Crowded, eh?" he observed happily. "When did you get here?"

"Today."

"You don't know who the hell I am," the stranger observed.

"No, I don't."

"Morgan Hanssen. Pleased to meet you."

"Hanssen. You're supposed to be looking after the rig."

The Scandinavian chuckled. "You're right. I'm supposed to be, but I'm here. I come down every now and then to haf a little party." He laughed again. He had to be over sixty, Spence thought, but this didn't prevent him from flirting like a teenager with the black girls at the bar.

"So who's looking—"

"What's that?"

Spence had to shout above the music. "Who's looking after the rig?"

"Oh, I got a couple of swampers keeping an eye on her."

"Can you trust them?"

"Why?" said the older man. "What they going to do? Put it in the back pocket and run away with it?" He roared with

laughter again, slapped his thigh, stuck out his tongue, and
reached deep into his blue cotton trousers for his wallet. "Haf
a beer. We'll talk about all that shit tomorrow."

Spence looked at him doubtfully. He'd already seen the
state of the jetty. Three months in the jungle could destroy
almost anything, and there was twelve million dollars' worth
of equipment up there.

"What kind of..." he began, but Hanssen couldn't
hear him.

"I've worked in yoost about every damn country in the
world," the old man shouted, "but never anywhere like this.
You see these people—they'd dance to anything. I seen them
dancing to some guy banging on a fifty-five-gallon drum—
yoost dancing, dancing, from asshole to breakfast. You know
why? They have an overdeveloped sex instinct—the mixture of
French with African blood. Good-looking guy like you could
haf any one of these little gals here—Nooni, Pushta, Germaine,
Martine—any one of them. And she'd never ask for money.
What do you think of that?"

The girls wore their hair in elaborate loops like pretzels,
and their shiny dresses were copied from French magazines.

"You been keeping it painted?" Spence asked.

"Keeping what painted?"

"The rig."

"Oh, we done lots of repainting."

"And greasing the cables?"

"Like they was new."

"What shape's the electrical wiring in?"

"Listen." Hanssen reached up and clapped a paternal hand
on Spence's shoulder. "You going to see it yourself tomorrow.
It's yoost exactly like they left it, and even if it wasn't, there's
nothing you can do. So haf a little fun. You're going to be a
long time dead."

"I didn't come here for my health," said Spence. He had
realized in Edmonton that it was only pride in his work that

kept him clear of the abyss, and he clung to it as a drunk clings to his lamppost.

"Sure you didn't. Yoost don't try and do too much too quick. That's how it is with you Americans."

"Canadian," Spence corrected him, but Hanssen waved this detail away.

"I met an American once up at the capital. He was sitting downstair in the Hilton, wrapped in a blanket, looking sorry for hisself. And he was one big-shot vanilla merchant. You know what happened to him? First day he was here, he got dropped off in Ampefiloha district, and someone stole his fancy watch. Well, he was madder than a bee. Started walking to the police station. Yoost got as far as the next corner, and two more fellows rob him. This time they take the whole damn lot: wallet, passport, traveler's checks, credit cards. So then this American goes crazy. He's in the middle of the road, and he start stripping off and shouting, 'Okay, okay, take the lot. Take my shoes, take my shirt, take my trouser,' and he's running around throwing them at people. Ended up in nothing but his underpant. That's the truth. Got hisself arrested. Police give him the blanket. Took him back to the hotel. Then drove off and kept all his clothes for themselfs—ha!" Hanssen rocked back against the bar, roaring with laughter and dabbing his eyes with a large, dirty handkerchief. A teenager in shiny green trousers came and said something in his ear. "This is Angeline. Angeline, this is Spence. She wants me to dance."

"Go ahead. I'm going to bed."

"What, already? The evening's yoost getting started."

"You look like you'll manage without me."

"You're damn right there. Ha! What time do you want to leave tomorrow?"

"As early as possible."

"Okay, I'll come around at seven."

"You sure you'll have the energy?"

Hanssen gave him a robust nudge in the ribs and said,

> When I was young and in my prime
> I used to do it all the time.
> Now that I am old and gray
> I only do it twice a day.

Spence said, "See you in the morning."

The old man headed for the dance floor, making clumsy ducklike movements with his elbows. The girl was dancing also, but with subtle, sensuous movements of her shoulders and pelvis. Spence paid the barman and left.

He was getting ready for bed, when he heard the door below him open and close. Perpetude walked out onto the veranda below him and stood looking out over the silhouette of the town, black on blue, stippled with the dull glow of oil lamps. Unaware of his presence, she adjusted her sarong, unwrapping it, then retying the knot across her breasts.

She walked down to the beach as a muezzin called from the mosque at the far end of town.

> God is Great.
> Allah is God.
> There is only one God.
> Praise be to Allah.

They departed at eight and drove out across the painful brightness of the tidal flats, leaving Morondava behind its mantle of ragged palms. Morgan Hanssen was driving, and Spence sat in the passenger seat with one foot up on the sill. They had taken on board two of Hanssen's assistants, who sat in the back with the supplies: watermelons, sacks of rice, and wicker baskets full of vegetables. Six live chickens, their feet tied together, sat resignedly in the shade of the fuel drum.

Along the ragged margins of the road the population of Morondava walked to work: women with pots and baskets on their heads. Children in the pink smocks of the mission school, and men in bright blue overalls.

"Where are these guys heading?"

"They work for me at the sugar factory," said Hanssen.

"Shit, how many jobs have you got here, Hanssen?"

"Oh, I don't go there much anymore. Two year back they asked me to train a local fellow. Son of a bitch is getting good. Pretty soon he won't need me at all."

"So, what will you do?"

"Who the fuck knows? I hoped you fellows would find us a bit of oil here so I could work on that. I s'pose a lot of people hoped that." Hanssen chuckled. "The president hoped it, and that's for sure. He knows as soon as that rig leaves the country, his government is going to look like a bunch of assholes."

"How come?"

"Yoost 'cause he promised all sorts of stuff when the oil came in. And nothing happen."

Spence said, "Strikes me they could have all the oil in the world and this would still be a poor place to live."

"Are you kidding? This is paradise, you know that? Paradise. Only trouble is, the politicians we got pretty keen on haffing their own fellows in the big jobs."

Big jobs. Spence disguised a smile. Foreman of some sugar factory in this remote patch of scrub. "I met one of them in the capital," he said.

"Who?"

"A politician. Minister for Minerals or something. Guy by the name of Velo-André. You heard of him?"

"I heard of him, all right," Hanssen guffawed. "You know what he used to be? A science teacher, professor of physics at the Lycée Nationale. A schoolteacher. Now he's head of gold and diamonds. Two guesses why."

"Dunno. He's related to the president."

"His brother," Hanssen said.

"Do they have gold and diamonds?"

"Nope," Hanssen laughed happily. "And no oil neither. Too bad for him. It's about the only thing that could haf safed this goffernment. Anyway, I hope this new guy Istasse likes foreigners. Otherwise the only way I can stay is if I marry some little honey. Probably end up planting rice with my ass hanging out of my trouser like these poor people."

Rice fields stretched from the road to the edge of the forest on their left and to the river on their right. Most of the rice had already been harvested. In one a man was plowing the stubble. In another a row of women were at work, their sarongs pulled up under them and tucked in at the waist, swinging their sickles in time to a chant.

"You could always go somewhere else," Spence said.

"Hell, no, this is where I'm supposed to be. You find out where you're meant to be, and you know this is it. And I got here by accident. Yes, sir. You gotta pay attention to accidents. They tell you where you're supposed to be going."

The road unfolded in front of them. Spence lifted his leg off the dash and maneuvered it onto the floor.

"This here's the road to the rig," Hanssen said.

They had turned off into the forest along the new dirt road constructed by the oilmen—dead straight and wide enough for two trucks to pass. It was cambered in the middle with drainage ditches on either side and occasional cuts from where the grader had taken extra earth. The red soil had been baked to a surface smooth and hard as brick.

"This road clear all the way?"

"Yep, there's other folks use it now. The tribesmen bring their cattle down it. Father Mitchell go up and down to the villages, teaching and preaching. These tracks is probably his."

"Who's Father Mitchell?"

"English churchman. You'll meet him, he's a friend of Pappatoot."

"Pappatoot?"

"She's the woman who runs the hotel."

"Strange name, Pappatoot."

"It's French."

"It don't sound French."

"Well . . . maybe it's African."

"How long's she been here?"

"Oh, she was born here. She went to some fancy college in Paris, got herself a husband. Came back here. Then the husband pissed off, and she stayed. Why're you interested? You want to fuck her?"

Spence didn't bother to answer that one.

"Why not? That's one damn attractive woman. I want to fuck her myself, but she always say no. Probably thinks I'm too old. I bet Father Mitchell wants to fuck her, but he's got his thumb stuck halfway up his ass."

"Well, I don't speak French, so that kind of rules me out too," Spence said.

"No, it don't. She speaks pretty good English."

"She didn't speak English with me."

"Probably just being awkward. You know what women is like."

A group of fat guinea fowl wandered onto the edge of the road in front of him, then hurried back in for cover. The road carved onward, sometimes following the straight course of the seismic line, at other times diverging from it to skirt a large tree or an area of swamp. Sometimes it took them through forest, sometimes savannah. Once they crested a rise, and the whole flood plain was spread out before them in a psychedelic carpet of red earth, greens, and yellows.

They stopped for a drink, and Spence took over the driving. With the driver's seat pushed right back, he could operate the brake and still reach the clutch. The road took them northwest now, off the floodplain and into dense green jungle. They bucked and jostled over roots and through shallow tannic streams, wove and scrambled through sand and mud, until finally the trees parted and they emerged into a clearing.

"There she is," said Hanssen.

Chapter 6

Spence got out and slammed the door behind him. The clearing was some five hundred meters square, leaving space beside the rig for the heavy machinery. From a distance it appeared that Hanssen had done his job. Most sections of the derrick had been newly repainted: brilliant white against the veined face of the jungle.

"Hello!" Hanssen shouted. "Anyone home?"

Spence left Hanssen to round up the guards and headed off across the lease, skirting the moist, dark earth where the mud and water reservoirs had been filled in. Beyond them an eight-foot length of casing protruded from the ground. The writing on it was a black bead of welding against the rusted steel:

NORCO OIL
MANSALAVA 1
42.06′w 12.64′s

At the center of the clearing, surrounded by the garrulous jungle, the well-marker took on a mystical significance. This rusting totem had cost forty million dollars and sixteen lives to erect. Spence considered it for a moment and limped on.

The flat ground was already being courted by the jungle's

emissaries—strands of broad-leafed creeper and some feathery saplings. At the edge of the lease this sparse foliage had already congregated to form a belt of green, which extended to the edge of the metalware.

"Avia . . . malak, malak!" It was Hanssen in the distance, yelling to the guards.

Spence started at the far end, opposite the shed that contained the rig's electrical plexus, and walked along the ranks of heavy equipment. Most of it looked in pretty good shape: Standing back from the draw-works, he could see that the cables had been bound and coiled on top of it with corrosion protectors over the connectors. There were three Caterpillar generators, two National mud pumps with sixty-horsepower electric motors mounted overhead, and three mud tanks the size of mobile homes. Finally, beyond the shale-shakers, desanders, and stacks of metal catwalk, the massive bulk of the sub—the iron substructure that formed a raised platform for the derrick. Disassembled, it still stood three stories high.

The derrick itself had been dismantled into a dozen colossal sections and laid out on timbers. The steel cable had been removed from the twenty-ton traveling block and spooled onto a drum. The grease on it was still tacky.

"Hello, Jean-Aimé?" Hanssen had emerged from the forest behind the trailers. Still shouting. His helpers were unloading the pickup. Still no sign of the guards. Spence turned back to the rig and continued along the northern edge of the rig site. Having been shaded all day from the sun, the ground was softer here, and his walking stick kept sinking into it. He labored on past the tongs and drill bits, the square-section safety railing, the high-pressure hoses and stacks of timber matting. Hanssen met him by the pipe racks.

"How'd it look?"

"Ask me in two weeks' time," said Spence. "There don't seem to be any major problems."

"Yes, there do," Hanssen told him.

"What?"

"Guards have all skedaddled."

"They've what?"

"They run away."

"Well. Don't suppose that matters now."

"Yes, it do. The trailers have all been broke into."

There were six trailers joined together on the side of the clearing, which were used as offices and living quarters for the crew. Spence followed Hanssen around all of them. Along the aluminum edges of each doorjamb were the dents where the locks had been forced with a crowbar.

In the superintendent's office the filing cabinet had been emptied of its contents. Spence rammed the drawers closed.

"You think there was something important here?"

"Just the manifest," Spence said, "just all the paperwork I need."

The room was warm and stale. The walls were lined with simulated-wood Formica. On the back of the door was a pinup of a big-breasted girl working out on a multigym.

"Those stupid people," Hanssen said. He was looking through the cupboards, as though in search of his missing guards.

"If you knew they were stupid, why didn't you stay here with them?"

"Would you stay here for a month and a half without coming to town?"

"If I was being paid for it."

"For forty dollar a day?"

"You took the job," said Spence. "It was your goddamn responsibility."

"You're damn right. My responsibility. So don't you come telling me what I should and I shouldn't haf done."

"Well, you shouldn't have hired a bunch of criminals to look after the rig."

Through the window he could see the helpers whom Hanssen had brought with him watching the trailer, listening to the foreigners arguing inside.

"Them was good boys," said Hanssen. "Nothing wrong with them boys. They wouldn't steal from here."

"Well, someone damn well did."

"Okay, but you can dammit well stop shouting at me. Pappatoot's right, we don't need you guys digging up the country with your big schemes and your we-know-what's-best."

In the hiatus that followed this outburst Hanssen left the trailer and stumped off across the rig site toward his pickup.

"You know where they live?" Spence shouted after him.

"'Course I do. We come through their village forty mile back there."

"Well, maybe you can find them and bring them back."

"Where the hell d'you think I'm going?" yelled Hanssen. He got in his pickup, ground the gears, and hammered off, leaving a curtain of dust hanging motionless over the entrance to the clearing.

The sound of the engine grew faint and disappeared. Their small pile of provisions sat on the baked mud. The chickens had pecked a hole in the watermelon, which was now covered with flies. By midafternoon they'd have lost the sun behind the jungle.

Fucking goddamn motherfucking piss-awful half-assed job in a piss-poor country.

The helpers were watching him, waiting for some lead. "Better get a fire going," Spence said.

Hanssen's helpers sat on their haunches regarding him, wide-eyed.

"Fire." Spence mimed rubbing his hands together. "Fire." He threw them his lighter. "Pronto, *jaldi,* quick-quick." His skin and hair and nostrils were full of red dust. The sandflies were beginning to bite. He picked up a can of fuel and went off to see if he could start the generator.

★ ★ ★

As the sun disappeared into the singing jungle, Hanssen's pickup
came swaggering out of the gloom. An ancient man with
rheumy eyes and a drooping lower lip was sitting beside Hanssen in the front seat of the pickup.

Hanssen jumped down from the truck. The old man remained in the passenger seat.

"I thought you said they were young guys."

"They was. This here's their father."

"Their grandfather."

"No, father. Twenty-three children. What d'ya think of
that?"

"What's he got to say for himself?"

Hanssen followed Spence back to the pickup. "You got to
be polite. He's the village chief."

"Does he speak English?"

"No."

"So what did you bring him here for?"

"He wanted to see the trailers."

"Morgan, he doesn't have to see shit." In the failing light
Spence tripped on an old tire mark in the mud. "He just had
to tell you where his sons are."

Hanssen ignored this and helped the old man down from
the vehicle.

"Sons," Spence said to him. "Where have your sons gone?"

The old man looked to Hanssen, and Hanssen turned back
to Spence. "I told you, he don't understand." He led the old
man off toward the fire and the trailers beyond it. Spence
trudged along behind them, making heavy weather of the hard,
rutted mud.

"Did you ask him where they went? Did you ask what
happened to the papers?"

"He doesn't know," Hanssen said. They had stopped outside the first of the trailers. The old village chief was inspecting
its damaged door like someone on a presidential visit. Spence

slapped a mosquito and went off to sit by the fire. The sky above their heads had separated into layers of blue and pink. Hanssen returned to the chief, who exchanged a few words of dialect with the helpers from Morondava.

"So, what does he reckon?"

"Later. You got to treat these people properly."

Hanssen put a can of water on the fire, and they all watched it boil. "You can't ask too directly. It's not polite. You tell them this. You show them that. Then maybe they'll say what they think and maybe they'll just go home."

"I still don't see why you couldn't have done this at his place."

"He never rode in a car before."

"Jesus." Spence dragged a hand through his hair and got his fingernails full of dirt.

The old chief sipped his tea contentedly. The light of the fire was reflected yellow in his eyes. From time to time he would cock his head and regard Spence with a penetrating look. Spence had seen the same lucid expression in the eyes of his father from time to time, after the nurses and doctors had pronounced the old devil mad. The other person who had looked at him that way was an old dirt farmer in Leduc, who'd taken him at five-card stud one night for two hundred and seventy-five dollars.

Unexpectedly the old man began speaking in French.

"What does he say?"

"He said no one around here would steal from those trailers."

"Well, someone did, didn't they?"

"He says it's *fady*. Bad magic. Taboo."

"*Fady*." The men from Morondava picked up on the word and repeated it in unison.

"Taboo what?" Spence asked. "What's taboo?"

"You can't steal the possessions of a dead man. Otherwise you die yourself. That's what their religion says."

"The hell with that. There's Christians here, ain't there? I met plenty of *them* who don't mind stealing."

"They might be Christians, but they haf the local religion as well. They do both, just in case."

Spence drew a pattern with his stick in the dirt. It sounded like a pretty thin story. "So why did they run off?"

The old man anticipated this question and began talking again without prompting from Hanssen. "Maybe someone chase them off, and they didn't come back because they thought I'd be angry at them."

"So he thinks his sons didn't do it."

"That's right."

"But they must have seen who did."

Hanssen put this to the old man. It seemed to take a lot of translating. Insects were still biting, but neither Hanssen nor the Africans seemed to be affected. Spence moved into the line of smoke.

"Maybe they did," Hanssen said at last.

"So who did they see?" Spence asked.

"He can't say," Hanssen translated. "The boys hafen't been home."

Spence blinked in the smoke. The old man smiled benignly and embarked on another long monologue, which frequently included the word *vasay*.

"*Vasay, vasay.*" Hanssen's men seized once more on a word in their own dialect.

"What's a *vasay*?"

"A white man."

"He thinks a white man was here?"

"Yes."

"When did he get here?"

Hanssen consulted with the chief and said, "Four day ago. Same day I left."

"So how did he get here?"

Another lengthy discussion followed. There were jokes that the helpers laughed at. The chief talked expansively, looking at the trees, the fire, the drifting sky, jostling a log till the sparks flew.

"What does he say?"

"He saw a green car."

"And?"

"That's all."

"Come on, Morgan, he must have said more than that."

"A green car went past the village. Maybe this white guy was inside it."

"He says 'maybe.' Is he guessing all this, or what?"

"Some of it."

"So where would he get a green car from? You know anyone in Morondava who owns a green car?" Spence asked.

"Oh, shit, yes," said Hanssen happily. "Everyone's got a green car. It's yoost about the only color of enamel they make here now. You look around Morondava and you can tell how old something is by the color they painted it. All the houses is pink and all the machines is green. Any different colors was painted more than five year ago."

"Well, how many white people are there in Morondava?"

"Altogether?" Hanssen stuck out his tongue. "Probably forty-something white like you and me, then twice as many white like Pappatoot. Anyway, who say the fellow come from Morondava? Could haf come from Maintirano, Antsalova, any of these places."

Spence gave up. Just when you thought you were getting a grip on something, the whole thing fell away in your hand. "The hell with it," he said. "I'll get the police to deal with it."

"So you staying here or coming back to Morondava?"

"I might as well hang around a few days," Spence said. "There's some stuff I can do while we're waiting for the paperwork. I'll give you a telex to McCabe's."

"We give the chief something to eat."

"Hell, yes," Spence said emptily. "Let's have a party."

Supper and a wash improved his mood. They sat around the fire, watching the sparks flow upward in the current of smoke.

Spence sat with his shirt undone, listening to the cracking wood.
The chief had refused a bed for the night and now snored
noisily in the shadow of one of the trailers. Beyond the flames
Hanssen's two assistants were resting on their spears. The cotton
blankets draped over their shoulders gave them the portentous
appearance of blackbirds. The jungle enclosed them. Its silence
was infectious, like the forest back home. In the old days Spence
used to do a lot of camping. Skippy and he would take a couple
or three horses up in the woods behind Fort St. John. Spend a
week hunting elk or maybe fish some salmon. They'd been
good times . . .

Spence swallowed some more rum and grimaced. The stuff
had been distilled locally, siphoned into an old Coca-Cola bottle
and stoppered with a wooden bung. "You want some more of
this?"

Hanssen drank. "You been in this business a long time?"

"Forever," said Spence. "I've got oil in the blood," he
added, smiling as he remembered Velo-André's experimental
English. "I started roughnecking around Alberta when I was
sixteen."

"Sixteen, eh? I got a girlfriend here who's sixteen. I'm sixty
and she's sixteen. You know how often sixty into sixteen go?"

"I can guess," said Spence, and Hanssen cackled delight-
edly.

"Where else d'you work?"

"Pretty much everywhere. Canada at first, then moved to
where the oil was: Alaska, Texas, Saudi, Indonesia, Peru, India,
Nigeria . . . "

"Didn't you ever get bored of it?"

"Bored, no. I hardly ever did the same job twice. Started
as a roustabout, moved up to derrickman, AD, driller, truck
pusher, tool pusher. . . . Before the accident I was rig supervisor.
This rig we had up in B.C., I built it, put the machinery together, hauled it up there. Had a hundred men working under
me up there." He patted his leg. "Then this bullshit happened."

"What happened?"

"Fell off a rig," said Spence.

"Was it bad?"

"Pretty bad. Smashed part of the bone clean out of my thigh. I still got the feeling in my foot, but they had to fuse the knee, and the muscles are all wasted."

"How did you fall?"

"Stepped backward on the drilling platform and fell out through the V-door. Dropped about thirty feet onto a bunch of steel piping."

"You get a pension for that?"

"Nope. I got fired for being drunk on the job."

"Why was you drinking?"

"Different reasons."

Spence swallowed another mouthful of rum. If things had gone differently, he'd be in charge of special projects by now— have himself an office, a couple of secretaries, and a seat on the board. He'd had big plans once. Now he was reduced to itemizing someone else's old hardware—machines that, like himself, had outlived their usefulness.

"Want some more?"

"You don't want to drink too much of this stuff." Hanssen took another swig from the bottle and spat some of it onto the flames. A patch of the fire flared briefly. "See what I mean?"

"Yup," said Spence. "It does the trick."

Hanssen chuckled. "You's what I call a serious drinker. You drink a lot, but it yoost make you serious."

Spence nodded. The bottle of rum was empty but for the last quarter inch. A thimbleful of rye. "I think I'll turn in now." He took a final swig from the bottle and blew lightly over its rim. The sound that came out echoed the hollowness he felt within.

Next day Hanssen returned to Morondava. Spence set up home in one of the trailers and inspected the derrick over two morn-

ings, before the steel became too hot to touch. Even at seven
A.M. the jungle would hiss and steam like a pressure cooker.
He worked methodically, using his arms and his one good leg
to climb through the lattice of girders, then sighted along each
strut to check that it wasn't buckled.

In the afternoons the stacks of pipe and casing were shaded
by the forest's western edge. Spence worked, stripped to the
waist, measuring them against a line held by the helpers and
marking each pipe with chalk, unscrewing the metal protectors
to check the threads.

Before lunch on the second day he fired up one of the
auxiliary generators and connected the air-con unit from his
trailer. When the sun came overhead, he lay inside dozing and
listening to the throbbing of the engines. The Africans were
drinking coffee around the fire pit. One of them was plucking
foreign arpeggios on a guitar made from plywood.

Spence fingered the gold puzzle ring on his left hand. Two
diamonds had been knocked out of the central band, and he'd
never bothered to replace them. He turned them to the light
from the window and examined the empty sockets. On the
other side of the partition the Africans shared some impenetrable
joke. In Canada he could at least catch the drift of the Indians'
dialect, but alone, with no one to talk to, there was little chance
he'd ever make sense of this cockeyed place. On reflection there
was nothing about this operation that wasn't strange: the music,
the scenery, the language... an entire rig crew killed, a government trying to buy a rig they couldn't afford to operate, an
empty camp looted. Spence looked at the ceiling and juggled
with fragments of memory.

Cora: "It's not just the crash. You know there was weird
stuff about that whole operation."

Velo-André: "We have two hundred million dollars' worth
of holes in the ground. ... The only benefit that now presents
itself is the chance to buy a rig of our own."

Morgan Hanssen: "The president knows as soon as that

rig leaves, his government going to look like a bunch of assholes."

It reminded him of listening to the cheap Motorolas they'd
used on the Alaska pipeline—the feeling that, among all the
half-heard conversations, there was an important message he
should be receiving.

Chapter 7

The last time Velo-André had been to a party chez Istasse, the house had just been completed. Istasse's French wife was an architect, and she had designed the place herself with swimming pool that started in the open dining area and led out into the garden. There were lights in the palm trees. Uniformed servants poured drinks and turned steaks on the barbecue. Despite the water ban Istasse's gardeners sprinkled this lawn for five hours a day.

The guests drifted over it, talking in French and English. They were all there: the French ambassador, Pascale Daumon, René Jancovici, the surgeon from the military hospital, the American ambassador, the Reuters bureau chief, the British consul—all the great and the good of Antananarivo, Istasse moved among them, blended in with them, occasionally signaling to one of the uniformed servants to bring over more champagne, more canapés.

Velo-André stood on tiptoe and looked around for someone he would feel at ease with. Istasse hadn't invited any of the *faux blancs*—the penniless Russian and Korean advisers who invariably got drunk and maudlin on imported Johnny Walker. Velo-André took some canapés and went off to stand by the swimming pool. He remembered the village parties of his youth in Manambato—wild boar and palm wine, bonfires and dancing to the sound of mandolins, a sarong and bare feet instead of this overstarched safari suit he was wearing. God, how he hated shoes.

He moved around the swimming pool to get a better view of the guests. He recognized a few fellow politicians from the FNDR, but none of his personal friends were among them. The guests all seemed to be drawn from those opposition factions whose support Istasse had already recruited. Remi Toamasina was helping himself to a steak from the barbecue. He could see Giselle Mahjasampho sitting under the travelers' palm and feeding her chicken bones to Istasse's black Labrador.

Velo-André stood with the reflections from the swimming pool dancing on his safari suit, munching another canapé and plumbing the shadows of the garden for some ally. Was everybody here on Istasse's side? The invitation had called it a *Soirée de l'avant-Noel,* but now, it suddenly looked to him like a show of hands. These people had gathered to show their support for Istasse in the spring elections. In which case, what was he, Velo-André, doing here?

"Drinking?"

"Oh. Claude. Yes. Thank you."

Istasse handed him a *coca désinfecté.* Velo-André had not been entertained by Istasse for two years, and he wondered how the man remembered this to be his habit.

"Sorry, Velo, I didn't see you arrive," Istasse said.

"I was with the president, working on the new manifesto."

"Is it different from the old manifesto?"

"Ha, ha. A bit."

"Well, I'm glad you could come," Istasse said. "These formal parties make me nervous."

Velo-André felt flattered by this confidence and instantly fought against the emotion. He was older than Istasse and politically more experienced, but he was also six inches shorter. Istasse was Merina, one of the tall light-skinned people of the plateau, descendants of the Hova monarchs, while Velo-André

came from the coast. Istasse had been educated at the Jesuit
school and the Sorbonne. Velo-André had passed his baccalaureate at twenty-two and won a scholarship to Yugoslavia. Istasse
had looks, sophistication, and the friendship of foreign states-
men. Velo-André had four children, a plump, adoring wife,
and the *faux blancs* for company.

"I hear you have a new friend."

"Do I?"

"This oilman, Mr. Spence."

"Well, I wouldn't call him a friend."

"No?"

"Actually, yes." Velo-André felt ashamed and corrected
himself. "I liked him. He was a very honest man."

"Did he advise you to buy the oil rig?"

Velo-André hesitated. He'd told no one except the president about the subtext to Spence's visit, but almost from the
outset it seemed to have been common knowledge.

Istasse nudged him playfully. "Come on, Velo. You know
there are no secrets in this place. That Reuters fellow, Davies,
can quote me the minutes of most of our council meetings before
they've been transcribed."

"I suppose you're right." Velo-André couldn't help liking
Istasse. At root they had more in common with each other than
with all the stylish expatriates of Antananarivo. "In fact, Mr.
Spence advised me against it," he admitted.

"I'm glad to hear it," Istasse said. "You had me wondering
why you were prepared even to entertain the thought. Do you
know something we don't?"

"Well, if I did, I wouldn't tell you," Velo-André said.

"Of course not." Istasse winked. "But I'd know anyway."

He would too. Last month Velo-André had taken his children to see the conjurer at the French Cultural Institute. Another
parent had been called up from the audience and stood bemused
as the conjurer magically removed the man's watch, produced
silver balls from his ears and doves from under his jacket tails.

Claude Istasse extracted truths with much the same dexterity, and Velo-André, despite himself, felt the same sense of foolish admiration. Something flashed. A photographer was taking pictures on the other side of the pool.

"He said I was pissing in the wind. That's a Canadian expression."

"Pissing in the wind," Istasse laughed. "I'll tell you an American expression, Velo. 'If you want to soar with the eagles, don't spend your time with the turkeys.'"

"Turkeys?"

"People like Mr. Spence."

"He is a practical man. I like that."

Istasse smiled, and it was an honest, affectionate smile. "You're not hard enough for minerals, Velo. If I were going to offer you a ministry, I'd put you in something friendlier. You should be in charge of Eaux et Fôrets."

Velo-André said "I hope that's not a job offer, Claude."

"Of course not."

"Actually I was wondering why you invited me. I hope you didn't imagine I could be encouraged to betray my brother."

"Velo, Velo. I invited you because I like you." Istasse patted his shoulder, with the same gesture brushing a morsel of canapé from the wide lapel of Velo-André's light blue safari suit. "I want nothing from you, Velo," he said. "Just your being here is sufficient."

Relieved, Velo-André turned to him and smiled.

There was another flash from across the pool as the photographer took their photograph together.

At five-thirty P.M. in Morondava drinks were served on the sandy yard behind the police station. Four bottles had been lined up on the plywood table in descending order of rank: a beer for the commandant, an Orangina for the lieutenant, soda for the second lieutenant, and lime-in-water for the corporal. Three prisoners lounged under the papaya tree, playing a game with stones on a hollowed wooden board. The commandant offered Spence his choice of the drinks, but he declined.

Spence continued on up the main street toward the Grand Hotel, stopping in at the PTT to book a call to Canada. The girl behind the desk wore her Bureau de Poste tunic over a sarong that had been printed with a public health breast-feeding advertisement. Hanssen had already telexed for the documents, and getting the connection to Canada would take an hour or two; they'd put it through to the hotel.

On the veranda of the Grand Hotel a bony European was sitting in one of the wooden loungers, sipping a glass of some red concoction that Spence didn't recognize. He wore a short-sleeved cotton shirt outside his gray flannel trousers. His long face was sunburned on its most prominent points: his cheeks, his chin, and his nose. A battered Panama hat lay beside him on the table.

"I'm Father Mitchell." He offered Spence the chair beside him. "Will you have a drink?"

"What is it?"

"Grenadine."

"I'll get a beer in a minute."

"You must be Mr. Spence. I believe you had some problems at the rig."

"Yup. I just been to see the police. Are those guys up to much?"

Mitchell shrugged. "Oh, I'm sure they'll do their best. Probably load the police truck up with beer and girlfriends and drive up to your camp to make an investigation. It's like everything else in this country. They've got the superficial procedures but not the fundamental concepts. Don't expect fingerprints or anything as sophisticated as that. It's all purely social. Most crime is sorted out among the tribe."

"The old chief seems to think none of the locals would have stolen from there anyway."

"Ah, yes. *Fady.*" The missionary rolled his eyes.

"You don't buy it?"

"Well, it's like all these things, largely a matter of expedience."

Spence lay back in his seat. He didn't have the energy to ask what expedience was. Having once sat down, he hardly had the energy to head upstairs for a shower. Somewhere in the background a bird sang repeatedly a sequence of five notes that sounded to him like a riff by Willie Nelson. The missionary's green car was parked beside Perpetude's jeep.

"I hear you go up there sometimes."

"Sometimes. Brother Szanto normally looks after that bit, but he was off last week on sabbatical in Warsaw."

"You got some churches up that way?"

Father Mitchell laughed dryly. "Not exactly churches. In most of the villages it's just a house assembly. I can always draw in a few pagans with the projector, but for three months of the year goodness knows what they get in the way of spiritual nourishment."

Spence poured himself a glass of water. Mitchell continued to talk, eyes narrowed against the glare, addressing the motionless trees.

"The most depressing part is that when you come back, you realize how thin is the veneer of civilization we've imposed in Morondava. If you scratch the surface here, you find all the same practices: polygamy, exhumation, short-term marriages, calling up the ancestors. I read in the paper from England they're worried about child abuse over there. Ha. In the Third World child abuse is normal."

Spence refilled his glass and drank again. He'd stopped listening after the bit about Brother Szanto from Warsaw. Warsaw was in Poland. Did that make him a Marxist or what? Over the past year he'd lost track of European politics. "Are there many of you working here?" he asked.

"Well, the mission was planned for four Europeans and six Malagasy district ministers. Now it's the two of us and three helpers. We've a few unpaid catechists, but it's difficult to persuade them to learn anything. Another two years of this, and we'll have to think of selling off the station to the Adventists." Father Mitchell smiled and wiped his forehead. "It's rather humbling to live on the credit extended by Muslim shopkeepers."

Some children had gathered on the far side of the street to look at him. Spence waved; they giggled and ran inside the covered market. He turned back to the minister. "Not too good on waiters here, are they?"

"Perpetude should be out in a minute."

"Actually I think I'll take a shower."

As he got up, Perpetude Peyrame emerged from the hotel. "Ah," said Father Mitchell. *"Notre copain voudrait une bière."*

"Il y en a au frigo."

"Help yourself to a beer from the fridge," Father Mitchell translated.

Spence headed into the hotel.

"Oh, while you're here," Father Mitchell called after him, "Madame Peyrame has had some problems with the air conditioner, which keeps the larder cool. We were wondering if you knew how to fix it."

On the mention of her name she turned her dark eyes on him again. Why did he find that neutral gaze so disconcerting?

"Maybe she could ask me herself," Spence said.

Afterward he took a shower in his room, and the mosquitoes which lurked in its cool, dark corners flew up to roost on the dusty beams of the ceiling. Voices filtered through the louvered blinds from the first-floor balcony that ran along outside.

He was dozing on his bed when a knock came at the door.

"Telephone." Madame Peyrame gave the word its French pronunciation.

"What?"

The door opened. *"Te-le-phone,"* she said again.

"I'm sorry, I don't understand French."

She left, closing the door behind her. Spence pulled on a workshirt and followed her downstairs.

The kitchen was built on the back of the hotel. Most of it had migrated outside the building, and most of the cooking now took place in a makeshift oven and grill, built like a garden barbecue out of smoke-blackened stones. Two fat guinea fowl roosted in the branches above it.

The hotel's only working telephone was a wall-mounted Bakelite affair just inside the back doorway. Spence picked up the receiver. Outside, Madame Peyrame stood humming to the radio and plucking a chicken.

Miraculously the PTT had got his call through to the right number. The line sounded as though someone were operating a Moulinex in the background, but he could hear Dennis clearly enough to detect that his voice was still croaky from sleep.

"Spence. What time do you call this?"

"'Bout six P.M."

"Not here it ain't."

"Sorry, Dennis. They didn't know when they'd get a line."

"Okay, I'm awake now. What do you want?"

"You hear about the manifest?"

"Yes, yes, yes. That Mansen guy telexed us. The stuff's on its way."

"Just, I can't do anything till it arrives."

"She'll be there when she's there. They'll put it on the first flight down to you soon as she arrives. Spend some time on the beach. How's the weather?"

"Ever been to Ras Shukheir?" Spence asked. Ras Shukheir was a godforsaken beachhead on the Persian Gulf. Most rig hands would have paid money not to go there.

"That good, huh? But I heard the local girls are pretty friendly."

"I guess some of them." Spence was looking at Perpetude Peyrame working in the kitchen. There was blood on her hands and chicken feathers, like tribal decorations, stuck in her hair.

"Myra's awake," Dennis said.

"See you in a couple of weeks, Dennis."

"You take care now."

Spence put the phone down. Dennis's cozy Edmonton suburb dissolved like a dream. Perpetude Peyrame looked up from her work. *"Qu'est-ce que vous voulez à manger?"* she asked.

"Listen. Can we drop this?"

"Quoi?"

"The police gave me a whole bunch of forms that I could use your help with. . . . I know you speak English. Morgan Hanssen told me."

She said nothing.

"Listen, I can buy the fact that you don't like Canadians. That's okay with me. I probably wouldn't like them much myself if I was you." He'd been to enough oil towns to know what it had been like here—a bunch of roughnecks coming into town twice a week, whooping it up and whoring and smashing stuff up and probably trying to seduce her. He softened. "All I'm saying is, I'm here to do a job, and it would make living here a whole hell of a lot easier if I understood you once in a while."

She considered him darkly. Two years ago the disheveled look had been fashionable in Edmonton. Somehow, with her hair full of feathers and the front of her skirt all crumpled, Madame Peyrame achieved the same effect. She washed her hands and dried them on her apron.

"Would you like to eat fish or chicken?"

Surprised by her fluency, he took a moment to answer. "Chicken."

She nodded and started stuffing the feathers into a bag. "The police forms are a waste of time. Most of them never get read."

"Thanks. I appreciate it." Spence turned to go. "So where's this air-con of yours?"

"The man will be here in a week. I can ask him."

"I'll look at it tomorrow," Spence said.

That evening he had no problem finding Hanssen. The old man was leaning against the bar in the Ambre Disco, laughing over the frenetic clamor of the music and inexpertly performing tricks with a coin.

"Spence, you come to haf a party?"

"No, I came to talk to you."

"Oh, shit, I'm in trouble again, huh? This is Martine and this is Sylvane."

Sylvane smiled at him. The girl called Martine moved away from Hanssen and went to dance by herself.

"You found those document yet?" Hanssen asked.

"Nope. Nothing from the post office either."

"Well, you probably had it till after Christmas."

"When's Christmas?"

"Tuesday."

Tuesday. Spence wondered how it had managed to sneak up so close without him noticing.

"You might as well stick around here till then. There's a dance with an orchestra here on Monday night."

"An orchestra?"

"Some fellows with guitars. They call it an orchestra. We might get you to relax a bit. Haf a beer."

The labels were stuck to the bottles with cheap glue, which, in the barrel of ice behind the bar, had taken on the consistency of wallpaper paste. Spence peeled the label off his hand and put the bottle back on the bar.

"So what you doing tomorrow morning?" Hanssen asked. "You want to come and see the sugar factory?"

"I thought I might take a trip to the airstrip, take a look at that crash site."

"What do you want to go there for?"

"Just curious. You didn't tell me you were there when it crashed."

"You didn't ask."

"You got any ideas how it happened?"

"They wrote some report on all that. You should read the report."

"I already did," Spence told him. "I want to know what you think."

"Shit, I dunno. The thing had taken off. I was towing the fuel drum back to the shed. Everyone's going home. Then there's a bang, and everybody looks at the plane. By this time the door has fallen off, and the plane is going like this."

"What kind of a bang?"

"Yoost a bang. An explosion. Like something exploded. That kinda bang."

"It didn't say anything about that in the accident report."

"Ach, well, you know what these guys is like," Hanssen said. "Come here, poke about a bit. Never tell anyone what they're doing. Make a lot of measurements, then go home. If they'd spoken to anyone, they'd know about the two explosions."

"So where was this first explosion?"

"I told you. I was towing the fuel," Hanssen said. "The people who saw it, they all say there was an explosion at the back of the plane, that's why the door fell off."

"You mean an explosion in the luggage section?"

"Ach, folk say different things, but something make that door fall off, that's for sure."

"The one they never found."

"Didn't they?" Hanssen asked.

"It says in the accident report they never found it."

"Oh, they found it straight away. The air force took it away with them."

"You sure about that?"

"Oh, yes, they took it away for testing."

Spence moved away from the loudspeakers, lights from the glitter ball swarmed over the bleached boards of the dance hall. He was finding it difficult to concentrate.

Suppose Cora was right. Suppose Norco was breaching safety regulations on the last flight. It was possible they had been getting out in a hurry and carrying explosives from the seismic work on a passenger flight. The rig inventory would have told him what equipment went out on that plane, but the inventory had been stolen. The state of the luggage–hatch door would give him some clue, but that was missing too.

"It said in the accident report it had been stolen," Spence said.

"What did?"

"The plane door."

"Stole? What's anyone going to do with a door off a plane? Anyway, same thing as your documents. The plane door is *fady*. No one wants to steal it."

Spence said, "I spoke to Father Mitchell about *fady*. He thinks it's horseshit."

Hanssen slapped his thigh and stuck out his tongue. "'Course he does. If they still believe that stuff, he's wasted fifteen years here."

"And you think he has been?"

"Well, what do you think?"

"I don't know what to think anymore."

"Well, that's what it's like here," Hanssen said. "The air force do one thing. The police do another. Someone come in from outside and do something else. Time you finish, you don't know your ass from your elbow."

"Tell me how I find the crash site."

"Yoost go to the airstrip, and she's straight ahead of you," Hanssen said. "I'd take you out there myself, but we got some problems with the new rollers at the sugar factory. Ask Pappatoot. She'll drive you out there."

"I'll take a taxi," Spence said.

"You making any progress with her?"

Spence drank his beer.

"No? Then you should shop around here."

Spence put down the bottle. Following Hanssen's gaze

around the throbbing dance hall, he noticed the girl called Martine—almond eyes, straight dark hair under a red baseball cap, dancing, drunk, absorbed in the music with her hands behind her neck.

"You like Martine? I'll introduce you. She was pretty friendly with one of those Canadian guys."

At that moment the girl looked up and saw them watching her. She dropped her gaze and left the dance floor.

Spence disentangled himself from Hanssen's grip and reached for his stick. "You go ahead," he said. "I got some sleep to catch up on."

At midnight beyond the salt flats the bleached boards of the shantytown were bathed in moonlight. Martine sat on her rattan bed, in her driftwood shack, surrounded by pictures from French magazines. .

When she unlocked the metal trunk, the package was still there: a bulky brown envelope. She looked at it petulantly. It was obvious that the Canadian knew something. It had been clear from the veiled look he shot her as soon as he came into the bar, from the way he was quizzing Morgan Hanssen and the covert glances in her direction while she was dancing. He was looking for the document, and Hanssen would have told him she was Ben's girl.

For three days now people in Morondava had been talking about papers that had been taken from the rig. If they found her documents, they would never believe she'd been given them by Ben, or that she'd once intended to post them.

She picked up the envelope, then sat on the edge of her bed in a welter of indecision, turning it over and over in her hands. She didn't dare go to the police or to the Canadian, and Morgan Hanssen was a friend of the Canadian, so she couldn't trust him either. The simplest solution would be to take it down to the beach and put it on the fire where they burned coconut husks.

She stood up and started looking for her sandals. Yes, she

would burn it, and then no one would know. Unless the Canadian already knew she had it.

The light from her oil lamp played gently on the walls of her hut, on the scrap of mirror, the calendar, and the fashion pictures she had torn from French magazines. One shoe on and one shoe off, Martine sat down on her bed again to think.

Chapter 8

From the airstrip the accident investi-
gators had cut themselves an access track to the site of the crash.
Spence proceeded on foot. His taxi driver leaned back in the
seat, pulled his straw hat over his eyes, and switched on the
radio.

Fifty yards into the forest the track took a bend to the right,
and the battered taxi disappeared from view. The sound of
music from its radio faded and dwindled as the singing forest
enveloped him. Spence limped along the track. Butterflies the
size of lurid paperbacks flapped lazily through the shadows. A
chameleon watched him pass, eyes swiveling like gun turrets.
On the silver tree its green and purple hide was an unlikely
camouflage.

The path wound on, through eucalyptus and baobab, acacia
and wattle. Those few days of hard work on the rig had done
Spence good. He felt fitter than he had in weeks.

Before he left Canada, he'd driven up to see Cora at the hog
farm. He'd found her under the poplar trees by the old barn,
feeding the sows from a plastic bucket. Cora wore a pair of
overlarge dungarees and a working hat crammed over her
hair. She often wore Skippy's clothes with the sleeves and
the legs rolled up, which made her look even more delicate
than she was.

He helped her with her chores, then they went out to look at the baby owls she'd found down by the muskeg swamp. This summer, she said, the place was crazy with birds: robins, orioles, wild grouse, eagles.

Back at the house she gave him the accident report and fed him tea. When he was leaving, she hugged him and forgave him and said, "There's only one thing that's really important in the world, Spence, and that's the love of friends. You can lose a lover and lose a leg and lose all your money and somehow you'll pull through. Losing the love of your friends is the one thing none of us can survive. Remember that, hey. There's not many of us left."

Near the crash site the ground became softer underfoot. Spence was approaching a dried-up pool. The few remaining patches of brown water were alive with armored insects. On its far bank, flanked by charcoal spikes that had once been trees, lay the remains of the aircraft.

Spence skirted the waterhole, pushing between the pandanus palms that still sucked moisture from its cracked margins. The aircraft stood where it had fallen. The right wing had been flung off to the side, and parts of it still hung in the tangled trees twenty yards away. Around him the forest insects fizzed and rattled. A thin matting of leaves covered the ground here, but, where his feet disturbed the surface, the charred earth broke through.

Inside the fuselage the remains of the seats had been removed in the search for blast fragments. They'd taken most of the cockpit electronics as well, leaving blind sockets in the dashboard from which there now sprouted nerves of blackened wire. Loose control panels hung from the ceiling where the accident investigators had left them. Protected from the flames, the insulated wires were still pristine—an unlikely splash of color in the gloom.

Spence peered in through the open hatchway to the plane's

crumbled cabin. Even now it held the dank smell of death. He walked on around to the back of the plane, where a few thorny plants were already beginning to grow through the charred earth. The tail section had sunk into the ground. Just ahead of it the luggage compartment gaped open. The hinges were twisted and buckled by whatever forces had ripped off the door. The inside skin of the luggage compartment had been stripped out, probably by the accident investigators, and the controlling rods to the ailerons were exposed. The rods themselves were so bent and buckled that it was impossible to tell if any of them had been damaged before the crash.

Spence bent off a section and put it in his pocket, then stepped back, brushing rust and soot from his shirt. If the plane had landed tail down, that would explain the damage to the aileron rods. And if, as the accident report suggested, the luggage door had been improperly shut and simply tore off in the breeze, that could easily have caused the crash. The balance of these small planes was critical. If luggage had started falling out, an inexperienced pilot could easily have panicked and stalled. It was quite possible that the sound of the door ripping off just sounded like an explosion. Was he merely trying to find something just to show Cora he'd tried? The trees all around him were a solid wall, creeping in, like the trees around the rig, to claim this scorched clearing. He turned and walked away, leaving the plane lying on its back with both wheels sticking up in the air like the ungainly legs of a murder victim.

The rains were four weeks late. The morning sky remained cloudless, but inside the covered market the air was charged with moisture, giving a thick, suffocating quality to the heat. Perpetude walked slowly through the reticulated darkness. Dusty shafts of light burned through the thatch onto dried sardines, eggplants, and manioc.

"Is that a bomb, Perpetude?"

She turned to find Father Mitchell fanning himself with his
Panama.

"It's a cylinder of coolant, for the air conditioner. The
Canadian is fixing it for me."

"Good to know he's making himself useful."

"And you?" she asked. Friday lunchtime was when he
normally trained the catechists.

"Collecting these." He was holding a sheaf of colored papers from the print works.

"Christmas decorations?"

"Election posters actually."

She could read the caption VIVE LE PLAN DE DIX ANS.

"You're seriously supporting Istasse?"

"We all have to do our bit, Perpetude. Is it time for a
grenadine?"

Father Mitchell sat on the veranda, fanning himself with
his hat. After a moment Perpetude came out onto the veranda
carrying a tray of drinks and a dusty brown envelope.

"What have you got there?"

"I don't know. Someone left it inside."

The minister took it from her and read the address. "Ben
Lowers. Does that ring a bell?"

"He stayed here. He was one of the Canadians who died
in the crash."

"Hmm. A message from the grave." Mitchell flexed the
package. "It's open," he said.

"I'll give it to Mr. Spence."

Mitchell ignored her and tipped the contents out onto his
lap. A clear polyethelene envelope fell out. The label said,
"Mansalava 1—Well summary." Father Mitchell unzipped the
polyethelene envelope and tipped out the computer readout—
a continuous folded sheet of graph paper covered with tracings
like those from a seismograph, which he couldn't understand.

He turned back to the cover.

"Confidential—Property of Norco Oil."

Perpetude poured the drinks. "I think you should put it back."

"Where do you think it came from?"

"I've no idea. Maybe it's one of the documents from the rig."

"Do you mind if I keep it?"

Perpetude stopped pouring. "You? Whatever for?"

"I promised Charles Hunter I'd make sure nothing went astray. . . ."

"When?"

"When the plane crashed. I said I'd make sure nothing got looted."

"Can I see it?"

He handed the document across. Perpetude put it back in its plastic and paper envelopes, then placed it on the seat behind her, out of his reach. "You can take your sense of patriotism too far, Father Mitchell." She raised her glass. *"Santé."*

Father Mitchell leaned forward, reverting to the tone he used at the mission for arbitrating in theological controversies. "What you have to understand, Perpetude, is that there are two different interests represented here. Charles Hunter and your Mr. Spence represent two different companies. Mr. Hunter is an executive for Norco, which paid for the whole operation down here. Mr. Spence merely works for the drilling company they employed."

"I do understand that."

"Ergo, Mr. Hunter is the ultimate authority."

She tapped on the wooden crucifix that hung over his chest. "I thought that post was already occupied."

Mitchell found this joke to be in bad taste. He gave her a thin smile. "You know what I mean."

"I'm sorry, I don't. Spence is here. Hunter is in London. We know Spence's looking for documents. Maybe this is what he needs."

"He told me what he'd lost was a rig manifest."

"Do you know what a rig manifest looks like?"

"Well, I know it's not that. That one says, 'Well Summary.'"

"Maybe they're the same thing. But I really don't think it's anything to do with us. If you've got some doubts about it, you should talk to Mr. Spence."

"Perpetude, why are you being like this?"

"Like what?" she scanned his face. "I just don't see why it's so important to you."

"It's not important. Frankly I don't give a hoot about it." Father Mitchell put his hat on and rose to his feet. "But I thought you and I had an understanding."

"We did." It was a slip of the tongue. "We do," she corrected herself.

"I'll see you anon," he said.

"Father Mitchell. You haven't finished your drink."

He left without looking back.

As the missionary made his way back down the street, Perpetude wondered how she'd managed to offend him. She never understood his little moods. You rub shoulders with someone for ten years and you assume that you are familiar with them. He had talked about his education: four years at New College in London, his enrollment with the Council for World Mission. She knew he came from a family of missionaries and had spent his first posting—ten years—in Senegal. She knew through their conversations the vague pattern of his yearly routine—the church services, the training of local missionaries and catechists, the schools committee, district and regional synods, the quarterly visits to the capital. She knew about his faith, his campaign against animism and syncretism, his loneliness, his prejudice against the Muslims, his long-standing and secret admiration of her. One Christmas several years ago, drunk on palm wine, he had admitted to her that there was a wife somewhere—Teignmouth, wherever that was—to whom, in name at least, he had remained married till her death last year.

But now, on reflection, it was the other facets of his life, the hidden facets, which were more important: his growing fascination with politics; his apparent self-doubt; his unlikely friendship with Charles Hunter; his increasingly public admiration of Istasse. Father Mitchell had changed in the last eighteen months into an entirely different kind of person. But, like the moving hands of the clock or the changing of the tides, it was a change so gradual and continuous that only after the event did she realize it had happened. The one person she thought she knew better than anyone in Morondava was suddenly a complete enigma to her.

The broken air-con unit was a rusting metal box bolted onto an outside wall in the palm grove at the back of the hotel. Its old nuts creaked and grated, showering Spence's hands with rust. The cowling eventually came off to a chorus of twanging complaints, revealing three decades of dirt and some pieces of bird's nest. Half an hour later he had gathered an audience of local urchins, who watched in silence as he worked. One of the older boys helped him to lift the unit away from the wall and lay it on some boards.

He ran some Freon through the system and listened for leaks, eventually discovering a crack in a concealed section of copper piping. With an old blow-lamp borrowed from the fisheries, he brazed the ends of the copper pipe together, then greased and tightened the nuts, reassembled the frame, bolted it on the wall, and cleaned the casing with a rag.

Evening found him perched on the end of the oilmen's disintegrating jetty, pulling on his bottle of rum. The sun was beginning to droop over the Mozambique Channel. Spence sat listening to the sea slapping against the rusting sides of the scuttled barge. A group of women were gathering on the beach. Far out to sea a little fleet of outrigger canoes was returning from the reef, their square sails pregnant with the onshore breeze.

A shadow fell over him. He looked up and found Madame
Peyrame standing above him.

"Thank you," she said. "It works."

He held the bottle out toward her. "Do you want some
rum?"

"You shouldn't drink that. It is very bad for your health."

"So everyone keeps telling me."

The wind caught her hair and blew it across her face. She
caught it and tied it in a knot. "Someone left this at the hotel,"
she said. "I think it's for you."

Spence took the package from her. He unzipped the plastic
folder and flipped through the document.

"Where did you say this came from?"

She shrugged. "It arrived at the hotel. Amin Bahera thinks
that one of the oilmen had left it with his girlfriend."

Spence turned over the envelope and read the address.

"Ben Lowers," he said.

"You knew him?"

"Sure. He was the logging engineer. He's the guy who had
the job of making these recordings."

"Recordings of what?"

Spence flipped back through the drilling log, glancing at
every other page. "Different stuff about the drilling," he said.
"What kind or rock, porosity, water content, any hydrocar-
bons—all that shit." At a glance it was a pretty standard record
of a dry well. What bothered him was not the log itself but the
address. Ben Lowers was sending a logging report home to his
own address.

"Well, I have to get some fish," she said.

Spence took another pull on the bottle and squinted into
the glare off the sea. The boats were drawing closer.

"Is something the matter?" she asked.

"No. It's just I knew this guy. I never thought he'd be so
stupid as to try and sell this stuff."

"Is it worth something?"

"Well, it's not worth nothing. I mean, it's the only hard proof in the world of the local geology. To anyone else who thinks of drilling here, this would be worth a few thousand dollars—just for showing them where not to waste their money."

"Father Mitchell said we should send it to London."

Spence pondered this. The last thing Ben Lowers's widow needed was a scandal on top of everything else. Ultimately there was no harm done. "Yeah, well, your mail doesn't seem too hot here." He said, "I'll send it to them from Canada."

When she'd bought her fish, Spence accompanied Perpetude back to the hotel. An African woman walked in front of them with a whole tuna fish balanced on her head.

Spence said. "So tell me about this plane crash."

"I didn't see it. I was at the hotel with Father Mitchell. What do you want to know?"

"I spoke with Morgan Hanssen last night. He said something about hearing an explosion before the plane hit the ground. I mean, by law they're not allowed to carry explosives on a passenger plane, but if he was right—"

"He is right. There were two explosions. A small one, then the bigger one. Everyone knows that." She looked across at him with the setting sun in her face. "There's a man in England who would be able to tell you about it," she went on. "A tourist from the hotel. He was there with a camera when it happened."

"What—he photographed the whole thing?"

"I don't know, but he was photographing the wreckage when I got there."

"Did the investigators talk to him?"

"No. He left the next day, before all those air-force people arrived. He's in the hotel register."

Luggage belonging to the afternoon's arrivals was being brought into the hotel. There was no mail from the capital.

Perpetude led him through to the office behind the reception desk and took out the huge leather-bound reception book.

They were all in it, all his old friends: Skippy, Al Parachuik, George Wilhelm, signing in for two and three days every time they were down from the rig to unload the supply boats. In August there was a long list of signatures, which represented the rig crew who'd come down for the last big dismantling job in Morondava. Then in September the same list of names when they had all signed out.

"Here," Perpetude pointed to a name. She was close enough for Spence to smell the shampoo she used.

"What, one of these guys here?" Spence asked.

"No, they were all the air-force men and the accident investigators. This is the man who took the photographs."

Between the list of oilmen and the incoming accident investigators, there was a single signature, written in bold capital handwriting: ELGIN KIRK. There was no address.

That night there were only two other guests in the Grand Hotel, and Amin Bahera had been given the evening off. A table for one was set in the dining room. Perpetude brought Spence a dish of tomatoes, onions, and prawns drenched in oil and vinegar. She watched him eat the first mouthful as though it were some kind of test.

"It's all right?"

"It's just fine."

"Your friends preferred tinned beans and toast."

"Why? Do you have tinned beans here?"

"No," she said.

"Well, I guess this'll have to do."

She saw that he was joking. It was the first time he'd seen her smile.

"What are you having yourself?" he asked.

"The same."

"Want to come and join me?"

"I don't eat with the guests," she said.

"I'm not a guest. I'm the man who fixes the air conditioner."

The lamplight caught the glint of a gold tooth in the corner of her mouth. That was the second time he'd seen her smile.

She came back with a plate and a salad bowl and sat opposite him with her back to the open doors that led onto the veranda. Above the door Amin Bahera had strung up Christmas decorations: some tarnished tinsel and a row of cardboard toucans with the logo GUINNESS IS GOOD FOR YOU.

"Your name's not really Pappatoot," he said.

"Peyrame."

"I mean your first name."

"Perpetude."

"Perpetude. I'd tell you mine, but I don't have one. My dad wasn't too organized in that department."

"You don't have a name?"

"Just Spence."

Perpetude ate with her fingers, pulling the heads off the prawns and separating the soft pink shells with her thumbs.

"Tell me about your father."

"Tell me about yours."

"I grew up in Belo," she said, "farther up the coast. My father was a tobacco planter. My mother was the queen."

"The Queen?"

"Well, they call it the Queen. She was the eldest daughter of the chief."

"No kidding. I never ate with royalty before. What's it like up there?"

"There's not much to see now. In the old days there were plantations, big houses, boats in the river. Now it's the same as here."

"Same kind of country as this?"

"Flat like this but no trees."

"I'm used to flat. You ever been to the prairies?"

"Where? Canada? No," she said.

"I grew up on the prairies. Kind of the same as here. Big skies. Except not so hot."

"Your parents were farmers?"

"My aunt and uncle. I grew up with my aunt and uncle. My mother died when I was born."

"What happened to your father?"

"Oh, he was everywhere and nowhere. He was a prospector."

"For gold?"

"Gold, jade, anything he could get his hands on," Spence said. "Galena, molybdenite, chalcopyrite. He couldn't spell the names of most of the rocks he came home with, but he sure knew how to find them. Someone would show him a little nugget of gold and he'd look at the texture and the color and he'd say, yes, this is from Massey May Creek or this one's from Moose Creek bar. And he was right too. When he died, there was a tobacco jar in his dresser full of gold dust from claims in the Northern Territories he'd never even bothered to stake. He just had a feel for the thing."

Insects were batting around the oil lamp. Perpetude wiped the oil off her fingers and moved it farther down the table.

"So where did you learn to speak English?" Spence asked.

"At the mission school. It has always been run by English missionaries."

"Did you go to college here?"

"France. When I was sixteen, my parents sent me to Paris to study for the baccalaureate. They were convinced that to be happy, I needed an education."

"You didn't agree?"

"Well . . . it was a strange time in Europe then—the end of the sixties. I look at photographs, and it all seems so ridiculous now. Clothes. Philosophy. Rich people pretending to be poor. Lovers pretending not to love. It was a very unimportant time."

"What were you studying?"

"Philosophy."

"I don't know shit about philosophy."

"You know about air conditioners," she said. "That's much more important."

He looked up from his food to see if she were mocking him, but her expression was perfectly serious. "If you saw Paris in '68, you'd known that was true," she said.

Outside, the moon rose over the covered market. "Why, what happened in '68?" he asked.

"Oh, it was nothing. The writers and philosophers tried to stage a coup. It lasted a week."

"What kind of coup?"

"It was just some student riots, really."

Something brushed his toe, and he looked down. Termites were hurrying around their feet, shedding their wings.

"Anyway," she said, "that's what finally made me decide to leave Paris. I came back here with Thierry and took over the hotel."

"Thierry's your husband?"

"He was just a friend then. We got married here."

"So where is he now?"

She hesitated. "In the end he went back to France."

"Do you still go back there yourself?"

"I'll go for a month at the end of January. It's quiet here during the rains."

"Seems pretty quiet here just now."

"It's enough. I don't get bored. I think work is like alcohol. In the right amount it can make you happy. But if you become dependent on it, it numbs the senses."

Spence mopped the vinaigrette off his plate with a wad of bread. A wind flapped the cardboard toucans that were hanging in the doorway. He could hear a politician on the radio, the low rumble from the generator behind the hotel. Insects clambered over the neck of his bottle of rum. Since they started talking, he noticed, he hadn't touched it.

Chapter 9

The Grand Bal de Noël wasn't due to start till after eight. For the early part of the evening Spence sat on his first-floor veranda at the Grand Hotel with the smoke from a mosquito coil winding around him. Fireflies appeared in the dried grass along the side of the hotel as lights and oil lamps began to go on all over town. It was the time of day when the clouds turned pink and the mango trees turned an impossible shade of emerald green.

As he sat watching, a memory returned of his childhood in Kiddersley. He'd sat then on a wooden veranda in almost exactly this position, watching the townsfolk returning from work. He remembered their voices hanging in the summer air, fireflies and mosquitoes. A baby crying, a girl's laughter.

What was it Hanssen had said on the drive to the rig about finding where you were supposed to be? Did he mean something as simple as these tiny associations? A shouted greeting, the sound of feet on a wooden walkway.

As the night deepened, the person on the far side of the covered market who had until then been playing religious music on radio Voice of America, switched to an African channel broadcasting Congolese music. From farther off, in the Villa Touristique, came the sound of the band from the capital tuning up their electrical instruments.

Groups of people in twos and threes began making their way to the seafront. The local girls congregated in the street below him, gathering in strength before they risked the dance hall. A group of young men drove past noisily in a pickup truck. Now he could hear faint dance music and snatches of song. In the past he had associated this feeling of nostalgia and regret with images of Nancy, but strangely now he found it difficult to reconjure her face. The sense of yearning persisted, but, like the pain in his leg, had become less acute and less focused—a nostalgia for other, less palpable things—community, friendship, tenderness.

At half past ten he made his way through the hotel, then out along the seafront to the Villa Touristique.

The Villa Touristique was bigger and more dilapidated than the Ambre Disco, though built along the same lines, open at its far end to the wind off the sea. There was a low stage on the left-hand side for the dais at the opposite side of the hall reserved for the notables of the town—the préfect de police, the chef de district and his deputy, the head of the mosque, and the Catholic priest from the leprosy hospital. The chair reserved for Father Mitchell was empty.

A few tables had been placed around the sides of the dance hall for anyone else who wanted to sit down, but most of these had now been pushed aside and the tables stacked on top of them to make room for dancing. Everyone was on the dance floor, performing a strange rocking dance that was halfway between a waltz and a jig. The band played frenetically on their accordions and guitars, and the dancers whirled and whooped and cannoned into each other. Hanssen was there, in an undiplomatic embrace with the buxom daughter of the head of the PTT. Spence could see Perpetude as well, being navigated around the dance floor by Monsieur Tsiromandidy, the commandant de police.

Time passed. The music changed. The dancers formed and

re-formed. Beers were passed over their heads to the far side of the hall. Hanssen caught Spence's eye and shouted something that Spence couldn't hear, then the dance enveloped him again. When Spence closed his eyes, he could clearly picture the Thanksgiving hop in Kiddersley—the violinists in checked shirts, the caller calling the dance steps, the children playing between table legs, the drunk and exhausted dancers tumbling off the dance floor.

"Spence?"

He opened his eyes. Perpetude was standing in front of him.

"Morgan Hanssen said you wanted to dance with me."

"He said what?"

"You don't?"

"Sure, I'd love to, but with this leg I can't dance worth shit."

"It's very crowded," she said. "You don't have to move around much."

As he stood, the band struck up a passable imitation in English of "Me and Mrs. Jones," the two girls singing in harmony words that they had learned phonetically from tapes and records.

"Why are you smiling?" she asked.

"This song, we used to play it when I was a teenager."

They danced, after a fashion. By supporting himself against her, he could sway backward and forward and pivot about on his good leg.

"They say that becomes the music of your life," Perpetude said, "the songs you hear at that age. When you first leave home, when you first fall in love."

"So what's the music of your life?"

"I don't know. Jazz, I think. Nat King Cole, John Coltrane, Miles Davis. Before I went to Paris, we didn't get much music here. The radio hadn't started broadcasting, and it was difficult to get records. But every month a different film came to town, and we would watch it four or five times, all the children, every weekend. So now I have the films of my life: *Ben Hur, Un Homme et Une Femme, Anthony and Cleopatra.*"

"I saw that one," Spence said. "I was in love with Elizabeth Taylor. You ever see *The Sandpiper?*"

"No."

"It's about a minister who realizes he's in love."

"And what happened?"

"Oh, I don't know—it doesn't work out. Where's Father Mitchell?"

"He didn't come."

"What's wrong? Too noisy for him here?"

"I don't know. He comes most years."

Through the crowd he could see Morgan Hanssen now wiggling against a huge woman in a blue patterned sarong.

"Morgan's enjoying himself."

"Morgan always does, it's his great talent," she said.

"You think I could take a lesson from him?"

She shrugged. "Some men are improved by sadness. But I think you should drink less. Thierry had that problem."

"How did he kick it?"

"He didn't. In fact he drank more and more once he got here. I think he liked the idea of living and working here more than he liked the reality of it. It's not a place for abstract thinkers. He got depressed. He left, came back, left again, came back again. Finally he left for good."

"How long ago was that?"

"The last time? Seven years ago."

"You think he'll come back again?"

"Actually he's dead now. He committed suicide."

"Oh. I'm sorry."

There was a problem of some sort behind the bar. Didier, the African barman at the Villa Touristique, was trying to catch her attention. Perpetude wound her way through the dancers to talk to him. She was away for some time, and Spence lost

her in the crowd. The music struck up again, and Spence retrieved his stick.

His shirt was sticking to him. He went to the back of the
hall and stood on the railing where the breeze came in off the
sea. A wooden stair ran down onto the beach, and a couple
stood pressed against the wooden wall of the dance hall in the
darkness below him.

He walked down the steps, onto the firm sand of the beach
and into the warm, steady wind that came off the sea. The lights
and music of the dance hall receded behind him. The tide was
out. He could see the phosphorescent waves washing over the
sand. Along the beach he could see the dark shadow of the jetty.
Behind that the Ambre Disco. Most of the town was in darkness. He could make out the Grand Hotel because there was a
light shining from one of the rooms upstairs, a flickering, moving light coming from one of the bedrooms. Spence stepped
sideways to see more clearly between the silhouettes of the
palms.

The light was coming from the end room on the upper
floor.

His room.

When Spence entered the darkened hotel, the old wall clock in
the front hall was striking eleven. Through the other side of
the dining room the central courtyard was deserted. The stairs
were cross-hatched by the dim, moonlit shadows of the banana
trees in the central courtyard. Spence climbed the staircase,
hauling himself up on the banister, trying to keep off the loose
and creaking boards at its center.

There was a gallery leading off to the rooms on three sides.
From here Spence could see torchlight under the door of his
room.

A board creaked beneath him, and the light inside his room
stopped moving.

He made his way around the walkway, keeping close to
the railing, putting as much weight as possible on his feeble left

leg in order to tread more quietly. He let go of the railing and took a step toward his door, placing his walking stick more heavily than he intended. It tapped sharply on the boards beneath his feet, and immediately the light inside his room was extinguished.

Spence stood where he was, halfway to his door, hardly breathing. Whoever it was in his room would be waiting, listening to see if he passed by.

He took a step forward, alert for every noise now. He could reach the door handle from here.

In his mind he was forming a mental image of the interior of the room. The intruder's most likely escape route would be via the French windows, which opened onto the common balcony at the front of the hotel. If Spence moved fast, he could intercept him before he reached it.

He waited three seconds, took a breath, then flung open the door.

Nothing.

The door creaked back on its hinges.

Light from across the street cast shadows through the louvered shutters. He strained his eyes into the shadowy recesses of the room, reaching for the light switch beside the door. When he turned it, nothing happened. He had switched off the lights via the switch above his bed, and the circuit was still broken at that point.

Spence moved cautiously into the darkness, prodding with his stick into the gloom behind the door. He was moving alongside the bed, when suddenly a figure came off the far wall and made a dash for the French windows.

Spence forgot the light switch and bounded across the room, bashing his good knee hard on the metal corner of his bed. The intruder was fumbling with the catch of the louvered doors. Spence dropped his stick, half falling, half diving toward him, and together the two of them burst through onto the balcony.

Hinges bent. Wood splintered. Spence took a fist on the

side of the head but managed to get both arms around the stranger's legs. Hauling himself around on a stick for three months had given Spence a grip like a vice. Now he dragged his assailant to the floor, scrabbling in the darkness for a better purchase.

The man was silent, determined, raining punches on Spence's head and shoulders. He dragged himself up on the balcony rail and kicked free.

One summer long ago Skippy and he had gone down to the Calgary stampede and taken part in the steer wrestling. Hanging on to a two-year-old bullock had been a stroll compared with this. As the young African made a bid for freedom, he managed to lunge after him again and catch his shirt. The shirt ripped. Spence took a knee in the chest and fell back, gasping. The intruder ran to the balcony railing and hesitated, unsure whether the sloping iron roof of the veranda would bear his weight. As he paused, Spence hauled himself upright and projected himself forward on his good leg. There was a rending of wood, and the two of them went through the railings, bounding onto the corrugated iron roof below.

Arms. Legs. The night crashed and resounded. From somewhere, below them, he could make out an approaching car engine. Headlamps raked the front of the hotel as, together, they rolled down the incline of the veranda roof. Spence felt the void opening beneath him, and he grabbed at the guttering for support. It came away in his hand.

Falling off the rig had been like this, the chill of terror through the soles of his feet and the palms of his hands, the moment when he knew he was doomed. The endless wait for the impact that he knew was going to cripple him for life.

The ground rushed up to meet them, driving the air out of his lungs. Lights and stars spun around his head. The younger man recovered first and ran off into the shadows at the side of the Grand Hotel. Spence tried to call out after him, but there was no air in his lungs. He heard shouts and running footsteps.

"Holà. Arrêtez!"
Then a face swam into view.
"Perpetude."
"Are you all right?"
"Where's the other guy?"
"Didier ran after him. Shall I call the doctor?"
"Hang on."
Spence moved his arms, he moved his legs. He could sit up now.

Looking up, he saw that he had fallen twelve feet off the veranda roof. The rubbish sacks had cushioned his fall. A gift from the people of America. The zinc guttering above him hung crazily from its supports, still creaking backward and forward from the force of his latest, despairing clutch.

Perpetude helped him sit up.

"I saw a light in my room," Spence said. "I was trying to stop him."

Breathing was difficult, and talking made his ears hurt. Spence tested his jaw.

"Come inside." Perpetude helped him to his feet. "I'll get the police."

"It can wait."

She put an arm around him and helped him up the steps. Every part of him seemed to hurt—his knee, his biceps, his back, the angle of his eye. When he breathed deeply, there was a pain in one of his ribs.

As Spence came inside, Didier, the African barman from the Villa Touristique, came back, sweating and breathing heavily. "It is too dark," he said. "I lost him on the beach."

"What did he look like?"

"I have no idea. From his clothes he was from out of town. What happened? Did he attack you?"

"I attacked him. I found him in my room."

"It happens this time of year. Have you still got your wallet?"

Spence felt his back pocket. "I've got it here. I'm okay now." He steadied himself against the balustrade of the veranda. "What did you come back for anyway?"

"They've run out of beer at the Villa Touristique," Perpetude told him. "We came to get some crates from the cold store."

Didier was inspecting his sleeve. "You are bleeding," he said.

Spence looked down and saw that he was right. A ragged graze ran the length of his right forearm.

"Stay there," Perpetude told him. "I'll clean it up for you."

Spence sat at the dining room table as Didier ferried beer crates past them, outside and into the waiting pickup truck. Perpetude returned with a magazine, some cotton swabs, and a bowl of disinfectant.

She laid out the magazine and put his arm on top of it.

"Morgan Hanssen told me once you had a theory about accidents," he said.

"Do I? What's that?"

"He said you reckoned it was God's way of telling you what you should be doing."

"And what's this telling you?"

"Not to trust the woodwork around here, I guess."

"Or to stay off the rum," she said.

"I hadn't had much."

Perpetude began dabbing at his arm with a wet flannel. The magazine bore a headline: GOVERNMENT TOUJOURS EN CRISE. There was a picture lower down of two African men at a party. It was blurred and poorly printed, but he recognized one of the figures.

"Ha. That's Velo-André."

Perpetude looked up from her work.

"Yes."

"The tall guy looks kind of familiar as well."

"That's Claude Istasse, the head of the air force. You've

seen him on those posters of Father Mitchell's."
"I thought he was the opposition."
"He is."
"So what are he and Velo doing together? Ouch."
"No idea. Sorry, is that painful?"
"Yes."
"I'm sorry," she said. "It's full of dirt."
Blood leaked across the picture of Velo-André. She dabbed
his arm with disinfectant. Spence winced. "So who are you
going to vote for?" he asked.
"Not Istasse."
"You don't like him."
"Oh, yes, he's a nice man. Actually we were at the Sor-
bonne together in 1968. He was a socialist then."
"So . . . ah! . . . tell me about that stuff. About these riots."
"You wouldn't be interested," she said.
"Maybe not. But it's less painful if you talk."
Her eyes flicked upward, met his.
"Well," she said, "it started off as a street fight between
some left-wing students and a right-wing group of thugs."
"What were they fighting about?"
She thought for a moment. "Who knows? Vietnam wasn't
our affair anymore. I think we'd finished fighting about Algeria.
They were just aggressive young men. Anyway, the police were
sent in to sort it out, and both sides turned on them. Then the
rector let the police follow them into the Sorbonne, and everyone joined in. So it became youth against authority, and the
rest of the city took part."
She rinsed the cloth in disinfectant again and returned to
his arm.
"At the beginning it was great fun. We marched through
the streets, and people threw chocolate and sausages to us. We
chanted slogans. Everyone became a young anarchist for a
week—even the old professors, even the bourgeoisie. Especially
the bourgeoisie. They loved it. They came out and took photographs of each other standing on the barricades; the Latin

Quarter was full of tourists." Perpetude looked up. "You really never heard about it? Les Enragés, l'Occident. Daniel Cohn-Bendit."

"Don't remember," Spence said. "I think I was working too hard. We had a boom going on in Edmonton about then."

Perpetude brushed an insect away. "Anyway that part lasted only a week. Then it became foolish. Everyone was on strike. Everyone had a slogan. The speaking clock went on strike. The Folies Bergère went on strike. The footballers went on strike. I remember them marching around the Place Vendôme with a banner saying, GIVE FOOTBALL BACK TO THE FOOTBALLERS. What do you think that means?"

"No idea."

"I don't think they did either." She rinsed the swab again. "It's quite deep here. Do you have strikes in the oil business?"

"Hardly ever. Where I come from you mainly just work with friends. Most of the bosses are your friends. It's kind of a family."

"Yes," she said. "I think that's how it should be."

"So?" Spence said. He liked sitting next to her, watching the expression of concentration on her face and listening to her low voice. She looked up, then continued dabbing at his arm, working from the center, gently brushing out the fragments of rust and metal.

"I don't know," Perpetude said. She recalled a meeting in the Grand Amphithéâtre, listening to Istasse, aged twenty-three, speaking to the crowd. "I think I suddenly lost the sense of it," she said. "Like watching a noisy film in a foreign language. It stopped making sense to me. People with big, important-sounding ideas were just creating chaos. Before that I suppose I was left-wing. I certainly didn't support de Gaulle, but afterward I didn't support anyone. It all seemed very stupid. 'Give football back to the footballers.' "

A praying mantis was balancing against the oil lamps, waiting for insects, slowly opening and closing its fragile forelimbs as the moths fluttered through them.

"At the same time the barricades got more violent. People started burning cars and chopping down trees to block the road. So the young anarchists became old bourgeoisie again and locked themselves in their apartments. The Sorbonne was full of litter and cigarettes. We had lots of earnest meetings to discuss football for the footballers and so on, but in private, people started hoarding food and complaining about the shortages. The rich ones left town, and everyone else complained about the rubbish and did nothing to clean it up. When de Gaulle finally returned, even the left-wing secretly felt relieved. Like a wild teenage party when papa suddenly comes home and takes charge again."

Outside, flying beetles swarmed around the streetlamp, the swift, dark shapes of bats foraging among them.

"So?"

"So I left them all to it. Finished," she said.

"*Tu veux y retourner?*" Didier had finished loading up the pickup and was about to head back to the Villa Touristique.

"*Allez-y,*" she said. "*J'arrive.*" Then to Spence. "This will sting."

She painted Spence's arm with Mercurochrome and held her hair to one side while she blew on it. In the street Didier's pickup truck reversed away from the hotel.

"How do you feel?"

"I'm fine. I appreciate it. I'll let you get back to the dance."

He stood up, and his knee buckled.

"Here." She took his arm. "I'd better help you up to your room."

The light was still on in his bedroom. She helped him to the doorway, and he hobbled to his bed. As she attempted to pull closed the broken louvered doors, Spence lay down painfully.

"Your bag's still here," she said.

"There's nothing in it anyway. Just clothes."

As she moved to the door, Spence raised his head and felt under the pillow.

"Son of a bitch."

"What have you lost?"

"That drilling log you found. I had it under the pillow, here."

"You should have given it to me," she said. "I'd have put it in the safe."

"I didn't reckon anyone would be that interested in it."

"Well . . . we can speak to the police tomorrow. If this burglar came down from the capital, his name will be on the flight list." She added, "You can check at Air Madagascar tomorrow."

"Or just wait till they're boarding and look for the guy with all the bruises."

"You think he was injured?" she asked.

"I darn well hope so."

There were about thirty people at the airstrip. Most of them were waiting to greet friends or to collect foods from the capital. Spence stood near the approach road, watching the new arrivals. Monsieur Tsiromandidy, the commandant de police, had delegated two young policemen to accompany Spence, on the off-chance that he might be able to recognize the man who had assaulted him.

He had already noted most of the passengers who were booked on the flight. The musicians from the capital who had played in the Villa Touristique two days before stood in a group with their instrument cases. The girl singers wore matching cotton suits with short, tight skirts and bodices that flared at the waist. There was an old woman standing guard over a pile of raffia bags. The other passengers included a father and his two daughters, who were playing in the shade of his parked Renault van.

There were two single men whose names were on the flight list. One of them was a thin man from one of the local villages who had won a scholarship to the university. There was no sign of the other man, although the Air Madagascar clerk had assured Spence that he was booked on the flight. His name, according to the airline, was Marcel Antansoa.

Spence watched the passengers as they filed inside. Still no sign of the missing man. The pilot checked his watch and conferred briefly with the Air Madagascar clerk, then he climbed back into the cockpit.

"Mr. Spence?"

He turned to see a clerk from the PTT.

"Package for you from the capital."

It was postmarked Edmonton and marked URGENT. For a second Spence looked at it in confusion. After the events of the last few days he'd almost forgotten why he'd come to Morondava in the first place. The package had been examined by customs and was now covered in government stamps. Spence tore it open. His manifest for the rig inventory had finally arrived.

"Got a Christmas present?"

"Hi, Morgan," he said. "What are you doing here?"

"Oh, yoost come to pick up some parts for the sugar factory. Fucking cane crushers all fucket up. You want a lift back?" Hanssen said.

"Sure. Thanks."

He helped Hanssen lift his spare parts over the tailgate of the pickup. His arm was still painful, but he could work with it again.

"What you doing here, anyway?" Hanssen asked. "Collecting your mail?"

"No. Mainly just looking out for the guy who attacked me."

"Who was that?"

"No idea. Went by the name of Marcel Atan something."

"Marcel Antansoa?" Hanssen said.

"You know him?"

"Not around here. I knew a guy called that in the capital."

"You did?"

"Young fellow, my height but skinny. Kind of sharp little face."

"That's him. How did you know him?"

"He give me a lift a couple of times."

"He's a taxi driver?"

"No, he worked for Norco. He was Charles Hunter's driver. Don't know who he's working for now."

As they drove back, Spence said, "So tell me about Charles Hunter."

"The big boss? I only met him once."

"Did you get on with him?"

"I didn't ever talk to him. He only came to Morondava a couple of times. Shook everyone by the hand. Had a hob and a nob with Mitchell. Visited the rig that last time to pick up coarse, then off in the private plane."

"Coarse? Coarse what?"

"No idea. That's what they said he was doing. Picking up coarse."

Spence let it drop. "Did you trust him?" he asked.

"Me? I don't trust anyone with polish on their shoes. Why? What's all the questions about? You writing a book?"

Next morning Spence loaded up the pickup with supplies and headed back to the rig.

Chapter 10

The Protestant mission sat in a palm grove on the west side of town—a rambling two-story building made of concrete and timber. The ground floor was of breeze-blocks with a few small windows. From this the living area extended on heavy teak stilts. The mission's green Toyota Land-cruiser was parked underneath. Perpetude climbed the wooden steps, tapped on the mesh door, and let herself in. She followed the sound of typing down a wide hallway, which was decorated, incongruously, with pictures of Spanish dancers.

Father Mitchell was sitting at the table in the front room. In the past when he greeted her, it had seemed to Perpetude that the stiffness would dissolve from the missionary's angular frame. Now she had the opposite effect on him.

"Ah, Perpetude . . ."

There was no breath of wind through the open windows, but he had taken the precaution of laying out a number of solid objects to prevent his papers from blowing away: a crucifix, a box of Nivaquine, and a paperweight that you could shake to produce a snowstorm over the London skyline.

"You're working?"

"Yes, quite. Just taking advantage of the school holidays. So," he said, "to what do I owe the honor?"

"I just wanted to talk."

"About anything in particular?"

"We had a burglar at the hotel on the night of the dance," Perpetude began.

"Yes, so I heard. Bad business. Would you like some iced coffee?"

Perpetude said, "The man who broke in:He was trying to steal the documents you asked me about."

"I see."

"I couldn't think who else might have known about them."

"Really, Perpetude." Father Mitchell poured from the thermos flask. Ice clattered out into the glasses. "I'm much too busy for this kind of thing."

"So you didn't tell anyone else?"

"Who would I have told?"

"I mean you didn't phone anyone in the capital about them?"

"Perpetude, how long have you known me?"

"Ten years."

"And on the basis of that knowledge, do you really think that I would get involved in some kind of intrigue?"

"You didn't call Charles Hunter about his documents?"

"Perpetude, my only interest was to point out to you who owned these things. They really weren't at all important to me."

"You haven't answered me."

"The answer is no. I never gave them a second thought. You can tell that to Mr. Spence. In fact I'll tell him myself next time I see him. To be frank, I'm rather insulted you should come here on his behalf."

"I'm not doing this for him."

"You're not?"

"It's for you really."

"In what way?"

"Because there are other rumors Spence doesn't know about."

"I don't know what you're talking about. What kind of rumors?"

"They say it was you who broke into the rig trailers."

"What!" He coughed and held a green paisley-pattern hand-kerchief to his mouth. "Who says that?"

"It's just a rumor. Just people in town. They're saying you were the only white man from here who goes up there."

"Really, Perpetude, this is too much," Mitchell interrupted. Tears were springing to the missionary's eyes. "I must say. I must just say . . ." Words failed him. He sat hunched in his typing chair, his bony shoulders caved in like a vulture's. She laid her hands across them.

"I'm not accusing you of anything," she said. "I know you wouldn't do anything wrong."

"You do, do you?" He turned and looked at her, dabbing his pale eyes with a handkerchief. "You do, eh? Should I derive some encouragement from that?"

"I think so."

"My only hope before I left this mission would be that I had established some kind of moral code. That I would be remembered as a moral person."

"You're not going to leave," she said, but Father Mitchell ignored her.

"You're telling me now that no one trusts me. That most people think I'm quite capable—of what? Vandalism, burglary."

"Of course we trust you," she told him. "Everyone admires you."

He shook his head. "No, no, no, they don't. I may be old but I'm not blind. They tolerate me. I know that perfectly well. I'm quite aware of it. They think I'm a joke. I give them employment and a bit of education. That's all. 'A godly life is the best sermon.' For how long? That's what I want to know. How long a godly life?"

He got up and walked to the window. Below them the cook was pounding manioc in a wooden pestle. "In the old days we paid them to become converts. *Plus ça change.* Spirituality counts for nothing. It's all economics, isn't it? You've known that all along. I've known it myself for two years at least. I was wrong to stay on when the oilmen came. I was wrong to try and compromise."

"You didn't compromise," she said. "We needed you here. We still do."

"No. No, you don't. You know you don't. Least of all you, Perpetude."

He turned, blowing his nose and looking at her in silence for a long time. "I've been meaning to tell you this," he said. "But I've been prevaricating, I suppose. I'm leaving Morondava next month."

"I know. It's your furlough."

"Leaving for good," he said.

She felt for a second as though the floor had shifted beneath her feet. "For good?"

"I was due for six months' leave anyway, so they'll have time to appoint another chap . . . if they decide to."

"What do you mean 'if they decide to'?"

"There's nothing here, this place is finished now. You know that as well as I do."

"It's not finished," she said. "You mean the mission? Of course it's not finished."

"I mean Morondava. This whole place. What else is there? The sugar factory? The fishery? The road to the capital won't last another rainy season. It's almost totally impassable now. The river estuary already silted up. The plantations are finished. Oil was the only chance this place had."

"We've done without it for long enough," she said.

"Perpetude. You know it's all in decline. When was the last aid project? Who wants to invest in Africa when they've got all Eastern Europe on their doorstep? Air Mad is cutting down flights from the capital to one a week. Then how long do you think the Grand Hotel will last? These last five years have been borrowed time, Perpetude. You can't keep a place going on faith alone."

"But you've done so much," she said. "You're rebuilding the roof on the schoolhouse, you're . . . "

"Holding back the tide," he said. "Just holding back the tide. That last trip I did—up to Manambato. When I got there, there was nothing to do. Visit the religious community? They had no religious community. The catechist hadn't been there in months. It's all going back to bush.

"So. They need you," she said.

"No, they need radio. They need telecommunications. What use is one man with a satchel full of books?"

"I . . . um." She looked around the room. It was all still there, but somehow, with the change in Father Mitchell, it suddenly seemed alien. She groped for words. "So what will you do?"

"Go to the capital," he said. "I've been offered a job."

"What kind of job?"

"Oh, you know. Administration. Actually I've been offered a seat on the Assemblée Nationale. Goodness knows we need more representation from the country's Protestants. The Catholics have had such a stranglehold for the past three years. We should change things at central level, that's where the real work's to be done."

"You're serious, aren't you?"

"Quite serious."

She picked up the snow scene of London and shook it. Plastic flakes fell on Big Ben.

"Don't go to the capital."

"Give me one reason why not."

"The Assemblée Nationale is a rubber stamp," she said. "The agenda is always set by the president. Down here at least you can see the results of what you're doing."

"There are no results," he said.

"You're sure about this?"

"Quite sure."

"There's nothing I can do to change your mind?"

"Not now."

"How do you mean 'Not now'?"

Father Mitchell cleared his throat. "You know the real reason I've been delaying."

"No."

"Of course you do, Perpetude. I could have moved up to the capital some time ago. I was delaying because of you."

"Because of me?"

"Our little chats over the years. I allowed myself to think . . . well, it's ridiculous really . . . I allowed myself to think that maybe I was important to you."

"You are. You know you're important to me."

"I mean in a different way," he said. "And after my wife in England died last year . . . "

She looked at his old, sun-battered face, wondering whether to look surprised, amused, or concerned.

He spared her by taking off his glasses and looking away. "But of course," he said polishing his glasses, "I can see now that it wasn't like that at all. I was more a sort of security, wasn't I? I suppose that's what I've always been for you, Perpetude. Isn't it? Since Thierry left. Our special relationship. I've always been your chaperone, haven't I? A father figure. A sort of protection against other men. No?"

"Of course not."

"Well, that's how I see it now," he said.

Perpetude drove back over the painful brilliance of the salt flats outside town. She passed a series of small wooden billboards, hangovers from Morondava's colonial days as a tourist resort. The boards were disintegrating, the paint weathered and peeling. MORONDAVA EST BELLE! said one. SOL ET SABLE read another.

She wondered as she drove if she had been using Father Mitchell. As a defense against the pushy irrigation workers and the loud tourists and Canadian drillers?

She had had affairs since Thierry left. And as manager of the hotel where people always came and went, it was easy to be discreet. Surely Father Mitchell didn't imagine she had no emotional life at all.

Then maybe he did.

Maybe, in a way, he was right.

She drove past the hotel and parked on the jetty, then set off walking along the beach, past the fishermen's huts, the coconut husks, the beached outrigger canoes. Father Mitchell was wrong about many things. He was wrong, whatever happened, to think that Morondava would just disintegrate. The life of these places had a way of sustaining itself in ways that were too intricate for politicians to understand. The life of a tree was just under its bark. The center might fall apart, but the margins would remain. Father Mitchell was wrong about Istasse, wrong about Madagascar, wrong about the future of this town. But maybe he was right about her.

A wind stirred the palms. The sea washed over the biscuit-hard sand. She took off her shoes and walked on the damp margin on the sea. She passed the volleyball net, passed the half-built fishing boat, propped on stilts, passed Tsiromandidy's remote little beach house. Her footsteps filled with water and were sucked back into the waves.

Perpetude walked off the beach and out along the sandbar, which now blocked all access to the harbor. Waves washed around her ankles. The wind blew at her hair and under her skirt. She turned to look out toward the reef and noticed something floating in the shallows. At first she took it to be a jellyfish, then a half-submerged plastic bag. A wave flipped it over, dragged it back, and nudged it farther up the beach. It was the clear plastic envelope that had contained the stolen drilling log.

She bent and picked it up.

The zip was still closed. The drilling log was still inside it.

★   ★   ★

It had taken Spence two days to inventory the contents of the first big container: checking the serial numbers on drill bits and stabilizers, tongs and pulleys, hoses, spools, swivels, collars, jars, fishing tools, and all the million spares and accessories that accompany a working derrick.

At the end of the second day he returned to the edge of the rig site to begin checking the heavy machinery. The sun was beginning to set, when he heard a vehicle approaching through the jungle. Spence walked across the clearing, past the fire where the new guards were preparing his evening meal. Perpetude's jeep was negotiating the last bumpy stages of the access road.

She parked in the shade and stepped down, barefoot, shaking the dust from her hair. He smiled when he saw her, suddenly full of a boyish enthusiasm he couldn't conceal.

"Perpetude. What are you doing here?"

"I came on an errand," she said.

Spence wiped the oil off his hands on the seat of his trousers and did up the buttons of his shirt. Perpetude was reaching for something under the dashboard.

"Well, we got food. You want something to eat?"

"Something to drink," she said. "Let me give you this first."

She reached into the glove compartment, the one that never closed, and handed over the plastic envelope. In the light of her confrontation with Father Mitchell it had assumed a malign significance, and she was glad to be rid of it.

"What do you know. The police actually found it?"

"No. I found it. It washed up on the beach. The man who attacked you must have thrown it in the sea."

"No kidding. I'll get you something to drink. You want to freshen up?" He felt he was talking too fast.

"I'll sit down first."

He left her sitting on one of the canvas chairs under the canvas awning he'd put outside his trailer.

When he'd washed, he came out to find her drinking lime juice and talking in dialect to the rig guards. They shook her hand and returned to cook dinner by the fire.

"You know these guys?"

"Oh, yes."

"What did you say to them?"

"I asked them what you were like to work for."

"And?"

"They said you didn't laugh as much as Hånssen."

"He's pretty hard to beat in that department."

Perpetude went to the cool box and got herself another drink. Spence sat down and unzipped the drilling log from its folder. The light was fading, so he lit the hurricane lamp, then he began unfolding the drilling log one page at a time.

"What are you doing?"

"I'm doing what I should have done the first time. Seeing if this is really worth anything. You want to see?"

She moved closer.

"Show me."

Spence turned back to the first page, brushing an insect out of the way. "Okay we start with this column here on the left— that's the drilling speed, so you see here they completed the first couple of hundred feet pretty fast. Then this mark is where they stopped to run in the casing.

"Then this column here shows the types of rock so"—he flipped some more pages—"you can tell that down to a thousand feet they were drilling silt, shale, clay, and sandstone at a speed of thirty-five feet an hour."

"You can tell so much?"

"Oh, yes, it's like a diary, this . . . see here . . . where the graph peaks. That's a gas kick. They hit some gas."

"Is that good?"

"Might have been, if there'd been more of it. It ran out after thirty feet."

A family of lemurs was sitting in the tall white girders of the rig. Birds whooped in the jungle behind them. The sky was turning pink.

Spence flipped on through the next fifty pages. They'd hit limestone now, and the rate of penetration had slowed to ten feet an hour. After a month on an unpromising site the last thing one hoped for was this kind of solid formation. The drill bits would be wearing out every thirty hours, and the whole six and a half thousand feet of pipe would have to be hauled up to replace it.

Spence could remember, from his own days as a derrick man, standing on the narrow platform two thirds of the way up the derrick, with the drilling crew like toy men below him, heaving the top of each pipe stand backward and forward from the monkey board—ninety feet of nine-inch-diameter steel pipe, bending like a fishing rod and wrenching his arms from their sockets. He could remember the cut of the rope harness around his waist and the whistle of the massive steel elevators as they came trundling up past his head. He could remember the crash and shudder of the pipe against the derrick and the half-heard instructions from the helmeted figures far below. The howling wind and the singing steel, the boots chafing his feet and the sweat stinging his eyes. He had never been happier.

"Something happened here."

Perpetude had been turning the pages for herself. On this page, out of more than a hundred, the printed columns were dense with tracery.

"What does it mean?"

Somewhere a trailer door banged shut. Spence frowned and rubbed his bad leg. "It means they had a second strike," he said faintly.

At just under seven thousand feet the chromatography column was suddenly showing gas again—more than ninety percent. Spence relocated himself—the lithology column showed mixed sands, and the drill rate had leaped up to a hundred feet an hour.

"There seemed to be a lot of it—no?"

Spence squinted at the glare off the paper. He was looking at a bed of hydrocarbon-bearing sandstone four hundred and twenty-five feet deep. The chromatography was going haywire. The visual porosity was consistently good.

Spence flipped back the preceding two pages and read through them again. It didn't make any sense at all—Mansalava had been designated a dry well. They'd capped it with a hundred feet of concrete and were selling off the rig. But only a fool would abandon a well like this. As far as one could tell from the drilling log alone, it looked like a surefire producer.

"Is there a problem?"

Spence rechecked the title page. The inscription "Mansalava 1" refused to go away. The same designation as was inscribed on the well marker sticking out from the center of the lease fifty yards in front of them. If the log really corresponded to this site, they were literally sitting on a fortune.

"The problem," he said, "is that this isn't the well they say it is. Either the report has the wrong title on it or Norco is lying about what they found here."

"Why would they do that?"

"Well, the obvious reason is so no one else drills here. You mention a possible strike and suddenly the country's swarming with oil companies wanting to buy all the next-door concessions."

The guards approached with the food—telapia and manioc. Spence fell silent until they had gone.

"So. What. You're saying they found oil, aren't you?"

Spence stalled. "No. Probably some balls-up. But it makes you wonder what that fellow was looking for when he broke into these trailers."

They ate, and in the silence Spence thought of Velo-André. Suddenly all the aspects of the job that had puzzled him were given new and sinister significance. If Velo-André knew of the find and had taken Norco's side against his own government, then he had every reason in the world for wanting to buy the rig.

But who in hell was he working with—Hunter? The president? The new man—Istasse?

The Norco boss, Charles Hunter, must have known about the find. As head of operations he was one person whom the news of the find would certainly have been reported to. Hanssen had mentioned once that Charles Hunter left Morondava two days before the accident. There was something else he had said— something about the helicopter that Hunter had traveled in. Spence strained to remember.

Nothing.

"What are you thinking?"

Spence roused himself. "Who else knows you found this?" he asked.

"No one. Well, unless anyone saw me coming back with it."

"Okay. If anyone asks, say nothing. Tell them it was just a bunch of scrap paper. I'll need to take this home and check it out."

She finished eating and pushed the plate away. "Thank you," she said.

"Thanks for coming out here."

"I was beginning to feel claustrophobic in town. It happens sometimes. I needed to get away."

Spence said, "If you want to take a shower, there's one over there behind that screen."

"And where can I sleep?"

"Any of these trailers. Or you could sleep with me."

"Thank you. I'll sleep on my own."

"Shit, I just blew it, didn't I? Now you think I'm like all those other guys."

"No. If I thought you were like them, I wouldn't have come up here alone. I think you're different."

"How different?"

"More sensitive," she said.

"I've never been called that before."

"Maybe where you come from it is not regarded as a compliment."

When she'd showered, he took her to her trailer and held the lamp while she unlocked the door.

"Good night," she said in the dusk.

He reached out and touched her arm. "Say your name for me."

"Why?"

"I like the way you say it. The way you did on the jetty that time."

"I don't remember. What time?"

"Say Perpetude."

"Perpetude."

When she said it, her lips made the shape of a kiss.

"Good night, Perpetude."

Next morning, after Perpetude had left, Spence searched in vain for some clue to what they'd drilled through three kilometers beneath him. From the contours of the site he could make out what had been the orientation of the rig. The substructure on its wooden mats would have created the shallow, square depression, twenty meters square, which centerd on the well marker. The raised areas beyond that marked where they had filled in the mud pits.

Mud pits were the artificial lakes, each the size of a municipal swimming pool, dug to receive the thousands of gallons of mud and chippings that were pumped out of the bore hole. Any oil that was allowed to escape from a successful well might have collected here, but, patrolling its margins, Spence found no signs of seepage.

This didn't prove anything. An oil strike these days was an undramatic affair—the underground pressures were balanced with a calculated tonnage of drilling mud, so even a massive strike would bring little oil to the surface.

Returning to the equipment containers, Spence found traces of heavy oil on some of the down-hole tools; but there was no way he could differentiate between what they'd used in maintenance and what they'd brought up from the well. As the sun began to drop over the western edge of the clearing, he had finally to admit that he had no way of verifying the Mansalava log. Its secret lay with the men who'd drilled this site, and they were all long buried. In the hypnotic play of sunlight through the trees, he fancied that he could see their faces—Skippy, Bob Leoppky, Billy Ross, George Wilhelm . . .

Returning to his trailer, listening to the noises of the jungle, he began to think again about the plane crash that had killed them. Suppose Cora was right and there had been something flaky about the plane crash? Suppose it wasn't an accident? Suppose—ludicrous thought—that the explosion in the luggage compartment was not simply due to the irresponsible transport of explosives? Suppose it was intentional, that someone had sabotaged the plane to ensure the secrecy of the oil find?

Spence switched out the lamp and stood outside his trailer watching the sepulchral figures of the guards gathered around the embers of the fire. The stoppered bottle of rum sat in the moonlight on the table under the awning. On an impulse he took it and poured some on the dusty soil at his feet. A beetle cracked against the wooden door behind him, and he whirled, aware of every tiny sound. The sensation of fearfulness was new and strange. He realized with some surprise that his own life had once more become precious to him.

Inside his own trailer he carefully unscrewed one of the wall panels and hid the drilling log behind it.

The first time he handled it, it had been an innocent ream of graph paper. Now it was the kind of information men would kill for.

PART
TWO

Chapter 11

Elgin Kirk stood on the corner of Fitz-
roy Street and Chalcot Road, his collar turned up against the
drizzle, exhaling steam and cigarette smoke into the damp
morning twilight. At seven-thirty he saw the lights go on in
the house opposite. Shortly afterward Mr. Waters opened the
front door briefly to take in the milk. Waters was a creature of
habit. Kirk still had another fifteen minutes to wait. He crossed
the road to the Indian newsagents and bought himself a cold
pork pie for breakfast.

Above the whitewashed terrace the London sky was turning from orange to gray. Kirk paid for his pork pie and a
newspaper, put his gloves back on, and crossed the road. He
had reached the sports pages, when Waters left his home and
turned briskly up Chalcot Road. Kirk followed him up past the
square and around the little tree-lined crescent to Regent's Park
Road. A delivery van was parked outside the grocer's shop,
obscuring his view, and Kirk hurried to keep up. He'd been
tailing Waters since Monday, and he already knew his route to
the tube station. Kirk picked up his pace as they crossed the
road. The great engines of the city hummed around him as
dawn flooded into Chalk Farm Road.

Inside the station door Waters stopped to buy a copy of
the *Telegraph,* then set off again. He showed his ticket pass and

went through the barrier, hurrying to catch the lift. The stainless-steel doors closed before Kirk reached them. He dodged
right and took the stairs.

The stairwell was lined with ivory-yellow tiles. Kirk clattered down it, his shoes rattling over the edges of the steps. If
he missed Waters this morning, he would have to wait all weekend, kicking his heels in the Holiday Inn before he got another
chance. He took the stairs three at a time, with his shoulder
pressed to the outside curve, and arrived in time to see the last
passengers coming out of the lift. Waters wasn't among them.

Kirk ran through to the Southbound platform, jinking between the commuters. Waters was a tall, stooped figure with
thinning brown hair. He was standing halfway up the platform,
reading his paper, about two yards back from the tube line,
with a young mother and her children in front of him. Kirk
slotted in behind him and waited.

The illuminated sign said, KENNINGTON VIA BANK 3 MINS.
Then two. Then one. Waters read his paper. Kirk stood behind
him, close enough to smell the damp wool of his overcoat. He
looked at the cinema posters. There was a gust of wind and a
rattling of wires, then the train came thundering out of the
tunnel. Waters took a step back; he was waiting, as usual, for
the direct train to Charing Cross.

The tube doors closed, opened and closed again, then, with
a sigh of its brakes, the train pulled off. Waters moved up closer
to the platform, but the young mother was still in front of him.
Kirk stayed close behind. The crowd was pressed around them.
It had occurred to him before that he could just about get away
with knifing the man, but it was impossible to make a knifing
look anything other than intentional, and murders attracted
police attention in a way that an apparent suicide on the Northern Line never would.

The warm wind came again, then the sound of wheels.

The mother pulled her child back from the platform's edge
and moved sideways, not quite far enough sideways to give

Kirk a clear push. The train stopped, and Waters moved inside. Kirk followed.

He stood, rocking to the motion of the train, in the standing area between the two doors. Farther up the aisle Waters unfolded his newspaper and looked back down the carriage, directly at Kirk. There was no recognition. Just the same guileless, freckled face that featured on the photograph in his file. Kirk looked away, scanning the faces of his fellow travelers. He'd been one of them himself, in the years between school and army. Eight-thirty till six, clocking in and out from the print factory, D.C. Thompson's in Dundee, knocking his pan in to support the wife and the child. It never ceased to surprise him that so many people still chose to live like this—that so few had woken up to the possibility of less conventional employment.

Kirk had been tipped off to the work by an ex-army friend, who brought his attention to the small ad that appears in the first issue of *Soldier of Fortune* magazine each month. The advert SAYS MAKE EXTRA MONEY and gives a box number in London. It relies on the ex-forces and martial-arts grapevine for a fuller description of the work.

It had taken Elgin Kirk two months to get a reply to his initial inquiries—long enough for them to check his army record. The friend had said they didn't want hotheads, and he'd been worried for a while about the two convictions for brawling off-duty in Biederfeld. Against that he had served four untarnished years in Northern Ireland, leaving Ballykelly with three stripes, his small-arms instructor's certificate and a second *dan* in *Tae-kwon do*, none of which gave him much of an edge in his subsequent employment selling baseball gloves to Lilliwhites.

Their first letter of reply had advised him to open a post office box at the central post office in Princes Street, and it was here that all their subsequent letters arrived. For his part all that Kirk knew of his employers was a box number in London.

The second letter was a bulky sheaf of printed sheets explaining, without reference to any organization, that the business of eliminating undesirables was extremely lucrative and largely risk-free. It hinted that such actions had the tacit sanction of the authorities and were therefore rarely investigated in depth. It gave examples of the kinds of people to whom the word *undesirable* applied—fraudulent businessmen, sex offenders, gangland thugs.

With each new assignment he would be sent a summary of the man, why he was to be eliminated, and where were the most vulnerable points in his daily routine. In Waters's case the tube journey was the obvious choice.

The train lurched to a stop at Euston Station, and Kirk glanced briefly down the aisle. Waters was still there, reading his folded newspaper over the top of his glasses. He didn't look like a blackmailer, but then you could never tell by appearances.

Three years ago Kirk's very first contract had been a shove off the Underground. A quick nudge off the platform at Sauchiehall Street Station had disrupted the Glasgow Underground for an hour one summer afternoon and successfully ended the life of a known child molester. For that first job Kirk was paid the equivalent of half a year's pay as an army sergeant.

For subsequent contracts he was paid slightly less, but the business of murder became less and less stressful. The sixth job—a poison needle, pressed into the shoulder of a Birmingham businessman as he jostled through the entrance gate to a football match—had hardly caused Kirk a single sleepless night.

The train had stopped at Tottenham Court Road. Someone pushed past. Elgin Kirk woke from his reverie and checked down the aisle again and cursed.

Waters had gone.

Kirk squeezed through to the door and looked outside. Waters was nowhere to be seen. People were pushing past him, onto the tube. Kirk nipped back inside and checked the seated passengers on both sides of the aisle. Still no sign of Waters. Kirk barged back out through the incoming passengers and ran

off down the platform, toward the signs saying WAY OUT and
CENTRAL LINE. Faces flooded past him: old faces, young faces,
black, white, and gray faces, lined and smooth faces. He ran
down the echoing corridor, past a busker playing Irish jigs on
the accordion, sidestepping an Indian woman with shopping
bags, a Sikh with a suitcase. At the end of the passageway there
was an escalator going up to the ticket hall and a corridor running straight on to the Central Line.

He couldn't see Waters on the escalator, so he ran on. A
train was leaving the Eastbound platform as he arrived. Kirk
ran the length of the platform, against the tide of arrivals, then
dodged through onto the crowded Westbound line. People
stood six deep, from the mosaic wall to the edge of the track.
Kirk climbed up on one of the red plastic seats that were bolted
to the wall and scanned the crowd. Waters was a third of the
way down the platform. He was standing a foot away from the
tracks.

Kirk pushed sideways through the crowd. All his attention
was focused on Waters now—the navy wool coat and the thinning shock of brown hair. The crowd shifted. Now he lost him
from view, now he could see him again.

Kirk was ten yards away when he felt the wind of the
approaching train. Five yards away, and he could hear the rattling of the tracks. Four yards away. He tried to squeeze forward, but the crowd was pressed tightly together here. A young
man in a pinstriped shirt accused him of queue barging and held
his jacket. Kirk brought his knee up hard into the side of the
other man's leg and felt the grip relax. The warm wind grew
stronger, the rattling of the tracks louder. Hot and breathless,
Kirk slipped in behind Waters at the moment the train's headlights rounded the corner. He waited a second, then walked
into Waters's back, tapping his ankles as the taller man pitched
forward.

He was already stepping back into the crowd as the train
blasted past him. A woman's scream rising above the shrieking

of the brakes. The crowd surged back, then forward, like the branches of a tree in a sudden gust of wind. A tall, blond woman was pointing at Kirk and shouting an accusation he couldn't hear. Time slowed. Kirk heard the train's engines being cut. Then the tube doors opened, and the new influx of passengers swept them apart. Glancing back, he saw the blond woman drowning like a swimmer in the noisy sea of heads and coats.

Now an alarm was sounding somewhere. Now uniformed men were pushing through the crowd on the platform. Kirk let himself be jostled up the stairs to Oxford Street, to daylight, the sound of traffic and the fresh, wet air.

Chapter 12

The Sucrerie Nationale de Morondava was a metal warehouse built around a complex structure of conveyors, tanks, and girders. Light poured in through the windows on either side and was caught up in the process of manufacture—given palpable mass by the haze of dust and vegetable fibers then chopped and bisected by the catwalks and railings. Over three stories dark men, stripped to the waist, would emerge from the machinery, make some adjustment, then disappear back into the machine.

Perpetude Peyrame walked to the far end of the central hall. From the spurs and balconies a dozen pairs of eyes followed her progress. She climbed upward through floors and subfloors, past wooden-clad vats discharging their cargoes of brown syrup into the centrifuges below. Here, watching the sugar being washed with steam, she found Morgan Hanssen.

"Pappatoot." He shouted, "Watcha doing here?" He found a fold of skin at her waist and squeezed it between his fingers and his palms. "Come to get a look at all these naked black boys?"

"Have I come to look at what?"

"You come to buy some sugar?" he shouted.

"No, I came here for a promenade."

Hanssen cupped a hand to his ear and shook his head. "Let's

go somewhere else, I can't hear myself fart for all this hissing and pissing."

He stumped off ahead of her along the row of wire-mesh shakers to where the refined sugar was cascading into sacks. Hanssen sat on one of them and patted another at his side.

"So how's the American?"

"What American?"

"Spence. I heard you went up to see him with his document."

"Who told you that?"

Hanssen shrugged. "Sorry. I wasn't meant to know, eh? You haffing an affair with him?"

"No."

"So—what—is there something important about these papers?"

"Nothing."

"Why are you looking embarrassed?"

"I'm not embarrassed. The papers weren't even worth keeping. He burned them."

"That's pretty stupid," Morgan Hanssen said. "He'll be running out of toilet paper up there pretty soon."

Perpetude laughed. On the ground floor she could see that the succulent cane was being squeezed through metal rollers. Hanssen looked at her sideways.

"You sure you're not haffing an affair with him?"

"Of course I'm not."

"Why 'of course'?"

"I don't know him, Morgan."

"What's that got to do with it? If you ask me, the Africans has got it right—you like a fellow, you sleep with him, you haf a baby . . . "

"Morgan, he's leaving here in a week."

"Okay, forget the baby. What else is the problem?"

Perpetude said, "He's not my type."

" 'Type.' Who's your type, Pappatoot? And don't say Fa-

ther Mitchell. You can know a lot of big words and still haf
small thoughts. You think Spence isn't smart enough?"
    "No, he's smart."
    "You don't think he's attractif."
    "No, he's very attractive."
    "Even with the leg."
    "I like his leg."
    "What then? You scared of him?"
    She wondered about that. There was a kind of tension in
him. She hadn't yet decided if it was aggression or suppressed
emotion. Below them the rollers ground to a halt and the operator started waving to Hanssen. "They need you," she said.
    Hanssen stood up, dusting sugar from the seat of his pants.
There was sugar on his shirt and in his side-whiskers. He looked,
she decided, like a contented old bee. He said, "You want to
know what your type is, Pappatoot? Me. I'm your type."
    She laughed and turned away from him. "À demain, Mor-
gan."
    Hanssen stood, wiping his hands on his shirt and shouting
after her, "Listen, Pappatoot. I can get a wash. I'll change my
trouser. I can—" but the rest was inaudible over the machinery.
    She walked away from him, smiling, following the con-
veyor belt that carried the desiccated stems to fuel the turbines.

At night the food the guards cooked Spence was repetitive but
edible—chicken with rice, alternating with zebu and rice. Once
they came back from the river with an evil-looking black telapia.
Spence ate, sitting on a log with his leg extended toward the
fire pit, listening to the unfamiliar conversation of the guards.
With each successive night he could feel the alcohol draining
from his system like thin, polluted oil, leaving in its place the
sediment of nightmares. He slept now on the nervous fringes
of unconsciousness and found himself waking with a start when
there was a noise in the jungle, when the air conditioner sighed
to a halt, or when a guard outside dropped another branch on

the fire. Waking, he'd lie staring at the ceiling till his limbs stopped shaking.

In this drained state he found he could remember things that had lain forgotten for days and weeks, which was how, on the fifth day, he remembered about Hunter's helicopter. Hanssen had said it was carrying "coarse," which at the time made no sense at all: but what if he was mispronouncing the word *cores*? Cores were samples of oil-bearing rock that one took from the bottom of a promising well. If Hunter had been carrying cores, he must have known there was something down there. In which case . . .

In which case, if the drilling log were accurate, if Hunter knew about it, and if he'd deliberately left early, wasn't it possible that he'd arranged for the drilling crew to be killed?

If, if, if. There were so many ifs that at times Spence worried the whole thing was just another paranoid fantasy provoked by his coming off the bottle.

Forget Hunter, he told himself. Assume only that someone wanted to keep Mansalava a secret, and the plane crash still seems ominously convenient. The idea made Spence's scalp crawl. It was the kind of story that got bandied around over a game of poker in some isolated Arctic drilling camp. It owed its terrible potency to the fact that everyone knew that, given a sufficiently large incentive, the multinational oil companies regarded people as their most expendable commodity.

Toward the end of the second week Hanssen turned up with supplies for the guards. Spence didn't press him to stay. Until now he would have been delighted to have company, but since the discovery of the drilling log, he no longer knew whom he could trust.

Had Hanssen somehow colluded in the break-in at the rig? If the drilling log was genuine, then Hanssen could be protecting the secret for Norco. Or was he trying to gather information for his political masters in the capital? He remembered that the old Dane had been openly critical of Velo-André. Could he be working for the opposition—for Istasse? Spence wasn't even sure that a conspiracy existed, far less who was involved in it. He had nothing for guidance except the principles of five-card stud—conceal your hand and let the other guy make his move.

Hanssen spent the night in the trailer that Perpetude had slept in. He left early the next day. Three days later Spence turned the final page of the rig manifest and realized he was finished.

It was four in the afternoon by the time Spence reached Morondava, and the backs of his hands were riverbeds of dust and sweat. At the hotel there was no sign of Perpetude. Amin Bahera said she had gone to Belo to visit friends and would be back late at night. He asked if there was anything Spence wanted. No, Spence said, there was nothing he wanted.

At Air Madagascar they told him there would be a plane the next day that would connect with the 747 from the capital. After that there would be nothing for a week. A small plastic fan stirred the hot air around him, fluttering the outdated time-tables on the clerk's desk and lifting the edge of an old Kenyan tourist poster.

The clerk was waiting for his response. A distant siren sounded from the sugar factory. It was six o'clock—time to close up shop. In the prison yard the police would be lining up their drinks. In the paddy fields the peasant farmers would be starting their long walk home. He found himself thinking of Perpetude Peyrame, the glow of her skin, the directness of her dark eyes, and the throaty melody of her laugh. In his memory her spirit infused the little town of Morondava. When he first came here, Spence would never have believed that he could come to miss the place.

Spence told them to confirm his ticket. He gave them his credit card. Yes, he would leave the next day.

By eleven at night Perpetude had still not returned. In his

room by the light of the naked bulb, Spence showered, then packed his carryall. He laid out his jeans, a laundered shirt, and his boots; closed the shutters and went to sleep.

He was woken at two A.M. by an explosion that rattled the timbers of the hotel. Spence found himself sitting upright. Water was pouring off the roof above him and flooding off the eaves beyond the balcony. He pulled on his trousers and fumbled for his stick. As he reached the veranda door, there was another flash of lightning—sheet lightning that covered the whole sky, as if a short had developed in the circuits that controlled night and day. Rain was spraying back at him off the balcony rail. Spence stepped back into the doorway as the sky turned magnesium-white again. For an instant he saw the row of palms along the beach and the white crest on each small wave, then blackness.

The rain was beating a deafening tattoo on the tin roof. To attempt to sleep was pointless. He picked up the half-empty rum bottle beside his bed and walked out onto the gallery. In the courtyard rain was clattering off the leaves of the banana trees. Spence walked across the deserted dining room. The marble still felt warm beneath his bare feet. As he came out on the veranda, as the lightning once more turned the sky inside out, Spence glimpsed, in its brief illumination, the silhouette of a woman.

She was sitting in one of the wooden armchairs, with a sarong wrapped around her. Her hair was loose, and her bare feet were propped on the table. At first Spence thought she was asleep, then he noticed her eyes in the darkness. He drew up a seat beside her and lowered himself into it.

"Perpetude?"

"Hello."

Spence lifted a foot onto the table beside hers. "I'm not disturbing you?"

She shook her head. "It's beautiful, isn't it?"

Beyond the veranda puddles were steaming on the warm tarmac. He could hear from the darkness the sound of shouting and children's laughter.

"You've finished your work at the rig?"

"Yes."

"I worried for you. You had no problems?"

"No," Spence said. "Except that I have to leave."

"Have to?"

"I bought a ticket," he said.

"Good. Then we're both safe."

"Safe from what?" he asked.

She didn't reply. Water was dripping through the corrugated iron above his head. He moved his chair a fraction toward her.

"Safe from what?"

"I didn't mean that," she said.

Another flash of lightning, another reversal of the night. He saw palm trees, the covered market, the outline of the water tower. A couple running. Then blackness.

"What were you doing in Belo?" Spence asked.

"Visiting a friend."

"What kind of friend?"

"A friend," she said, smiling.

"Sorry. It's none of my business."

"It was a woman I know."

Rain rattled on the roof above their heads. It fell like a screen onto the sand in front of the veranda.

Spence said, "I wanted to apologize to you about what I said up at the rig."

"What did you say?"

"About asking you to sleep with me?"

"I took it as a compliment."

"I mean, I wouldn't like you to think I'm the kind of guy who sleeps around all the time."

"I didn't think that," she said.

"I mean, when Nancy and I were together, I was away a lot, for sure, but I wasn't a guy who messed around—you know." He laughed. "I mean, I'd have liked to be sometimes but I wasn't. Why am I saying all this stuff?"

"You've never told me about Nancy," she said.

"What do you want to know?"

"What happened between you and her. Why you split up."

Spence hesitated. His breakup with Nancy was something he had never spoken about. The subject was locked up in some steel-bound part of him, and to open it now felt like a physical act of vandalism.

"You don't need to talk about it."

"There's not much to say. We'd been married six, seven years, when she started saying she wanted me to give up the oil business and spend more time at home. I told her I couldn't do it. Part of the reason I married her was because I thought she'd understand that. All my life I'd worked tours: two weeks in every four, in every eight, that kind of shit, sometimes all winter at a stretch. The time I got into oil, you could just walk down the road and some guy would give you a job. Anyway Nancy said she was lonely, and she didn't want me to keep going away, but I guess I didn't listen to her. . . . "

Spence paused and leaned back in the chair. The old hardwood struts creaked under his weight.

"My friend Clyde used to call and see her while I was away, and people started telling me she and him were getting more than friendly, but I didn't listen. I guess I couldn't believe there was anything wrong between her and me. During the times back we'd go camping or skiing up by Slave Lake, or Clyde and Skippy and me would take the camper and go shooting moose out west of Edson.

"Then one time I was out on a wildcat in B.C.—that's British Columbia—I got drinking with some of the boys, and they started telling me about how everyone knew about Clyde and Nancy. We'd been playing cribbage all night. One of the

guys said they were spending the weekend together down at
Elk Island Lodge. I knew that was where Nancy was, but she'd
told me she was going with a girlfriend. 'Ring them up,' they
said. 'Ask for Clyde Schoepp. You'll see if he's there or not.
"At first I wouldn't do it. I guess I was scared I'd prove
them right. Then eventually I made that call, and sure enough
he'd booked a room for the two of them."
"So what did you do?"
"I got into the Blazer and drove all the way down there—
some nine hundred miles. Got in at five the next day. I'd been
drinking coffee all night and smoking all day, and when I got
there, I was just flying. I hardly knew what I was saying. They
told me what was going on and let me storm around, smashing
things, till the management came to see what was going on.
That's when she said she was leaving me."
"What did you say?"
"At the time I think I told her not to let the door slap her
ass on the way out. It wasn't till afterward I realized how much
I loved her. The times I was home, it seemed there was no
point in doing anything, but the times I was away, there was
nothing to look forward to. Like half the fun of going away
was looking forward to coming home. Anyway . . ."
Spence got up and stood at the balcony, looking out over
the dark, steaming tarmac of the street. He pressed an eye with
the palp of one finger and in the half-light examined the moisture
that appeared on it.
"Yes?"
"That's all," he said.
He heard a plank creak behind him, felt her hand on his
shoulder.
Spence wiped his other eye with the back of one finger.
"This is stupid. I hadn't thought of her for . . . well, not since
before Christmas. How long ago's that?"
"Three weeks."
"Three weeks. Seems longer." He turned toward her. The

glossy skin of her neck and shoulders. Those dark, grave eyes.

Rain hammered off the sand beyond the balcony and rose in a fine mist around them.

"Perpetude."

"Yes?"

He hooked a finger over the knot of her sarong, meaning to draw her toward him, but when he pulled, the knot came undone and she was naked.

Spence drew her close.

Her lips tasted of salt, and her skin was burning hot, as though, like the beach, it had stored the heat of the sun all day, waiting to give it up at night.

"Perpetude."

"There are people in the street," she said.

In her room she lit a single candle and stepped out of her dress. With his withered leg his own undressing seemed clumsy and unsensual, but she laughed when he lurched onto the bed, and she helped pull off his trousers. Naked, she lay along his side, tracing his thickened scars with her fingers.

"Your fall off that rig must have been very painful."

"Not really. Most of the nerves were torn out. At first they were going to amputate, then they found I had a bit of feeling in the foot, so they reckoned they could save it."

"Can you feel me touching here?"

"Yes."

"Here?"

"Yes."

"Here?"

"Ah. Yes."

"It's not so bad, then."

"It's not so bad. Once I started using it, I started to get the feeling back."

"Ah, yes," said Perpetude. "That is also how it goes with the heart. Once you begin to use it, the feelings return very quickly."

"You think you can mend this one for me?"

She put her head close to his chest and said, "Oh, yes, I can hear it stronger already."

He ran his hands through her thick, strong hair. "I still don't understand what a woman like you is doing on her own."

"You think I need a husband?"

"Don't you miss sex?"

"I have sex sometimes," she said with a smile, and Spence felt an unreasonable spasm of jealousy. Then she drew him toward her, and he forgot everything except the salt taste of her skin and the soft resistance of her mouth and her breasts.

Music drifted over from the Ambre Disco. Shadows moved across her face, across the green shutters and the blue walls of her room. She knelt on top of him, her hips pushing on his pelvis, her breasts close to his face—illuminated by the oil lamp. Hands on his shoulders, she rocked backward and forward, the rhythm of the tides. They were floating underwater. Her hair waved like seaweed around him. His hands found the curve of her waist.

"Perpetude."

"Spence."

Her smooth breast brushed his cheek.

"Perpetude."

"Yes, I'm here," she said.

Tiredness was gone. Dust, frustration, fear, and pain were gone. Confusion was gone. Characters tumbled through his mind. Hanssen, Mitchell, Velo-André. Dancing, skipping, cartwheeling, Istasse, Hunter, Skippy, Cora, Dennis . . . laughing, trailing streamers. Faster and faster they danced. Shouting, waving.

This strange blend of peace and frenzy.

He craved her. He devoured her.

"Tell me your name."

"Perpetude."

"Perpetude. Say Perpetude."

"Perpetude."

"Again. Say Perpetude."

She shook her head and smiled. Her brow was furrowed as though in concentration.

He gazed at her. "Perpetude," he said.

"Yes?"

"Yes?"

"Yes." She looked into his eyes.

She smiled as his body flowed into hers. Then she lowered herself toward him and lay motionless on top of him, with her head in the hollow of his neck, and Spence felt an unfamiliar tranquillity more profound than he had ever achieved with alcohol.

Dawn was a wash of watercolor blue. Blue-slatted light on the mosquito net above them. A dark breast exposed by the blue sheet. Perpetude lay heavy with sleep against him. He kissed her, and she enfolded him without waking.

"Is it morning?"·

"Not yet."

With a finger he traced the outline of her face. "You're very beautiful."

"And you also."

"No, I'm an old wreck."

She smiled, opening her eyes. "I like old wrecks," she said. "Why do you think I have stayed in this hotel for so long?"

"I don't know. What keeps someone in one place? I never did understand that."

"Not even in your own home?"

Home. The word sounded unfamiliar. The place he'd stayed in had always been the house. Even when Nancy lived there, it was their house. "I don't know if I had a home," Spence said.

"Home is where you miss."

"I'll miss this place."

★   ★   ★

A great force picked him up and propelled him forward. His ears were full of noise. He watched, helpless, as the landscape hurtled by.

At the end of the runway Perpetude stood waving with both arms and shouting something he couldn't hear. In that fraction of a second he formed her name with his lips.

Once, as they made love for the second or was it the third time, he had looked down and found her watching him with an expression of childish wonder that made his heart turn over. There was so much they would never know about each other. Now she was a speck in the distance. Now she was a memory. Now she was a weight in his chest—at once disturbing and reassuring like the weight of the drilling log in the carryall on his lap. As the plane climbed, he could feel the temperature dropping. Clouds obscured the window. He was going back.

Chapter 13

The main hall at Ivato International Airport had been built as a series of lofty arches in order to create an impression of space; viewed from ground level, however, the press of humanity entirely confounded this illusion. Spence wound his way through the tangle of interwoven queues, stepping between piles of suitcases, bags made of hessian and woven palm, car tires, squatting families and a knot of fatigued, embattled tourists.

Here was the crack vanguard of the regiment of hustlers and souvenir salesmen who garrisoned the capital. In the thirty yards between ARRIVÉE and DÉPART one could buy leatherware and jewelry, evil fly-blown confections, French romantic paperbacks, rum and Three Horse beer, erotic carvings, table lamps, tortoiseshell and crocodile skin, postage stamps, raffiawork, and pressed flowers.

The noise of barter stabbed through the chaos of the departure hall, drowned only by the deafening squawks from the public-address system. Spence found what he was looking for: a stringed instrument of which the sounding box was a length of bamboo. He paid without arguing about the price and headed for the taxi rank.

In his room at the Hilton he unpacked his carryall. Every time he handled the drilling log, he found himself rereading it to reassure himself of its authenticity. But there it still was, in blue stencil, documentary evidence of what could be, given the right underground structure, the most promising wildcat well in East Africa.

Spence turned back to the title page and tore it off. He made the tear as ragged as possible so that, when matched, it would marry with the rest of the continuous sheet. Then he turned to the back two pages—the ones that related to the oil-bearing strata. These three pages he put in a hotel envelope and addressed to himself in Canada.

Next he took his knife and cut out the circular base of his souvenir musical instrument. The rolled-up drilling log fitted inside it. Spence put it in a plastic bag and took it down to reception to be locked in the safe. He posted his letter and asked the desk clerk to call Velo-André at the Ministry for Mineral Resources. The line was out of order. Spence checked his watch: one-forty. With a bit of luck Velo would be out of his office.

"Numéro deux. Rue 26ème Août 1960" sounded to Spence like a telephone number. When the desk clerk wrote it out, it looked more like a date. In fact, it was the address of the Ministère des Ressources Minérales—a three-story building on the far corner of the Place de la Révolution.

The taxi became stuck in a traffic jam of ancient Peugeots and Citroëns outside the Hôtel de Ville. A small crowd of students was marching down the main street, handing out leaflets and taking turns to shout through a megaphone. Spence paid the driver and proceeded on foot through the Zuma market, picking his way through the forest of white canvas umbrellas, stopping frequently to check that no one was tailing him. He stopped outside the ministry and paid off with tiny brass coins the two urchins who had been pestering him for money.

Close up, the Ministry for Mineral Resources looked less distinguished than it had seemed from the far side of the square:

tiles were missing from the steep roof and less than half of the
tall, slim windows retained their shutters. The lyre-shaped steps
that led to the main door were chipped and eroded, and, in
places, the wrought-iron railings had broken off and fallen into
the cobbled courtyard below. The building's title had once been
set in brass letters above the door, but more than half of these
had by now disappeared, leaving a collection of misaligned
consonants above the architrave. In the foyer a uniformed concierge was whittling a stick.

"I'm looking for Velo-André," Spence said.

The concierge frowned.

"Velo-André," Spence repeated.

The concierge said something in French that Spence didn't
understand, then mimed eating with his penknife.

"Can I go to his office?" Spence asked. To his surprise the
concierge waved him upstairs.

From the first-floor landing an arched window looked out
over the Zuma. He tried the mahogany door to his left and
found it locked. The passage led off to his right, so Spence
followed it. It led him through a series of large, partitioned
rooms. Once there had been paintings on these ceilings and
elegant floral cornices, but now the grand halls had been condemned and boarded off. The walkway led Spence to a door
at the rear of the building, inscribed with Velo-André's name
and title.

Velo-André's assistant was a handsome young man in a
yellow Lacoste T-shirt. When he smiled, he displayed a set of
brilliant false teeth.

"Is this Velo-André's office?"

"*Il n'est pas ici*. He is departed for lunch."

"My name's Spence. I'm a consultant with McCabe. I was
wondering if you had some documents I could look at."

"In which documents are you interested?" The young man
looked eager to help, but Spence already knew he'd find nothing
here. The room contained two wooden desks, two swivel

chairs, and an ancient, duck-green filing cabinet. There was nothing on the paneled walls except withered propaganda posters, arranged in a configuration that suggested they had been used to cover cracks. The floor was uncarpeted. Norco evidently hadn't lavished much attention on their Third World partners.

"Anything you can show me on Mansalava. A drilling log?"

"Drilling log?"

"Or a well summary?"

"Well summary." The young man repeated the unfamiliar syllables with care, then shrugged. He had large eyes and a shock of dark hair. "Monsieur Velo-André returns after three o'clock."

"My plane leaves this evening," Spence said. "I won't have time to come back."

"Can you telephone?"

"I tried earlier, but I couldn't get through."

The young man picked up the Bakelite handset, rattled it, listened briefly, and put it down again. "The telephone is broken," he explained without surprise.

"Maybe you could just show me the papers relating to the Norco job. Your boss said he would do anything he could to help me."

Velo-André's assistant walked over to the filing cabinet, pulled out a middle drawer, and stood back.

As he leafed through the files, Spence said, "Have you worked here long or . . . "

"Since Norco came here." The young man made an apologetic gesture that encompassed the run-down state of the office. "Maybe not too much longer."

"Did you ever work for Norco itself?"

The young man shook his head.

"You didn't know one of their drivers—guy by the name of Marcel Antansoa?" Spence wondered if he'd got the pronunciation correct. As with the Cree Indians back home, these surnames began to sound like a section of the same obscure incantation. Rakoutouson, Tsiromandidy, Antansoa...

The young man was shaking his head again, but Spence wasn't looking at him. There, amid the bills, receipts, and official letters, sat a pristine geological display.

"You don't have a logging report as well?"

"Everything is kept here."

"Don't you lock this up?"

"The lock is broken."

He picked up the geological display and limped over to Velo-André's desk with it. The young man had to heave his typewriter onto the floor to make room. Unfolded, it covered the wooden tabletop. Spence leaned his walking stick against the chair and moved sideways so that the sunlight from behind him would fall on the chart.

The geological display was a three-dimensional plan of the whole area Norco had prospected. This one included a contour map of the area within a twenty-mile radius of the Mansalava well, gridded with the courses of seismic lines and the heavier black markings that denoted geological faults.

In the top right-hand corner was a lithological profile. The sequence of rocks certainly matched the drilling log he'd obtained in Belo—limestone, sands, and shales, with an igneous basement at ten thousand feet. Spence turned his attention to the seismic display. He knew all about the practicalities of drilling, but most geology was outside his province. His limited knowledge of the subject had been picked up as fragments of geologists' conversation at planning conferences, in bars, and across the Formica tops of countless camp diners. He remembered one crucial fact: an oil field, to exist, requires the coincidence of three geological accidents: a source rock, an enclosing structure, and an underground seal. Here, in front of him, was the full house: an underground blister of rock sealing six hundred meters of sandstone and shale between the cap and the base. In the dead center of this natural dome was the thin, straight line which marked the site of the Norco well.

"Have you got a pen?"

The young man turned his clear eyes on him.

"Pen . . . pen," said Spence, making scribbling movements with his right hand. The young man rummaged in the desk drawers and produced half a pencil. Spence took a blank corner of the geological survey map and began jotting down calculations: Say the pay area was thirty thousand acres, with a vertical closure of six thousand feet. Assume twenty-five percent porosity with a net pay of at least three hundred feet, it worked out that Mansalava contained . . . sixty billion barrels of oil.

Spence stopped, scratched his nose, and checked the zeros. Even in his wildest dreams he hadn't expected anything this big. He remembered the tremor that had run through the industry when they'd discovered the Ninian and Forties fields in the North Sea of Scotland. The logging report plus this geological display added up to a field bigger than either of those, and nobody knew a damn thing about it. More than ever before, Spence felt scared and alone. He longed for Perpetude's dark wisdom or Morgan Hanssen's lusty vulgarity. Here in the capital he was without a friend.

"Do you have a photocopier?" He realized, even as he asked it, that it was nervousness that prompted such an absurd question. Predictably Velo-André's assistant went blank again. Spence checked his watch—twenty past two.

"Paper," Spence told him. "I need paper."

The boy found him two sheets of lined paper from an exercise book, and Spence began to make copies of the diagrams in front of him. It was a soft, blunt pencil, and freehand drawing had never been Spence's strong suit. Despite the open window the room was hot and stuffy. The sun shone directly on his back, and sweat from his palm smudged the lines he drew. Velo-André's assistant watched him draw in the minutes of the seismic lines around the anticline, then he lost interest and left to go to the lavatory.

Spence studied his handiwork and realized that, as a serious document, it would be virtually useless. He folded the original carefully and slipped it inside his shirt. Then he took from the filing cabinet a document of approximately the same size as the folded geological survey. As Velo-André's assistant came back through the door, Spence ostentatiously returned this to the filing cabinet and closed the drawer. "Finished," he said, assembling his pencil copies.

"You have a message for Monsieur Velo-André?" the young man asked him.

"No, I'm leaving this evening. I might ring him from Canada."

As Spence headed back through the partitioned-off halls, he heard the solid clatter of the typewriter start up behind him.

Spence made his way back to the Hilton on foot. There had been a traffic jam around the Zuma market when he arrived at the ministry, but by now it had grown to epic proportions. Some of the drivers were standing outside their vehicles. Others opted to remain seated in the crushing heat, leaning on their horns.

He climbed the steps over the wide ridge that separated the Zuma market from the lake. On top of the ridge, in the parched gardens by the cinema, he stopped and looked back. The knot of students had swelled to a small demonstration that was now blocking the center of town. Their chant floated up in the flux of smog and rotting vegetables. *"Vive Istasse. Vive le plan de dix ans."*

The tiny figures of the hopelessly outnumbered gendarmerie ran around ineffectually blowing whistles. Up here, above the melee, the balustrades were lined with soldiers, joking, smoking, and laughing at the feeble attempts of the police to disperse the crowd.

At the Hilton he retrieved his musical instrument from the safe and hid the geological survey inside. Afterward he changed into swimming trunks and found a lounger by the pool. He wrote a card to Perpetude, then lay watching the marbled patterning of the water and wondering about Velo-André. His memory was of a pleasant, uncomplicated man but nonetheless a man who had offered to buy the rig: that, surely, was ample cause for suspicion. Even if Velo-André was as naïve as he seemed, it would be risky to share any information with him. The fewer people who knew of the drilling log, the easier it was for Spence to control things. If his information in the hotel was accurate, it could quite possibly change the political complexion of the whole country, and Spence wanted to be on home ground when it happened.

His thoughts were interrupted by a vaguely familiar voice: "Mr. Spence. Taking the sun, I remark."

Spence turned, squinting upward into the painful white of the sky, from which there emerged the smiling, chubby face of the minister for mineral resources.

Chapter 14

Velo-André was wearing a white shirt, a sober tie, and a lightweight gray suit that was slightly too long in the leg. He hitched up his trousers and sat on the lounger opposite Spence, blinking in the glare from the water. "Ah," he said, loosening his shoelaces, this is the life—you have the chance."

"The chance to what?"

"The chance . . . good fortune."

"Luck."

"Yes, luck," said Velo-André, summoning the waiter. "What will you have?"

"I'll have a soda."

"With whiskey?"

"I've given up spirits."

"I'll have the whiskey," said Velo-André. He took off his jacket and tie. As he was doing this, he noticed someone he recognized on the far side of the pool and beamed at him. The waiter appeared, and Velo-André gave his order in local dialect.

"You have injured yourself," he remarked.

The scab had come off Spence's forearm, but the new skin was still smooth and white with a pink flare in the center. He touched it and thought of Perpetude. "It's nothing serious," he said.

"So." Velo-André mopped his brow with a handkerchief. "I believe you called to see me. Pardon me for not being present. So much work."

Spence pulled on his shirt and rolled up the sleeves. "It didn't matter. Velo, you needn't have come here. I just called to say good-bye. I would have just rung, but the phone was broken.

"My assistant said you were interested to see some documents."

"Well, while I was there . . . I was just curious."

"He tried to describe to me the document he showed you."

"It was a geological survey," Spence said.

"I thought so, but the foolish duck could not find it."

"It's there somewhere," Spence said. "I just made some rough copies. Geology is kind of a hobby of mine."

"It's no problem," said Velo-André, embarrassed by the accusation he had barely articulated. He ran a hand over his shining face and changed the subject. "So. How did you enjoy your stay in Morondava?"

"Good—it was good. The rig's in pretty good shape. I made a couple of friends . . . a woman called Perpetude Peyrame and a fellow called Morgan Hanssen."

"Ah, yes, Hanssen, at the sugar factory."

"That's the guy," said Spence. His mind was full of unasked questions about the Mansalava field, and small talk did not come easily. "There was a bit of demonstration going on downtown this afternoon," he said.

"Ah, yes, students. They have gone now."

"What were they protesting about?"

"Oh, it was just a . . . what would you say . . . a demonstration of support."

"For the other guy."

"For Istasse."

"Well. There wasn't a whole hell of a lot of them."

Velo-André shrugged. "The problem with a young country like this is you don't have to convince many people. Even when you include the students, there are less than a thousand people in this country who know anything of economics. Istasse persuades five hundred that he knows how to change their lives and . . . pan . . . out we go. Small boats are very unstable."

"And if you had oil?"

"Aha—if we had oil there would be fewer waves. Anyway," he said, "enough of my problems."

"I'm interested," said Spence. He was thinking of Velo-André and the president sitting in some decaying tropical council room while the promise of oil revenue drifted out of reach and the opposition bayed for blood.

A German girl walked past them wearing a loose shirt over her bikini. She had skin the color of cinnamon and heavy, fluid breasts. Velo-André watched her till she reached the umbrellas on the lawn, then he looked back to Spence with a boyish smile.

"Tell me about geology," said Velo-André.

"What do you want to know?"

"The geological survey—what you thought of it."

"I'm just an amateur, Velo."

"Well, tell me as an amateur."

"It's complicated," said Spence.

Velo-André sensed that he was stalling. A cloud passed over the African's face. "It was not a good spot?" he asked.

"No, quite the opposite. It was a very good spot, very good."

"But not good enough—*hein?*"

The drinks arrived—a whiskey and ginger ale for Velo-André and a small bottle of soda for Spence. He poured it himself and had to drink to stop it from frothing over. "Tell me," he said, wiping his mouth with the back of his hand. "Did Norco ever show you a logging report?"

"*Comment?*"

"A logging report. It's a blue sheaf of papers about yay thick, and it unfolds to show what they found at various depths."

"Oh, yes," said Velo-André. "I believe I saw such a document."

"Did they tell you what it showed?"

"Oh, yes." He smiled wryly. "But there wasn't much to tell."

"Nothing on it? No gas kicks? No evidence of oil?"

"Nothing big enough."

"Are you sure?"

"I'm sure that's what they told me." Here Velo-André oscillated his glass. "As with politics, we are short of experts, we are largely dependent on the visiting oil company."

"And they said there was nothing?"

"Nothing. The head man, Hunter, was very frank with me." Behind him the reflection of a fluffy cloud drifted across the windows of the Hilton.

"And yet you still want to buy the rig?"

"If you like, I had a . . . what is the word . . . a hutch?"

"A hunch."

"I had a hunch," said Velo-André.

"In this business hunches aren't good enough."

"I know, but there has been oil exploration here for twenty years. For the French and others to spend so much, surely the signs must be favorable."

"I'll give you that."

"If the truth were told, we govern by hunches. These large companies offer us deals on powdered milk, on medicines, on irrigation schemes. We judge them and choose this or reject that. Sometimes we trust the wrong people."

Spence nodded and looked away. A huge beetle was trundling over the mosaic tiles at his feet.

"And sometimes," Velo smiled, "we are lucky enough to meet an honest man."

Spence looked at him and saw a face as lacking in malice as the tropical day. Surely he could speak freely. A tiny whirlwind rummaged through the stems of bougainvillea and carried a monogramed napkin across the lawn. "Tell me," he said.

"Have any other companies bought concessions here?"

"Not here. Here I am told the rocks are too old. But on the coast near Mansalava, yes. Exxon has a concession inland from Mahajanga." He drew a vague outline on the table with the soda Spence had spilled. "And the Italians—Agip—down here in the south."

"And when do these concessions run out?"

"Very soon—one month, two. They bought them when Norco started drilling."

"And they have no plans to renew them?"

"No, when Norco put the rig up for sale, everybody lost interest. Hunter told me when we last met that if they hadn't found oil, then nobody would. I suppose the other companies thought so also."

Spence said, "And Norco was happy when you offered to buy the rig?"

Velo-André laughed. "Happy? I don't know. Amused, maybe. Like you, they think I am pissing into the wind." He laughed, pleased to have remembered the figure of speech.

"And Norco definitely isn't coming back here?"

"Not with oil prices so low. Unless we managed to attract them with a more favorable deal."

"Like what?"

"Well, on this exploration they had agreed to split any revenue fifty-fifty for the first five years. Maybe if we offered them seventy percent . . ."

"I'd hold fire on that one," said Spence.

"Why do you say that?"

"Just a hunch."

"You told me that . . . hunches . . . were not sufficient in this business." Velo-André was regarding Spence with interest. "For an amateur you have been asking some strange questions," he said. "You do not have some professional interest?"

Spence laughed and rubbed his leg. "No . . . no," he said.

"You didn't notice anything at Mansalava that made you suspect—"

"Nothing."

"Or on the geological survey?"

"Like I said, Velo, I'm just interested in the process. I like to know how these things work."

"I believe you. I am sorry if I have appeared suspicious." Velo-André seemed to relax and looked away. The German girl had slipped into the pool and was swimming lengths with a lazy, powerful stroke.

Spence looked at his watch. "I have a plane to catch, Velo. I need to go and pack if I'm going to catch the check-in."

"Go . . . pack," said Velo-André. "I will wait for you here, and we will drive to the airport together."

"Really, there's no need."

"It would give me pleasure. Besides, my house is in the same direction, and these hotel taxis are not a reliable mode of transport."

Spence flung the towel around his neck and picked up his stick. "Okay," he said. "I'll be ten minutes. See you in the lobby."

"I'll be here by the pool." Velo-André gave a sly wink. "I prefer the view."

From his window on the eleventh floor Spence looked down on Velo-André lying in a position of blissful repose. It was impossible to mistrust a man who wore his trousers too long, who drank Jim Beam whiskey, who didn't have a pen in his office or a lock on his filing cabinet. If he found anything to pin on Norco, then Velo-André would be the first to know.

They drove to the airport in the back of Velo-André's old black Mercedes. Beyond the Zuma the houses were open to the street. Shops doubled as living rooms, living rooms as shops. Children and dogs rooted in the gutters, and women with water containers gathered around the public standpipes. The warm air flowed and eddied through the open car windows, bringing with it the smells of dust and jasmine, cooking and sewage.

At the entrance to the airport car-park, the guard lifted a

barrier and saluted as they passed. The driver brought them
opposite the main entrance and got out to open Spence's door.

"Hey, Velo," he said, attempting to shake hands. "I really
appreciate it. Maybe contact you again."

"On you go," said Velo-André. "I'm coming with you."

"Really, it's not necessary."

"*Allons-y,*" said Velo-André, giving him a gentle shove.
"Customs, money control... I can prevent you many problems."

Spence grabbed his carryall, and they made their way together into the swarming heat of the airport. A guard joined
them at the main entrance, and, on Velo's instructions, forged
them a path to the departures desk. Velo walked in front of
Spence, turning repeatedly to ensure that Spence was coping
with the crowd. They squeezed past the main queue and arrived
at the customs station. Naked light bulbs hung precariously
from the dusty ceiling high above. Customs men were working
at half a dozen benches, unlocking suitcases and untying parcels,
then sweeping the piles of clothes and possessions out of the
way. At the far end of each bench, tourists were hustled into
the waiting area, still stuffing socks and shirts into the gaps in
their violated luggage. The air was heavy with dust and official
impatience. Spence saw a customs man groping inside an ornamental vase.

"Really, Velo, I can handle it from here."

"Tch." Velo-André dismissed this with a smile. A bubble
of tranquillity seemed to surround him in the chaos. One of
the benches was cleared for him, and he beckoned for Spence
to come forward. The customs man was a scrubbed, unnaturally
thin man in a uniform starched to the shape of a cornflakes
packet. Velo said, "Money form."

Spence took out his wallet and handed over the buff form.
Velo handed this to the customs official, who studied it with
elaborate care.

"You need to show your currency," said Velo-André.

Spence handed over the bills in his wallet. As the customs official counted them, Velo made a joke in dialect. "All in order," he said to Spence, returning the money. "Now your bag. Only a formality."

"I don't have diplomatic immunity?" Spence asked.

Velo-André laughed lightly at the joke. "In a country as changeable as ours, there is no such thing as diplomatic immunity."

The customs official opened the bag. He carefully removed two checked shirts and a pair of jeans, then unzipped the shaving kit.

"How much would you pay for that razor in Canada?" asked Velo-André.

"Forty dollars."

Velo-André translated this for the benefit of the customs officer, who made a clucking noise and shook his head.

"Tell him he can have it if he wants it."

"Ah, no, that would not be proper. Aha. A souvenir. Do you play?" Velo-André picked up the bamboo musical instrument and plucked one of the strings. It made a dull, thwacking sound that hit Spence like a whiplash. The customs official heard it too. He held out his hand, and Velo-André handed the instrument over.

All around them the clamor of voices continued, but Spence could hear every scrape of the official's thumbnail as he picked at the bottom of the bamboo tube. The base fell out onto the bench between them with a clatter like the roll of a military drum. The official fussed and picked at the papers inside. Slowly there emerged the logging report and the geological survey.

"Just some papers I was carrying," Spence said.

The official flipped through them and handed them to Velo-André.

"The blue one's an old logging report," Spence explained.

Velo-André was examining the official stamp on the geological survey. "You removed this from my office?"

"I must have. I intended to return it."

"And this one? The blue, where did it come from?"

"It's just an old report that I found at the rig."

"But important perhaps?"

"No. I don't think so."

"The front page has been removed," Velo-André observed. "Did this come from my office as well?"

"No, Velo. Can we go and discuss this somewhere else?"

"Please, Mr. Spence, do not embarrass me further by appearing to have my complicity."

"Well, what can I say? This is yours, and I shouldn't have taken it. The other one's not important."

Velo-André looked tired and disillusioned. "It is important, because it looks important, and you appear to have been hiding it."

The customs officer had been following this conversation with his eyes. Now Velo-André spoke to him in dialect. From his tone he was offering an apology. He handed the officer the documents.

"Velo, listen to me. I need those."

"In that case you should not have stolen them. If you had been open with me, there would have been no problem. Now it is outside my control."

"I'm on your side, Velo."

"My side against whom?"

"I don't know. Norco maybe? Someone's trying to cheat you."

Velo-André smiled wryly. "We own this country, Mr. Spence. That is not something we can be cheated out of. Why is it that dishonest people are the first to accuse? Norco has at least been direct with me. I assumed you were also a man of principle."

"Velo, I can help you. You asked me to help you once."

"That was when we trusted each other."

"I was taking those reports to be interpreted."

"I have no doubt of it. I believe such espionage is quite highly paid."

Together they watched the customs official mark the reports with red pencil and lock them in a strongbox.

"Please listen to me. I think you may have oil in Mansalava."

"Enough."

"At least get these reports reassessed."

"Of course. I will ask Norco to reexamine these. I am sure that if they suggest anything new, Mr. Hunter will inform me."

"You're making a mistake."

"Good-bye, Mr. Spence."

"Velo!"

But Velo-André had already turned and was making his way back across the airport's main hall. Spence started after him, but two military guards blocked his exit. Over their heads Spence saw Velo-André head back into the crowd. Some of the optimism had left his rotund form, and he was stepping on the backs of his trouser legs.

Spence turned again. The customs official was dealing with three other passengers. Spence pushed the shirts and the shaver back into his carryall. Beyond the heavy glass doors the Air France 747 was waiting on the tarmac.

Chapter 15

"Clyde?"

"Yes" said the voice on the phone.

"It's Spence."

A pause, then, "Hello, Spence."

"Can we meet up and talk?"

"What do you want to talk about?"

"It's about work."

"Go ahead."

"I'd like to come and see you."

"Yeah. Last time you did that, you took a swing at me, remember?"

Spence said, "I think it's time we forgot all that bullshit."

"You serious about that, or is this just some new kind of stunt?"

"I'm serious," Spence said.

It was three months since he'd last seen Clyde and been thrown out of the restaurant they were in. Driving downtown to his offices on 102nd Avenue, he began to feel nervous about the meeting. He had felt on the flight back into Edmonton that something fundamental in him had changed. That he was no longer in love with Nancy. That he no longer wanted to kill himself. That his life had purpose. But a lot about his relationship with Clyde was the same: their twin burdens of guilt and blame, the scars and tender areas left by the severance of their friendship.

Clyde was wearing an expensive tartan pullover. It looked like the kind of thing Nancy would have bought him for Christmas. He lit a cigarette and started fiddling with the blinds while Spence sat down.

"So. You been in Madagascar. How was it?"

"Fine. Just fine. How's Nancy?"

"She's fine. I told her I was seeing you."

"You been doing any hunting?"

"Not a lot."

The conversation refused to flow. The questions dropped like lead weights, and the silences carried their echoes. It was odd how someone who had been close to you could become a stranger. Spence shifted in the leather chair and came to the point.

"I wanted to ask you about this Madagascar crash."

"Yeah, I kind of figured you'd come about that," Clyde said. "You know I didn't have anything to do with that investigation."

"That's okay. This is just off the record. What's the inside word on all that?"

"Well, you know how it goes, Spence. You can never get the truth about these things. Often you just settle for the most you can know for sure."

"Which is what?"

"Which is what it says in that accident report I gave Cora."

Spence said, "While I was out there, I heard a couple of things that aren't in it."

"Like?"

"Like some folks figured there was an explosion on board before the plane went down."

"Yeah, I heard that."

"Also that the door that blew off got taken away by the air force."

"Yeah, I heard that too."

"So why isn't it in the report?"

"You know the reason as well as I do, Spence. If there's any chance of negligence, it makes it a whole lot more difficult for the wives around here to get compensation. Best we could do was keep it simple."

"You mean the whole thing's a crock?"

"I mean it's all we could find out. The charter company was just as keen as anyone to get to the bottom of it. Their top guy in London was pushing for a further investigation, but you know—what can you do? The place is a long way away. The witnesses are spread halfway around Madagascar by now."

"You know who headed up the investigation?"

"Some English guy went down there. I can probably get you his address."

"You think in the meantime you could get your labs to look at this?" Spence rummaged in his pocket and handed Clyde a broken section of steel rod.

"What's this—a piece of aileron rod?"

"I took it out of the crash."

"What do you want them to look for?"

"Explosives."

Clyde ran the rod between his finger and thumb. "What you after, Spence?"

"Nothing. I said I'd do it for Cora. I guess you owe me one."

"It's dead now, Spence. Best to leave it at that," but he put the rod in a plastic envelope from his desk drawer. When Spence got up, Clyde came around the desk and shook his hand. "You should come out and see us some time."

An ambulance passed in the street far below.

"Maybe after a while." Spence turned to go, noticing, as he did so, the picture of Nancy on the wall under a photo of a plane wreck. He didn't recognize the clothes she was wearing. She looked like someone else's wife now.

"I don't suppose you feel like lunch," Clyde said.

"I'm seeing Dennis. See you around."

"Sure." He opened the simulated-wood door. "Bye, Spence. Thank you."

"Thank you for what?"

Clyde pulled his nose. "I dunno. I'll tell you if we find anything."

Spence drove west along 104th, with the sun to his left appearing and disappearing between the mirrored tower-blocks. At each stop sign he looked across at the other drivers swaddled in wool and fur and denim, their faces set against the winter. He remembered Perpetude, walking barefoot to the sea, her hair blowing in the dusty African wind, the magical ease with which she undressed and the warmth of her naked skin.

He signaled left and turned off before the old railyard, adjusting the sun visor against the glare.

Spence had booked a place downtown called the Victor Hugo, which turned out to be a fancy new restaurant with lots of windows in the roof and plants on the walls. The waiters and waitresses were dressed alike in bow ties, black trousers, and white aprons.

Dennis came in, looking around him as if he'd taken a wrong turn somewhere. From an alcove in the corner Spence watched him stop a waiter and ask for directions. The waiter pointed to Spence's table, and Dennis headed toward it. "What the fuck is this?" he whispered.

"It's a French restaurant. Dennis, you've been to French restaurants before."

"Not unless I have to. What's wrong with us just going out and having a burger?"

"I wanted to eat somewhere French."

"What the hell for?"

"'Cause I got used to French food, okay? Madagascar's French. I got used to it. Sit down and stop attracting attention.

If you objected so much, you could have told me on the phone."

Dennis sat down reluctantly. "You didn't tell me it's French."

"Well, what do you think Victor Hugo sounds like?"

"Sounded to me like a couple of good old boys," said Dennis. "Victor and Hugo. I figured they'd be serving steaks and have a guitar picker." He scowled across at the violin player, who was sitting on a stool, playing a muted selection of classical music. The kind of fiddle music Dennis liked was played by musicians like Mo Bandy. "Leave the waiter a couple of dollars and let's get out of here."

"Relax, Dennis. Everywhere's packed at lunch hour. Least-ways we got ourselves a table."

Dennis parked his cap under the aluminum chair and looked at Spence over the wine list. "Well, you're looking good anyway," he conceded. "That African climate must agree with you. What did you do—find yourself a squaw?"

"I stopped drinking spirits," said Spence.

"Hmm, maybe I should try that myself someday. How was Morondava?"

"Interesting."

"Interesting, huh?" He examined Spence's face for irony. "Interesting" wasn't the answer he'd expected. He looked down again at the wine list. "Don't seem like they've got any beer."

"Just behave, okay, Dennis?"

When Dennis's business meetings demanded it, he was perfectly capable of acting sophisticated. He was playing the hick to punish Spence for choosing a restaurant he couldn't relax in.

Dennis signaled to the waitress, and she came over—a busi-nesslike girl with her hair in a ponytail. "You got anything to drink here?"

"That's the wine list in front of you, sir."

"Okay, we'll have some wine."

"What kind of wine?"

"Any wine," Dennis told her. "You choose."

"I'll bring you house white."

When she'd gone, Dennis said, "Okay. Tell me what kind of shape was the rig in?"

"Pretty good. I'll send you my report for Mandy to type up. That's not what I wanted to talk to you about."

"Well, if you're looking for more work, there's nothing much doing," Dennis said. "Since this price-war bullshit, we already lost three contracts."

"I'm not looking for work. I wanted to ask you about Madagascar."

"Ask away, but you've been there yourself. I probably can't tell you a whole lot more."

"I know they drilled five wells, and that Mansalava, near Morondava, was the last. I know they said all the holes were dry, so they said they were pulling out and selling the rig."

"Yup." Dennis looked wary. "That's what I know too."

"What'd you say if I told you there's oil there? A bunch of it," Spence said.

Dennis adjusted the position of his seat, and it wobbled precariously. "I'd say, 'Who says?'"

Spence fished in his wallet and took the pages of the drilling log out of an airmail envelope. He passed it across the table, together with the freehand sketch he'd made of the geological survey. Dennis put his glasses on and inspected each paper in turn, holding them at arm's length and pushing out his bottom lip.

"Who sent you this?"

"I sent it to myself."

"Well, I guess that's one way of getting mail."

"So what do you think?"

"I think you've got part of a drilling log and a drawing of a survey without a title on it."

"There's a title page for the drilling log . . ."

"Sure there is. It says Mansalava One, but that don't add

up to an oil well either." He handed it back. "Where's the rest of the log?"

"Customs took it while I was leaving."

When Dennis smiled, it was like watching paint crack and blister under a blowtorch. "What, and that bit got ripped off in the fight? Oh, what we got here?"

"Muscadet," said the waitress, showing him the label. She poured a dash in the bottom of his glass.

"Must be powerful stuff."

"That's just to taste."

"So what happens if I don't like it?"

"We throw the bottle away."

"Might as well fill her up, then," said Dennis. "Give a guy something to make up his mind on."

She filled the glass, and Dennis swigged it back. "Okay, she's good," he said, wiping his mouth with his napkin.

The waitress shook her head and poured Spence some wine. She refilled Dennis's glass and asked. "Do you want to order now?"

"Sure, what have you got?" He opened the menu and frowned.

"Shall I translate for you?"

Spence said, "You do steaks?"

"We have *entrecôte café de Paris*."

"What's that?"

"It's a filet steak cooked with a mousse of butter, garlic, onions . . ."

"Okay," Dennis broke in. "Scrape off the butter and garlic and we'll have two."

Spence said, "I'll have mine like it comes," he said.

"How about Potatoes Dauphine?"

"Whatever—but fry them," said Dennis, enjoying himself.

"I'll see what I can do," she said tolerantly and left.

"So where did you get this from?" Dennis was referring to the pages of the report.

"Ben Lowers was sending it on to himself," Spence said. "He probably left it with someone in Morondava to send on to him."

"Ben Lowers was doing that? Bullshit."

"Well, that's who it was addressed to."

"He'd never do it," Dennis said. "He wasn't that stupid."

"Maybe he was desperate," Spence suggested.

"Desperate for what? To get himself run off?"

"To get some kind of a message through."

Dennis scratched his forehead. "You're not making sense, you know."

"Okay," Spence said. "Here's what I've been thinking. Suppose they drilled this well at Mansalava. It's a tight hole, okay. They make a big strike, but no one's got to know. They hit here, but they don't do flow rates or anything, just cap her off straight away—they're treating it like it never even happened."

"Why'd they do that?"

"Let me finish," Spence said. "Ben Lowers gets suspicious about something. Maybe he doesn't like the way they're doing things. Maybe he just wants something to fall back on if something goes wrong."

"It doesn't occur to you the log could be a phony and he's just sending it home for—I don't know—something for his kids to play with."

"Dennis, you know that's bullshit. You know this has got to be important."

"How do I know?"

"'Cause." Spence gathered his thoughts. On the long flight homeward he'd constructed a perfectly logical argument, but somehow the facts were now coming out in the wrong order. "Okay," he said. "Start at the beginning. As soon as I arrived in Madagascar, there was weird stuff going on. I was in the capital, and they had some guy following me."

"Sure they did. It happens in a lot of these places. The

government gets some tame Westerner to tag along with you just so's you'll tell him everything. They probably had some insider keeping an eye on Norco all the time they were there. You know that, Spence. They're all paranoid." Dennis laughed. "Shit, if I was a Marxist these days, I'd be paranoid too."

"Okay," Spence said. "Okay, listen to this. I get down to the rig and all the documentation's gone. I go back into town," Spence continued, "I get hold of this thing Ben Lowers left behind and someone tries to steal that too."

Dennis refueled his own wineglass. "Spence, you go to Africa, and there's no shortage of guys who'll rip you off. I went to Yemen that time and got myself robbed once every week. What did they take? Twenty dollars, a guidebook, a bunch of old machinery specs . . . "

Spence said, "You're not listening to me, Dennis. The guy who tried to rob me was an African kid from the capital. He used to drive for Charles Hunter."

"So?"

"Look at it this way. Just look at it my way for a minute, okay? Let's just say there's some kind of cover-up, and they're worried about what the documentation's going to show, so they send someone down to the rig to get rid of any papers before I arrive. Then this drilling report turns up, and they send a guy down to get it back off me too."

"Wait a minute. 'They,' who's 'they'?"

"I dunno—let's say Norco."

Dennis raised an eyebrow. "Norco? I thought we were talking about the government. If Norco was worried about security, why didn't they send one of their own people? And why didn't they do it a lot sooner?"

"They weren't expecting anyone to go there."

"Come on, Spence. It's a Norco rig. Someone would have to inventory it sometime."

"Well, maybe they didn't think we'd come in so soon. What do you think?"

"I think you've been watching too many movies, Spence. That logging report you got is probably scrap paper. They probably had some other well logged onto the computer, and someone stuck the Mansalava handle on it."

"Look, Dennis, I've got a copy of the geological survey here. The formations match."

Dennis glanced briefly at the crude pencil sketch. "Of course they do," he said. "It's a standard oil-bearing sequence, that one. Every well in the world looks something like that."

"Dennis, I know this is the Mansalava log. There's all kinds of shit that doesn't add up in the Norco operation there. The government of the country doesn't know an oil well from a muskeg hole. Every single person who knew what was happening on that rig got killed in the plane crash, and you know who wasn't on it? The company man, Charles Hunter. And you know what he carried out with him? Cores."

"Here's your steak," said Dennis.

Their waitress came around the pot plants, carrying two steaks with French fries.

"Is this what you wanted?" she asked.

"Set her down," said Dennis.

"How's the wine?"

"Hundred percent."

As she turned to leave, he called, "Hey, got any relish?" The waitress stopped, turned, and said with no hint of sarcasm in her voice, "Do you want me to run down to Burger King?"

"Can you do that?"

"Kiss my ass, cowboy," she said sweetly, handing him the salt and pepper.

Dennis looked after her with a wounded expression as she made her way around the potted birch trees to a table of suited businessmen. Afterward he would leave her a ten-dollar tip. He was only playing at being a redneck.

"Eat up, it's good," he said, but Spence's mind wasn't on his food.

"So, what do you think?"

"Of this Mansalava thing, not a whole hell of a lot."

"You think I'm shitting you?"

"I think you should sleep on it a couple, three nights. The way I see it, there's Ben Lowers—don't ask my why—keeping himself a copy of the log; there's a white guy you meet in the capital who's maybe checking up on you or maybe he's just fishing for business intelligence; and there's some African kid who's got used to Western wages breaking into your room at night and stealing something he's got no use for. I mean it sounds like you had an exciting time over there, but whichever way you look at it, it don't add up to a conspiracy."

"Listen, Dennis. I ain't told you half of it."

"Yeah, well, if it's more of that other stuff you just told me, I know a farmer who sells it in sacks."

Spence said, "That plane crashed because the back door blew off. No one proved why and—what do you know—it's the only piece they couldn't find. Plus this guy Claude Istasse is head of the—"

Dennis already had his hands up. "Hey, keep the plane crash out of this, Spence. I'd just about gotten over that."

Spence continued. "I'm telling you, the way it looks is that someone sabotaged that plane to keep this well secret. If the charts are anything to go by, there's six billion barrels under there."

"You're talking bullshit."

"Listen to me, Dennis."

"No, you listen to me," said Dennis. He leaned forward on his elbows and jabbed the air with his fork. "You're telling me—what now? You think Norco killed sixteen guys to keep an oil find secret? Is that what you're saying? 'Cause if you look at it, it's kinda hard to believe. I mean I know everyone's got a hard-on for these big companies, but big companies are what? They're just a bunch of guys. And everyone's got principles, least most folks have, some more than others. If they're going to get into mass murder, it's got to come from the top, and I don't see that happening. The top guys have all got too much to lose."

"On a little overseas job it would only take the operations manager and the geologist..."

"Besides," said Dennis, ignoring this, "if they'd had a find that size, they'd be hanging on to that rig."

"Maybe they're just trying to bluff Exxon and Agip into pulling out. If they do that, they can buy two more concessions. Maybe they're trying to rip off the local government."

"Yeah and maybe you spent a little too long in the sun." He broke off and looked in amazement at a table near the center of the restaurant. "Holy shit, we got ourselves a blowout."

A neighboring diner giggled. Her partner leaned across and whispered, "That's called *flambé*."

"Yeah? They can come around my place on barbecue night and see that for free."

Spence said, "Did you ever get any mail from the guys out in Morondava?"

"We still talking about that African shit?"

"There's just too many coincidences."

"Spence, you carry on like this and you'll end up a paranoid crazy old fucker like your daddy. You know as well as I do how logging reports get messed around. You don't have to kill guys to keep them secret."

"I still don't feel happy about it."

"Well, get happy. Because if you go rooting around with those kinds of ideas, you're going to make yourself unpopular with a lot of important people. And I don't have to tell you, it's getting difficult to find work in the old patch."

"If they get pissed at me, that's their problem."

Dennis laughed. "You're an ordinary son of a bitch, aren't you?"

"Skippy was a good buddy of mine," said Spence.

"Hey, hey...I know that. He was a buddy of mine too,

remember. I knew every one of those bastards on that rig—
Walter Neish, Al Parachuik, Gill Winters, Steve Wyse, Dennis
Smith . . . You want me to go on? I hired most of those guys,
and I sent them on that job. So how do you reckon I feel
about it?"

"Sorry, Dennis."

"That's okay." He let his belt out a notch.

"I'm still going to find out what happened."

"You know where I think you should go, Spence. I think
you should take your pickup and head up into the hills around
the Keg River for the weekend. Take a hike, do some shooting,
get back in tune with the real world. See how you feel after
that."

Spence ate a French fry, mulling this over. "Yeah," he said
at last, "that's not a bad idea . . . I might just do that."

Chapter 16

All along the McKenzie Highway the frosted birches sparkled like crystal. Spence drove with the windows down, the collar of his lumber jacket up, and the heater on full. Snow still lay thick on the fields and the rolling hills beyond: it smothered sheds and fences and formed frozen crags on either side of the freeway. He drove north and west, through the towns of Slave Lake and High Prairie. The hills became higher, and the spruce and poplar denser. On Peace River some children were playing ice hockey.

At Highway 35 he turned right and carried on north through Dixonville and North Star. Just before Carcajou he branched off through the pine forests toward Skippy's place.

As Spence arrived, Cora came out of the farrowing shed wearing a pair of rubber boots covered in hog shit. She had on one of Skippy's old donkey jacket, and her red-brown hair was stuffed into an old trapper's cap.

"Hey, Spence."

"Cora. What do you say?"

"I can't hug you," she said. "I'm covered in pig."

"I never liked this jacket anyway," he said, embracing her.

She took a step back from him and held his arms. "Hell, you look good, Spence. You look like you used to. What happened to you? You fallen in love?"

"Shit, no."

"Well, I'd pay to know what it is you're taking."

"You don't need it. What are you doing?"

"Oh, messing out. We've got half a dozen sows fixing to deliver."

"Where are the boys?"

"Alexander's gone off for the weekend. His Uncle Jim Yuskin has to blow up a beaver dam, and he wanted to see it. Patrick's out on the loader, putting some of this good stuff on the big field. God, it's so good to see you, Spence, I could just pinch you. I'll just get rid of this shovel, then we'll go on up to the house."

"Throw it in the back."

"Okay."

She climbed in and rode up to the house with her boots sticking half out of the door.

The house was on its own on some high ground surrounded by trees. The yard, the main hog shed, and the vegetable garden were at the bottom of the slope below it, separated from the fields by a narrow creek. When Skippy first bought the quarter, Spence had helped him clear some of the lumber. By the time he died, he had three good-sized fields, sixty hogs, a few dozen hens and ducks, and two sons. While he was out on the oil patch, Cora would look after all of them.

The house itself was fifty years old and built of cedar. Skippy had put new shingles on the roof and built an open veranda along the front and around the south side. Spence could see it now—white against the black-green of the spruce trees. At night the lights of the top windows were visible from the far side of the property. For Spence they were the lights of family, of sanctuary. He'd spent more evenings than he could now remember sitting around their old pine table, listening to the roaring of the stove and the creaking of the house's old timbers, drinking bottles of Moose Head beer, telling stories, playing cribbage. And even after Skippy had died, his tousled,

grinning spirit still shambled around the house, looking for
cigarettes and pieces of string.

Inside the front porch Cora kicked off her boots and shook
out her hair. "What are you looking at?" she asked.

Spence said, "I'm just thinking how you don't ever look
any older."

"I feel it, I can tell you. This winter seems to have gone
on all year." She watched him as he unlaced his own boots.
"When did you get back?"

"'Bout a week ago."

"Come in where it's warm."

Outside the kitchen windows the boys had cleared a path
through the snow to the chicken coop. Cora made tea and talked
about the bears pillaging the rubbish tip, her running battle with
the Alberta hog-marketing board, the trouble she'd been having
tidying up the last of Skippy's legal affairs.

"Do you still miss him?" Spence asked.

"Sure, I do. It's funny. I'm so used to him being away.
But it's having someone, somewhere, even if you can't see
them. That's what I miss. You must have felt the same when
Nancy went."

"No, I don't think I felt the same. I had a lot of other
things—guilt, revenge, jealousy. It was all that that screwed
me up."

"You sound as if you've got over it."

"I guess I have."

"How come?"

"Well, it's like you say—someone, somewhere, who cares
about you."

"So you are in love, you old coyote."

Spence shook his head. "I didn't say that. I just met someone who helped me sort some things out."

"A woman."

"Yeah, but it wasn't anything."

Cora said, "You guys, you think it's such an admission of defeat to depend on someone. Skip was just the same. Everyone loved him because he was such a raggedy man and he'd do anything and didn't have a care in the world. Then when we were in bed, he'd put his head on my shoulder and tell me all these stupid little things he worried about and he couldn't tell anyone else but me, because he thought they'd despise him for having hang-ups like normal people."

"He didn't have hang-ups."

"That's what I mean, he couldn't even admit it to you, and you were his closest friend. I've never met an oilman yet who'd admit to having a heart. You go off for weeks, drinking and gambling and fighting and whoring, and you're never allowed to admit that you love your wife and miss your family."

"Skippy always said he was crazy about you."

"Yeah, but he always made out he was joking . . . " Cora smiled. "Except to me . . . I knew he wasn't joking."

"Well," said Spence. "This woman in Africa . . . "

"What's her name?"

"She was called Perpetude."

"There, I knew it."

"Knew what?"

"You kind of light up when you say her name."

"Bullshit."

"It's not bullshit. You went out there looking like an old man, and you come back looking like a teenager. Beats me why you left her."

"Really, Cora, it was nothing."

"Well, if you think that, Spence, you must be stupider than you look. I can forgive a guy for losing one good woman, but not two. I don't suppose you've even written to her."

"I wrote a card from the capital. Then I tried to phone her from here a couple of times, but you can never get through."

"Ever heard of writing?" she asked.

"I guess so."

She shook her head and poured him some more tea. "So what's new on your property?"

"Aw, not a whole hell of a lot. I don't really feel so attached to her anymore. Maybe I'll move somewhere else."

"Like Africa?"

"Okay, that's enough."

"Just teasing."

"I liked it better when it was more isolated," Spence said. "Seems every year Edmonton gets closer. Time was there was just a few old ice-fishermen on the river, now it's all kids with Ski-doos."

"I thought you liked machinery."

"I like machinery that does a job."

"Well, how do you feel about diggers? We've got a burst oil seal. Patrick bought a new one, but I think he'll need some help with it."

"I'll do her tomorrow."

"You're a honey, Spence."

Patrick came in just as the sun was setting. He was twelve years old and had his father's shock-headed charm, though he was quieter and more serious than Spence remembered him. Later, when he had gone to bed, Spence and Cora sat up by the big log fire listening to a raccoon scrabbling for grubs on the shingles of the chicken coop.

Cora said, "Did you visit the place where they crashed?"

"Yeah, it was just a hole in the brush."

"Was the plane still there?"

"It was all burned out."

"I hate to think of him burning," she said, staring into the logs.

"I'm sure he'd have died before that."

"I mean even his body burning..."

They were sitting as they always sat—Spence on the left of the fire and Cora on the right. She and Skippy would usually share an armchair, one of them sprawled over the seat and the other leaning with his back to it. Spence noticed the way her arm still wandered, as if to touch Skippy's knee or rumple his hair.

"Did he use to write a lot?"

"Yeah, most weeks."

"Have you still got his letters?"

She smiled. "Oh, yes, I've got a shoebox full. I don't ever read them."

"Would you mind if I were to look at them?"

"What for?"

"Just interested."

"Ha, you're kidding me."

"Really, I would."

"They're just romantic nonsense."

"Did he ever write about what they were doing on the rig?"

"Not a hell of a lot. I mean an oil well's just an oil well, isn't it? Sometimes he'd say things about the other guys and sometimes...well, you know...they were just love letters."

"Would you be embarrassed if I read them?"

"I guess not. Some of them get a bit steamy." She laughed. "Especially toward the end of each hitch. I still don't see what you're looking to learn from them."

"I just want to check up on something."

"Check what?"

"A theory."

"Hey, come on, Spence, if I'm letting you read my personal mail, the least you can do is tell me why you're interested."

"I found out some interesting stuff for you."

"For me?"

"You asked me to go, Cora."

"Oh, that." She looked embarrassed. "I thought that

through afterward. I figured you were probably right. It just hurt at the time."

"Right about what?"

"About me interfering. Maybe I was just kinda trying to kick-start you. Maybe I wanted somebody to blame for Skippy dying. I don't feel so bad about it anymore. Besides, it don't seem to have done you any harm."

"I told you, I think you were right. I think there was something kooky about that plane crash."

"Spence, you don't have to—"

"I'm serious, Cora. I think you were right. I mean, how often does the back door blow off a plane?"

She said nothing. Watching for some sign that this was a black joke.

"They said in the report some African stole the thing, but the folks there say no one would do that. Because of their religion. They say it got taken away by the air force."

"Why would they do that?"

"'Cause I reckon Norco found oil down there. Everyone says it was a dry hole, but I found something that says it wasn't."

"Oh, they found oil, all right."

"They what!"

"Yeah, I'm pretty sure his last letter said they did. I'll get it for you."

She went upstairs, and Spence heard her feet padding across the floor of the bedroom above him. She came back down carrying a shoebox tied with a red ribbon.

"Here they are. The last one's on the bottom."

"Do you want to read it to me?"

"No, I couldn't, I'd just get silly."

Outside a coyote howled in the woods. Spence took the shoebox and dug through the letters, mostly in company envelopes, sent home by the company courier and posted from the UK. The last one was different. It was written on airmail paper and had been posted in French East Africa.

Spence read:

Mansalava
September 25th

My darling,

Seems like you didn't get the last two letters I sent. Seems the company post is all screwed up. I'm giving this to one of the swampers to post in Belo. Maybe it'll reach you. I got your letter you sent end of June. Tell Pat real well done with his school exams. I wrote to the boys also, but maybe they didn't get that neither. Tell him he should figure on becoming an engineer. One thing I regret is I never did go for that degree. I guess I'd never of got the math anyhow. Must be he gets his brains from his mother.

Hey, you remember that real wizened old guy who used to run the store in Moosejaw? Tell Steve there's a monkey out here looks just like him. He's a yappy little mother too. I told Iain, the derrickman, we could maybe train him to throw pipe. Iain says the monkey's training to be a rig superintendent—just sits on his ass all day watching everybody else working. That's how much respect I get around here.

I think of you every day. Gets kind of lonely being in charge—can't goof around like I used to. Sure wish I had you here to talk to and all that other good stuff. It's winter here but it's still hotter than a bitch. I guess back home it's hot enough to swim in the creek. When I come home, we'll sneak off at night and go skinny-dipping. Remember that one tree we made love against and you got that rash all over your ass. I get a hard-on just thinking about you with your hair all wet and your skin shining in the moon and your arms around my neck. A lot of the guys bring girlie magazines out

here, but I just have to look at your picture and you
get me all steamed up even all those miles away. I'm
going to have to stop writing this stuff or I'll need to
go take a shower. I'll be home in a couple, three weeks.
Soon as the boys are at school, we can get in the
hammock and you can fuck my brains out. That don't
sound very romantic, but it's meant to be.

Sounds like the hog prices are all screwed up
again. I guess you should hang on to those weaners
and sell them next year as feeders. Maybe we should
sell the hogs and get ourselves some cattle. If I was to
quit the oil patch next year, we could buy another
quarter section with my bonus, then we'd just about
have enough land. That brush between us and the
Indian reserve is all vacant.

Hey, guess what? Looks like we struck oil. The
company man's a moody son of a bitch and he's telling
us there's nothing on the log, but we all know it's
there because you can see it in the mud pits. I guess
we'll be doing flow rates for a week now, so don't be
surprised if I'm not home for your birthday.

You look after yourself, darling. I love you more
than I can tell you and I miss you real bad. I dreamed
we were in bed together and woke up chewing on a
piece of my arm. Somehow it didn't taste the same as
your neck. Tell the boys it won't be long now and I
miss them all. I guess I might just pack her in next
year and become an old cow-poke like your daddy —
can think of lots of worse ways to grow old.

You take care now
I love you
Skip

"Well," Cora said, "did you find out what you wanted?"
"I don't know if it's what I wanted, but I guess I found it."

"Will you stop looking like that, Spence? You're scaring me."

"Like what?"

"Like you're spooked."

Spence folded the letter and tucked it under the others, then slowly retied the shoebox with ribbon.

"There's an oil field in Mansalava," he said. "I've seen the reports. It's real big—no, not just big, it's colossal. Skippy knew they were onto it. Norco had a fifty-fifty deal on any finds going with the government of French East Africa. Thing is, they never told the government there was oil there. And all the guys who could have let the story out were killed in that plane crash. The only folks who know now are you and me."

Spence picked up another log and threw it on the fire. A shower of sparks streaked up the chimney.

Cora said, "Tell me you're not serious."

"I'm serious."

"No. They wouldn't have done that."

"You'd be surprised what people would do for three billion dollars."

"Not kill their own people. Surely not that."

"I wouldn't say this just to scare you, Cora. You know I wouldn't. I keep wanting to prove I'm wrong. But every time I try to do that, I find something that points the opposite way."

In the morning he helped Patrick change the oil seals on the digger arm of the backhoe. The kid obviously knew what he was doing, and Spence was careful not to take charge. They had the heater on full in the machine shed, but it was still so cold that they could hardly feel the elm screws through their gloves.

"Your dad ever tell you about working in the Arctic?"

"Sometimes."

"It was so cold there that if a guy touched anything metal, his hand would stick to it."

"So how could a guy work, then?"

"We had these big tents, hey, bigger than a Kenworth, made of parachute material, and we'd blow them up with hot air and work inside that. You saw them from the outside, and they looked real weird, out in the middle of nowhere, couple of guys working inside a soap bubble."

"Can you hold that?" said Patrick.

"I've got her." Spence held on to the casing while Patrick pulled off the end plate and extended the cylinder arm. "Sometimes you'd be working in there and an old polar bear would come along to see what was happening."

"I shot a bear last week with the Mannlicher." Patrick was trying to pull out the oil seals, but his fingers weren't strong enough.

"Here," said Spence. "Let me pull on that. . . . What did you do with that bear of yours, did you skin him?"

"No, he was kind of mangy. Uncle Jim Yuskin chopped him up, and Mom fed him to the pigs."

"I didn't know these pigs ate meat."

"For sure they do. They're fierce, pigs are. Old Mr. Penwarden, he got in a fight with one old sow who'd just had a litter, and she knocked him over in the corner of the pen and took a bite out of his hip about yea big." Patrick made a circle with the thumb and forefinger of both hands.

"Holy shit," said Spence.

"He was in hospital for four weeks. They said he could have bled to death."

"No kidding?"

"They're just like a shark on dry land. They get a smell of blood, and they'll go for you."

"You be careful with those old pigs."

"Naw, I just get 'em with the cattle prod if they get too frisky. Most times they're pretty tame."

"I think I'll stick with machines," said Spence. "They're a whole lot safer."

"No, they ain't," said Patrick, and it was only when Spence stepped outside and saw a vapor trail scratched across the sky that he realized what kind of machine the boy had been referring to.

"So what are you going to do next?" Cora asked.

"I've not really had time to think it through. I contacted the accident investigators last week, and they couldn't tell me anything. The only other thing I can do is confront this guy Hunter."

"Where would you find him?"

"Their head office is in London. England."

They had walked across the frozen creek and up to the fence of the big field. The dung that Patrick had spread lay in knotted lines across the snow. "Wouldn't it be better to phone the guy?"

"It would sure be easier," Spence said, "but I wouldn't be able to see if he was sweating."

Cora pulled her collar higher and hunched her shoulders. Her red hair was fanned over the rabbit skin and the wind had brought a pink glow to her cheeks.

"You be careful, Spence," she said. "I couldn't sleep for thinking about what you told me. If it's true, they'd kill you, too, for sure."

"The doctors said I was indestructible."

"Yeah, and you've been trying to prove them wrong ever since."

"Hey, I stopped drinking, haven't I?"

"So you want to die sober?"

"No one's going to kill me, Cora. I don't even know how I'm going to get to London. Probably need to wait till a job comes up in the U.K."

"I don't suppose I can persuade you just to leave it be."

"I don't suppose you can. I'm like an old hog who gets the smell of blood."

She laughed. "Patrick's been telling you about Mr. Penwarden, hasn't he? When the boys heard that story, their eyes grew big as dinner plates. Suddenly pig farming was something to tell your buddies about."

"Sounds as though you should be careful with those animals," Spence said.

"I am. I'm real careful. And I know more about pigs than you do about billion-dollar crime."

Spence smiled. He put his arm around her shoulder, and she leaned her head against him. A coyote came out of the spruce and ducked back in again. Four snow geese flew over the treetops, beating across the frozen sky toward Paddle Prairie.

Chapter 17

Life was a bitch. She was a red setter, aged four months, and no matter how often you tapped her on the muzzle, she would come back and unlace your shoes. Myra had actually named the dog Lief after a sheepdog her grandfather had owned in Norway, but Dennis had renamed it Life, which was pronounced the same way. Now, when people said, "How's life?" he could reply, "We just had her wormed" or "Still chewing on shoelaces." He dragged her from under the table where they were sitting and deposited her on the carpet behind him. They were eating in the dining room because the McCabes were having the kitchen rebuilt, and the kids were watching TV in the lounge. In normal circumstances the McCabe dining room was hardly ever used for eating, which was why Myra allowed Dennis to put his trophies there: two cups for bowling, the stuffed head of a moose he had killed, a perch in a glass case, and a signed photo of Dennis shaking hands with Red Adair.

"You applied for a job *where*?" he asked.

"The North Sea."

"The North Sea of Scotland?"

"Is there another North Sea?"

Dennis shook his head in disbelief and bent to retie his shoelaces. Requesting the North Sea at the end of January was like requesting Ras Shukheir in July.

Myra offered Spence the rice.

"But the North Sea," Dennis said, surfacing.

"I'm sure Spence has his reasons for going there."

"That's what worries me. You not still on about that Norco shit?"

"What? Oh, that. No, of course not," said Spence. "For Christsakes, Life." The dog had found its way under the table and was pulling on the hem of his jeans.

"Here, I'll take her." Myra put the dog through with the boys and closed the door. "So how's Cora?" she asked.

"She seems fine," Spence said.

"I worry about her, all on her own up there."

"I asked her had she thought of moving back into town, and she said, 'And do what? Drive through twenty miles of stop signs to get to some office?' Up there the only place she has to drive is the general store, and all she needs to worry about is hitting an elk. Besides, if anything goes wrong, she's got those guys who work on the farm."

"The ones who stay in the trailer?"

"The Indian guys, for sure," Spence said. "They're good hands."

Myra pulled a face. At the welfare office she was an outspoken champion of Canada's minorities. At home she was cynical about integration and protective of her friends. "Just seems awfully far away this time of year."

There was a loud burst of laughter from the sit-com on TV in the next room. Life was barking to get back into the dining room.

Spence said, "She was on her own most of the time when Skippy was away."

"I wasn't too keen on it then either."

Dennis gave her a craggy smile. "Anyway." He sawed on a chicken leg and turned to Spence. "Why do you want to go to the North Sea?"

"For the scenery," Spence told him.

★ ★ ★

That week the winter tightened its grip on the Alberta countryside. Out past Fort Saskatchewan the sloughs and farmland
that surrounded Spence's house had long ago disappeared under
a uniform blanket of snow, broken only by the feathery stands
of poplar along the horizon and the single-lane blacktop that
the snowplow kept clear.

Snow gathered along the telephone wires and the tops of
fences. Icicles formed on the eaves and the silvered wooden
drop-siding of his house. Spence salted the paths and repaired
burst pipes. He spent three or four days cutting birch logs with
the chainsaw and stacking them along the side of the house.
The logs froze solid at night and had to be prized loose from
the log pile with the blade of his ax. Each morning he chopped
them for the fire, bracing himself against the trestle so that the
backswing didn't pull him off balance. Under each blow of the
ax the frozen white wood splintered like glass.

Toward the end of the week Clyde phoned to say that tests
on the aileron rod had yielded nothing. The independent investigator who'd gone to Madagascar hadn't returned their calls,
but maybe Spence could write to him in England.

On Friday night Spence went down to the happy hour at
Jake's Bar in Edmonton. He drank two Budweisers and watched
abnormally tall black Americans playing basketball on TV.
There had been a time he couldn't call in at Jake's without seeing
at least someone he recognized, but companies changed location, and guys moved on to work elsewhere. Unless you were
working, it all drifted past you.

On Saturday morning he went for a tour around the house,
looking for jobs that needed doing. There wasn't much he could
do on the roof till the thaw. He took the snow shovel and
recleared the path between the house and the woodshed, then
changed one of the snow chains on the pickup. In the afternoon
he put on a jacket, packed up his fishing gear, and went ice-
fishing on the river.

On Sunday afternoon the Oilers were playing at North-
land.

That morning and evening he tried to phone Perpetude in Morondava—he couldn't get through to her. Memories of the little town kept coming back to him: Africans playing *boule* at sunset, light reflecting off the sea. Dogs and brown, potbellied children; the sound of guitars at night; kapok blowing off the trees. Perpetude.

Perpetude.

On a couple of occasions since his return Spence had sat down at his father's rolltop desk and tried to write: when he read these letters back, the voice on the page never sounded like his own. He burned each attempt. At night, lying waiting for sleep, he would talk to her in his imagination, trying to reconjure the details of her face against the pillow, the sound of her voice, the feel of her skin.

Each morning he checked his mailbox. There was no response to his job application.

Midweek he drove into Fort Saskatchewan and bought some two-stroke and some fence wire. The liquor store was right next to the hardware shop, but he managed to get past it without weakening. He continued on into Edmonton and ate in the basement of the legion hall where Korean War veterans limped around the pool table or fell asleep on the Formica-topped tables. Outside, the downtown area looked deserted. These days, with the temperature hitting minus ten, most people stayed off the sidewalks. They shopped out of town at West Edmonton Mall or traveled between blocks on the pedways and subways. Spence called in at Richler's and bought a couple of ax handles and some paraffin. He drove home and watched the TV for a couple of hours, then sat, dozing, beside the fire, thinking of Morondava.

It had been three weeks now since he visited Cora. He didn't like her to think he had nowhere else to go. Maybe next weekend he could take a trip up there again.

That Friday the temperature dropped another five degrees. Cora was snowed in. Spence stayed in most of the weekend, flicking through the TV channels, watching everything—the sports channel, the religious channel, the shopping channel. He tried to phone Morondava again, but, as always, the French switchboard defeated him.

On Monday a letter finally arrived from Geosource to say they didn't want to see him for the North Sea job. His application had been processed, and they would keep it on file.

Like hell they would.

On Tuesday he had a hospital appointment.

Since his discharge from the Walter McKenzie Hospital, Spence had been back for more than a dozen appointments, but the place still unsettled him. Memories of the time of the injury still returned—strapped to a stretcher, exhausted, disoriented, high on morphine. With every jolt of the hospital stretcher he had felt the shattered bones in his leg grating together. Waiting for his appointment, it all came back again: the smell of antiseptic, the noise of shoes on the rubberized floors, the continual whump of the swing doors.

"So—let's have a look at you."

The doctor was an East Coast guy whom Spence hadn't met before.

"Where's Dr. Cox?"

"He's moved on now." The new man didn't look up from his notes. "I see you missed your last appointment."

"I was working in Africa."

Spence lay on his back in his undershorts as the doctor mapped out the sensation of his bad leg, dictating into a tape recorder on the shelf by the couch.

"Four months ago this patient fell thirty feet from a drilling platform, crushing two thoracic vertebrae and sustaining multiple compound fractures to the left leg and a fracture in the occipital region of his skull. The arm is now completely healed, as is the skull, with no central neurological deficit. He has some pain on full rotation of the spine and some numbness over the T-nine dermatome.

"Regarding the left leg, all superficial tissues are healed. There is clinical union of the femur with two centimeters of shortening. The ankle is fused in the position of function and there is minimal range of movement at the knee—twenty degrees extended, thirty degrees flexed. He enjoys good range of movement in the Charnley hip replacement, which was installed on this side. There was some tissue loss at the time of injury, added to which there is now substantial muscle wasting in all compartments of the thigh and foreleg. Superficial sensory loss in the distribution of the peroneal nerve. He is, however, getting around well with a walking stick."

"The hell I am," said Spence.

The doctor afforded him a thin smile and switched off the Dictaphone. "As well as can be expected," he said.

"It might be as well as you expect, Doc. It's not as well as I expect."

"I see. So what exactly do you want us to do?"

"You're the doctor."

"Correct." The doctor consulted his file. "I notice you never turned up for any of your social-rehab appointments."

"I figured I could do that on my own."

"Well, the truth is you probably can." The doctor closed his file. "Seeing you're mobile now, I don't really think there's much more to be gained by—"

"Listen," Spence interrupted him, "I can't climb a ladder. I can hardly chop wood. Who's going to employ me like this?"

"Well." The doctor stole a look at his watch. "Have you ever thought about a desk job?"

"A desk job?"

"You have to learn to adjust to disability."

"I'm not disabled. I just broke my fucking leg."

"Mr. Spence, I'm sorry, but in no way did you 'just break your leg.' You suffered multiple trauma and arrived here in very poor shape indeed. By rights you're lucky to be alive."

Spence put his pants on, lassoing his left foot with the

waistband of his trousers. "Just book me for physiotherapy. I'll do the rest myself."

"I've already told you. That isn't going to help now. We can't expect much more mobility at the foot or the ankle. If you carry on with the isometrics at home, you may be able to rebuild some muscle bulk, but apart from that—"

"You're saying I'll always be a cripple."

"That's rather a pejorative word."

Per what? At least Dr. Cox had used words he understood. Spence hopped around angrily, looking for his stick. The doctor polished his glasses.

"Can I ask you how much you drink, Mr. Spence?"

"None of your business."

The doctor smiled indulgently. "I know the accident was alcohol related. I wonder if you shouldn't be seeking another form of help."

"As a matter of fact, I'd gone on the wagon."

"Until when?"

"Until today."

The approach to Spence's house lay down a gravel track that ran off Highway 15 and lost itself in the belt of protected forest. Now, with the leaves off the poplar trees, you could see Edmonton from the end of the driveway, when the mirrored tower-blocks caught the low autumn sun. Dennis McCabe pushed the doorbell and found it wasn't working. The hanging chimes tinkled as he crossed the porch. The main door was unlocked, and he let himself in.

Inside, a McDonald's sat half eaten on top of the TV set. A copy of *Oilman* lay open at the help-wanted page. There were circles marked around a couple of supervisor's jobs, but all the circles had been scored through.

"Spence!"

In the kitchen the fridge was empty. Dennis closed the freezer door, stepping in a small pool of blood and water, which had trickled from a defrosting piece of venison. The sink was

full of dishes. He could hear country music and the sound of
chopping wood.

Spence was in the yard, wearing his jeans and hunting shirt,
splitting logs with his sleeves rolled up to the elbow.

"Hi, Spence, how's it going?"

"It's going good, Dennis. It's good."

"I tried to call you. Your phone was out."

"Yeah, well, you know how it is. You lose one invoice
and next thing you know they've cut you off. How's work?"

"Actually I got a problem. Spence, we need a guy pretty
urgent. They're stripping a semisubmersible, and they want
someone to supervise. The ship's on standby, but the fellow
we had lined up got injured."

"Is it anywhere warm?"

"No."

Spence put another log on the chopping block.

"How much does it pay?"

"We've got a problem there. They're having to pay this
injured guy anyway, so you'd be surplus. The most they could
offer you is two."

"Two thousand Canadian? Do I have to pay my own boat
fare?"

"I didn't fix the price. Spence, I wouldn't have bothered
to suggest it if you hadn't said you wanted to go to the U.K."

"You didn't say it was in the U.K."

"Didn't I? Well, it is. I'll phone Aberdeen and tell them
you   "

"Hey, hang on a minute," said Spence. "If it's in the North
Sea, I'll do it. When would I have to leave?"

"Tomorrow."

"Okay. Ask Mandy to get me an open return and book
me a couple, three days in London on the way home." Spence
put down the ax. "I'll get you a coffee."

"Hey, one thing," Dennis said as they walked back to the
house. "You still off the juice?"

"You caught me just in time."

"Two things. You promise me you've not still got a hard-on for Norco."

"No."

"'Cause if you make yourself unpopular, you're nothing to do with us."

"Someone, somewhere, cares about me, Dennis."

"Sure." Dennis clapped his gloves against the cold. "That's because they don't know you as well as I do."

Chapter 18

The big Sikorsky was a relatively quiet helicopter, but no one felt like talking. There was room for the six of them to spread out, so most of them took window seats, sitting in the outsized orange survival suits, staring back at the receding granite of the Aberdeenshire coastline and ahead to the granite water of the North Sea.

The rig, a twenty-year-old semisubmersible, rolled heavily in the swell, the crown of its derrick tracing slow ellipses on the sky. They disembarked. The helicopter rose, tipped, and wheeled off into the distance. When the pilot waved, few of them bothered to return the greeting. A gray mood. A gray day. The only splashes of color were the orange flares of two Norwegian platforms to the west.

The skeleton crew of twelve was already on board. Spence took his team down to the materials man's office and allocated them rooms from the accommodation plan. Half an hour later they started work.

By day helicopters and supply boats that serviced the fields steered lonely tracks across the sky and water. By night the hard sea clanged against the metal legs, and sparks dripped into it from their welding equipment and grinders. The flares of distant rigs, invisible by day, appeared along the horizon.

There was a fax machine in the communications room from which Spence sent a message to Norco in London asking for an appointment with Charles Hunter. He also sent a letter to the address Clyde had given him for the man who'd headed up the plane-crash investigation. Four days later, still awaiting a reply from Norco, he sent another fax.

During their meals in the windowless canteen they talked about work and food. On dock the wind and rain penetrated the necks and sleeves of their oilskins.

By the middle of the second week they had uncoupled the motor, the mud tanks, the generators, and the winding gear. They unbolted the dog house, lowered and dismantled the derrick. Still no word from Hunter.

Another week went by. There was a letter from the sister of the accident investigator. She regretted to tell him that her brother had died recently in an accident on the Underground and therefore would not be able to meet him.

Still no reply from Norco. Spence sent another fax.

Day by day the big crane swung sections onto the waiting supply boat, a tiny target on the rolling sea. From this height a container looked like a child's building brick.

They stripped the platform bare, then started on the living quarters. A Portuguese roustabout got knocked out by a swinging length of girder and had to be evacuated. On the phone to Aberdeen, Spence asked them to contact Norco for him.

Over the next four days the rest of the men left in twos or threes. Spence and the crane driver were the last to go.

In the Aberdeen company headquarters he signed the papers that terminated his contract. Still no word from Norco. He phoned London himself and was told that Mr. Hunter was not available.

The Aberdeen secretary offered to reschedule his flight out of Glasgow, but Spence said he'd go down to London anyway. After three weeks of freezing his ass he was damned if he was going to leave the country empty-handed.

★ ★ ★

London on the twenty-fifth of January was marginally warmer
than Aberdeen, though just as wet. Spence took a taxi from
Heathrow to the hotel that Dennis's secretary had booked for
him. He'd asked her to find him a room in a Holiday Inn.
Fletcher's Hotel in Mayfair was just the kind of place he'd been
trying to avoid: a small, gloomy place full of pillars and mirrors
and men dressed as undertakers. As he signed the register, the
desk clerk looked pointedly at Spence's hands—still ingrained
and scarred from two weeks of hauling on boomers, chains,
and cables. The clerk's own writing was minute and as perfect
as crochet. Beside it Spence's signature looked like the work of
a vandal.

　A boy with an unfashionable haircut insisted on carrying
his bag up the hallway. Spence looked into the dining room as
they passed and saw white tablecloths, austere arrangements of
single flowers, a carpeted platform with music stands and a
surgical array of silverware. A chandelier the size of a Christmas
tree hung over the central table. Spence made a mental note to
eat elsewhere.

　The paneled lift was just big enough for himself and the
boy. They stopped on the third floor, and the boy checked
his fingers in the ancient folding gate. Spence pressed a number
of unfamiliar coins into the boy's hand and let himself into
the room. He found a single bed, a lot of dark, carved furniture, a couple of watercolor paintings of Scotland, and a
deep, reenameled bath with brass taps. The window looked
out on a cobbled street and the baroque façade of the Burmese
embassy.

　Spence turned on both taps of the ancient bath. While it
was running, he dialed a London number.

"Norco Oil International."

"Hello, could I speak to Mr. Hunter?"

"Which Mr. Hunter do you require?"

"Charles Hunter, your boss."

"What is your name, please?"

"Can you just tell me if Mr. Hunter's in the building?"

"Your name, please," she repeated with no change of tone.

"My name's Spence."

"Which company do you represent?"

"I don't represent anyone. I represent myself. Surely you know whether Mr. Hunter's in the building?"

"Putting you through to his secretary," said the receptionist.

There was a pause, then a voice said, "Mr. Hunter's office. Caroline speaking."

"Is Hunter there?"

"Who's calling, please?"

"Is he there? I mean, he's either there or he isn't."

"I'm afraid I have to have your name, sir."

"Spence."

"Which company are you with?"

"McCabe Drilling. Didn't you get my messages? I faxed you three times from Aberdeen, trying to arrange an appointment."

"I'm sorry, Mr. Spence, we didn't receive any messages. There was a call from your Aberdeen office, but Mr. Hunter wasn't available."

"Well, can I speak to him now?"

"I'm afraid Mr. Hunter is not in the building."

"Now you tell me."

"He's a very busy man. If you leave me a number where I can contact you—"

"I've kinda lost faith in that system."

"I'm afraid it's all I can do."

"You can tell me when he's going to be back. Does he come in in the mornings?"

"Sometimes."

"Is tomorrow one of them?"

"I'm afraid I can't say."

"Can you say if he's avoiding me?"

"I'm sure he's not doing that," she said pleasantly. "I'll tell him you rang."

"No, tell him this. I'm in London. I'm at Fletcher's Hotel in Mayfair. I'd like him to call me back this afternoon. If I don't hear from him, I'll call by."

"And this is concerning what?"

"It's all in the fax I sent."

"We didn't get the fax."

"Tell him it's about Madagascar."

He put the phone down and turned off the taps.

At three-thirty he gave up waiting for Hunter to ring back and left a message with the hotel clerk to expect a call for him. He walked the length of Oxford Street and bought himself a new pair of jeans. At Tottenham Court Road his leg began to give up on him, so he caught a taxi back through the rush-hour traffic. It was six o'clock when he got in. Still no word from Hunter.

"Will sir be wanting dinner?"

"No, sir's going out for a McDonald's."

Friday dawned gray and damp. Mayfair to the Strand was less than two kilometers on his street map, so Spence went on foot. The narrow streets were jammed with taxis trying to avoid Park Lane. Spence limped along at a brisk pace, heading roughly west across Berkeley Square and stopping to check his map when he hit New Bond Street. The narrow streets were booby-trapped with umbrellas and packed to the gutters with small European cars. Spence stepped on and off the pavement, in and out of the pall of exhaust fumes. The shops here sold jewelry and expensive suits.

On the corner of Piccadilly a newspaper seller was shouting in an unfamiliar accent. Spence headed on through the press of shoppers and out-of-season tourists. Motorcycle couriers threaded in and out of the vehicles. Cyclists dodged the motorcyclists.

Everything about London was smaller and more cramped than he had pictured it, like a composite travel poster in which all the city's main attractions had been compressed into one: Soho's sex emporiums spilled into the edges of theater land and Piccadilly, the interstices filled with shops selling records, souvenirs, and leatherware. Eros was dwarfed by its plinth, which was dwarfed in turn by the extinguished circuitry of neon signs. In Trafalgar Square he expected to find Buckingham Palace rubbing shoulders with the National Gallery and Big Ben.

Behind Charing Cross Station he finally emerged into open space. Spence passed under the trees and across the wide boulevard of the Victoria Embankment. Beyond the river wall a small launch was struggling against the slow bulk of the Thames. Spence checked his map again and headed left toward Waterloo Bridge. Five minutes farther on he found himself opposite a tall octagonal building in white concrete. The bright gray sky reflected off the windows, giving them the appearance of highly polished steel. The main doorway was two stories high. Just inside it hung five gold letters: NORCO.

Spence recrossed the road. Through the huge glass frontage of the Norco building he could see a central reception desk, two broad flights of stairs, and a uniformed security guard. Spence stepped forward, and the door opened automatically in front of him.

Music was playing in the carpeted foyer. A glass case between the two staircases held a twelve-foot-high gilded model of a jack-up rig. Ten yards to the left of reception was a row of lifts with stainless-steel doors. Spence headed for one of them, and the security guard moved to intercept him.

"Could I see your pass, please, sir?"

"Sorry. I'm just visiting."

"Visitor's passes from reception, sir."

The receptionist was a glamorous, highly varnished girl

with hair that seemed to be spun from glass fiber. Spence had met her in oil-company headquarters in Calgary and Edmonton, Dallas and Houston. She spoke with the same mid-Atlantic accent and regarded his thick jacket and woollen shirt with the same veiled mistrust. It was a measure of the feudalism of the oil industry that in head offices you rarely saw a man without a tie, while in the field you'd rarely met a man who even possessed one. These young executives now entering the lift would roll up their sleeves and undo a top button to show that bean counting had not turned them soft, but the tie remained an obligatory insignia of rank.

Spence said, "I've come to see Mr. Hunter. Charles Hunter."

She consulted her VDU. "Is he expecting you?"

"No, but he knows me. The name's Spence."

"One moment, please."

She swiveled on her chair and picked up an internal phone. Spence looked around him. The guard had lost interest in him and was pacing out the distance between the lifts and the stairs, his hands behind his back and his head lowered, as if in thought. The receptionist was talking on the phone to Hunter's secretary. She had lowered her voice and now shot him a doubtful look. Spence knew from that glance that Hunter was going to be unavailable once more.

To his left a bell rang, the lift doors opened, and a bald man in a brown suit stepped in. The receptionist had turned away from him again, the guard was inspecting his blunt fingers. Spence made for the lift—ten paces, levering himself forward on his stick. The door began to close, the receptionist shouted, "Hey," the guard looked up too late. Spence hopped—eight, nine, ten—and landed in the lift, as the steel doors locked shut behind him with a contented sigh.

The bald man looked up from the control panel.

"I hate waiting for these things," Spence told him.

"Which floor do you want?"

"I'm going to see Charles Hunter."

"You want number six."

The lift pulled upward. Spence watched the numbers. If they didn't stop at any intervening floors, he'd have about a minute to find his man.

The numbers rolled past, one to six.

"Second on the left," said the bald man helpfully. Spence thanked him and was off bounding down the carpeted corridor. As he passed the top of the stairs, he could hear heavy footsteps and voices. The second door on the left was marked, CHARLES HUNTER—CHIEF EXECUTIVE, LONDON.

Above the secretary's desk was an African ritual mask carved from dark wood. The expression on her face as Spence burst in was almost identical—the eyes wide circles and the mouth a perfect O.

"My name's Spence. I'd like to talk to Charles Hunter."

"Mr. Spence, I've been on the phone to reception and . . ."

"Where is he . . . this way?"

She stood up. Her chair rolled back on its castors and into the file cabinets behind her.

"I'm afraid it's just not possible."

"Just five minutes is all I need."

He had his hand on the handle of the communicating door, when a security man came down the corridor at a run. Spence tried the handle and found it locked—operated by an electrical release behind the receptionist's desk. She smiled sweetly.

"Open the door."

The security guard took a step toward him, and Spence stopped him with a look.

"Open the door," Spence said to the receptionist.

The security guard was a reasonable man. "Come along, sir, we don't want any trouble."

"I don't want trouble myself."

"I've told you," the receptionist repeated. "Mr. Hunter is not available."

As she spoke, the communicating door opened from the inside. Charles Hunter stood in the doorway, illuminated from behind by the metallic daylight that filled his office. "What's going on here?"

Spence had expected an older man, but all the same there was something about Hunter's face that seemed vaguely familiar. For a man in his midforties he retained his boyish good looks. The groomed blond hair was accentuated by his ski tan. When he spoke, there was silence.

"This is Mr.—"

"Spence?"

"Yes."

Hunter looked Spence up and down, then addressed the security guard. "Five minutes," he said.

The windows of his office ran ceiling to floor, taking in the Thames and the monolithic architecture of the South Bank. On the opposite wall was a massive map of the world, colored to oil concessions and ongoing exploration programs. Like the colonial powers of the past, the oil majors had divided up the globe. Saudi was blue for Aramco. Gabon was yellow for Shell. Angola was red for Elf.

"Coffee?"

"No."

Hunter crossed to the coffee machine and poured himself a cup. "Have a seat, Mr. Spence. Now perhaps you'll tell me what all this is about."

"Perhaps you'll tell me why you've been avoiding me."

Hunter checked his Rolex as he poured. The gesture was for Spence's benefit. "I believe you're interested in Madagascar," he said.

"You haven't answered my question."

"If you mean those faxes you're supposed to have sent, then we've got no record of them. I can only assume that your machine wasn't working."

"You got the phone calls?"

"Yes, we got your phone calls."

"And—"

"And I ignored them, I'm afraid. To be honest, Madagascar wasn't a very happy experience. We lost a lot of money there, not to mention a lot of good people, and the problem with disasters, as you know, is they tend to stay with you longer than your successes." He glanced down at Spence's injured leg. "I think that now I just want to bury the whole affair."

"Seems like you did that pretty well," Spence said.

Hunter sipped his coffee and placed the cup on the metal corner of his desk. "Come again?"

"Like you buried the fact there's oil in Mansalava," Spence said.

"Oil in Mansalava?" Hunter smiled ruefully and raised an eyebrow. "You're probably right. I just wish we'd found it."

"You did find it. You cored the well."

"What makes you think that?"

"A guy out there told me."

"Out where?"

"Morondava."

"Who was that?"

"Name of Hanssen."

Hunter searched his memory. "Hanssen, Hanssen? Ah, yes. Hanssen. He's a character, isn't he? Not the most reliable of people, though."

"Well, did you core the well?"

"We did, as a matter of fact. Not, of course, that I make a habit of coring dry wells, but—"

"It wasn't dry."

Hunter said, "I assure you that I wouldn't have come home unless it was."

"I read the drilling log."

"Then you'll know what I'm saying is true."

"I read the *real* drilling log," Spence said.

Hunter looked confused. "We're talking about the same place. Mansalava One."

"Yes."

"Mansalava One is a dry well. I know that for a fact. I was in Madagascar for two years operating the program there, and I visited Mansalava three days before we capped it."

"You visit all your exploration wells or just the producers?"

"Mr. Spence, you've got two more minutes of my time. I don't see how anything can be gained from our talking around in circles. Mansalava is dry as a bone. Our files on it are closed."

"So why did you have someone checking up on me when I went out there?"

"Checking up on you?"

"In Madagascar. Why did you send that driver of yours down to Morondava?"

Hunter frowned and brushed the blond hair off his forehead. With that gesture Spence suddenly remembered where he'd seen the man before: on the steps of the United Reform Church in Edmonton, three months ago, giving a press interview before the memorial service. "This is getting surreal."

The intercom started ringing. "You've got one thing right," Hunter said before picking it up. "I did check up on you. But I did it long after you were back from Madagascar, when we got the first phone call. Human Resources at Amoco told me about your injury. They also mentioned that you were an alcoholic and rather a difficult character. That's why I didn't want to see you." On that Hunter picked up the intercom. "I'll be right there, Caroline. Mr. Spence is leaving now."

"I'll leave when I'm good and ready."

Hunter replaced the handset. "I'm sorry," he said. "You're leaving right this minute."

As he spoke, the door opened, admitting the two guards who had been waiting in the outer office—the thick-set gray-haired man from the lobby and a younger, sharp-faced boy with a walkie-talkie on his belt. As they advanced, Spence stood up.

"Come on now, sir."

The receptionist stood rooted in the doorway, unable to drag herself away. Spence kept his eyes on Hunter. "I've come three thousand miles to speak to you, and I've been trying to get a handle on you for two weeks. I just wanted five minutes of your time."

"That's what you've had. Now I'll give you five seconds to stop this nonsense and get out of here. What do you think this is, a rodeo?"

The guards had separated, and the younger one was closing in, one from the side of the window and one between the potted palm and the desk. Spence slammed his stick on the desktop so hard that the phone receiver jumped off its rest. The younger guard took a step back.

"You can throw me out, Hunter, but you can't get rid of me. You know there's oil in that well, and you know what caused the plane crash."

Hunter spoke without raising his voice. "If you want my opinion, Mr. Spence, you need psychiatric help." He glanced over at his secretary. "Call the police."

"Yeah and tell them your boss is a fraud and a murderer, tell them that."

The young guard made a rush from the right. Spence caught him on the ribs with his stick, then lashed backward, snapping the top off the potted plant. The older man came around Hunter's desk, catching Spence under the arm and throwing him back against the wall. Suddenly everything was elbows and confusion. As Spence went down, a punch knocked the wind out of him, and his head smashed against the side of the desk. When his head cleared, he was on his knees with his head between the spinning castors of an office chair and one arm twisted painfully behind his back. Some papers had been thrown onto the floor, and blood from his nose was dripping on them, making a noise like a snare drum. He heard the older guard breathing heavily and apologizing to Hunter for the disruption.

"Come on, sir," he said sympathetically. "On your feet now."

Spence's head swam. Amid this hazy confusion a card caught his eye. He grabbed at it before he was hauled upright.

"Make sure he stays out of the building," said Hunter, "and Caroline, ask someone to come and clear up this mess."

"I'll be back," Spence mumbled through a bruised mouth.

"I'd strongly advise you against it," Hunter scowled, wiping coffee from the cover of a dossier. With that Spence was shoved through the secretary's office and out into the hallway. In both directions people were looking out from their office doorways, trying to make out the source of the disruption. Spence's nose was bleeding, but with a guard on either side, he couldn't reach up to stanch the flow. He let himself be marched to the lift, leaving a trail of red dots on the oatmeal-colored carpet.

Chapter 19

Every February, two or three weeks before her annual trip to France, Perpetude would spend a day going through her room at the hotel, putting aside everything that was worn out or redundant or had lost its significance. She had opened the windows to the veranda and the door to the central courtyard. A breeze blew through the room as she worked, catching the pages of the paperback novels she had discarded, magazines and newspaper articles she would never read, odd scraps of material she would never use.

In the conch shell on her dressing table she found a handful of Canadian coins that she had collected when the oilmen left. She put them in a tin for the church collection, along with a broken earring and some beads from a necklace. In among the beads she found a small gold lapel pin in the shape of an oil rig that Spence had given her when he left. She put it in the tin for the church, then, as an afterthought, took it out again and stuck it in the wooden frame of her dressing-table mirror.

"Anyone at home?"

Morgan Hanssen stuck his head around the door.

"You're back."

"Yoost got in," he said. "You haffing a spring clean?"

"There are some books there if you're interested."

"Books. What would I do with books? I brought you some

mail off the plane. Can I get a beer in the fridge?"

"Get two," she said.

Hanssen stumped off to the kitchen as Perpetude leafed through the mail he'd brought her. There were three or four invoices, a letter from her cousins in Brittany, which had, according to the postmark, been posted five weeks previously, and a small white envelope from the capital with a government seal on the back.

Antananarivo 25 Feb.

My dear Perpetude,

How goes it with you? Apropos of the election campaign in Morondava, I found myself talking yesterday with one of our delegates to the Assemblée Nationale, an Englishman called Mitchell. Your name came up, and it made me think how much I enjoyed seeing you again. Do please call on me if you are ever up here in the capital. The above is the direct line to my office. My life has become rather frenzied recently, as you can imagine, and I value the support of my oldest friends.

As ever,
Claude

She had last seen Istasse the previous year, when he came down as part of a government delegation to visit the rig. He'd insisted then on taking an hour off from his official program to walk along the beach with her and talk about old times. She'd been flattered by his attentiveness, but there remained a part of Istasse she mistrusted. He was a consummate politician and the join between genuine friendship and expedience had become so seamless as to be invisible—even to Istasse himself. "The support of my oldest friends"?—was that an attempt to recruit her to his political campaign? If so, he was out of luck. Even if she supported his party, she would be out of the country now until just after the elections. All the same, she would be passing through the capital on her way to France, and it would be interesting to talk to him again. She put the letter with its envelope in the pocket of her skirt as Hanssen returned with the beers.

"You want to sit here or on the veranda?"

"It's cooler here."

Hanssen opened the beers with the heel of his pocketknife and lowered himself into one of the raffia chairs.

"Ah. It's good to be back."

"I thought you liked those visits to the capital."

"Ach. It's mad up there. Can't go anywhere now without some fellow drifting past with a loudspeaker. Can't even go dancing without they want to make some political announcement." Hanssen drank from the bottle. "Your garden's growing well."

Since the beginning of the rains the greenery in and around Morondava had been burgeoning. The grass along the road to Mohabo was already chest high, and the vines in the hotel's central courtyard were growing at a rate of six inches a day. Perpetude stood up and pulled at some of the tendrils that were growing up through the floorboards.

"Did you get your visa renewed?"

Hanssen shook his head. "That's what else was wrong with up there. They give me another three-month yoost."

"Then what?"

"Then I got to go back with my cap in my hand again. Maybe Father Mitchell was right. Maybe there's not enough jobs to go around here."

She said, "I hear the mission is finding it difficult to get a replacement for him."

"Fuck. You think I should apply?"

She laughed. "I don't think they're that desperate."

"I don't think I am either. You get any Valentine cards?"

"No."

"What about that good-looking Canadian fellow? He ever write to you?"

"Spence? He was not the kind of man who writes letters."

"Wonder where he is now," Hanssen said.

"I wonder."

Spence lay in the bath, operating the brass taps with the toes of his right foot. Through the open door of the bathroom he could see evening light playing on the sheets of his bed. Steam rose off the surface of the water in thin ringlets and trailed up to the patterned ceiling. He could hear, faintly, the muted toot and rumble of London traffic inching home from work. The phone in his room had been ringing for almost a minute. Spence rubbed the soap out of his eyes and eased his stiff joints and muscles out of the bath. He collected the phone from his bedside, carried it through to the bathroom, lowered himself back into the bath, and picked up the receiver.

"Mr. Spence?"

"Yes."

"Long-distance call for you."

"Uh huh."

There was a pause, a crackle, then Dennis's voice. "Spence, where the hell have you been? I've tried to call you all day and all night. It's ten in the morning here, and I've been tearing my hair out for the past twenty-four hours."

"I was in jail," said Spence. "They charged me with disturbing the peace and put me in the cells for the night. I didn't get any sleep either. It was colder than a bitch and they kept the lights on all night. I saw the judge this morning, and he fined me a hundred and twenty pounds English. I've been asleep all afternoon with the phone off the hook. I still don't feel too great."

"My heart bleeds for you."

"I'm telling you where I've been."

"I've heard the story, you asshole. I had Norco on the phone yesterday afternoon. You realize how much work we do for these people, Spence? You want to know how much your drunken expedition is going to cost us?"

"I wasn't drunk."

"Tell it to the marines. You wreck a guy's office, you beat up on two security guards . . . "

"They're exaggerating."

"Spence, I got this from the horse's mouth. He was on the phone for twenty minutes, chewing my head off and spitting in the hole."

"To hell with the guy and everyone who looks like him."

"To hell with you, Spence. We're pitching for a three-year contract with Norco in Bangladesh. If Hunter pulls the plug on that, I'm finished, finito."

"Tell him I'm nothing to do with your outfit."

"Oh, yes, and you expect him to believe that when you've been stampeding around his office, yelling about Madagascar? I told you to leave it alone, Spence, why couldn't you leave it alone?"

"I'm sorry, Dennis, but really it's nothing to do with you."

"Fucking right, it's to do with me. You think I've got five-million dollar contracts to give away? You think I don't need a job—"

"Dennis."

"You think that, Spence? I'm a twenty-year . . . "

"Dennis," said Spence. He was trying to interrupt, but, with the slight time delay in the satellite link, he kept mistiming the pauses in Dennis's tirade.

" . . . man, hey? I've been in this business twenty years. You think I need this bullshit? Spence, a guy tries to do you a favor and you just piss on him. Go buy yourself another bottle of Scotch."

"I told you I've not been—"

"And I hope you choke on it."

"I'll phone you when I get home." Spence said.

"Don't bother."

The line went dead. Spence dropped the receiver and sank lower into the water. After a while he got up and inspected his bruised face in the bathroom mirror. He wrapped one of the hotel's towels around himself and went through to the bedroom. The sky above the Burmese embassy was a livid orange. Spence sat on the edge of his bed and picked up the crumpled, bloodstained business card he had somehow retrieved from the floor of Hunter's office. It read:

> Norco Oil International
> Charles R. Hunter
> Chief Executive, London
> 227 Hampstead Avenue, London, W2

At his home there would be no security guards: he'd have to talk. On the other hand, there was Dennis to think about.

Spence studied his fingertips. Even after half an hour in the bath the fingerprinting ink they'd used on him was still deeply ingrained.

If he was wrong about Hunter, Dennis would never be able to forgive him. If he was right, he'd never be able to forgive himself. The hell with it, he was too far in to stop now.

Spence stood up and began to get dressed.

The area that bordered on the north edge of Hampstead Heath reminded Spence of Westridge in Edmonton—mature gardens and three-car garages. In the floodlit driveways instead of Lincolns and Cadillacs there were Rolls-Royces and Mercedes convertibles. Outside No. 227 there was a new Peugeot and a black Jaguar with the license plate CH1. A muted light shone from the conservatory and from between the glossy white pillars of the front porch.

Spence pulled the bellpull and waited, positioning himself

to get a foot in the gap. There was a pause, then footsteps approached. It was Hunter's daughter who opened the door—a sporty-looking girl of thirteen or fourteen in jeans and a football shirt.

"Charles Hunter live here?"

"Yes."

"Can I have a word with him?"

"Is he expecting you? He's having dinner."

"Sure. I work with him."

The girl looked doubtfully at the bruises on Spence's lip and on his cheek. Spence had worn a jacket and tie, but his appearance obviously failed to inspire confidence. The girl began to close the door.

"You mind if I wait in the hallway?"

"Um . . . yes, all right." She let him in, and Spence closed the stained-glass door behind him. It was cold in the hallway. Spence had noticed in Aberdeen that for some crazy reason British people kept switching their central heating on and off all winter, as though folks had never heard of thermostats. He could hear classical music playing.

At the end of the T-shaped hallway there was a mirror with a scrolled gilt frame. There were oil paintings on the walls—ordered English landscapes. As the door in the left-hand arm of the hallway opened, he heard voices from the dining room and cutlery being put down, then Hunter emerged carrying a napkin.

Spence said, "We didn't finish our talk."

"Get out of here."

Since the fight and the conversation with Dennis, Spence felt strangely liberated. He no longer had anything to lose—not even his pride. "Like I said, we've still got some talking to do."

"I think I've said everything that I want to say to you, Mr. Spence."

"Yeah!" Spence raised his voice. "Well, I ain't said the half of what I want to say to you!" The crystal droplets of the chandelier above him struck up a descant harmony. In the dining room conversation stopped as though a switch had been thrown. A woman appeared behind Hunter's shoulder. She had a square, aristocratic face and straight dark hair turning gray.

"This is the madman I told you about." Hunter said. "The fellow who came into the office."

She looked at Spence, and a shadow crossed her face. He was unused to inspiring such fear. "I'll call the police," she said.

"I just want to talk to your husband," Spence said. "If he's got nothing to hide, I don't see what the problem is."

Hunter's wife went back into the dining room. "The problem is, I'm not going to be blackmailed," Hunter said.

"Seems I tried every other way to get to speak to you."

The phone extension beside Spence chirruped as Hunter's wife dialed a number in the next room. Spence picked up the hall extension, canceled the line, and left the handset off the hook. Hunter's daughter had come out to stand beside her father. She was watching Spence in wide-eyed amazement. Spence could see Hunter wavering between the indignity of a brawl and the humiliation of surrender. He looked like a strong, fit man, but he was probably unaccustomed to fighting.

"Go next door with your mother, Claire."

"What does he want, Dad?"

"Just do what I say, will you?"

Spence answered the girl's question himself. "I want to know why thirteen of my friends got killed in a plane crash. That's first off. And I want to know why your father's too damned scared to talk to me about it."

"Go out the back way," Hunter told his daughter. "Ask the Marsdens if you can call the police from there. Tell them we've got an intruder."

The girl slipped back into the dining room. Spence said, "You're just storing up trouble for yourself, Mr. Hunter. If they lock me up again, I'll be back again. The more you refuse to talk with me, the more sure I am you've got something to hide."

"Mr. Spence, as I think I already explained to you . . . "

"You ain't explained anything," Spence interrupted. "What have you explained? You ain't explained why their government's so keen to buy that rig. You ain't explained why Mansalava One was such a big secret. The whole reason I'm here is because of all the stuff you ain't explained, Hunter. Now, either we can wait till the police arrive and then have a fight in your hallway or else you can sit me down and give me some straight answers for ten minutes. What do you say?"

In the dining room to his right the record finished and switched itself off. Hunter threw his napkin on the floor. His eyes didn't leave Spence's. He looked like a man who could kill.

"The study's through to your left," he said.

Spence had expected armchairs and leather-bound books, but Hunter's study was equipped for work. There was a word processor and two computerized phones on the desk: behind that a laser printer and another computer screen. A fax machine sat in the scalloped alcove by the window, and there was a large, heavy safe built into one wall. Below the heavy cornicing the walls were white and lined with chart cupboards, filing cabinets, and ranks of ring-bound files. There were some fancy longitudinal blinds screening the window and architectural lighting on the wall charts and bookshelves.

Hunter shut the door behind them.

"I didn't want to have to do it this way," Spence said.

"It's a bit late to apologize."

"I'm not apologizing."

Hunter pushed his hair off his forehead and sat on the edge of his desk. "All right, let's go back to the beginning again."

Spence took a seat below a pastel portrait of Hunter's wife. He took the phone off the hook and positioned himself where he could keep an eye on Hunter, the window, and the door. "I was in Madagascar four weeks ago. I was sent out to itemize the rig."

"I know that."

"While I was in the capital, I ran into a fellow by the name of Velo-André."

"I know Velo-André," said Hunter.

"I bet. He's supposed to be your partner. Seemed to me like you raped him."

Hunter took out a pack from his pocket and lit a small cigar. "And what gave you that impression?"

"I go down to Morondava and I find the rig accommodation has been broken into. Someone has been paid off to clear out all the documents. Then, back in town, we find what he was trying to hide—a buckshee drilling log report. And what do you know, the dry well that the government of the country can't give away, that finally persuaded Exxon and Agip to throw in the towel . . . it isn't a dry well at all."

Hunter looked nonplussed. "You said a logging report. I don't suppose you've got a copy of it."

"I've got a part of it."

"May I see a part of it?" Hunter said with elaborate patience.

Spence took his wallet out of his inside pocket and tossed Hunter the pages of the log. Hunter unfolded them, laughed dryly to himself as though something had been explained, ran a hand over his eyes, then refolded them, and said, "Didn't it strike you as odd that we'd have left a document report like this kicking around the rig?"

"You didn't. Ben Lowers had it. He was trying to send it home to himself."

"You think he wanted to sell it?"

"Ben Lowers was a friend of mine," Spence said. "I don't think he'd do anything illegal without good reason."

"I'm sure he wouldn't," Hunter said. "So why do you think he was sending it home?"

"Because he thought there was a cover-up."

"Or because he knew it was worthless, and it would take

too long to explain the whole thing to customs."

"Explain what?"

"I gave him the log," Hunter said.

"You gave it to him?"

"As a present. A birthday present. It was his birthday then. What date was it? Well, if you're so pally with him, you should know. They had a party for him." Hunter stood up and walked around the desk. "You see, Ben Lowers was a friend of mine too. We had some good evenings together. A few times in the capital, one down at Father Mitchell's place in Morondava. He told Alan Skipton that the best birthday present he could get would be an oil find. So that's what we gave him, organized one for him."

"You knew Al Skipton, huh?"

Hunter drew on his cigar. "Of course. We worked together for two years. I liked him a lot."

"Bullshit. I read his letters," Spence said. "He wrote a lot of letters home. You were stopping all the company mail by then, but he got some through by the local post. He said the whole operation was screwy. He told his wife there was oil there."

"I don't suppose you've got these letters."

"No. But she still does."

Hunter's cigar had gone out. He relit it. "Actually, come to think of it, I probably wrote a few letters saying the same thing myself. Right up till the end we were sure we were on a winner. Why do you think we tightened up security and laid off the number-two crew?"

"Because you had a strike."

"Because we thought we were going to. We had an early gas kick; we were drilling through a perfect formation: it was the last well in the program out there, but suddenly it seemed as close as you can get in this business to a sure thing. Then what? We drill the last five hundred feet and—nothing. Right down to the basement, and it's dry all the way."

"The log said—"

"You're not listening to me, Mr. Spence, the log was a fake. We gave it to Ben Lowers for his birthday. The logging engineers were a pair of comedians. George and René from ExLog—you probably knew them too."

"No."

"They were on that plane as well unfortunately. They were as certain as anyone we were going to find something at Mansalava, so as a joke we made up an impossibly favorable report and had it printed out."

"You're shitting me," said Spence.

"I'm sorry, but I'm absolutely not 'shitting' you, Mr. Spence. It takes about three hours to draw a bogus log report. You can do it in the field on standard equipment. You just program the computer with what you want to find, then you run it backward. If you'd investigated this business in any detail, you'd know that yourself, but I don't suppose you had the patience, did you? You look to me like a man who prefers action to words. Preferably the kind of action that involves threatening people with a stick."

"So how come you never told me this before?"

"You never said anything about a log before. I didn't know what you were on about. You burst into my office, shouting and throwing your weight around. You never mentioned a drilling log. I'd completely forgotten about it."

There was a knock on the door, and Hunter called, "Yes, what is it?"

The door opened, and a fat man wearing carpet slippers and a dark blue cardigan came in. He carried a shotgun, broken, under his arm. "You all right, Charles?"

"For God's sake, Peter." Hunter introduced the stranger. "Peter Marsden, my neighbor, this is Mr. Spence."

Spence didn't feel in a mood for introductions. The fat man eyed him warily, then turned back to Hunter. "Nicola's in a hell of a state—I got the idea you were being . . . well, I don't know what I thought. You're all right, Charles?"

"I'm fine. Just about." Hunter looked at the gun. "Have you got a license for that thing?"

"Of course."

"Is it loaded?"

"Yes."

"Well, for God's sake, get rid of it, or we'll all get arrested. Has Nicola phoned the police?"

"They'll be here any minute. You sure you're all right?"

"I'm fine, Peter." Hunter ushered the other man to the door. "Tell them I'll be through in a minute. We're just getting all this sorted out." He closed the door and looked back at Spence. "Aren't we?"

Spence said, "You took cores. You don't core a dry well."

"You do if you're dealing with a man like Velo-André, who insists on having everything demonstrated to him. I don't suppose he mentioned that he insisted on seeing rock samples from every well we drilled."

Hunter knocked the ash from his cigar into a black glass ashtray. Spence could feel his self-confidence beginning to fracture. He scanned his memory for landmarks. He pictured Skippy's face, the crash site, Perpetude. "You're bullshitting," he said. "There's an oil field out there, and you killed these guys."

"I killed them?"

"The plane blew up. I can prove it."

"If you can, I'd be more than grateful. Our consultant, Waters, was on at the Malagasy Air Force for months to tighten up that accident report. I dare say it's partly what drove him to suicide. They never did find the door from the luggage compartment. I wouldn't be a bit surprised if the plane was carrying something it shouldn't have. Between you and me, I wouldn't be a bit surprised if they were carrying some dangerous cargo."

"So why didn't you push it?"

"Because I had no evidence." Hunter put out his cigar and

brushed the hair off his face. "Why? Do you? Or have you come all this way to torment me with some scrap of a bogus log report and a lot of misplaced aggression?"

"I don't believe you, Hunter."

Hunter opened his arms. "Well, what more can I say? Tell me what proof you need. What do you want me to show you? Do you want to see the real logging report for Mansalava One? Is that what you want to see?"

Without waiting for Spence's reply, Hunter walked to his computer terminal, punched in some codes, and waited.

"You want to look at this or not?" he asked.

Spence got up and walked around to the other side of Hunter's desk. On screen the central Norco computer was processing Hunter's personal access code. The screen changed, and the computer offered him some menus. Hunter's fingers flitted over the keys.

"That's Mansalava One," he announced, calling it up on screen. "That's the real log, straight from central records. You push that button to scroll."

Spence scrolled through the drilling log. Each page was numbered and labeled with a red "classified" flag. The first five pages were a replica of the log he'd read that night in Morondava. It showed mixed shales and sands. On page eight, above the limestone, there was the tiny hydrocarbon deposit Spence had pointed out to Perpetude.

"Otherwise dry as a bone," said Hunter.

From outside Spence could hear a siren approaching. He scrolled on through the log. On pages eleven through fourteen, where he'd once seen oil, there were repeated beds of shale and siltstone to the basement. The drill rate was fifty feet an hour. The resistivity was next to zero.

"That's the real log," Hunter said.

Spence stared at the screen. There was something else he'd meant to ask Hunter, but now his mind had gone blank. "Sorry, I just kinda had the impression—"

"You got a lot of impressions, by the sound of it, Spence, and they were all wrong. Excuse me."

Hunter left the room, and Spence stood listening to the sound of his own breathing. In ten minutes Hunter had demolished his entire theory. Had it really been so feeble? He remembered his father's last months, a frail old man dying of alcoholism in the unnaturally clean sheets of the Edith Wardell Nursing Home. The paranoid delusions, the daily humiliation of madness. Outside, he could hear Hunter talking to the police. The door opened, and Hunter came in with a constable in tow.

"As I was saying," Hunter said, "just a bit of a misunderstanding. My colleague here was just about to leave now anyway."

The policeman looked at Spence, then back at Hunter. There was a tired expression in his eyes. "Okay, if that's fine with both of you."

"Really, it's all more or less sorted out." Hunter looked to Spence for confirmation. "Isn't it?"

Spence sat on the edge of the desk. Hunter was offering him a truce. Spence nodded. Hunter escorted the policeman to the door. In the hall he said some words to his wife and daughter. In the silence Spence could hear the policeman outside making his report on the car radio. Hunter came back into the study.

"Thanks," Spence said. "I guess maybe I jumped to conclusions. I was certain I was right, or I wouldn't have taken things this far. I guess there's no way I can apologize for what's happened. Just as long as you know I'm nothing to do with McCabe Drilling. Dennis McCabe phoned me this afternoon and made that pretty clear. Anything I did, I did on my own."

"You'll get a taxi at the bottom of the road," said Hunter. "You know where the door is."

From the end of the hallway Hunter's wife and daughter watched Spence leave the study. It seemed to take all his strength to lever himself across the hallway and out the front door.

★   ★   ★

Hunter stood in his office till Spence was safely through the front gate. Then he lit another cigar.

Hunter knew oilmen. He knew their tenacity. He knew the black sullenness that would descend on a drilling crew on those rare occasions when the bit got stuck irretrievably in the hole, when several thousand feet of pipe sheared off and the well had to be abandoned. He knew their obsession with seeing the job through, getting to the final depth, arriving at the basement. To drillers like Spence—real drillers, born drillers—an abandoned well was like a miscarriage that could never quite be exorcised. He'd known drilling superintendents travel back at the end of an exploration program to the one rig site they'd had to abandon. He'd seen them kick the marker pole and swear at the earth, knowing it was unlikely they'd have found oil even if the well had progressed, but grudging even that. That outside chance.

And the same gambler's obsession would stay with Spence, undulled by alcohol. He'd go home and try to forget about it, but he would never really let go, and if anything happened to reinforce his belief, he would have to come looking.

"Charles."

His wife Nicola was at the study door.

"Are you all right?"

"I'm fine," he said. "Just calming down."

"Who was he?"

"He was no one," Hunter said. "I'll be through in a minute."

His wife closed the door.

Hunter picked up the phone and dialed a number in Edinburgh.

Chapter 20

Only fifty passengers disembarked from the Canadair flight at Edmonton. The rest were flying on to Vancouver. Kirk walked through baggage reclaim, signed for his car, zipped up his padded jacket, and walked out into the frozen afternoon.

Highway 2 from the airport was an eight-lane motorway coiling through the snowbound prairies under an endless expanse of sky. The fields were deserted. In the distance he could see low wooden farm buildings stapled to the horizon. Kirk set the cruise control to 100 kilometers per hour, keeping pace with the goods train to his left. He passed the grain elevators, the billboards, and the prefab warehouses: PJ'S PET CENTER, FOOD FOR LESS, TOYS "R" US. He moved into the center lane, following the big green overhead signs to the city center, and switched on the car radio.

"You're listening to John Mack on KT Nine-nine-oh drive-time radio. It's a quarter after four with a low of minus ten . . ."

Edmonton appeared in the distance, its mirrored tower-blocks catching the low evening sun. Cars were passing on both sides now: Chryslers and Cadillacs, Fords, GMCs, and Oldsmobiles. Beyond them, to the right and left, roadside signs flashed and rotated: FAMILY TIRE, MOHAWK PETROLEUM, SOUTHGATE MOTOR INN. Kirk found himself pressing on the accelerator again, drawn forward by the hoardings, the lights, the flood of traffic. The road was crossing and recrossing the railway line now, pushing on under telephone lines and overhead traffic lights. The shining tower-blocks beckoned in the distance, and the solid phalanx of traffic swept him toward it. Rock music filled the car, and Kirk beat time to it with the flat of his hand against the steering wheel. He was traveling. He was on another contract. He was happy.

Long ago, when he had just turned twenty and his wife of two years was divorcing him on the grounds of domestic violence, he'd gone for three appointments at Ninewells Hospital with a psychiatrist called Jane Stacey.

"*Psychopath* is not a word I like to use," she said. "It's not a psychiatric diagnosis at all, really. It's just a label given by society according to its values. If Napoleon were doing your job in the print works, he'd probably be inappropriately violent, and they'd probably call him a psychopath. If you find it difficult to control these aggressive impulses, maybe you should find a legitimate outlet for them. Maybe you should join the army."

He'd taken her advice three months later and never regretted it.

The highway narrowed and the traffic grew denser. It crossed the railway lines for the last time and dipped down and right into the river valley of the North Saskatchewan River. A sign on the right said TEAMSMANS SPORTS CENTER. The road narrowed again to two lanes and rattled over the Walter Dale Bridge, then up through the trees of River Valley Park, with the low red sun catching his wing mirrors and illuminating the tall buildings above him, and the radio at full volume saying, "Join the Eskimos this Sunday afternoon as they take on the Hamilton Tigercats," and the overhead traffic lights all still on green. He hit 105th Street and almost immediately saw the sign saying RAMADA RENAISSANCE HOTEL CUSTOMER PARKING. Kirk pulled right across two lanes, up the ramp and straight into a parking space.

From his picture window on the fifteenth floor he watched the mirrored tower-blocks opposite turning blue-green and gold in the cold evening light. He showered and put on a bathrobe, then switched the TV on to the adult film channel, turned the sound down, phoned room service for a club sandwich and a beer, and stretched out on the bed with his maps and documents.

From the route-planner Spence's place, Fort Saskatchewan, was just half an hour out of town. He'd leave that till his return from the break-in job. Paddle Prairie was three hundred miles north of Edmonton. He could get there in a day.

The phone rang while Cora was up to her elbows peeling vegetables. She crossed the kitchen, trying to keep drips of muddy water from running off her gloves and onto the newly polished floor. She juggled the phone off the wall, tried to hold it against her ear with one wrist, dropped it, and caught it again.

"Cora? I caught you in the middle of something."

"Heck, no, it's good to hear you. Let me turn the radio down." She reached it with one hand. "You at work, Myra?"

"I'm sitting here in the office, but no one wants to see me this morning."

"If you want a job to do, you should come up here."

"We might just do that. Dennis could use the therapy. He's like a bear with a sore head these days."

"What's the problem?"

"Oh, different stuff. You heard about this nonsense with Spence?"

"No. What? Is he back?"

"Oh, sure, he's been back a week. It seems while he was over in England, he went rampaging around London insulting people."

"Did you say assaulting or insulting?"

"Bit of both, insulting them, then assaulting them."

"Who?"

"I don't know. Half their royal family, from the way Dennis is taking it."

"So how's Spence now?"

"No idea. Dennis says he's never going to speak to him again."

"Dennis said that?"

"That's what he said."

Cora whistled. For all his gruff demeanor, she knew Dennis had an essentially forgiving nature.

"I'll give Spence a ring."

"Can you do that? And tell him from me to find himself a good woman instead of trying to destroy himself."

"I thought he already had."

"Destroyed himself?"

"Found himself a woman."

"Well, it's time she got herself over here."

After she rang off, Cora dialed Spence. His number was written in felt tip on a board above the phone. When she dialed it, she got a continuous tone. Either he'd left it off the hook or his phone was still cut off.

She was about to call the operator when a car she didn't recognize pulled into the yard. The man who got out was short and wiry with blond curly hair down to his shoulders. He wore jeans, sneakers, and a leather-trimmed logger's jacket. As she watched, he looked around, then walked off into the big barn.

Cora went out onto the deck and called down to him.

"Hello!"

He came out again, looking pleased to see her, and climbed the wooden steps toward her.

"Careful you don't break your neck," she called. "I was going to put salt on them."

He picked his way carefully up to the doorstep, stepping on the patches where the snow had thawed.

"I got lost, I wonder if I could use your phone."

"Sure thing." She turned, and he followed her indoors. "You want to see a map?"

"No, I've got one in the car. I just have to call some people to say I'm on my way."

"Sure. That's a Scottish accent, isn't it?"

"Edinburgh."

"My grandfather was from Dumfries."

"Is that a fact?" He was knocking the snow off his sneakers. "You keep pigs in those barns or what?"

"Hogs," she said. "We call them hogs."

"They take much looking after?"

"I'll say."

"You got anyone to help you with it?"

"Why, you looking for a job?"

"Oh, no." He laughed pleasantly. "I've got a job. Just thought it seemed like a big place for you."

"I got a couple of local hands during the week," Cora said. "And my two boys help out after school. There's a phone on the wall there."

"Is there one anywhere else I can use?" the stranger asked. "It's slightly private."

"Sure. There's one in the study. Straight down the corridor and turn right."

When he'd gone, she returned to the sink. She heard him go down the corridor and open the lounge door.

"On the right," she called to him.

"Sorry. My mistake."

He came back out of the lounge. Cora reached across to turn up the radio. Whenever Skippy was around, they used to have the radio tuned to the country-music channel, but since he'd died, she preferred not to listen to it. Most of those songs were so brimful of emotion that it only took the plangent whine of a slide guitar to make her cry. Most other things she could cope with.

The knife she was using was blunt, so she chose a sharper

one from the drawer. It was a funny thing, emotion, the way it crept up behind you when you were least expecting it.

"That's that, then."

She turned with a start. With his sneakers on, she hadn't heard the stranger returning.

"That was quick."

"They're not at home. I'll try again farther down the road. Can I use your loo?"

"My what?"

"The what do you call it. The washroom."

"Oh, yes. It's upstairs, left on the landing."

He thanked her and left again, closing the door behind him.

Cora was used to helping lost travelers, but it was almost always mostly folks traveling north who had turned off the McKenzie Highway too early, looking for a shortcut through to Rainbow Lake. If, as he said, the stranger was traveling south, she wondered how he could have got lost. The nearest intersection was fifty miles north at High Level. There were no other major turnoffs in that direction, so it would have been pretty difficult to go wrong. She heard a board creak above her head. Obviously had no sense of direction—he'd somehow taken a wrong turning into Patrick's bedroom.

A couple of minutes later he came downstairs again.

"You found it?"

"In the end." He had a nice smile. "Something smells good."

"I made some cookies earlier—you want one?"

"Thanks." He helped himself.

"Take a couple. You got far to go."

"Athabasca. Wherever that is."

"Lord's sakes. Where have you driven from today?"

"Up north," he said vaguely. "Do you get away much yourself?"

"Sometimes," she said. "Our farmhands go back to the

reservation most weekends, so most of the time I stay up here."

"You ever feel trapped?"

"Oh, no. Most Sunday afternoons we go visiting down at Twin Lakes or La Crete. Saturdays we often have people coming to visit."

"Looks as though you're expecting some people now."

She looked at the pile of vegetables in the sink. "Oh, no, I'll put most of this in the freezer."

"Well." The stranger slapped his chest with both hands. "I'd better be getting on down the road. Thanks for everything. Be seeing you."

"Probably not."

He laughed. "You're right, probably not."

Kirk drove out of the Skipton property and turned south toward Peace River. It was a two hours' drive to the rooming house he had found, but it was far enough away from the Skiptons' house for no one to remember him till he was safely out of the country. For now he'd achieved most of what he'd set out to do. He'd got a vague idea of the layout of the house and established that Sunday afternoon would be the best time to find the property unoccupied. There was no burglar-alarm system, and there was an easy access through an unsecured window he'd found on the first floor. The room she used as a study had been set up for dealing with all the commercial business of the farm. He'd decided that the personal letters he'd been asked to retrieve were much more likely to be kept either in her bedroom at the back of the house or in the shelves and rolltop desk in the living room. He'd return on Sunday afternoon through the woods. One of these little side roads would surely offer a secluded place to park. It wouldn't take more than an hour to get into the house, find what he was looking for, and be off again. Meanwhile all he had to do was wait.

★   ★   ★

In Fort Saskatchewan Spence had run the pickup into a ditch on the third day he was home, cutting his forehead on the inside mirror and wrecking the vehicle's front suspension. Now it sat in the yard, jacked up on bricks, but he didn't have the energy to fix it.

For the week since he got home, he'd been drinking more or less continuously. The kitchen table was littered with cans, and the mail now formed a drift underneath the coatrack. On top of these, had he been sober, Spence might have noticed an airmail letter from East Africa. The stamps were colorful, badly aligned prints of agricultural machinery, and the address was written in Perpetude Peyrame's loose italics. It read:

> Morondava
> 26ème février

My dear Spence,

> This is the last letter I will write to you. The post here is unreliable, so I cannot know if you received the other two I sent. No problem. I wrote them for myself as much as for you.
>
> Much has changed here. Father Mitchell is now in the capital, and Morgan Hanssen is worried that he will soon be out of a job. I am going in two weeks to the capital and then to visit my family in France for one month.
>
> Also what happened about your grand theory concerning the rig? I'm sure there was a logical explanation. Conspiracies only really work in fiction. Real life is much too unpredictable, thank God.
>
> Write to me in case you get this.
>
> I send you my love. I hope you are quite healed.
> Perpetude

This letter had been lying on the floor since he got back from London. When Spence finally got around to reading it, melted snow had seeped through the envelope and smudged the ink, and he found it difficult to focus on the words. Perpetude, Africa, the beach at Morondava—it seemed like another world, another planet.

Since his return to Canada Spence's mood had lurched between stupor and self-loathing. From ten at night till four in the morning he was pleasantly fuddled by booze. From four till twelve he slept. In the early afternoon he treated his hangover with alcohol. In the evening he attempted to drink himself to death.

In his more lucid and, correspondingly, most desperate moments, he asked himself how he could ever have constructed such a ludicrous theory around Skippy's death and the drilling log. It seemed to him now that he had been clutching at something, anything, that would revive his withered sense of self-worth. He wanted the oil companies to be villains. He wanted to play the courageous victim; it was a bizarre psychological trick he'd devised to obscure his own failure.

Often he remembered, with piercing embarrassment, details of his father's decline into madness. What had Dr. Cartwright once called it? The trick of proving deception with deception? Spence couldn't remember the word, but he remembered the device. He remembered the old man with urine-stained trousers and the pathetic, childish transparency of his lies.

He lay on the couch, staring blankly at the TV screen. The television announcer said good night. She said that today had been Saturday. Tomorrow was Sunday.

Chapter 21

That morning Kirk had found a spot about three hundred yards away from Cora Skipton's house among the pine trees that surrounded the farm. He'd driven there at eight A.M. and parked off the main highway, where the car would be out of sight, then picked a route through the trees that brought him out opposite the house. It had been a strenuous walk: in places the snow had drifted, thigh-deep, under the trees, and elsewhere a delicate film of ice concealed deep, boggy trenches. One leg was now cold and damp below the knee, but generally he was comfortable enough. He could get a good view from here of the trailers to the south of the farmhouse, where the Indian farmhands stayed during the week. There had been no activity around these all morning, and the deep tracks in front of the caravans showed where a pickup truck was customarily parked.

She'd mentioned two sons, and now he'd seen them both: one about thirteen, the other eight, walking from the house to the large stainless-steel barns that housed the pigs, then transporting hay for the horses out on the far field. Just before eleven o'clock the boys had finished their chores and gone inside again.

Kirk heard a noise behind him and turned, startled, but it was just another load of snow sliding off the fir trees. A family of deer appeared, tentatively, on the far side of the big field—

a female and two young. If Kirk had a rifle, he'd have a perfect shot at the female from here. He liked Canada. He liked the no-nonsense spirit and the enlightened attitude toward guns. Maybe one day he'd come back here for a holiday.

His leg was going to sleep. He unlaced the boot, peeled off the sock, and massaged the calf back to life. The sock still felt damp and in places was caked with half-frozen mud. He rubbed it over the leg of his jeans to dry and clean it, then put it back on again. He was doing this when his attention was drawn back to the house. Cora Skipton and her sons were leaving the house. The boys were fighting about something; at this distance he could make out the sound of their voices but not the words. He watched their mother turn and speak to them as she locked the front door, then the family descended the wooden steps to the yard and get in the pickup, all three of them sitting along the wide bench seat. The oldest boy, who'd apparently lost the argument, was made to sit in the middle.

Kirk waited fifteen minutes after the sound of the engine had died, then pulled on his tan leather gloves and made his way down the slope.

Jim Yuskin owned a quarter section on the west bank of Peace River. In the yard behind his house there were a dozen old cars and assorted pieces of farmyard machinery. In spring and autumn his property looked a mess, but in winter, when the clutter was disguised by snow, and in high summer, when the tall grass reclaimed it, the place looked almost respectable. Just down the road from him was the roll-on roll-off ferry which took cars across to Buffalo Head Prairie and beyond. When Cora arrived, he was sitting in the front porch, cleaning his second-best shotgun. He'd promised to take the boys skeet shooting.

Even before Skippy's death Uncle Jim Yuskin had been an honorary father to the boys. He was a rangy, untidy man with a shock of brown hair and piercing pale blue eyes which, when he smiled, became almost invisible. He cracked jokes with them, slipped them half dollars when their mother wasn't looking and involved them in dangerous, irresponsible escapades. He was the acknowledged local expert on dynamite, and local lore was rich with the stories of his exploits. Once, trying to crack the base of a septic tank near La Crete, he had hoisted into the air a column of effluent that fell like rain over the town half a mile away.

The boys loved him to the extent that, even before they arrived at his house, they would begin to imitate his slow, laconic drawl and his laid-back demeanor. When they pulled up outside his house, he came out to welcome them. Cora rolled down the window.

"You okay with these guys till five?"

"Ain't you coming too?"

"No, the feeder's choked up again," she said. "I got to go back and feed them by hand."

"Can't they wait a couple of hours?"

"Well." She wavered for a moment. "No, I'd better be going," she said. "If I get out of the car, I'll be here all afternoon."

"You suit yourself," said Jim Yuskin. "If it's late, can the boys stay here overnight?"

"Sure, just as long as you get them to school Monday morning."

"You know me," Jim Yuskin said.

She laughed. "That's why I'm worried." With that she rolled up the window, waved the boys good-bye, and set off home again.

Back at the Skipton house Kirk had managed quite easily to scramble over the wooden tiles of the back-porch roof and, with a penknife, to slip the lock of the bathroom.

This side of the house faced the sun, so there was no snow in which he might leave footprints. It was his habit to buy an entire outfit from one of the biggest chain stores as soon as he arrived in a new country, just to make life difficult for any forensic investigators; the prints from his sneakers and the material of his clothes could have come from any one of a hundred branches of Eaton's, anywhere in Canada. This was in many ways an unnecessary precaution: he knew that only a fraction of all crimes got solved. In the kind of apparently motiveless crimes in which Kirk specialized, the proportion was much smaller, and among those crimes that crossed international boundaries, the number that were ever solved approached almost zero. He'd have done both jobs and be out of the country before things went any farther than the local police force.

Kirk clambered in through the bathroom window, wiped his feet with a piece of toilet paper, closed and relocked the window, and made his way downstairs. He made no attempt to move quietly. He'd been watching the house for long enough to know there was no one inside.

The lounge was painted a warm, pink color with pine bookshelves and a couple of old leather sofas. There was an animal head above the fireplace. The tall windows faced south and east, over the fields and the panorama of treetops beyond that. Kirk started in the lounge with the rolltop desk. It was an unsophisticated lock with a hinge mechanism, which he was easily able to sweep aside with the blade of his knife. Inside there was a release lever that opened the side drawers.

His instructions had said to find a bundle of letters sent from Madagascar over the past year or so, no doubt connected in some way with the last Madagascar job he'd done. Kirk didn't know exactly how, but it gave him a satisfying sense of continuity. He rifled through the papers. The gloves he wore were of fine, expensive leather with seams that didn't run across the tips of his fingers.

In the desk's upper drawers he found stationery, pencils, and bits of household junk: string, paper clips, a pair of sunglasses in a case, a guitar pick. In the drawer below that there were photograph albums and a sheaf of drawings by the children. He tried the other drawers with no further success—one held knitting patterns, another a plan for an extension to the house. The third held equipment guarantees.

Kirk closed the bottom drawer and then stood motionless. A clock in the dining room was chiming the half hour, but, beyond that, he thought he'd heard a car engine. The clock stopped chiming. He crossed to the window and looked out. Snow was slipping from the pine trees that encircled the yard. Melting ice dripped off the eaves. He was alone.

He stood on a chair to check through the contents of the pine shelves: books, cassettes, records, some board games belonging to the children. He climbed down again and put the chair back where he'd found it. In the cupboards by the fireplace he found photographs, farming magazines, a wedding album, some holiday snaps. For a brief moment he thought he'd found the box he was looking for, but it contained nothing but school reports. He pulled the drawers shut and carefully closed the rolltop desk, then walked out into the corridor. He'd try the bedroom next.

There was a photo on the bedside table of the woman with her husband, laughing together in a rowing boat. In the bedroom cabinet on her side of the bed he found a book about the history of Alberta and, buried under her assorted underwear, a box containing her diaphragm. The drawers on her late husband's side of the bed were empty. Kirk turned his attention to the wardrobe. The one next to the window still contained all her husband's clothes: shirts pressed and folded, a suit still in its plastic bag from the dry cleaners. Drawers full of socks. Kirk closed the doors carefully. As he did so, he heard the sound of a car door slamming.

Kirk left the bedroom and walked quickly to the far end of the upstairs corridor. His trainers made no sound on the carpet. From the hall window he saw Cora Skipton's pickup truck parked in the yard outside. The door on the driver's side was open, and he could hear her now letting herself into the kitchen below him.

Kirk cursed and moved quickly to the window at the opposite end of the hall. It was nailed shut. Suddenly she was coming up the stairs. Kirk doubled back and into the bathroom, thinking to leave through the window, but remembering too late that he'd closed it behind him. He heard a plank creak on the landing, and he climbed into the bath, letting the shower curtain fall back into place behind him.

He could feel the blood forcing through his arteries.

Damn, she was coming into the bathroom too.

He heard her walk past a foot away from him, put down the toilet seat and unzip her trousers. As she peed, she hummed softly to herself.

Kirk didn't breathe. He'd been in some crazy situations in his time, and this was certainly one of them. He remembered two years ago, staking out a night-club boss in Liverpool and ending up locked in the dancers' dressing room for the night. One of these days he'd write his memoirs.

She'd finished now. She zipped up her trousers, closed the toilet seat, flushed the loo, and, as an afterthought, pulled back the shower curtain.

Kirk was on top of her before she could scream, clamping a hand over her mouth and pushing her back against the wall mirror. His hip caught the edge of the washbasin, and she was able to wriggle sideways, eyes wide and straining around at him like a frightened horse. She got halfway around the door, but he managed to grab her wrist.

"I don't want to hurt you," he said. "I just want to . . . Jesus!"

Somehow she'd twisted around behind the door and managed to slam it back against his wrist. His grip slackened, and she yanked herself free.

Kirk followed her down the stairs. He cleared the first steps to the first landing at a single jump, slamming into the far wall and smashing an aeriel picture of the farm with his shoulder. At the bottom of the stairs Cora turned. Kirk bounded down the stairs in twos, slipped on a loose rug, and fell the length of

the hallway. Cora slammed the door of the lounge. He heard
a key turn in the lock.

"Mrs. Skipton."

"I'm phoning the police."

She was bluffing. He knew from his previous visit that
there was no phone in the lounge.

"Mrs. Skipton."

"Go away," she shouted at him. Then, "Hello, hello,
RCMP? I'd like to report a break-in."

He tried the door handle. "Mrs. Skipton?"

She wasn't replying.

He put his ear to the door. Through the paneling he heard
a window being raised. She was leaving the house.

Kirk padded away from the doorway and through to the
kitchen. He stepped out through the porch and onto the decking
beyond. Below in the yard the pickup stood with its door still
open. Kirk stayed pressed against the wooden wall of the house,
watching the near corner. She appeared suddenly on the bank
to his right, sliding down its snowy surface. Kirk was ready
for her. He projected himself away from the wall and raced
down the wooden steps. He slipped and fell the last six rungs,
then got to his feet in the slush and gravel at the bottom. She
looked across at him. There were thirty yards between them.
The car stood in the middle of the yard, slightly closer to him
than it was to her. She could see she wasn't going to make it.
Her breath crystallized in front of her, there was color in her
cheeks, and her auburn hair was wild.

"What the hell do you want, mister?"

"I told you—I just want to talk."

"Get the hell off my property."

"Really, I can explain."

He took a step toward her.

"Stay right there."

Kirk sprang forward. In the army athletics teams he'd once
been the number-two sprinter. He'd thought he could catch her

before she reached the nearest barn, but she was faster than he thought and reached it ten yards ahead of him.

Kirk stopped in the doorway, waiting for his eyes to get used to the light. Cement walkways ran between the pens. There were about four hundred pigs inside, and now they all thought they were about to be fed, honking and squealing and slamming their huge bodies against the metal sides of the pen.

Kirk strained his eyes against the gloom. The air was heavy with the sweet smell of animals and straw. He found a bank of light switches and switched them all on. One by one the sectors of the vast shed were illuminated.

Cora Skipton stood twenty yards away from him, holding an electric prod.

Kirk was relieved. For a moment he'd thought it was a gun. He came toward her over the wet, salted concrete.

"Stay right there, mister."

Kirk kept coming forward. Show no fear, think yourself into winning. When she saw it was hopeless, she'd drop the prod.

"I'm telling you, mister, you wouldn't like the feel of this."

"Listen." He lowered his voice. "I'm sorry I frightened you. I don't mean to harm you, but you've got something I want."

"There's no money on the property. It all goes straight to the bank. And I don't have any jewelry worth stealing."

"That's not what I'm after."

"That's far enough," she said. "What do you want?"

Kirk stopped. He knew that if he asked her outright, then he'd ultimately have to kill her. On the other hand he'd wasted too much time chasing her around the farm.

"I want the letters your husband sent from Madagascar."

"You what?"

"Just a few letters," he said softly. "I'm sure that's not worth getting hurt for."

Cora said, "So Spence was right."

Kirk watched her. He was barely listening. He moved closer. The woman kept babbling.

"They found oil, and they wanted to keep it quiet. The plane crash was rigged. They wanted to keep those men quiet. Now you want to keep me quiet too."

Kirk moved another step forward. His quarry was backed against the pens now. There was just the cattle prod between them. Kirk made a lunge, and she jabbed at him with the prod. She caught him on the upper arm and the surge of volts almost spun him around. He came back again, weaving in toward her. She was trying to keep the prod directly toward him, but it was shaking wildly. The huge hogs behind her were going wild. Now one of them slammed into the wall just behind her knees, and in that instant's distraction Kirk came in and grabbed the prod halfway up its shaft. She tried to kick him, but he turned her easily, getting her arm behind her back and her chin in the crook of his elbow.

He spoke in her ear. "I don't want to hurt you. I just need to know where the letters are."

She choked. "It makes no difference anyway. Everyone knows about them. Norco'll never get away with it."

Kirk said, "Just tell me where the papers are."

He waited till she breathed out and increased the pressure on her windpipe. She panicked and struggled. He released the pressure enough to let her talk.

"They're in the bedroom."

"Where in the bedroom?"

"In a shoebox. There's a suitcase under the bed."

Kirk relaxed and let her begin to twist out of his grip toward the left. Then, with her chin in the crook of his elbow, he jerked her head violently around to the right.

There was a crack as the uppermost vertebra came off its moorings, and Cora fell limp.

It was a satisfying procedure when it went right. You sometimes had trouble with men with big, muscular necks, but on women it usually worked a treat.

Kirk took her shoes off and carried them back up to the house.

The letters were where she had said they would be. In the porch he picked up Cora's Wellington boots and left her shoes, then locked the door behind him.

In the pig barn her body was already going cold. It was difficult getting the boots on her limp feet, though he managed after a struggle. Then he put the prod in her hand and lifted her into the pen that contained the largest sows. When he dropped her, she fell in at a suitably accidental posture with her head in the corner of the pen. The pigs came over to sniff at her. Kirk left them to it and headed off, switching out the lights behind him. He closed the door of Cora's pickup and picked his way up through the woods again.

Chapter 22

Whenever she was passing through the capital, Antananarivo, Perpetude stayed with her friends in Amparibe district. She called Istasse's office from there, and he arranged for his driver to collect her that evening.

The elections were only a month away. Illuminated banners were strung across the Rue Jean Ralaimongo, and smàll groups of students were gathering in the dusk outside the cafés and restaurants along Avenue de l'Indépendance. She recalled the same kind of urgent street-corner debates on the Boulevard Michel in '68. She remembered Istasse then, at the time when she first knew him, and his sudden transformation from outsider to celebrity.

Overnight the German Jew, Cohn-Bendit, had made it fashionable to belong to a racial minority (*"Nous sommes tous des Juifs Allemandes,"* they chanted, three beats of three, as they marched shoulder to shoulder over the Ponte de la Concorde, sweeping aside the men of the CRS). Istasse, as an articulate black intellectual from a colony that was pressing for independence, was a ready-made hero. She could picture now the moment of his baptism into politics—the moment he had climbed onto the stage in the Grand Amphithéâtre, with his loud friends, the Enragés from Nanterre, waving red flags from the balcony and cheering every time he pronounced one of those large words like *freedom* and *comradeship*. She had stood on her own, to one side of the auditorium, quietly fascinated by his metamorphosis, from the brooding, tentative man she had slept with the night before.

Ironically this was the beginning of her own total disillusionment with politics. She remembered now all those earnest, hairy gatherings that followed in the classrooms of the occupied Sorbonne. Outside, people were being stoned in the street. Inside, they were debating whether philosophy belongs in the factories. She had decided then that philosophy didn't belong anywhere, that she cared less about Sartre and Marcuse than she did about the trees that had been hacked down to make barricades on the right bank or the policeman she'd seen killed by a falling slate, or the little kiosk they'd burned in the square of Rue des Écoles, or the paving stones, much too heavy to throw, that had been ripped up around the Luxembourg Station. Dissent was easy. Plans and theories and opinions were easy. Reconciliation was the difficult thing.

They drove past the embassies. It was one of the few stretches of road in the capital that was completely free of pot-holes. At Istasse's house a guard opened the gate for them. When the driver opened her door, she noticed a recent scar on his forehead. She walked through Istasse's floodlit garden, across the ornamental bridge. Claude Istasse came out of the front door to greet her.

"Perpetude." They kissed on both cheeks. He was dressed in the European style, the cuffs of his shirt turned two careful turns up his forearms. For a man on the threshold of the presidency he looked extraordinarily relaxed.

He led her across the tiled courtyard, then out into the dining room with the floodlit swimming pool and the garden beyond. He had switched off the lights in the garden so that the only illumination to the palm trees came from the turquoise water in front of them and the moonlit sky behind. The table by the water's edge was set for two.

"I'm sorry you've missed Mimi," he said. "She's off to Nosy Bé for a week."

"So it's just the two of us?"

"Is that all right? I spend so much of my time surrounded by people these days, I thought it would be nice to entertain you *à deux*." He pulled out a chair for her and took her shawl.

The wine he poured was imported from South Africa.

"You look well," he said. "I'd almost forgotten how attractive you are."

"It's rather difficult to forget what you look like, Claude."

"Thank you."

"I meant all the posters I keep seeing with your face on them."

Istasse made a dismissive gesture. "You know that most of the peasants are illiterate. I have to give them something to focus on."

"You could visit them in person," she said.

"I intend to. I might even get as far as Morondava someday."

"Do you have any special interest in Morondava?"

"Apart from you?" he said.

"Will you drill for oil again?"

Istasse chuckled. "Oh, that. God, no. That's Velo-André's little fantasy. I hear you've become quite friendly with one of the oilmen."

"Have I?"

"Velo's man. Mr. Spence?"

"You're certainly well informed."

Fireworks exploded in the sky above the city center. Istasse leaned back in the canvas chair. "Actually it was your friend Father Mitchell who told me."

"How is he?"

"He's a funny old man. I think he had quite a soft spot for you."

"Is he happy in his new job?"

"Probably not. Men like that are never happy. Pleasure makes them uncomfortable."

"And you?"

Istasse smiled and sipped from the crystal glass. "Oh, yes. I'm happy. Within the normal limits."

"So why spoil it all?" she asked.

"Pardon?"

"By running for president. You've got a nice house here, an attractive foreign wife. What do you want to be president for?"

"Because I'll be good at it. Because I believe in my principles. Because this used to be a great country and could be again."

Perpetude smiled. These were exactly the reasons he had given to *Jeune Afrique,* and he had recited them in the same order. "I remember you were also good at poetry," she said.

"It didn't pay the rent."

"Is money the fourth reason?"

He laughed and dabbed his moustache. "I'll get the salad."

The salad was *cœurs de palme* in oil.

"You knew Charles Hunter, didn't you?" she said.

"Who?"

"Charles Hunter. He was the head of Norco, the oil company."

"Oh, yes. Of course."

"How well did you know him?"

"Well enough."

"Did you trust him?"

"He seemed a reasonable-enough fellow. Why?"

"The oilman, Spence, had a theory that Norco had not been perfectly honest here."

"On what level?"

She watched his face but saw no sign of tension. "Oh,

some odd things happened when he was doing the inventory on the rig," she said. "He began to think the well had been more promising than they admitted."

"I don't see how that could benefit them," Istasse said. "They stood to gain as much from it as we do."

"Yes."

"And if your fellow had unearthed anything, I'm sure we would have heard about it by now."

"I'm sure."

Bullfrogs chirruped in the greenery. She could hear the driver locking up for the night. "I'll ask Velo-André, if you're serious," he said.

"No," she said. "I'm sure you're right."

Istasse finished his salad and stood up. "Excuse me. I'd better go and check the main course."

He was some time in the kitchen. Perpetude got up from the table. She walked around the lawn and trailed her hand in the water in the pool. A dog barked somewhere, and, among the frangipani trees, Istasse's black Labrador stirred itself from sleep.

Istasse returned with a casserole and put it on the metal table. "You can have a swim if you like. I'm sure Mimi's got a costume here somewhere."

"Would that be wise?"

"Wise?"

"Now you have your political reputation to protect."

He laughed and said, "I'm sure your being here would only enhance it."

She smiled. "I wouldn't push your luck, Claude."

"You mean on a personal or a political level?"

"'The personal is the political.' Remember that one? Or does the new right have a different slogan?"

Istasse served the food. "It was a perfectly innocent suggestion. I was just remembering what a good . . . swimmer you were." He couldn't resist that pause.

"Yes," she said. "I wouldn't rely too much on that gambit either."

"What gambit?"

"The *double entendre*."

Istasse laughed and served the vegetables. "Perpetude. You surprise me. I don't remember you being so adversarial."

"Yes, you do. It's why you were attracted to me. I was a worthy opponent, someone you could spend a few weeks learning to dominate."

"Dominate? Me? I was a shy, retiring communist."

"Come on, Claude. That was your way of attracting women. You were never a communist. At least not privately. You were a bedroom imperialist."

"A bedroom imperialist?" Istasse tested the phrase. "That's rather good. I'll say one thing. All that sun down there hasn't fried your lovely brains. *Bon appétit.*"

" 'My lovely brains.' " She laughed. "And *Jeune Afrique* called you sophisticated. Did you cook this?"

"Of course."

"It's good." She blew on a piece of chicken. "I should give you a job at the hotel."

"Actually that's why I invited you here, Perpetude."

"To ask for a job?"

"To offer you one. You're wasted down there. We're short of intellectuals, as you know."

"A shortage of intellectuals. That's an interesting idea. What kind of job did you have in mind?"

"How does the Foreign Office sound?"

"Foreign," she said.

"Okay. Name your department."

"I don't want a department, Claude. You know how I feel about politics."

"No. But I know you're an intelligent woman. And I can't imagine what you're doing at the Grand Hotel in Morondava."

"I run the place. I go swimming in the sea. I buy my own

supplies. I know it's just a shabby hotel, but it's something I can touch. It's not a theory. I can see when the hinges need oiling or when the termites have eaten the floorboards. I know when we need more rice. These are things I can encompass. They make me happy."

"It's called parochialism, Perpetude."

"We're all parochial. You live in a small world of politicians and corporate men. I've met wealthy, cosmopolitan people in Paris who are the most parochial you could imagine."

"But Morondava. Perpetude, it's a tiny dot on the map."

"Well." She looked around the garden, at the black silhouettes of the travelers palms standing out against the Milky Way. "I've tried living in a bigger dot, and it didn't make me happy. I hated Paris. I hated the idea of being part of some big consensus. I felt that the big crowds, the random barrage of ideas, was not how we are meant to live. We belong in small social groups, Claude. That is my only political opinion. That we should forget big cities and complex plans. We know that grand schemes never work. We should return to village life where we know who our friends are, where we can see the physical results of what we do."

Istasse guffawed. "Perpetude. You're talking about going back twenty years. You're talking about Marxist collectives."

"Am I? Well, if that's what a Marxist collective is, then I think the idea was ahead of its time. We just didn't have the technology to make it work then. We didn't have the transport. We didn't have the communications. In ten years' time people will be able to make a living anywhere. Even in Morondava. We'll be able to return to the villages."

"So who's going to run the country?"

"Do countries need to be run nowadays? It struck me when there was that cyclone at Toamasina that the problem was solved internationally. If you have information and commerce, what do you need government for? It reminded me of the flood in Belo when I was a girl, and all the nearby villages came around to help. Not because anyone told them to, but because they heard about it and they knew it affected all of them. That's what's happening in the world now, Claude. What's happening in the West. It's not the end of communism. If you ask me, it's more than that. It's the beginning of the end of national government. It's the devolution of power. It's happening on the right wing as well as on the left, except that right-wing politicians are too full of themselves to notice it. Europe is breaking up into city-states and villages. People are tired of wild theories, of big political movements. They can make their own decisions now. Life doesn't have to be complicated." She stopped, feeling slightly breathless, and said, "I don't know. Does that make sense?"

"None at all. But I'll drink to being less complicated." Istasse raised his glass. "To the end of complications," he said.

She smiled and toasted him, sitting in the shifting reflections from the swimming pool. After all was said, he was her old friend, and she liked him. "The end of complications," she said.

And strangely, at that moment, though neither of them recognized it, they both thought of the same person.

When Spence set out from his home to the Saskatchewan Bar, it was already dark. The night frost had its grip on the frozen mud, transforming the rutted track into an infernal giant saw blade off which his boots scraped and slipped. Flat ground turned out to be ice, ice turned out to be water, and the beam his flashlight cast was deceptive, jerking shadows over the treacherous surface. He made slow progress, breathing heavily, with his breath frosting on the inside of his wool collar and his walking stick stubbornly embarking on detours of its own.

He fell at least once and realized he'd have difficulty getting a bottle back intact to the house. Looking back, he found he'd come just under halfway. Behind him lay nothing but blackness. He forged on, motivated by masochism and by the fear of

spending the night sober. To his right he could hear wads of
snow sliding through the spruce trees and thudding on the
ground below. Black clouds obscured the black sky. The lights
and music of the Saskatchewan came as a relief.

Inside he found himself a stool at the end of the upstairs
bar. They were playing loud rock music on the lower level.
The huge timbers of the place absorbed the higher notes, but
transmitted the base beat like the engines of a captive riverboat.
Outside, red-colored lights stained the cold, black water. Icicles
had formed, broken, and re-formed on the wooden balustrade.
Spence kicked the frost out of his toes and bought himself a
double rye. Jugs of beer were handed backward and forward
around him. Some Indians were getting drunk in a corner, and
a group of local kids were playing shuffleboard along the far
wall. There was warmth and color and the sound of laughter.
Spence thought of the cold, awkward hike home and the deserted house that was waiting for him. He unbuttoned his jacket
and ordered another double.

It was half past eleven and the car-park was emptying fast,
when he finally staggered out of the main door. He stuffed the
half bottle in his pocket. The buttons of his jacket were done
up wrongly, but he couldn't find the correct configuration, so
he put his gloves on and left it as it was. It took him a few
moments to get his bearings, then he identified the track on the
far side of the highway and aimed himself in that direction. Ten
minutes previously he'd had an incoherent argument with a
stranger at the bar, and now he was replaying the exchange in
his mind. The boundaries between speech and thought had
become blurred, and he shouted or muttered things he'd said
or the other man had said or he should have said. Then he got
cross with himself for having such a damn-fool argument and
told himself so. A car turned its headlights on him, and he
flailed at it with his stick, then turned and headed on his way.

If the path had been treacherous on the way to the Saskatchewan, it was positively malevolent on his return. The

spiked mud seemed to buck and shift under his feet, pitching him into snowdrifts and puddles of slush. A mile on from the pub his hips and knees were too bruised and painful to continue further, so he sat down on a drift and took out the bottle, which had miraculously survived the journey. He may briefly have fallen asleep, because the next thing he was aware of was the pain in his freezing right hand and the damp ice penetrating the seat of his trousers.

Spence pushed himself into a sitting position and peered into the darkness. The eerie gray snow looked the same all around him, and he couldn't remember which way was home. He felt around for his stick and struggled to his feet. He could hear something now—a car engine. It had to be coming from the road. Spence started out in the opposite direction. Suddenly there were shadows all around him. Looking back, he saw two yellow pinpricks like the eyes of a prowling beast. The car was coming toward him. Spence continued walking away from it. He could hear the growl of the exhaust and see the pitching of the shadows as the vehicle negotiated the ruts. Nobody came up this track. Certainly not this time of night.

The headlights were growing bigger. The vehicle was gaining on him. Spence tried to clamber out of the track, but the drift between him and the fence was waist-deep. Further on there'd be a gate. He had a bad feeling about this stranger on the tracks so late at night. Spence found a rut and hobbled into it. Behind him the lights grew brighter and the noise of the engine more distinct. He turned and waved with his stick, then pitched on again, his stick rapping off the pinnacles of frozen mud and his boots knocking into each other. The car was gaining, his bruised legs tiring. What did the bastards want with him? He turned again, still moving forward, tripped and fell. It was too cold. There was too much pain. He closed his eyes and lay back.

The vehicle advanced till it was almost on top of him, then it stopped, the lights blazing, the engine breathing steam. The door opened; a man got out and came toward him.

PART
THREE

Chapter 23

Light filtered down through the metal grilles and stained-glass skylights, reflecting off the inlaid pillars. The noise of a squash game echoed around the swimming pool, but the pool itself was deserted except for two men. Robert Heckterman III stood on the marble steps splashing water on his arms and chest. The scar on his sternum left by the heart bypass had all but disappeared under a mat of fine gray hairs. He liked to surprise people by telling them his age, which was seventy-six.

"So how was Sydney?" Hunter asked him.

"Oh, Sydney's Sydney. We did some yachting."

"How's Barry?"

"He's fine. Living with some other young thing now. I'd feel happier about him if he had children."

Robert Heckterman III still tended to talk about his three chief executives as though they were his sons. And, Hunter reflected, as they swam abreast up and down the center of the monumental swimming pool, he did tend to think of the other two men as stepbrothers, with all the sibling rivalry that relationship implied.

Heckterman had always refused to nominate a successor. Now, in the year before his retirement, the old goat liked nothing more than playing the three of them off against each other.

In Houston, some time in the next two years, at one of the quarterly board meetings, he would rise to his feet, tap his signet ring on the table for silence, and nominate one of them as overall head of the company.

Hunter was the youngest of the international chiefs, but he knew that the presidency was within his grasp. The other two men, Sandy Greer in America and Jake Stevens in Australia, had come up through accounting, while Hunter shared Heckterman's background in geology. Geologists were fundamentally different from accountants. They were tougher, they had a grander, simpler vision of the world; they didn't hedge their bets. Heckterman had built the company from nothing with just this approach, and Hunter had sensed, even before his promotion to chief executive, that the way to impress Robert Heckterman was to play the big game with the same ruthless panache, the same ferocious selfishness. He knew Heckterman respected him for this. But, inevitably, he also mistrusted him, which was one reason why the old man was here.

Until now no one had questioned his holding on to the Madagascar concession. It was understood that every oil company kept a couple of unlikely projects on hold. There were various reasons for backing these apparent losers, sometimes for political reasons, sometimes as a tax loss, sometimes merely to attract rivals away from the real geographical focus of the company's attention. Norco U.K. retained concessions on several unlikely territories, and, uncannily, it was these outside-chance projects that Robert Heckterman had been focusing on during the last few days of his visit to London. Now, as he stood at the shallow end, he said, "So tell me about Madagascar, Charles."

"What do you want to know?"

"Planning told me you're keeping a window there. I thought we'd ditched the place."

"That's what I'm asking you. Do we want to keep the concession?"

Hunter sank up to his neck in the water, leaning back

against the side of the pool. "I've got a soft spot for the place," he said. "It's where I got promoted from."

Robert Heckterman laughed. It was Heckterman who had promoted him. "A soft spot, eh? That's a part of your anatomy you keep pretty well hidden."

"It's a good place. They're nice people."

"Nice, eh? How far out of the trees are they?" Heckterman had given over two million dollars' worth of African art to the University of Texas, but his views on that continent remained unreconstructed.

"Let's say they're not Saudi, but they're not Burkina Faso either." Hunter submerged and came back up, pushing his hair back out of his eyes. Heckterman refused to drop the subject.

"What are you telling me, Charles? They're smart enough to do business with, but not so smart we couldn't make a profit?"

"Something like that."

"So what? We're taking a flyer there, or is it charity work?"

"Neither."

"So it's political."

"You don't want to know the answer to that, Bob."

"Try me."

"Let's go and get some lunch," Hunter said.

"The hell with lunch. Why are you clamming up on me, Charles?"

"I'd tell you, but it wouldn't be good for your health."

"My health's fine."

Hunter signaled for one of the pool attendants to bring over his towel, then Hunter lifted himself out of the pool. "You want a hand up?" he asked.

"Just tell me this, Charles. If I was a shareholder in Norco U.K., should I keep buying shares or sell them?"

"Sell them," Hunter said. "Sell them to me."

Robert Heckterman reached for a hand up. "You're a devious son of a bitch, Charles," he said.

But his eyes were smiling.

★　★　★

Spence woke with his eyes closed. He was lying on an unfamiliar, soft mattress and could hear the hum of traffic outside. His body ached and his mouth tasted stale. He opened his eyes and saw a Flying Fortress diving at him out of a clear blue sky.

He was in Dennis's house. This was the boys' room. There were hockey pads in the corner and a poster of the Edmonton Oilers above the dresser. A dog was pulling at a corner of one sheet. He reached down and patted its head.

"Hello, Life."

Spence got up and sat on the edge of the bed, looking for his clothes. There was a teenage boy's dressing gown on the back of the door that, when he put it on, barely reached past his elbows. Spence smoothed his hair and walked downstairs.

He was already bracing himself for a frosty reception. Myra had worked as a welfare officer for too long to retain any sympathy with alcoholics. He expected to find her stomping around the kitchen, crashing cutlery, equally enraged with Spence for having fallen off the wagon as with Dennis for having picked him up again.

But when Spence walked into the kitchen, he encountered a somber atmosphere that was entirely untypical of the McCabe household. Dennis was sitting at the pine table trickling syrup on a pancake he seemed to have little intention of eating. Myra was at the sink looking out through the bare trees on Wellington Crescent over River Valley Park.

"Morning," Spence said brightly.

Dennis looked up. "Sit yourself down."

"Morning, Myra," said Spence.

"Good morning," she said without turning.

Spence helped himself to some coffee. "I guess that was you in the van, hey, Dennis?"

"Yup. That was me."

"I thought you were someone else."

"You were unconscious," Dennis said.

"I saw the vehicle coming. I don't remember anything after that."

"You'd probably have frozen to death out there," Dennis said, passing him the milk.

There was silence as he shook out the cereal and poured milk on top of it.

Spence looked toward the sink and said, "Something wrong, Myra?"

"Yes."

Spence looked to Dennis for elucidation, but Dennis was also avoiding his gaze. Life pulled at his shoelaces.

"I guess it was pretty late," Spence said. "What were you doing out there?"

"I was coming to tell you something."

"Tell me what?"

"Cora's dead." It was Myra who had spoken. Spence looked in disbelief from Dennis to Myra and back to Dennis.

"Cora Skipton?"

"Yup."

The mug slipped from Spence's finger. He caught it as it fell, slopping coffee over the toast rack. "What happened?"

"The boys were away for the weekend," said Dennis. "She was on her own at the farm. They reckon she must have fallen in the pens and knocked her head. The hogs got to her. When they found her she was . . . Well . . . "

Myra put the tea towel down and left the kitchen.

"She was what, Dennis?"

Dennis sawed through his pancake. "There wasn't much of her left."

"How did you hear?"

"Patrick found her when he got home from school. We got the call last night from the RCMP."

"Where are the boys now?"

"They're staying with Jim Yuskin."

Beyond the river valley Emily Murphy Park was cloaked

in snow. Cars sparkled like rhinestones on the Groat Road.

"I should go out there," he said at last.

"There's nothing you can do," Dennis said. He gave up carving his pancake, took it over and scraped it into the dog bowl, then turned around and met Spence's eyes. They looked at each other for a long time.

"What's going on, Dennis?"

"You tell me, Spence. Just seems all the people a guy feels close to..." Dennis turned his back on Spence, looking out the window and making a pretense of washing his breakfast plate. "The plane crash. Then Cora. You." He looked down. Life was slurping noisily over his pancake. "Every time I turn around these days, someone else has died. Just can't help feeling somehow we got on a bad roll, and we're never going to get off it."

Spence got up from the table. He crossed the kitchen and put a hand on Dennis's shoulder. "I ain't dead yet, old buddy."

"Sure you are. You just don't know it."

Life finished eating and looked up, expecting more. Dennis nudged the dog aside with his foot.

"Can I borrow the Dodge?" Spence said.

"The overdrive's busted. How far do you want to go?"

"Cora's place."

"What for?"

"Just to see what happened."

"I told you what happened."

"To see the boys are okay."

"Jim Yuskin's looking after them."

"I'd like to see them," Spence said.

Dennis reached for the hook next to the towel rack and handed Spence a bunch of keys.

"Just drive carefully, okay?"

Spence retied his shoelaces and left.

★   ★   ★

Planes drifted overhead, coming in to land at the municipal airport. Spence tuned the radio to the *Bobby Nunn Show* and headed out past the garden centers on Highway 2. Opposite St. Joseph's Cemetery he passed a car accident. A paramedic was directing the traffic. Spence reached out into the scythingly cold air and adjusted the sideview mirror. A message along the bottom of it said, OBJECTS IN THE MIRROR ARE CLOSER THAN THEY APPEAR.

Free at last of the endless grid of suburbs, he drove on through the rolling hills past Flatbush, then westward along Route 43, with the Pelican Mountains rising to his right. On the frozen banks of Lesser Slave Lake he pulled in at a truck stop, bought himself a submarine and a Coke, and ate them as he drove. He opened the windows, switched the heater on. Fiddling with the unfamiliar controls of the radio, he came across a French Canadian music channel. It was a weak signal, and he didn't understand a word of the song, but strangely it made him feel better. He'd met Jim Yuskin on a few occasions with Skippy. Three years ago they'd gone on a fishing trip together in the lakes up north in the Cariboo Mountains. In the summers he and Jim had helped out with bits of heavy work on the hog farm—putting in fence posts around the paddock, laying the concrete base for the new pumping shed, or digging drainage ditches with a hired digger along the side of the big field.

When Spence arrived, night had fallen, and the boys were sitting up around the fire in their pajamas, drinking cocoa. Patrick shook his hand. Alexander went off to sit in a corner, fiddling with the pieces of the jigsaw he had started.

Until the boys went to bed, Spence and Jim Yuskin tried to avoid the subject of Cora's death—joking about the social worker who'd come snooping around to assess whether Jim was fit to look after the boys. Fit or not, Jim had decided that the boys were staying with him. They'd hire a manager to look after the hog farm, and maybe one day the boys would inherit it. Meanwhile, he said loudly, he was training Alexander to be an explosives expert.

Alexander put down his piece of jigsaw and said he was going off to bed.

When both the boys were asleep, the two men put on their jackets and went for a walk outside. A full moon had risen over the house. They could see from here the dim-blue glow of the night-light in the boys' room. Farther down the river the lights of the ferry trolled slowly backward and forward across the slow, cold waters of the Peace River.

"The boys're better than I thought," Spence said.

"They're bad and good. Patrick's okay most of the time. Alexander's pretty difficult. They both have nightmares a lot. You know, it was Patrick who found the body."

"I heard. How bad was she?"

"Well. The hogs had made a bit of a mess of her. Mainly her legs and around her middle. I just hope she was unconscious till she died."

"They reckon, what, that her neck was broke?"

Jim Yuskin nodded. "Looks like she tripped and fell. I had to sign a form for them to do a post-mortem. After that we can get the body back for the funeral."

"You need some money for that?"

"Hell, no. I tell you what, though. If you're looking for a job, how do you feel about managing that farm for a bit?"

Spence shook his head. "I'd say yes, but right now I think it would drive me crazy. It's staying in one place that's got me all messed up."

Jim Yuskin looked at him. "You never thought that maybe it's moving around so much that did that?"

They had reached the wooden jetty. There was a crust of ice at the water's edge. Farther out, in the main current, ice floes were drifting down from farther up river, ghostly shapes in the moonlight.

Spence said, "There wasn't anything odd about Cora's death, was there?"

"What kind of odd?"

"I don't know. I saw a patrol car outside the approach road when I was driving up here. I just worried if there was anything they weren't sure about."

"Like what?"

"Like whether there was anyone else around at the time."

"You mean she was murdered?"

"Yeah."

Jim Yuskin gave a hollow laugh. "Shit, Spence, why would anyone murder Cora Skipton?"

"No reason."

Next day the patrol car was no longer there. Spence drove off the main road and down the gravel track. Once, he'd helped Skippy to clear back the brush on either side here. Now there were patches of ice where the path had thawed and refrozen. Icicles hung from the pine trees. When he slowed down, he could hear, above the noise of the engine, the sound of birds calling softly from the woods.

A lot of vehicles had been down this path in the last few days, police and forensic, the ambulance, neighbors and friends. But, when he broke through the trees, he found the yard deserted.

Spence called out, but no one answered. Spence tried the door of the house and found it locked. He cleared a space on the frosted window. Inside, time had stopped. A jersey of Cora's lay over the back of a chair. On the table there was a full shopping basket with a newspaper in it.

The back door was also locked.

Spence walked back down to the main barn. The hogs had been fed recently. Midway into the shed some striped red tape, of the type used by the RCMP for cordoning off the scene of an accident, was tied between the tubular steel railings of an empty pen. Spence looked into the pen. In one corner the muddy cement floor was stained red.

He heard a sound and looked around. A figure stood in the far doorway, silhouetted by the crystal light behind, a shotgun under his arm.

"Who's that?"

The figure stood motionless. Spence hobbled back down toward the door, shielding his eyes against the glare of the snow outside. As he got closer, he recognized the young Indian in a woollen hat.

"Hi, Joe."

"Oh . . . it's you, Mr. Spence." Joe was one of Cora's farmhands—a dark, powerful man in his early twenties. He came up the cement walkway, his high-heeled boots scraping on the rough surface. "Sorry about the gun," he said. "I didn't know who you were."

"That's okay. How are things?"

"Not so good. The RCMP were on the phone just now. They're not sure it was an accident."

"You don't say."

"Seems there was something about the forensic. They're saying the way her neck was broke, it couldn't have been done in a fall . . . or the bruises weren't the right side or something." He leaned back morosely against the barricade opposite Spence. "Anyway, there's a whole lot more guys coming down here this afternoon to go over the place again." Joe took off his hat and ran a hand through his long, dark hair. He looked nervous. "I kinda knew it would go this way."

"How do you mean?"

"Oh, nothing. I just had a bad feeling. There was a car parked down by the river the morning she got killed. I thought then it was just some guy out hunting, but now I think maybe it wasn't."

"Why didn't you tell them that before?"

"Didn't think of it. I sure wish I had now. As soon as

there's anything suspicious, the first person they're going to suspect is an Indian. This Indian."

"You didn't see this guy in the car?"

Joe shook his head. "It was early. I had the day off. I was going back to the reserve. Even if it was some guy poaching, I didn't have time for a lot of hassle."

"You got a key to the house, Joe?"

"Yes . . . why?"

Spence laughed. "Shit, take that look off your face. I know you didn't do it. I just want to go up and have a look around up there."

"Looking for what?"

"Just some stuff Cora was keeping for me."

"What kind of stuff?"

"It's nothing, Joe, it doesn't matter. We'll wait till the police get here."

Joe was still watching him. There was concern in his hooded dark eyes.

"Really, Joe," Spence said. "I don't know why I mentioned it. It was just some letters she had of Skippy's that I was interested in. Some letters in a shoebox. Tied with a red ribbon. It can wait. I can get them some other time."

Joe reached slowly in his jacket pocket. "This the ribbon?"

Spence felt a cold current run through his veins. He felt suddenly breathless. He took the ribbon and ran it between his fingers.

"Where did you get this?"

"I found it yesterday." Joe was watching him carefully. "It was stuck on that fence at the bottom of the big field. I guess the wind must have blowed it there."

"Near where the car was parked?"

"Near enough. Why?"

The ribbon was frayed and crumpled from frequent tying and retying. There was a blot of ink along one edge.

"What letters were these, Mr. Spence?"

"Nothing. They were love letters."

Joe misread Spence's air of distraction. "What, between you and her?"

"Shit, no. Of course not. Between her and Skippy." There was a ring to his indignation that even to Spence himself, sounded vaguely insincere. "Listen, Joe," he said. "You know there's no chance Cora Skipton and I were having an affair. You been here, what, Joe, two years?"

"Almost three."

"And how often you seen me out here?"

"Sure, Mr. Spence, I know. I know. Let's go outside. I'm not saying nothing. I just was thinking. I just wondered what it was with those letters."

"It's a long story, Joe."

They began walking to the shed door.

"You think the police are going to want to hear it?"

"I doubt it. But if they want me, I'll be at Jim Yuskin's till tomorrow."

He left the Indian standing in the yard, a solemn, solitary figure in a checked shirt, Sears Roebuck boots, and a donkey jacket. Spence had worked with lots of Indians, but suddenly, for the first time, he knew what it felt like to be one. If you knew in advance that no one was going to believe you, then why even bother trying to explain things?

Chapter 24

Every day there was a different convention going on at the Ramada Renaissance Hotel. Tuesday had been skiwear manufacturers. Wednesday was book publishers. Today was flower arrangers, and the lobby was full of flamboyantly dressed older women wearing name tags. Kirk threaded his way between them on his way back to his room. The nylon carpets stored electricity, and he got a shock of static when he touched the button for the lift. It wasn't the first time this had happened. The hotel was beginning to irritate him.

Kirk stood alone in the lift, looking at his reflection in the mirror. Maybe he could use up some time by going for a haircut. He'd been out to Fort Saskatchewan three times since his return to Edmonton, but there was still no sign of Spence. Over breakfast he'd read a report in the Edmonton *Sun* saying that further investigations into the cause of Cora Skipton's death were now in progress. "Further investigations" bothered him. What Kirk wanted now was to get rid of Spence so that he could leave the country.

A bell rang, and Kirk stepped out onto the fifteenth floor. If Spence still hadn't turned up by tomorrow, then he knew he would have to delay his own flight out of the country.

In his room he phoned Spence's number. The line had been reconnected the previous day, but there was still no one answering the phone. He replaced the handset and lay back on his bed, disconsolately flicking through Spence's file. Under the section that usually indicated why his target should be eliminated, his handlers had simply written, "Internal security." They'd given the same reason for sabotaging the plane in Madagascar and for retrieving the letters from Cora Skipton. Kirk wondered, not for the first time, what a lady pig-farmer and a lame oilman have to do with internal security. He closed the file and got up again. He didn't like having time on his hands. When he had time, he began to wonder daft things—like whether or not he really was working for the good guys.

Kirk took a tour of the room. He switched on the television and switched it off again. He stood in front of the picture window on the fifteenth floor, leaning against the glass with his hands, looking at the toy cars below him scuttling like ants around downtown Edmonton. He tried Spence's number once more, then he put on his jacket and went out to explore the town.

West Edmonton Mall was an endless, multistory complex of magnolia cement and glass cupolas running along the north side of 87th Avenue. Outside Entrance 23 the thermometer read fifteen degrees below. Inside, people were sitting in swimming trunks around the water park. There were waves and a sandy beach and tables under the palm trees. There was a pool for performing dolphins and a full-size reconstruction of the *Santa María*.

Kirk wandered down a reconstruction of Bourbon Street and bought a doughnut in one of the restaurants there. He visited the bird aviaries and the water fountains and played nine holes on the indoor golf course. He walked down to the aquarium under the water park and had a look at the sharks. When he came back up to ground level, it was half past one.

Back in his room he dialed Spence's number again. He'd let it ring a dozen times and was about to replace the receiver when a voice answered on the other end.

"Hi, sorry, you just got me on my way out."

Kirk said, "Who's that?"

"This is Spence. Who am I talking to? Hello? Is anyone there?"

The sign that read MC CABE DRILLING was made of stainless steel and set on a cement plinth. It had been designed to sit directly outside the front of the building, but when he saw the finished article, Dennis had disliked it so much that he had it moved to one side of the car-park. Spence leaned against it, waiting for Dennis to come out and join him.

"Spence, what am I doing out here?"

"I need to talk to you."

"So let's talk where it's warm. What's wrong with my office?"

"This is private."

"My office is private. Also we won't get frostbite there."

Spence handed him the newspaper. "They killed her, Dennis."

"Killed who?"

"Cora."

"What are you talking about? Who killed her?"

"Norco."

Dennis threw down the paper. He stepped forward and gripped Spence by the arm. "Hey, Spence, you quit that now, hear me, I thought we'd heard the last of this."

"I told Hunter that Cora knew about the well, that she could back me up. I told him she had some letters to prove it. God, I'm a stupid son of a bitch."

"Shut up, you hear me?"

"It all makes sense, Dennis."

"The hell it does," said Dennis with sudden fury. "You just got that East Africa stuff fixed in your mind, and you can't shake it off. This has nothing to do with Norco, okay? It's nothing to do with them. We've finished discussing all that."

Spence said, "Skippy dead, now Cora dead. Don't you think that's a coincidence?"

"I think it's a goddamn tragedy, Spence. I really liked that woman. I liked them both—her and Skippy—I liked them a lot. I liked you, too, before you started cracking up. And the one thing I don't need is for you to mix them up with your mad-ass bullshit."

"I'm not mad, Dennis. And I'm not drunk. I swear I'm just as sane as you are. I was right all the time. I just let Hunter turn my head around. Maybe he was bluffing, Dennis. Maybe *his* log was the phony one."

Dennis dropped Spence's arm, then turned on his heel and began striding back toward the building. Spence followed.

"Dennis . . ."

"I've told you, Spence, I don't want to hear any more of this."

"It's possible."

Dennis stopped and rounded on him again. "It's possible," he said, "that you've finally gone over the rim. Now, shut it or I'm telling you . . ." He looked down and unclenched his fist. "Aw, fuck it. I've got work to do."

Spence let him go and watched him stride back into the building. The glass door swung back behind him, reflecting the trees and the white sky behind him.

Every time he drove across it, the vibrations in the metal structure of the Walter Dale Bridge made his artificial hip ache. Spence could have guessed that Dennis would react like this. The newspapers and the police were even less likely to believe him. In the eyes of the world he was at best a drunkard, at worst a harmless lunatic.

Maybe Dennis was right. Maybe they were all right. Spence could no longer tell, and the only positive proof lay at the bottom of a fifteen-thousand-foot hole on the other side of the world. Short of waiting to see if Norco tried to murder him, there was no way he could ever discover the truth without going back to Madagascar.

He pulled into the little park in front of the Legislature building and cut the engine, looking out over River Park, over the Teamsmans' sports center and the water-purification plant. To his left the glass and steel of the new convention center went tumbling down the hill. It was a crazy piece of architecture, but you had to admit that the designer had balls.

Spence thought. In the past, risk taking had got him into nothing but trouble. But equally he knew that the decisions he was certain to regret were the ones where he backed down for lack of courage. If you never go the full distance, you never know. If you never drill to the basement . . .

Every five or ten years there comes a time when you have to bet everything on your beliefs. And if you let those rare moments pass, your belief will remain untested, and you will remain forever uncertain of who you are. You will end up like those old guys in the basement of the legion hall, sitting at the red Formica tables, sipping soda from the fountain and waiting for their pacemakers to stop.

Spence leaned back in his seat, looking at the glass pyramids of the Muttart Conservatory and the eastern horizon beyond.

Kirk left Edmonton at midnight and drove out along Highway 63. The snowplow had been past recently. Fragments of gravel flicked against the bottom of the car, and the loose ammunition rattled in his glove compartment. He had brought cartridges for the Remington 306 that he knew Spence kept in the house. On the backseat he had a sheet of plastic to carry the body in. They'd told him to make it look like a suicide, but if things didn't go according to plan, then he might have to put him in the trunk of the car and dump him in the river.

He could see the white smoke from Dow Chemical against the black sky. He drove through Fort Saskatchewan and across

Highway 21, then out along the road to Spence's place.

Just beyond the poplar trees he pulled off the road. He put on his leather gloves, took a pocket flashlight from the passenger seat, then jogged back down the road to the mailbox.

Tire tracks led into the old barn that served as a garage. There were no lights in the windows. Kirk skirted around the house, hanging under the shadow of the trees. He watched for a full quarter of an hour until he was sure there was no one awake inside, then climbed up and disconnected the cable to the telephone lines. He'd been caught out once before when his quarry bolted himself in a back room and telephoned for help. Kirk had had to kick the door in and strangle the guy, but it had been a sweaty, nerve-racking business and he never wanted to go through it again.

He lowered himself back onto the ground and used his knife to slip the catch on the parlor window.

Inside, the house felt cold. On the wall of the hallway there was a hat rack made of elk antlers. His flashlight caught a picture of a cowboy in a pearl-buttoned shirt leaning against the slips at a rodeo. Kirk tested the door of the gun cupboard. It was unlocked. He took out the Remington, broke it, and loaded it.

The back room was empty. The front room too. Spence had to be upstairs.

Kirk milked the leather gloves tighter over his fingers and climbed the stairs. A wind stirred the chimes in the porch. He stood for a moment on the first-floor landing, breathing lightly, summoning his energy. The door to Spence's bedroom stood ajar. Kirk nudged it gently. It made no sound as he slipped inside.

The bed was made and some clothes were folded on top of it. Kirk saw a figure move in the door of the wardrobe. He had the gun raised to hip height before he realized there was no one there. Just his own reflection in the tarnished glass of the mirror.

Kirk lowered the gun. Then he closed the door softly, crossed the landing, and checked the spare room.

Empty.

He returned to Spence's bedroom, not bothering to move quietly now, and stood there for a moment or two thinking. There was something about the house. It didn't just feel unoccupied. It felt deserted.

Kirk went downstairs again, relocked the pantry window, and checked the fridge for food. It was switched off and defrosting. The rubbish bin was empty as well. He returned to the hall, unloaded the Remington, and put it back in the gun cupboard.

He left by the front door and walked down the snow-covered track. On the track that led into Spence's property he now noticed, under a light powdering of snow, three plastic rubbish sacks tied at the neck. He was contemplating these, when some lights appeared around the trees at the end of the track ahead of him.

The car slowed as it approached, then stopped alongside him. It was a blue and white Chevrolet Caprice with the emblem of the RCMP on the door. The policeman in the passenger seat shone a flashlight in his face.

"You got your ID, sir?"

"No, I'm a tourist here. I just called to see if my pal Spence was in."

"Is he?" The driver switched the light on inside the car. Both men were wearing beaver-skin hats and Gore-Tex parkas.

"No."

"Kind of late to be visiting," said the big man in the passenger seat.

Kirk blew on his hands. "He's a difficult man to get hold of."

"Where do you figure he's gone?"

"No idea. There's some rubbish down the way there. It

looks like he might have cleared off for a bit," Kirk said. "Why? Are you looking for him yourselves?"

The driver nodded, looking down the track at the darkened wooden house ahead.

"Is it serious?"

"It's in connection with a murder," the big man said. He looked like someone who was having a bad evening.

"Murder. Jesus."

"Have you got a car, sir?"

"It's parked just off the road." Kirk waved a hand in the direction of the poplar trees. "I didn't want to risk the ice here."

The policeman in the passenger seat nodded, turned off his flashlight, and rolled up the window, then the police car moved away.

Kirk walked on toward the moonlit road. Looking back, he could see, through the poplar trees, the flashlights of the two policemen playing on the frosted cladding of the house.

At eight the next morning Kirk went down to the gym for his daily workout. Typically there was some flabby executive hogging the Nautilus, so Kirk did fifty push-ups on his fingertips, then hammered out his aggression on the punching bag. He'd done twenty-five pull-ups on the wallbars and just about succeeded in shaming the other man into leaving, when a youth in a hotel tracksuit came in carrying a telephone.

"Call for you, long-distance."

"I'll take it outside."

On the rare occasions that they called him directly, Kirk would try to pin a face to the voice on the other end of the phone. There was no identifiable accent, and he could never hit on the age of the speaker. For some reason he'd formed a picture of a pale man with thick, wet lips and pebble glasses. The man was ex-army—he could tell that from the accent. There was another quality to the voice, a sort of dampness to one of the vowel sounds that suggested some illness or injury to his throat.

Kirk said. "So what's the plan, mate?"

"We'd like you to return home."

"So the job's off."

The voice said, "You will be contacted with further instructions." The voice always spoke in these officious, rather formal constructions. Ex-army, or ex-police.

"You mean he's left the country?"

"Message ends," the voice said.

"Message ends to you, too, mate." Kirk put the phone down and wiped the sweat off the receiver with the end of his towel. They'd lost Spence.

Chapter 25

There was a half-hour connecting flight to France, then a three-hour delay at Orly. The departures hall was full of Madagascar residents returning home for Christmas with their booty of car tires, microwave ovens, food mixers, and hi-fi sets. Spence waited in the bar for an hour, then checked in for the second leg of the journey.

In the airless clamor of the customs hall at Antananarivo, he labored through the formalities of money declaration, endless forms to be filled in triplicate on fragile, off-white paper. On the wall in front of him was a mosaic showing the country's progress since independence. The plaster they had used was of such inferior quality that large parts of it were blistering and peeling off. The floor under the wooden tables was littered with painted fragments: a combine harvester, a nurse, a group of peasant farmers. Over one of the gaps in the mural was plastered a picture of a handsome man in collar and tie with carefully trimmed moustache, clear eyes, hair receding from a widow's peak. The caption read, VIVE ISTASSE. VIVE LE PLAN DE DIX ANS.

There was a wooden bench by the lakeside, across the road from the Antananarivo Hilton. Beside it, under the jacaranda trees, shadowy figures were selling food and nursing infants. The smell of roast peanuts and hair oil mingled with the corrupted smell of the water. There were preelection banners strung across the road, and from some distant part of town there came the noise of shouting and drumbeats.

Spence angled his watch to the light. They'd agreed to meet at nine P.M., and Velo-André was already half an hour late. Over the phone the minister had sounded distracted and suspicious. Spence wondered now why Velo-André had specified this place, rather than somewhere more respectable, like the Hilton bar. It occurred to him that the African might have been fobbing him off or—worse still—setting him up.

A gang of local youths came strolling along the darkened lakeside path. Spence remembered Hanssen's story of the American who was mugged in the capital. He was thinking of crossing to the lighted side of the street, when a black car pulled up by the curbside and Velo-André got out.

Spence seized his walking stick and stood up to greet him, but Velo-André either didn't see, or didn't choose to accept, the handshake.

"I'd almost decided you weren't going to turn up," Spence said.

"I almost was not, but I was curious."

"About what I told you on the phone?"

"About you," said Velo firmly. "Shall we walk?"

He headed off briskly, and Spence tried to keep pace beside him. On benches, set at intervals along the cinder path, illicit lovers clung to each other in the velvet night.

"I was in contact with Charles Hunter. He told me you had some psychological problems, that you were *alcoolique . . .*"

"Did he tell you about that drilling log I found?"

"The one you have tried to steal? Yes, he told me also that this log was . . ." Velo groped for a word in the dark, pungent air. *"Fabrique . . . artificiel . . ."*

"I think Hunter's a crook."

"A what?"

"A villain, a bad man."

"And he thinks you are the same."

"So it's my word against his."

"Not exactly. Mr. Hunter has invested a large amount of money in this country. He is a respected businessman. I have known him for longer time than I have known you, Mr. Spence."

"You said once that you didn't trust him."

"Well." Velo-André shrugged. "In this business that is the problem. Nothing is certain. We can only guess if there is oil here or there, if it will make us rich or poor, if our advisers are *digne de notre confiance* . . . so many guesses. And nothing to guide us. There is a principle in physics called the uncertainty principle of Heisenberg, which states, I believe, that in certain complex experiments one part of our calculations will always be wrong. In politics also that is a universal law: perhaps one day it will be regarded as the only universal law. What do you think, Mr. Spence?"

"I don't know anything about physics, Velo, but I know about oil. I think Hunter's trying to rip you off."

"Comment?"

"To swindle you."

"You keep saying this. You said this two months ago. Have you proof now?"

"No, but I can find it."

"How?"

"By going down to Mansalava. By setting up the rig again and drilling out the plug for you, to see what's really under there."

Velo-André laughed lightly at the absurdity of the idea. In the center of the lake one of the spotlights illuminating the Independence memorial had ceased to function, giving the sculpture a precarious, lopsided appearance. "How much did you imagine I would pay you for this service?"

"I don't want to be paid."

"Everyone wants to be paid, Mr. Spence. I have been a

politician for only some years, but, in that time, I have learned
that . . . how does it go . . . 'There is no such thing as the free
dinner.'"

"There's no such thing as a free lunch."

"Lunch. Exactly."

Farther along the path an old woman was frying eels in a
tin can. Spence said, "If I were looking for a free meal, Velo,
this country is the last place I'd come to. I'm not doing this for
money. I had a lot of friends in that plane crash."

"Revenge is not a very reliable motive."

Spence said, "Also, I need to prove that I'm not going
crazy."

"I would say that, as a motive, that was less reliable still."

"I guess," said Spence. "But if I'm right, Velo, your government is sitting on a gold mine."

"We are not sitting on it. We have abandoned it. Norco
also. If it had value, why would they allow that?"

"I don't know."

"Moi non plus."

They were approaching the stretch of road that ran along
the bottom of the palace grounds. Far above them, on the pink,
crenellated battlements, a guard leaned on his rifle and lit a
cigarette.

"Consider this also," said Velo-André. "Elections in less
than one month. Even if you were correct about Norco, it was
my government that invited them into the country. Now is not
the time to denounce them. If you are wrong, we will upset
one of our foreign allies."

"No one needs to know about it."

"Now you are talking about espionage."

"I can have that rig up and the well drilled in just over two
weeks. You know what communications are like over here.
Half the time you can't even make a phone call from Belo, and
there's no one living within miles of the rig. I could drill out
the plugs, and no one would be any the wiser."

"And the money for this operation?"

"I'll pay for it."

"Then you must be richer than I thought. Did you not tell me one time that my country could not afford to drill oil wells alone?"

"We're not talking about drilling an oil well, we're talking about taking out a cement plug. All I need are a couple of old drilling bits, a few sacks of mud, and a thousand feet of pipe. We've got all that in containers on the site. I can afford to pay the laborers. From what I remember, there's about a dozen guys on Morondava main street fucking the dog all day."

"Doing what?"

"Nothing—wasting their time."

"Fucking the dog?"

Spence laughed. "It's a Canadian expression, Velo—I wouldn't use it in polite company."

"Am I not polite company?"

Spence turned toward him and noticed, by the light of the palace floodlights, that he was smiling. "I know it's a long shot, Velo, and I know you feel I betrayed you, but you've got to let me do this thing. What have you got to lose? Everyone's saying you're going to lose these elections. I'm giving you a last chance maybe to turn this thing around."

"No. You are asking me to risk a diplomatic catastrophe," Velo-André said. "You must appreciate my position, Mr. Spence. I am still a government minister. I cannot endorse the theft of foreign property."

"We're not stealing anything, we're just borrowing Norco's rig."

Velo-André glanced nervously toward the palace. "Please don't say 'we.' I cannot associate myself with this."

"You can't?"

"Absolutely not."

Spence leaned heavily on his stick. Without Velo-André's implicit support, the job would have been risky. With his explicit disapproval, it was more or less impossible.

"You sure you mean that?"

"Quite sure."

A black silence fell over them. Spence prodded at the path with the end of his stick. "So what are you going to do now—deport me?"

"No. This is still, thank God, a free country. You are free to spend time here."

In the darkness he couldn't see Velo-André's eyes.

"Spend time?"

"You are free, I mean, to go where you like and get involved in whatever illegal activity pleases you. That is what democracy means."

A car's headlights swept briefly over them. Spence had imagined Velo-André to be smiling. In fact he looked solemn and rather worried.

Spence said, "You're a good guy, Velo."

"Please. You don't know me. We met only once—three months ago."

"I hear you."

"But this time . . . "

"Yes?"

"If you find oil, you will let me know."

"For sure."

"Au revoir," said Velo-André softly, *"et bonne chance,"* he added as he slipped into the shadows. When Spence next saw him, he was on the other side of the road. A guard saluted as Velo-André hurried through the palace gates.

Spence sat in a window seat on the flight to Morondava. The rains had left a patina, like verdigris, on the dun hills below. Spence watched the landscape unfolding and thought of Perpetude.

He had noticed some boxes for the Grand Hotel being loaded at Antananarivo Airport and wondered if she would come herself to collect them from the airstrip. He hadn't tried to phone. He knew from past experience that it would take him two hours to get a connection to the coast, and, even with a clear connection, he never felt confident with words. If anything still existed between them, he would know when he met her.

From the air he saw her vehicle parked by the airstrip.

Spence ducked out of the plane. His ears were still blocked from the flight, and the impairment of his hearing gave him a vague sense of dissociation as he walked toward the jeep. In the small crowd of African faces there were one or two who seemed to recognize him. No sign of Perpetude. The air was cooler and the surrounding foliage denser than he remembered it.

He reached her jeep, immediately recalling the details that made it personal and intimate to her—the dents in the offside door, the cracked wing mirror, the ancient triangular windscreen sticker for some long-defunct French touring organization, and the collection of dust and dead insects that gathered between the dash and the windscreen.

"Excuse?"

Spence turned. It was Didier, the barman from the Villa Touristique.

"Mr. Spence. Ya! Welcome. You are come back."

"That's how it seems. Are you collecting someone?"

"Just picking up some stuff. Perpetude will be sorry to have missed you."

"She's not here?"

"No. In France. She is visiting some family."

"Oh."

"The Honda's *en panne,* so I borrowed her jeep. Let me load up these things for the hotel. Are you staying for long?"

"Just a couple of weeks," Spence said vaguely. He shielded his face against the glare off the airstrip. Suddenly it seemed like a barren, uninteresting place. "Is Morgan Hanssen still here?"

Didier laughed. "Oh, yes. Hanssen's here. Hanssen will die here."

★   ★   ★

As Spence approached, the turkey outside Morgan Hanssen's
house rose to its feet and stalked off underneath the defunct
tractor, making a noise like a carpet beater. The bungalow was
painted yellow, with faded green shutters and doors. The sandy
yard, shaded by a single tamarind tree, had been raked and
brushed clean.

Spence knocked on the door. Beside the tamarind tree there
was rice laid out to dry on a raffia mat. Inside the chipped
doorway there was no sign of life.

"Hanssen?" Spence stepped over the threshold into the
cool, tiled interior. The furniture was carved in local wood to
a vaguely Danish design. Printed sarongs served for curtains.
There was a cluster of empty beer bottles on the table.

A board creaked. A sultry wind was blowing up from the
river estuary, rattling the blinds. Spence looked down and found
a cat threading itself between his legs. He walked through to
the living room. A double mattress was laid out in the center
of the floor, and there, asleep in the plump arms of his cook,
lay Morgan Hanssen.

The cook awoke first, drawing the sheet around herself
and nudging Hanssen awake.

"Who's that?"

Spence walked forward into the brighter light from the
veranda doors. "How's it going, Morgan?"

"Ha. Spence. Whaddaya know. Ha. What the hell are you
doing here?"

"It's a long story."

"That's goot. I like stories." Hanssen scratched under his
arms and rubbed his face. The hair was sticking out from his
temples like two furry horns. "What time is it?"

"Two o'clock. I figured you'd be home from the sugar
factory for lunch."

"No, I don't come back for lunch now, and I don't go to
work. That young fellow finally took over. Now I yoost grow
bananas and keep my head down." Hanssen cackled and slapped

his cook's generous rump. "This is my lunch now. Ha."

She scowled at him and said something in dialect. Hanssen pouted and adjusted the knot of his sarong. "She's angry with me now. Let's go outside."

On the veranda, under a trellis overhung with vines, Spence lowered himself into one of the slatted teak armchairs. There was a big Calor-gas fridge standing outside the back door, from which Hanssen took two bottles of Zebu beer. The slope from the house down to the river had been planted with papayas and banana trees.

"You know Pappatoot's not in town," he said.

"I heard she was in France."

"She'll be back in three or four weeks. You should have told her you were coming."

"She wasn't the reason I came back."

"How d'you know that? She might have been, you never know."

In the heavy peace of the tropical afternoon, Spence looked at his beer and pondered this remark. At the river's edge, cattle waded knee-deep in lilies.

"So what about this story you promised me?" asked Morgan Hanssen, and slowly, like a man unfamiliar with the parts attempting to reassemble a complex machine, Spence told the story of the rig. He talked about Father Mitchell and the rediscovered drilling log, about Velo-André and Dennis. He talked about Cora and Skippy and the plane crash and Cora's death. He talked about Hunter and his own abortive trip to London. At times he wondered if Hanssen was really listening, but when he finished, the old Dane cackled and wiped the beer from his chin and said, "So now what you telling me? You're planning to hijack the rig?"

"I guess so."

"Sounds to me as though you could upset a lot of people."

"Maybe."

"Hell of a big job for one man too."

"That's true."

Hanssen rocked back on his chair and looked at the woven screen above them. A gecko was stalking a butterfly twice its size, advancing centimeter by centimeter on delicate, padded feet.

"Smoke?"

"No thanks."

Hanssen rolled himself a cigarette, working the tobacco between his short, broad fingers and chuckling softly to himself. "I never worked on an oil rig before."

"You can run a crane and a digger," said Spence, "and you speak the language. There's got to be a dozen locals around here who used to work for McCabe. We take two pickups and head up there, we'd be finished inside three weeks."

"That's a long time to spend up-country."

"You could come back now and again. There would be two or three periods when I wouldn't need you."

"Ha, you got it all worked out."

"I'll pay you double what Norco was paying you, Morgan."

"Well, that's twice fuck-all." He ran his tongue along the cigarette paper. "Anyway I don't need money yoost now."

"Well, you're going to eventually. If we found oil here, there'd be work here for the rest of your life."

"And if we don't?"

"If we don't, we don't."

Morgan lit his cigarette and picked tobacco off his tongue. "I'll tell you what happens if we don't. If we don't, we both go to prison. So far it seems they've forgotten about my visa, but if I get in trouble now, they'd probably deport me. Then where'm I going to go?"

"I guess that's the risk you take."

"Me! I don't have to take any risks at all. I'm happy yoost keeping my head down."

At the bottom of the slope some local children, sleek as

otters, were diving off the wreck of an old riverboat. Their shrieks wafted up on the hot breeze. Hanssen settled into the chair and leaned his head back. Sunburned and disheveled, he seemed completely at home in both the house and the landscape.

Spence said, "You're right, Morgan. I can't expect you to help me, but I'm committed to this thing now, so if you change your mind, I'd surely appreciate—"

"What do you mean, change it? I've not made it up yet."

There was a scuffle above their heads, and a large brown and red wing floated down to the table. Under the canopy the gecko had the moth in its toothless jaws.

"Holy shit," said Spence.

"You call that a goot omen or a bad one?" Hanssen asked.

"Don't know. If I were a butterfly, it would scare the shit out of me."

"Ha," said Hanssen. "You're like me, you ain't a butterfly and that's a fact."

"Must be a good omen, then."

"Must be." Hanssen walked over to the gas fridge and took out two more beers. "Ach, what the hell," he said, opening them. "Let's do it. I kept my nose clean too long anyway."

"You mean it, Morgan?"

"Once I drink this, I'll mean it."

"When can we leave?"

"You in much of a hurry?"

"Some."

"Okay. Have another beer, then we'll go down main street and round up some fellows for tomorrow."

"You think they'll come at such short notice?"

"Oh, shit, yeah. The volleyball season's finished."

Chapter 26

They arrived in the clearing at Mansalava at four o'clock the following afternoon. Over the past three months the jungle had begun to thread itself through the girders of the rig and to break like a wave over the back of the accommodation trailers.

Spence turned and looked back. Climbing down from the back of the second pickup, the men he'd hired looked like the members of a renegade army. Many of them still wore, as a sort of badge of office, some part of the Western outfits they'd once been given by Norco or McCabe's: faded overalls cut off at the knee, Western T-shirts advertising Coca-Cola and Ferodo brake linings, and an assortment of headbands, native jewelry and baseball caps—incongruous souvenirs of Halliburton Well Services and Moosehead beer. Three of the men had work boots; the rest wore thong sandals or went barefoot.

After lunch Hanssen put the guards to work hacking the vines and creepers off the rig machinery. As evening fell, Spence paced up and down the site, measuring it off and marking it out with roughly fashioned wooden staves. He had no blueprint to work from, nor did he need one. The standard layout of these rigs had, over many years, been imprinted on his memory, and it pleased him to find it was still clear in his mind. As they pushed back the tendrils that had obliterated the site, he found trenches, drainage ditches, and the depressions left by heavy machinery.

One of the local men had been trained to drive the bull-dozer. On the second day Spence put him to work pushing earth out of the mud and water pits. Spence started up the mechanical digger and dug around the marker pole in the center of the site. After two or three hours he was getting into the swing of it, using both steering levers and both foot pedals simultaneously, losing the jerky robotic movements of the arm and combining the whole movement—lower, scoop, sweep—into a single fluid action. When he'd dug to three feet, the marker pole fell over, and they dragged it out. At twelve feet he hit the well head. Digging around this sunken core, he reex-cavated the moon pool—the circular pit over which the rig would be built.

Later he sat with Hanssen by the trailers guzzling water.

"Don't look like much, do it?" Hanssen said. "Two days' work, all we got is some holes in the ground."

Spence refilled the tin mug and drank. "She'll come."

In the morning Hanssen coaxed one of the Kenworth trucks back into life, and they winched the timber matting onto the back of it. By the evening they were laying out these slabs of steel-bound timber, four yards by six and the thickness of rail-way sleepers, which would form a level platform for the rig.

Along the edge of the clearing Hanssen's men climbed over the rig machinery, greasing, oiling, and tightening bolts.

On the third day Spence took over driving the Kenworth truck and hauled in the two main "subs." These heavy steel frames, each thirty feet high, were shunted onto the matting on either side of the moon pool to form the rig's substructure. The mas-sive spreader bars were positioned and secured, making a solid square base for the rig, the A-legs were hauled upright and bolted in place. They were assembled when the sun set, standing three stories high in the center of the clearing, the feet of the colossus.

He found Hanssen back at the trailers. The old man was clutching the small of his back.

"You okay, Morgan?"

"Shit, yes."

Hanssen looked around the rig site. They had started hauling some of the large machinery into position, and now it lay strewn around every corner of the lease, as though some giant child had emptied out his toybox and left them to tidy up the mess. "Two weeks, you think?"

"Give or take."

"You mean if it don't kill us first?"

In London Hunter stood in his office scowling down at the Embankment, with the receiver tucked under his chin. The time difference gave him only two short windows in which he could put private calls through to Madagascar. He'd been trying to get hold of Claude Istasse for most of the week, but each time he phoned, he'd been told that Istasse was unavailable—visiting one of the provinces on his final preelection campaign. Hunter listened to the phone ringing and flipped a pen between his fingers.

Killing the Skipton woman had been a serious blunder. It may have been all Spence needed to convince him he was right all along. It was highly unlikely that the Canadian had headed back to Madagascar, but it was a possibility Hunter desperately needed to rule out.

The phone continued to ring. He was on the point of replacing the receiver when a voice said, *"Oui, Istasse."*

While the government in power made use of the country's outdated telephone exchange, Istasse had his home connected to the military satellite link. His voice was clear and precise.

"Istasse. This is Charles Hunter."

"Charles." He spoke near-perfect English with a slight American twang. "How is everything?"

"I have a minor problem."

"I'm sorry to hear that."

"The Canadian I told you about. We've lost touch with him for now."

"I see," Istasse said. "How can I help?"

"It occurred to me that he may have visited your country again. I wonder if you could check with immigration."

"I'll do that." Istasse chose his words carefully. "But you know it would be inadvisable for anyone here to deal with the problem."

It had always been Istasse's policy to keep his hands clean. It suited Hunter to keep it that way. A mercenary like Kirk could be relied on for confidentiality. He couldn't be linked to either of them, and furthermore, he could be eliminated at a stroke if things went wrong.

"You don't need to bother about anything else," Hunter said. "If our Canadian is in the country, I'll send my own man over to find him."

"You may have a problem. Madagascar is a big place."

"We know his contacts over there," Hunter said. "It shouldn't be too difficult to trace him."

It took two more days to correctly position the mud tanks and the heavy equipment, hauling them up onto the flatbed, then lowering them back into place. Creaking over the tailgate of the Kenworth came machines the size of small houses: the draw-works and pumps, the generators and fuel tanks. Four of the local men were appointed to push and swing these machines into place, while Hanssen operated the winch.

Even without Hanssen pointing them out, Spence could now recognize the men who'd worked on the rig before. The new men ran about wildly, scattering if the huge containers swung too near and trying to pull on the guide lines as the steel was pulling away. The experienced hands worked in close, using the momentum of the load to bring it into alignment. From these men Spence learned the vocabulary of about thirty words that had evolved from the Norco job—"stand by," "okay," "come here," "stop," *"malak-malak,"* *"vita,"* "no fucking good," "same-same," *"beaucoup,"* *"petite"*—a composite argot of French, English, and local dialect.

The derrick—the tower of the rig—was assembled horizontally from great hinges on the drilling platform, ready to be winched upright. They began to put it together on the fifth day, starting at the A-legs and building the twenty-foot L-shaped sections outward toward the jungle's edge. Spence brought in the crane, balancing each section on the ten-foot-high trestles, then inching them together till the holes married. Then the supporting trestle was moved along and the next part swung into place. Slowly the vast latticework stretched across the clearing, men working inside and over it like ants, knocking in the securing pins with sledgehammers. This was what Spence had been born to—the growl of the diesels, the ring of steel on steel, the mesh of girders swarming with workers. A shouted command, a cable tensing, a sledgehammer thrown in a lazy arc across the sky, a wave, the slings dropping to the ground, and the crane hook swinging free. They worked from dawn till noon, broke for an hour, and worked again till sunset, when the mosquitoes began to bite.

Showered, Spence lay in the hammock he'd rigged outside the accommodation trailers, listening to the sounds from the jungle and the laughter of the rig hands around the camp fire. A big night bird flapped across the square of sky above the darkening clearing. Hanssen took out a pocketknife and started paring his toenails by the light of the hurricane lamp.

"So how did you get here in the first place, Morgan?"

"Where, here? Morondava? Same way as you. By accident."

"It's a long way from Sweden."

"Denmark, Denmark, I was born in Denmark," Hanssen said. "My mother die when I was four years old." He slapped an insect on his neck and laughed. "Shit, that was sure as hell a long time ago."

"Where in Denmark?"

"East coast. Near Fredericia. We lived in this fancy house on a nice green slope above the town—thirty-two-acre patch. My father bought it for five cents a square meter and then he sell those square meters for twenty and move into town. I preferred it when we had the land. So I run off to sea when I was fourteen. Wanted to go to your place—America."

"Canada."

"Canada, America. What's the difference? Anyway, I got the wrong boat and ended up in Singapore."

"I've been to Singapore," Spence said.

"They wouldn't let me off, so I decided to stay in the navy. Got bombed de next year by some damn Korean, just for minding my own business. That's where I got this." Hanssen turned sideways and showed off a knotted white scar down one side of his belly. "Piece of three-inch pipe went straight through there. Lost my spleen and kidney. Yup." Hanssen put down the knife and stretched back in the canvas chair. "Twenny year in the navy after that. British merchant ships—that's where I learned English. I finally quit in Australee. You ever been to Australee?"

"Sure."

"Hell of a place," Hanssen said. "Married a shopkeeper and started up a trucking company. 'Nother fifteen year I made real goot money. Then the recession come and everything go wrong at once. Wife diet of meningitis, company went bankrupt, and my partner run off with half a million dollar. Paid some city-slick lawyer everything I had to sort out that bullshit. Spent my fiftieth birthday with some old ginny in a shack outside Darwin. Six months afore I'd been making twenty thousand dollar a year."

The hammock rocked him gently. "Yes, that's the way she goes," said Spence.

"No, sir, that's not the way she go. That's the way she went. You never know how she going to go, you only know how she went." Morgan Hanssen cackled to himself in the darkness. "No, sir, that's not the way she goes . . . "

"So what happened?"

"Nothing happened. I packed up and left. I was too old to go back in the navy, but a friend of mine gave me a job as second engineer, one-way to Madagascar. We land here in Morondava, and I thought, 'This is the place for me.' Got myself a job in the sugar factory, and I've been here ever since. That's the way she goes. And I'll tell you a funny thing. It didn't strike me till afterward. Then I realize. It was yoost the same as Denmark."

"Where, here?"

"That place of mine on the riffer in Morondava. Yoost exactly the same. Dead flat. Little slope above the town. The riffer. Little wooden schoolhouse. Like my father's thirty-two-acre patch yoost got lifted up and moved here. Like it's been waiting for me all this time. Like I've been fifty years traffeling all around the world yoost looking to find that place again, where I was happy when I was a kid. I guess a lot of people do that, hey? You still awake . . . Spence."

Chapter 27

On such brilliant spring days Edinburgh always looked her best. A northern sun hung over the monuments on Carlton Hill, dazzling Kirk as he walked eastward down Princes Street. It was a morning of Hellenic clarity. On the other side of the gardens he could see, razor sharp, each crag and crevice of the castle rock. Half a mile in front of him the Scot monument was a bayonet against the pale sky.

Kirk made his way down Princes Street toward the central post office. The agreed waiting period was almost up, and still there was no word from his handlers. Either they'd been having trouble tracking the man Spence down, or else they'd decided not to bother pursuing him. Either way Kirk would be glad of some news. He crossed to the south side of the street, where the pavements were less congested with Saturday-morning shoppers. At the side of the art gallery the self-appointed pundits were declaiming on religion and politics. Sprigs of greenery sprinkled the black branches of the chestnut trees, and the ice-cream vans had returned with the warmer weather. Pigeons were being lured off the railings with bags of corn. They scattered as Kirk walked through them, his head down, his hands in the pockets of his tan leather jacket.

At the central post office he asked for the key to his post office box and was led down into the vaults. The buff envelope he found there was thicker than usual, and, untypically, it contained an air ticket for a flight leaving the following morning. Kirk wondered what the rush was for.

He looked at the destination and pulled on his lower lip. Madagascar again.

When the final section of the derrick was pinned into place, Spence gave Hanssen the job of stripping down the mud pumps, while he had the catwalk drawn under the derrick. It took both the cranes to position the traveling block. Then they began the laborious job of threading the guideline through the block and up around the crown. By eleven o'clock he was ready to winch the main drilling cable through the pulley system.

With the cable threaded through, he walked the length of the derrick, squinting up at the joints between every section, checking that the securing pins had been hammered through and fixed. The loops of steel cable from the crown to the traveling block sagged under their own weight, almost touching the ground at the center of the derrick. Spence climbed up the metal ladders to the drilling platform and checked the traveling block—a massive block and tackle the size of a small car. Normally it would carry lengths of pipe up and down the derrick, but now it was secured to the drilling floor. The derrick lay horizontal, hinged at its junction with the substructure, so that when the cables tightened, it would pull itself upright.

The bridle lines were attached. The safety lines to the crown were in place. Spence fired up the generators and heard the colossal electric motor of the draw-works wake from its long slumber. The six-foot-diameter spool of steel cable began to unwind onto it. The cable started moving off its wooden spool, two hundred feet along the derrick to its crown, then back to the traveling block and back to the crown, then back to the traveling block and back to the crown. When he had enough to spare at the foot of the derrick, he put one and a half wraps on the main drum and had the laborers bolt the free end to the dead-man inside the A-legs.

Spence slipped the clutch. Deafened by the machinery and

dwarfed by the draw-works, he saw the steel ropes take the strain. It always seemed to him impossible that these slender inch-thick cables could raise the monster.

He walked along the catwalk to check them one final time, and his heart sank.

Spence returned to the drilling platform, switched off the engines, and shouted to one of the rig hands to switch off the main generator.

He was leaning against the railings, unwrapping a piece of gum, when Hanssen hauled himself up the metal ladder to stand beside him.

"What's the problem?"

"I got a line crossed."

"What kind of a line?"

"One of those steel cables to pull up the derrick. They're supposed to all run parallel. I got one of them crossed."

"Is that so bad?"

"It's a basic mistake. I shouldn't have been hurrying so much."

Hanssen stepped to one side and looked down the line of the derrick. "Can't you yoost leave it?"

"Nope. When we come to lowering the pipe down the hole, this old block here will be shooting and down all day. You got one of them crossed, she'll wear through in no time."

"So what you going to do?"

Spence put the gum in his mouth. The African laborers had wandered out onto the lease to sit in the shade of the machinery. They were getting tired. "Undo the whole line and string her up again."

"Will that take long?"

"A day."

"So," Hanssen said. "What's a day?"

Spence looked at the date on his watch. He was already running late. A day could mean everything.

"Anyway. Lunch is ready," Hanssen said.

"Go ahead. I ain't hungry."

While the laborers ate, he put the engine in reverse and unwound the draw-works. When the men finished eating, he rewound the drilling line onto the spool, and the whole sequence started again.

Hanssen found him at nightfall standing on the sub by lamplight, tightening the bolts on the dead-man.

"You got her finished?"

"Just about."

"You going to raise her now?"

"Too dark. We'll do it tomorrow."

"Then we ready to drill?"

"Hell, no." Spence rubbed a hand over the knotted muscles at the base of his neck. "We still got all the small stuff to do: rigging the floor, putting in the walkways, fixing the electrics—there's about a hundred power lines to be laid out and connected."

"Ha." Hanssen surveyed the rig site, still littered with the dark shapes of machinery and metalware. "There's more to this shit than it looked."

Spence gave the bolt a final turn and climbed down. A million insects were batting against the glass of the lamp. His fingernails were chipped and torn. He picked slivers of metal out of the black ingrained ball of his thumb and wondered if all the effort he was expending would prove just as futile.

In the morning, as dawn broke, Spence was limping around the lease like a cantankerous ship's captain on the eve of departure, checking cables, testing nuts. The mist above the trees was tinged with pink. Spence climbed onto the drilling platform and restarted the electric motor of the main winch. Like a giant stretching, the cables tensed, the huge joints of the derrick creaked and cracked, the engines thundered through the cool morning air, and, by degrees, the crown of the derrick lifted off its trestle. A spontaneous cheer came up from the laborers

as the derrick lifted higher and higher into the pastel sky—a
Gulliver, dragging twenty slender wires.

He eased the clutch, spooled in the last few feet of line; the
derrick teetered on its great creaking ankles, then stamped its
steel feet down onto the sub. Spence took a sledgehammer and
knocked in the securing pins himself. He disconnected the traveling block from the sub, then engaged the clutch. The generators belched smoke, sparks whirled in the guts of the winding
machinery, the steel ropes twanged and grated, and the traveling
block went thundering up and down the inside of the derrick.
It was working. Spence hopped down the ladder from the drilling floor, taking his weight on his arms and jumping down the
rungs with his good leg. The thing was working. He was finally
getting somewhere. He took his stick and walked out the far
side of the lease, then looked back at the rig.

Hanssen was winching the shale shaker onto the back of
one of the Kenworth trucks. When Spence approached, he cut
the engine and leaned out of the window. His face was speckled
with mud and oil, but he was smiling.

"You happy now?"

"Just checking she's vertical," Spence said. "Can you move
these mud tanks, Morgan? There should be a cement fixing to
attach the geronimo line somewhere around here."

"What's the geronimo line?"

"Dieudonné's bringing it."

Farther back, by the mud pits, a rig hand in a baseball cap
and tattered green overalls was struggling across the clearing
toward them. The wire he was pulling over his shoulder was
attached to a tiny platform near the top of the derrick. Hanssen
shaded his eyes against the sun and followed the long loop of
wire up toward it.

"What's it for?"

"It's an emergency escape. If you're stuck up there on the
monkey board and the rig catches fire, it's so you can get back
down. You sling a harness over the geronimo line, then slide
down to the ground."

Hanssen laughed. "I don't know what you're saying all this 'you' for. You're not going to get me climbing up there."

"I hope we won't need anyone up there. If they're no problems, we can do it all from the drilling platform. It's only when you're tripping pipe back out of the hole that you need someone up the derrick."

"You mean what, if you need a new drill bit?"

"Or if the pipe gets stuck."

"Does that happen a lot?"

"It happens enough."

Dieudonné, the rig hand, was approaching, turning now and walking backward, still hauling on the wire. Spence headed off across the corner of the lease to inspect the alignment of the rig from another angle.

Chapter 28

Kirk sat in the conservatory at the back of the Antananarivo Hilton, drinking black coffee and leafing through the *Herald Tribune*. His contact turned up ten minutes early—he was a man in his mid-twenties with a sharp face and strangely pointed ears. He pulled up a chair, sitting with his back to the bamboo-paneled wall, framed by climbing plants.

"Mr. Kirk."

"That's me."

"Can I see your passport?"

Kirk pushed his passport across the table. "I had shorter hair then." Kirk took his passport back, glimpsing briefly at the photograph. The army haircut, the thin tie, the unlined face. He folded it and put it in his pocket. "Have you got something for me?"

The other man reached into his bag and passed over a thin folder containing maps, car-hire details, and airline addresses. It was the kind of information any tourist might receive.

"Is this all?"

"That is what I was given."

"Where do I pick up the gun?"

"There is no gun."

"No gun."

The waitress came. Marcel Antansoa declined to order. When she left, he said, "Handguns are illegal in this country."

"Bugger illegal. I thought you guys were supposed to be helping me," Kirk said.

"No one is helping you, Mr. Kirk. Politically this is a sensitive moment in our country."

"I thought that's why I was here."

"No, you are working for a private concern."

"A private concern. So what about transport?" he asked.

"The details are all here."

Kirk flicked disconsolately through his thin file of maps and tourist information. "You mean it's a do-it-yourself job."

"I was told that you had been here before."

"Jesus."

When he had flown down to the west coast in December, to clear out the rig trailers, Kirk had taken a charter to Maintirano, then hired a jeep. But he had no guarantee that either of these vehicles would still be available.

"So where's the man? Where's Spence?"

"Spence."

"Aye, Spence. Who I came here for. Don't tell me you've never heard of him."

"Oh, yes, I've heard of him," Marcel Antansoa said. "He gave me this." He touched the scar on his forehead. "I was sent to retrieve a document he had stolen."

"Hard man, is he?"

The other man fell silent. Some tourists had come in to look at the conservatory. Kirk waited till they had passed. Gun or no gun, Spence was a cripple. And on the face of it, there were only two places Spence was likely to have run to: Morondava or the rig site.

Kirk could cope. He could always cope. But he liked to feel he was working for people who had their act together. It occurred to him that his handlers seemed to have left him to wander out on a limb.

★ ★ ★

In the morning he took a taxi up to the airport. They turned right before they reached the terminal building and took the unsurfaced road that followed the perimeter fence. The road ended at a wire-mesh gate. Most of the brass letters had fallen off the sign, but their outlines remained visible on the bleached, painted board: CLUB AÉRONAUTIQUE D'ANTANANARIVO.

Beyond the gate there was grass growing between the concrete sections of the runway. To either side of the strip sat the rusting and cannibalized wrecks of small planes. To the right there was a modern prefabricated hangar with four serviceable airplanes standing outside it. A bearded man in shorts and knee socks was working on the engine of a Cessna four-seater.

"Hello, André?"

The man looked up from his work.

"Elgin Kirk." Kirk reminded him.

The bearded man held up his hands, gloved in dark engine oil. "Kirk. Yes. Excuse me when I do not greet you."

"You having problems?"

"Gaskets," André told him. "Not too serious."

He bent and changed the socket on his spanner. The tools were laid out on a piece of canvas in the small patch of shade under the airplane.

Kirk stole a look through the open door of the plane and noticed that the dashboard had been unscrewed.

"I came to ask if you could fly me down to Maintirano again. Looks as if you might be some time."

"Are you in a hurry?"

"A bit."

André fitted an extension to the socket and fed it deep into the guts of the engine. "Have you tried Air Mad?"

"They don't have any flights for a week."

André was still struggling with the seized nut. Kirk walked around the Cessna. Close up, the flimsiness of these small planes always worried him. This one had to be at least twenty-five

THE RIG   311

years old. It was made of riveted aluminum and painted brown and yellow. The leather cover on the air-speed probe was frayed and perished.

Kirk ducked under the other wing and stood there in the shade.

"So what about those other three planes?"

"Huh?" André looked up from his work.

"Those other planes outside the hangars. Who owns them?"

"Those? They are not for charter. Just this."

"Just this." Sun played on the stress cracks in the blue Perspex windscreen. "Come and see me tomorrow."

"Tomorrow?"

"Okay. I'll see you then," Kirk said. "You reckon she'll make it?"

"No problem."

No problem. Kirk took a final look at the brown and yellow plane and the tatty PVC upholstery. Oil was dripping out of the engine block and falling on the socket set. André was nothing if not an optimist.

At the rig the elation that had followed raising the derrick had been short-lived. Spence had spent the rest of that day trying to do three things at once: work out the correct order of the electrical cables, construct the walkways, and supervise the pinning together of the drilling platform. The first job on its own would have stretched him to the limit of his ability—circuitry was normally the province of the rig electrician. Unaccustomed to the color codings, Spence had to work out everything from the manual. He loathed these rubber cables with a passion—each was one or two inches thick, and, in addition to the mental exhaustion of figuring out where to place them, he was soon physically exhausted from lifting them to the board and back.

Meanwhile Hanssen kept requiring guidance on how to position the metal walkways over the mud tanks. In all there was about a mile of the stuff, and it had been stacked out of sequence. The sections were frustratingly similar but not quite similar enough to be interchangeable. In places the markings had scraped off, and Hanssen ended up on more than one occasion standing in his stained shorts and work boots among the massive iron jigsaw, cursing it in English and Danish.

Spence finished the electrical work on Tuesday. The next day he started rigging the drilling floor. He had dressed the pumps and changed the pistons and liners to accommodate five-inch pipe. The bore holes and down–hole pumps were back in service, and now the mud tanks were full of water. Spence stood above the caustic mixer, watching the laborers relay sacks of barite up the walkway and empty them into the agitators. Hanssen had been racking drill pipe all morning; now he came swinging up the metal steps and stood wiping his hands on the front of his shirt.

"What you doing now, then?"

"Mixing the mud."

"I'd have thought out here mud was the last thing you needed."

"We use it for the drilling. You pump it down the hole through the bit, and it washes all the fragments you drill out back up to the surface. It comes out here, shale shakers get rid of the chippings, then the mud goes back down here into the tanks."

Hanssen was still looking at the mud. "Looks as though it's going to be pretty thick."

"It's meant to be. If there's oil down there, then the weight of the mud is all that stops it from gushing out."

"So we're yoost about ready to drill, eh?"

"All I got to do is nipple up the stack and test the choke manifold."

Hanssen laughed. "I don't know what the hell you're talking about."

A laborer slit open another sack, and white plumes of dust blew back at them. Spence moved away, and Hanssen followed him along the metal catwalk above the steaming, churning mud, then up the second flight of steps toward the drilling platform.

"So what's for lunch, Morgan?"

"A handful of rice. We're joost about out of that too. One of the guards caught a lemur we could eat."

"Does it taste any good?"

"Depend how hungry you are."

On the drilling platform Spence cleaned his hands with Swarfega. The tall stands of drill pipe towered above him, ready to be swung across the drilling platform and fed down the hole in its center. Hanssen walked around the platform, swinging the heavy pipe tongs that hung on chains there, leaning back on the safety railing, looking down to the ground sixty feet below them, and peering up along the line of the flimsy metal ladder to the distant summit of the derrick.

"What's this?" He had found a leather harness on a wire, suspended from high in the derrick.

"Called a derrick climber. You strap it on when you climb up the ladder there. There's a weight comes down inside the derrick, counterbalances you if you fall."

"You're still saying that 'you.'"

Spence smiled. "Actually I was thinking, Morgan. Once I get to drilling, you might as well take some of these African guys back down to Morondava. They're just going to be getting in the way here. If we get rid of most guys except the drilling crew, we'll probably have enough food to last us."

"Suits me."

Spence wiped his hands on a rag. They were climbing down from the drilling platform, when a noise attracted their attention, and they looked up. Slightly to the left of the derrick a small plane had appeared in the sky. It flew high above them, finally disappearing behind the trees as the noise of its small engine faded.

★ ★ ★

Charles Hunter was sleeping when his wife, Nicola, nudged him awake.

"Charles."

"What is it?"

"The business line's ringing in your office."

Hunter opened his eyes. He could hear it now. He pushed the pillow to one side and stole a look at the glowing numerals of the clock.

"It's been ringing for two or three minutes now," she said. "I thought it would stop."

Hunter savored the warmth of the bed for another few seconds, then he pulled on his dressing gown and made his way down the stairs. There was a fault in one of the streetlamps beyond the front garden, and its orange light was flashing on and off, visible now through the glass panel above the front door.

In the hallway he unlocked his office door and picked up the phone.

"Yes?"

"Mr. Hunter?"

He had never met Kirk's handler, but he recognized the voice. The telephone number on which he left messages for him was somewhere in Surrey.

"Speaking."

"I have some urgent information," the damp voice said.

"Go ahead."

"Mr. Kirk surveyed the rig location as requested. He reports that he found it operational."

"The rig's running?"

"Affirmative."

Hunter was wide awake now. He'd imagined, at best, that Spence had simply gone to ground in Morondava, at worst that he was rampaging around the capital trying to bend the ear of Velo-André. This third alternative, that Spence had actually gone on the offensive, had barely seemed a real possibility.

"Hello?"

"Yes," Hunter said, "I'm still here."

"Do you have any further instructions?" the voice said.

"The instructions are the same," said Hunter. "Except obviously there's some urgency now."

He checked the Perspex calender on his desk. The quickest Spence could possibly have assembled the rig and redrilled the hole was twelve days, say ten days. If he'd left Canada on the day they lost touch with him, the longest head start he could possibly have was seven. They had at least seventy-two hours to stop him.

Nicola was still awake when he got back into bed. She turned toward him.

"Who was that?"

"Business," he said.

She was unsurprised. Hunter's overseas colleagues often miscalculated the time differences. She closed her eyes and turned away from him. Hunter lay on his back, looking at the ceiling. "I might have to go out to Madagascar a bit early," he said.

"Why's that?"

"You know Claude Istasse invited me to be his guest of honor for the elections."

"Have they changed the date?"

"No, but I might have to be there beforehand."

"Why?"

Hunter didn't reply.

"There's a flight on the fourteenth," he said.

"You'll miss the kid's half-term," she said as she drifted off to sleep.

Chapter 29

There was a mango tree in the center of Maintirano, and the ground around it was littered with the flat, fibrous seeds of the mango fruit. In one corner of the village square a man was binding up the car tires on his bullock cart with strips of inner tubing. Behind him, from the dark opening of the village forge, came the noise of a blacksmith hammering metal.

Kirk walked down the street that led to the river. The roads were of mud here, burnished smooth by feet and cart wheels, worn and cracked by the yearly rains. On the banks to either side the exposed and burnished roots of trees gripped the clay. He'd been in the village for three hours, long enough for André to refuel and head back to the capital. Long enough for Kirk, sweating in the local post office, to get a call through to his handler in Britain, but not yet long enough for the local people to lose interest in him. As he passed, men looked up from their games of dice, and women pulled aside the screens from the doorways of their mud and wattle houses. A gaggle of children followed wherever he went, laughing and scampering for cover whenever Kirk turned to look back at them. He remembered himself at that age, playing kick the can on Keir Hardie in Cumnock—those small-town days when every visitor was a celebrity.

The only four-wheel drive for hire in Maintirano was

owned by a local trader called Mani, a short, smiling Indian in
his mid-thirties. Kirk found him in the courtyard behind his
mud house, sitting in the afternoon sun, playing checkers with
two friends. His hair had been shaved and was now growing
back like a covering of emery paper on his oval skull.

He recognized Kirk from the Scotsman's original visit.
"Ah, my friend. Welcome."

Kirk drew up a carved stool. Chickens pecked the ground
underneath the table.

Mani said, "You are returned to pay respects."

"No. Business, really. I'm just here a day or so."

"Aee, always so short. You should come for longer, Mr.
Kirk."

"Maybe some other time."

Mani made his move on the checker board. The pieces
were small squares of glazed pottery. The board itself was red
and black, scored and grooved from countless games. "Were
you wishing to hire the jeep?"

"If it's possible."

The Indian shook his head. "It's not possible."

"Not possible."

Mani made another move and took three of his opponent's
pieces. He made a joke in dialect, then stood up, laughing, from
the table. "Come. Come," he said.

They walked out the back, through the shell of what had
once been a French colonial farmhouse. The gaps in the stone-
work allowed Kirk to see the outlines of ancient cornfields in
the brush along the river, now overgrown and replanted with
clumps of manioc and banana. Outside, by the side of the old
house, where it joined with the new, sat the wreckage of Mani's
Land-Rover. It had run into something head-on, and the electric
winch that had once sat on the front bumper had been driven
back through the radiator grille. Both front tires were flat, and
the front half of the chassis was bent, giving the headlights a
comical, cross-eyed appearance.

"My nephew," Mani explained. "A month ago he gets

drunk and takes it without asking. Even if we had the *pièces de rechange,* there's no one here who can fix it."

"Shit."

"Exactly, shit."

"So where else can I get a vehicle in Maintirano?"

Mani rubbed a hand over his skull. "Well. There are four vehicles in town. Mine. The police, the hospital clinic, and the chef de district."

"Where can I find the chef de district?"

"In fact, I should not say the chef de district. Chef de district's vehicle is all smashed up."

"Him too?"

"That's who my nephew hit."

"So what about the police vehicle?"

"I think they would never lend it."

"So what about the clinic?"

Mani shrugged. "If you have dollars, we can try."

Kirk looked at his watch. The afternoon was drawing to a close. "Can you take me there now?"

"Ah, no. The nurse is in Antsalova. He has to treat the people there."

"When's he back?"

"Tomorrow night, with luck."

"And without luck?"

"Maybe the next day."

"The next day." Somewhere a cockerel crowed. Kirk had the impression that some divine force was willfully obstructing him from ever getting to the rig.

"Would you like a beer?" Mani asked.

They sat outside while one of Mani's children ran off to the bar. All around them, in the pink evening light, the mud huts were turning deepest magenta.

"There's no one here with a motorbike?" Kirk asked.

"Motorbike is no use on these tracks. Too much sand."

Kirk threw a stone at the rainwater tank. A pig rushed out from behind it and escaped between the gnarled wooden posts of the fence. Sand was not the only problem. As he remembered it, the journey to the rig was a nightmare of rock and savannah and overgrown tracks. He had no alternative but to wait for a vehicle.

"So you're sure this fellow from the clinic'll be back tomorrow night?"

Mani smiled confidently. "Almost sure," he said.

The local hotel was a blue cement shack with a wooden veranda and a sign outside that read HOTELY. The best room contained a single iron bed, a torn mosquito net and a homemade wardrobe carved with native designs.

Kirk slept badly and woke at dawn. Light was streaming through the shirt he had hung across the window. He sat for a while on the edge of the bed, scratching his insect bites, then pulled on his shorts and went for a run.

He did some more exercises while he was waiting for breakfast—push-ups and sit-ups on the cement floor of his bedroom, then pull-ups on the wooden lintel of the veranda.

Later in the morning he walked around the village, but there was nothing happening, and the women in the little market had nothing to sell—a few bars of soap, some strips of cloth, a jumble of outdated drugs and cosmetics. He found one thing he could use—a length of fishing line—and in the afternoon he sat as he had sat as a youngster dangling a worm in the river. Fifty yards downriver a girl slapped her laundry on the warm, flat stones. Another filled a bucket with water, balanced it on her head, and walked up the baked steps that had been cut into the mud of the river bank.

He'd intended to fish for only an hour, but he stayed there all day, watching the women come down the steps from the village, putting worms on his hook, and watching his bit of cork float down river. Sun filtered through the overhanging trees and scintillated on the water. He caught nothing all day, but it didn't bother him.

Next morning he heard that the male nurse from the clinic had finally arrived back in town.

The clinic's vehicle had once been a Toyota Landcruiser. The engine was leaking oil. The tires were bald and lacerated so badly that in places the inner tubes showed through. There was almost no brake or clutch fluid left in the reservoirs, and there was a worrying amount of play in the steering wheel. On a drive around the square, Kirk found that the vehicle pulled to the right, and the back end had a tendency to drift on corners. When he got out and slammed the door, a shower of rust fell out from under the wheel arches.

"Not a very good vehicle," Mani observed.

"It's a piece of shit," Kirk said. "How much does he want?"

"A hundred dollars for the day."

"I'll give him a hundred for two days."

"Self-drive?"

"Why, are you volunteering?"

"Aee, no!"

The road beyond the village had been forged by bush taxis: tiny converted Peugeot vans, crammed with villagers. After an hour on the track, Kirk passed one of these battered, overloaded vehicles coming the other way, then nothing for the rest of the morning.

Up on the savannah, the countryside rolled on endlessly toward the limestone plateau in the north. He'd last driven this road in the dry season, when the grass was low and sparse. Now it brushed the window sills and dragged under the chassis. Kirk drove carefully, listening to every creak and squeak of the suspension, skirting around the gaping red potholes that appeared in the laterite surface of the road, and accelerating over the long stretches of soft sand where the heavy, underpowered Landcruiser often threatened to stall.

By midafternoon he had reached the second river.

Kirk stopped the Landcruiser and left the engine running. When he'd last been here, the river was dry. Now it was two feet deep and about twenty yards wide. Kirk glanced up and down the banks, looking for crocodiles, then waded on through the warm, chocolate-colored water.

The river bottom felt solid beneath his feet. The worst part of the crossing was actually the far bank—a stony ridge just wider than the vehicle, which fell away sharply to the right. Kirk stood on its summit. There was a collection of mud huts on the next escarpment. Beyond that, a thin band of jungle stretched across the horizon.

He rolled a boulder off the road, then waded back through the river. At the Landcruiser he checked the height of the exhaust and the clearance of the sump; then he climbed back in and restarted the engine.

The battery was almost flat, and he had to try several times before the engine would catch. Kirk pumped the clutch, forced the gear selector into low, then eased the rattling, creaking wagon down the riverbank and into the water.

In midstream the engine spluttered. Kirk declutched, revved, gave it some choke, and it scrambled on. The water was deeper than it looked. If he failed to get up the ridge, he would find it difficult to reverse back into the river without submerging the exhaust. Kirk looked up from the water, judging the height of the far bank, and saw two nomad children on its summit, standing in the center of the track.

Kirk leaned out of the window and yelled at them to move. They watched him, standing motionless, hand in hand. The boy was about seven years old. He wore a pair of faded pink shorts. His little sister was naked except for a string around her belly.

The rise was only a few yards away. He couldn't stop now. Kirk put his foot down on the accelerator and leaned on the horn. The big vehicle lunged out of the river and up the rocky slope. He saw the children scramble to one side and disappear behind the summit. The Landcruiser hit an outcrop of rock, and the jolt bounced him off his seat. When he regained his balance, the front wheels were rearing over the summit. The vehicle lost traction for a moment, then the tires gripped suddenly on the narrow plateau, pitching the vehicle forward into the downslope. Kirk stamped on the brakes, but nothing happened. He wrenched the wheel around, following the rocky path of the road. The Landcruiser teetered precariously to one side, and Kirk glimpsed, out of his nearside window, the two native children standing in the drainage ditch to his left. He saw them shrink into the dry thorny undergrowth as the Landcruiser hung above them. Then the front nearside wheel hit a termite mound, wrenching the steering wheel from his grip and throwing the Landcruiser back onto the track. Kirk hit the windscreen and fell back. The engine stopped abruptly, and the Landcruiser seemed to sink forward on one knee.

Kirk sat back in the driver's seat. He prized his hands off the steering wheel. The children had scrambled out of the ditch and were gazing at him in wide-eyed silence. Kirk tried the engine again. It restarted on the second attempt, but the Landcruiser wouldn't move.

He got out and walked around the front of the vehicle. Crouching underneath, he saw that the front offside suspension had completely sheared through. The tire was flat and pressed into the wheel arch. There was nothing to be done with it.

Kirk shifted into neutral and, by manipulating the steering wheel, was able to nudge the Landcruiser down the slope into the drainage ditch. Then he slung his carryall over his shoulder and, with the children trotting behind him, continued along the road on foot.

At the little cattle-herders' village on the escarpment he traded in his spare jeans for a bed for the night. Next morning they gave him some bread and fried fish for breakfast and some boiled water for his water bottle. Kirk left the bare dusty village behind him and set off to cover the last fifteen miles on foot.

The edge of the forest was farther away than he had estimated. At ten o'clock he was still toiling toward it across the wide, baking savannah. Flies fussed around his face and sweat collected underneath the strap of his shoulder bag.

Slap, slap, slap. His shoes fell on the parched surface of the track. A buzzard wheeled and circled in the rising heat.

"Never let your head drop," his sergeant major used to say. "If you let your head drop, you look tired, and if you look tired, you start feeling tired." Kirk fixed his gaze on the approaching wall of the jungle and kept walking at the same even pace, feeling the yards and miles disappear under the soles of his trainers. Maybe this would be his last job for a while. He had enough in the bank now to relax. Maybe he'd go abroad—somewhere like the Seychelles or Sri Lanka, find a place to hang out, do some diving or a bit of sailing. He had always fancied that he might buy a bar somewhere, marry a local girl, maybe run a scuba-diving school. There was a place along the coast from Hikkaduwa where he'd been happy for a while—a coral reef, hard white sand, turtles on the beach.

The wall of trees drew closer. The sun was directly above. The cool of the jungle beckoned him.

Have no doubts. Feel no pain. Show no fear. As the big trees drew slowly closer, his feet kept up the rhythm on the baked dirt of the track. If this was going to be his last job, he needed first of all to survive it. And if he was going to survive it, then he needed to be in the mood. He needed anger. He needed hate.

Hate made the world go round. Hate gave him purpose. Hate gave him energy. Kirk felt thirsty, but he didn't stop to drink. He needed the thirst. He needed the discomfort. He began to concentrate now on the way the sides of his trainers chafed his ankles, on the tiny insects that fussed around the sweaty margins of his hair. He concentrated on the sunburn on the back of his neck and the dull ache in the soles of his feet. He remembered now the days spent kicking his heels in the Ramada Renaissance Hotel, of the hours reconnoitering Spence's house. He thought about the week he'd spent waiting in Edinburgh, the long haul back to Madagascar. Two more days hanging around Antananarivo with only the whores in the Hilton Hotel for company.

He'd been wasting his time. He'd been letting himself go soft.

He was entering the jungle now, the parallel tire tracks stretched ahead. Kirk's pace quickened. His trainers ate up the yards. Hate smoldered inside him and caught fire. He thought now of all the things he most disliked in the world—those smug rich Englishmen who ruled Scotland, intellectuals, French tourists, jazz musicians, army drill, Japs, landladies, tax collectors, NCOs, Paddys, wops, skinny-hipped pop stars, game-show hosts.

He walked faster, following the faded tracks through clay and bog and leaf mulch, ignoring the branches, the insects, the pools of stagnant mud. As the sun lowered itself into the trees, he felt his hate continue to grow and swell until it was possible · to convince himself that Spence was responsible for divorce lawyers, herpes, bureaucracy, tearful women, social workers, screaming kids.

Spence, whoever he was, was to blame for all of these things.

Spence was dead.

He heard the rig before he saw it. But what he heard was not the mechanical hum he'd expected, but a roaring and bellowing, like a huge beast in pain—a terrible howl of metal grinding metal as a thousand feet of steel pipe were allowed to slip, then checked, then allowed to slip again. Kirk left the path, walked for fifty yards through the trees, and parted the foliage.

Two hundred feet of illuminated steel now dominated the

clearing, as incongruous as the Eiffel Tower among the ancient trees. Lights were suspended in the steelwork, reflecting the vast reservoir below it. Steam rose from the machines and the mud pits, mingling with smoke from the generators and forming lambent clouds around the huge gray legs of the sub. Above this a tiny figure stood on the drilling platform. At this distance Kirk couldn't make out his face, but he knew with a killer's instinct that this was his man. Kirk ducked back into the trees and began slowly to skirt the clearing.

Chapter 30

The drilling crew had started work before dawn and had been tripping pipe all day: throwing in the slips, swinging in the tongs and hauling on them till they bit, spinning off the kelly, then manhandling the next section of pipe over the neck of the last one. All day the huge traveling block thundered up and down inside the derrick, the steel pipes came swinging across the drill floor, the pipe spinner wheezed and belched, the tongs swung back on their chains and clanged against the derrick.

They'd kept up the punishing pace for fourteen hours. Spence hadn't once dared to stop. If they stopped rotating, there was danger that the bit would get stuck in the hole. Normally he could pull back and just circulate the mud till the crew got some rest, but his supply of mud was already running low and to leave the drill idling would further deplete the tanks. As the afternoon wore on, the crew moved in a daze, stumbling into the massive tongs and leaning on them as they steered them against the pipe. Often they didn't have the strength to make the teeth bite and needed to haul them back and swing them in again.

Spence stood at the brake handle, pressing on the lever that allowed the drill pipe to drop, foot by precious foot. He kept one eye on the mud pressure and one on the drill weight, listening for any change in the noise of the machinery, shouting instructions to the floormen. As each length of pipe disappeared into the hole, the floormen would clamp its neck, then manhandle the next section over it. Then, using the rotation of the drill floor, they would spin the two sections together till the threads locked. As exhaustion set in, a careless driller could mangle a floorman's hand or chop off a finger; and as the sun set behind the derrick, Spence felt truly exhausted, mentally and physically. He no longer felt that he was running the rig—the rig was dominating all of them, this angry behemoth, standing astride their tiny platform, yelling its discontent across the jungle.

Now it was almost over. Half an hour previously they had drilled through the ESCV packer—the rubber and alloy bung that supported the bulk of the cement. There could not be more than thirty feet to drill. This length of pipe would probably be the last they required. Spence sent one of his floormen to watch the Koomey. He had already sent one of the remaining two men to keep an eye on the mud pit. That was fifteen minutes ago, and the man still hadn't returned. Spence knew he would soon need help on the drill floor. With one eye on the clock, he sent his last helper to look for the missing man. Alone on the drilling platform, he now watched the traveling block inch toward him down the derrick. All noise was drowned by the draw-works engine, and around this brilliant floodlit stage the whole world seemed to be holding its breath. The jungle was lost in the darkness. A warm, constant wind was blowing from the direction of the camp, giving the impression that the whole universe was rushing past them—this brilliant tower the only constant point in the shifting cosmos.

The ground below the rig was cross-hatched with the shadows of girders. From his vantage point high on the platform Spence scanned it once more, but his men were still nowhere to be seen. He could make out the gleam of water in the pit, the outline of a crane, the lowered blade of a bulldozer, and now, emerging from the steam above the mud tanks, a stranger.

Spence tied the brake handle to the automatic driller and limped across to the railing. He had thought for a moment that it was Hanssen, returned from Morondava, but he saw now that it wasn't. It was a blond European man whom, at this distance, Spence couldn't recognize. Spence looked along the edges of the mud tanks, but he saw no sign of the African rig hands. He looked back to the stranger, who now started climbing toward the drilling floor. As he did so, Kirk looked up, and their eyes met.

Spence hobbled back to the brake and retrieved the flare gun. He put in two cartridges and snapped the muzzle shut. When Kirk reached the drilling floor, Spence was waiting for him.

"Mr. Spence." Kirk stopped at the top of the steps. He seemed pleased with himself. "Jees. I canny tell you the trouble I've had finding you."

"Stop right there."

Kirk seemed to notice the gun for the first time. "Any chance of a drink?"

"Who are you? What are you doing here?"

"The name's Kirk. I came to give you some advice."

Spence glanced at the walkways behind him. Kirk seemed to be alone. A warning light was flashing on one of the dials on the drilling console. The mud pressure was rising.

"Different from this, though." Kirk turned toward him, moving a fraction closer. "Cold as fuck. I used to think all oil rigs were at sea. Did you put all this up yourself?"

"Just get back down these steps, mister. I don't have time for talking."

Kirk took another step forward along the line of the railing. His back was to the halogen lamps. Steam rose around him like a shroud. "I came to help you."

"Bullshit. You were down at Morondava when the plane crashed. You're part of this whole thing. Who are you working for?"

"British intelligence."

"That's bullshit too."

"You want my army number? You want my rank? Ask me. Try me."

To his right the drill pipe dropped a foot, and the brake screamed.

"I want you to get off this platform," Spence said.

Kirk seemed calm. "I'm telling you. You don't know who you're up against. I know who caused that plane crash. I know about Norco. If you listen to me, you might just get out of here alive."

"I'm going to count to three."

"I've been following you, Spence. I've been gathering information. I know what you've been through. I know about Cora Skipton."

"One."

"And there's more you don't know about, pal. If we sit down and talk, I can help you get out of this."

With his thumb Spence cocked back the hammer on the flare pistol. "Two," he said.

As he spoke, the drill penetrated something, and the traveling block above their heads lurched down another foot. Instinctively Spence turned to the drilling brake, and Kirk pounced.

Spence was driven back against the drilling console. Kirk had both hands on his wrist. Spence got in a punch with his left hand, but Kirk ducked under it and slammed Spence's hand once, twice, on the metal railing. The pistol went off, and a ball of red magnesium went careening through the metal walkways and into the mud pits far below.

The gun recoiled upward. As Kirk grabbed at it, Spence sent him sprawling. Kirk fell back, the gun skidded out the lip of the rig platform and down through the substructure.

There was a pipe wrench hanging on the railing. Kirk's hand closed around it. There was blood on his lip now. He looked pleased.

Around them the rig roared and creaked. Spence was un-
armed. He cast around for an escape route, but there was no
way he could descend the far steps and run across the uneven,
muddy ground before the stranger caught up with him. His
eyes lit on a sledgehammer lying in front of the gap in the open
railings called the V-door. Spence hopped around the rotary
table, dropped his walking stick, and took the neck of the
sledgehammer in his free hand.

Kirk was already ducking under the mud pipes, coming
around the other side to meet him, adjusting his grip on the
pipe wrench.

Spence edged away from the V-door and leaned against
the railings. He realized now that the sledgehammer was an
impossibly cumbersome weapon. The first swing would throw
him completely off balance.

Kirk realized this too. He stopped on the other side of the
V-door, waiting for Spence to make a move. Thirty feet below,
their shadows confronted each other across the pipe racks.
Spence raised the sledgehammer to shoulder height. His hands
and arms were shaking in anticipation.

"You're working for Hunter, aren't you?"

"No idea, pal. I was just told to stop you drilling."

Above them the traveling block shuddered and descended
again.

"Let me past," said Spence, "and I'll shut her down."

"Sure you will," said Kirk, not moving.

The brake creaked. The string of pipe vibrated.

"We're almost through to the bottom. If I don't shut her
down, the well could blow."

"Is that a fact?"

"We're sitting on an oil reservoir here. If anything goes
wrong, the whole rig could melt like a candle."

"Keep talking," said Kirk, edging forward.

Spence took a pace back and found himself alongside the
air-powered winch. He sidled around behind it. To his right

was the steel ladder up to the monkey board. To his left was the railings. There was nowhere to go but upward, and anyone could climb faster than a one-legged man.

Kirk took another step toward him, and Spencer raised the sledgehammer above his head. There was no way he could hope to win a fight. His floormen were still nowhere to be seen— maybe the blond man had already dispatched them. Spence judged the length of his swing. His eyes were still on Kirk, but in one corner of his field of vision he could just see the winged nut that connected the air hose to the winch. Spence braced himself and brought the hammer down on it with all his strength.

The union spun apart, and the two-inch rubber pipe blasted free, whipping across the drill floor under five hundred pounds per square inch of compressed air. Kirk leaped back just as the steel connector whisked past his knees, clubbing dents in the metal railings and striking sparks off the drill floor. Behind the flailing rubber Spence fumbled with the greasy, clumsy buckle of the derrick climber.

The safety harness was connected by a pulley to a metal weight that ran down inside the derrick. It was not intended to hoist a man, only to partially counterbalance his weight as he got off the superstructure. To move upward out of Kirk's reach, Spence had to kick with his good leg and pull with his arms, hopping from rung to rung on the narrow metal ladder. It was faster than he could have managed unaided, but it was still slower than a fit man could climb. From twenty rungs up he saw Kirk negotiate the flailing hose and come after him.

Spence dropped the sledgehammer. It missed, bounced off the railing, and clattered through the steelwork to the ground far below. Spence didn't wait to watch it. He was climbing now, hauling himself upward with both hands, bruising his shins on the metal rungs. If he could reach the monkey board, he could escape on the geronimo line. But Kirk was already gaining, and the geronimo line was designed to be used by derrickmen—the industrial equivalent of trapeze artists—not by exhausted cripples.

Spence hauled with his hands and pushed with his good leg.

Forty feet, fifty. Above the level of jungle canopy the hot night wind came whipping through the wires. Breathlessness was making his head spin. He felt himself shaking and realized now that the derrick itself had begun to vibrate—the traveling block was moving again. As Spence climbed, the kelly spooled past him, descending to the floor. The automatic driller had drilled right through the plug. Whatever was down that hole was being held in place now by the weight of the mud alone.

Spence kicked with his leg and pulled with his arms. He had to get down. If the rig blew, they were both dead.

Kick and pull, kick and pull.

Unrelated, crazy pictures raced through his mind.

Cora in a cloud of soya flour, feeding the hogs.

Dennis with a golf putter scraping the elk droppings off the putting green before he could shoot the ball into the hole.

Skippy and him, years ago, driving Ski-doos around the surface of the lake. Shouting, hallooing, laughing like madmen.

Kick. Pull.

Kick. Pull.

He was tiring. Kirk was gaining. Spence glanced down through the white web of the derrick. A hundred feet below him the traveling block, supported on its cables, hit the drilling platform and crashed out through the V-door. The whole derrick shuddered. Spence tore his eyes away and pulled himself upward. He fancied that he could hear his pursuer breathing, louder than the wind, louder than the batting wires.

Kick. Pull.

He remembered Perpetude undressing him.

Kick. Pull.

Her eyes widening as he penetrated her.

"Tell me your name."

"Perpetude."

"Tell me your name."

"Perpetude," she whispered.

Kick. Kick.

His foot appeared to be trapped.

Turning, Spence saw that Kirk had grabbed his ankle. Spence summoned all his energy, jerked his foot away, and, to his horror, saw the ladder in front of him begin to separate from the derrick.

In his haste to get the derrick up and running, Spence had been unable to supervise every little detail. A hundred feet above the floodlit metal of the drilling platform, the safety ladder was not bolted to the framework of the derrick. Opposite Spence's hands the angle irons were held in place by one-inch nuts alone. Their bare threads were slipping through the holes in the girder.

Below him Kirk hammered his calf with one fist. The bolts slipped another quarter of an inch.

"No. She's coming away."

Kirk couldn't hear him. His fist kept hammering into Spence's good leg. Spence kicked back with his heel. Spence kicked again with his good foot. His wasted leg gave way, and for an instant he was clinging to the rung with his hands. One bolt in front of him sprang free, the other grated, held, then exploded past his ear, as the ladder began slowly to drift backward. Spence made a last despairing grab for the bottom of the next section, but it was already outside his reach. They swayed crazily. Far below, the tiny derrick platform seemed to spiral around the base of the tower. Kirk released his leg, yelled, swore, drifted away from him. Spence let go and launched himself into space.

The harness of the derrick climber gripped under his arms and dragged him clear of the metalwork, swinging him around in a wide, crazy arc and clubbing him against the girders of the derrick. As he was lowered, spinning, to the drilling platform, he saw his assailant, still gripping the detached section of the ladder, arc outward from the rig and crash through the shale shakers into the mud pit beyond.

Dazed, bruised, sprawling on the drill floor, Spence fumbled with the buckle of his harness. His fingers were like putty. He limped across to the control panel and checked the pump pressure. He spooled back the traveling block till it hung just a few feet off the rotary table, then cut the pumps and watched the pressure drop to around zero. He opened the HCR valve, closed the Hydril, retrieved his walking stick and headed for the steps.

At the edge of the mud pits he found two of his three floormen. One seemed to be regaining consciousness. Another was sitting with his head between his knees and a bloody rag pressed to his head. The illuminated rig was reflected in the water. Ripples were still spreading from the twisted length of derrick ladder. Next to where it pierced the glassy surface Spence could dimly distinguish the form of a man.

He kicked off his boots and half swam, half waded, toward it. The fluid in the mud pit was warm as blood, thick with barite and pungent with chemicals. Kirk was floating facedown. Spence managed to grab an arm of his clothing and drag him toward the shore. He staggered up the steep bank and collapsed next to his victim. A gelatinous fluid clung to his hair, his skin, and his clothes. He could see now that the same black film covered the whole surface of the reservoir. It was not just effluent from the drilling. It was oil. They had struck oil.

Chapter 31

As Spence drove over the salt flats into Morondava, the charcoal sellers were walking homeward. They parted to allow his vehicle to pass. The African driver stopped opposite the Grand Hotel, and Spence climbed painfully out, then the pickup pulled away, leaving Spence standing on the hotel veranda.

"Perpetude?"

His voice died in the soft timbers of the Grand Hotel. There was no reply. Spence walked through the marbled foyer and through the courtyard to her room at the back. He knocked on the door and tried the handle. Inside, the blinds were closed, her bed was neatly made. Spence closed the door carefully and limped back through the courtyard. The old man Amin Bahera had materialized in the center of the dining room.

"I'm looking for Perpetude."

"*Elle n'est pas ici.*"

"Madame Peyrame."

"*Pas ici. En vacance.*"

"She's still on holiday?"

"*Oui.*"

"When's she coming back?" Spence asked, but could get no reply.

He signed in, bought a beer, then walked down to the sea

and lay on his back in the shallows, letting the water massage his battered body.

Afterward he walked along the beach to the estuary and back through the palm groves to the docks on the riverbank. He sat on a bollard looking out over the silted harbor, trying to imagine the place as Perpetude once described it—a thriving port, a market town for the plantations upriver. With some money and a bit of motivation a mechanic like himself would be able to salvage quite a lot of the old machinery—these little dockside cranes, the dredger rusting at anchor.

"There you are," a voice said.

Spence turned. "Hi, Morgan."

"What happen to my swamper? He's got a gash in his head five-inch long."

"He was hit with a pipe wrench. They sent a man to stop us drilling."

"So where this fellow now?"

"He's dead. We buried him up there."

For once Morgan Hanssen was speechless.

"It was an accident," Spence said. "He came after me up the derrick and fell off. He was trying to kill me. It was either me or him."

"Holy cow. Who do you think sent him?"

"Hunter. There's oil there. We found oil."

"Holy cow," said Morgan Hanssen again. "You going to be a national hero."

"I wouldn't bank on it. Norco still has a whole lot of influence here. I still have to convince the government I'm telling the truth."

"How do you plan to do that?"

"I guess I'll fly up to the capital tomorrow and try to talk with someone." Spence regarded the cuffs of his own tattered work shirt.

"Might see you up there. I'm coming up for the elections," Hanssen cackled. "Besides, there's couple of little honies I haf to visit."

They walked together back to the hotel. Spence said, "I heard Perpetude's not back yet."

"I bet you was looking forward to seeing her after all that."

Spence squinted at the sun through the palms. Yes, since leaving the rig he had been aching to see Perpetude. But also, he reflected, he had been dreading it. Dreading that she would not be the desirable woman he remembered. Dreading even more that she would be.

That night he slept in her bed. Next morning he went to the post office and telephoned the capital. To his surprise his call got through, and he managed to leave a message at the Ministry for Mineral Resources for Velo-André.

The sun set behind him as the Dakota flew toward the capital, casting bizarre shadows among the crumpled hills below. If Spence looked at them for long enough, it was possible to believe that these strange black shapes had some magical significance, like tea leaves in a cup or the shapes that Eskimos cast with seal bones.

Darkness fell, and the shadows of hills gave way first to the black geometry of paddy fields, then to the scattered bonfire of the town.

Spence walked along the tarmac to the terminal building. A line of people was leaning over the railing above him, waiting for the 747 from France. Velo-André was not among them.

He joined the queue outside domestic arrivals. Behind him the darkness was filled with the roar of jet engines. There was a young girl in front of him wearing a red dress with a bow at the neck. She clutched her father's leg and smiled shyly at him, as though she alone shared his secret. Spence smiled back at her.

"Mr. Spence."

A young gendarme was standing at his elbow. *"Suivez-moi, s'il vous plaît."*

"Did Velo send you?"

"Allons." The policeman set off across the front of the

airport building. Spence hesitated, then followed. The little girl with the bow on her dress waved bye-bye.

There was an unmarked car parked just inside the airport. The security gates had been opened to let it through.

"Velo-André?" Spence said as they approached.

The policeman opened the door. *"Entrez."*

"You're taking me to Velo-André."

"Oui. Velo-André," the policeman said.

Spence ducked inside. There was another uniformed man sitting in the back of his car. The door shut behind him, and the other policeman leaned across to shake his hand. As he did so, he slipped a handcuff over Spence's wrist, then he tapped on the wire screen in front of them, and the car drove off.

Chapter 32

The cell they put him in was twelve feet square. It had a metal door and a crumbling concrete floor. The walls were whitewashed and decorated with graffiti. There was an abandoned hornets' nest in the far corner of the room. The bars were made from concrete-reinforcing rods—half-inch steel with a roughened spiral pattern on their surface. Sitting on the wooden bed, Spence could see a brilliant oblong of blue sky through the window on the opposite wall. Hauling himself up till his chin was level with the window ledge, he was able to see the perimeter wall of the prison, with the paddy fields that surrounded the town beyond it.

Sound traveled poorly in the heat. Occasionally he thought he could hear a distant voice or the sound of a car from outside, but when he shouted out, there was no reply. Nor was there any echo. His voice seemed to disappear in the still, dusty air above the exercise yard.

The first day, after he'd been shouting for two hours, a soldier came to his cell door and told him in broken English that if he continued to make a disturbance, they would move him downstairs to the basement.

A key turned in the lock, and an orderly, different from the one he saw yesterday, came in for his food tray. The fish was mainly bones in a thin, salty gravy. The manioc was a gray, congealed paste.

"I'm a Canadian citizen," he told the new orderly. "I need to contact my embassy."

"*Il est sourd,*" said a voice in the shadows. Beyond the door, in the dark, airless corridor that smelled of urine, a soldier was standing with a gun. "*Sourd,*" he said again, and pulled his earlobe to indicate that the orderly was deaf.

"I got a right to contact my embassy," Spence said. "I am Canadian." Then, because this seemed to cut no ice, he tapped himself on the chest and said, "*Américain.*"

The soldier spat on the floor. The deaf guard collected Spence's slops pail. His right hand had been badly burned in the past and was now an inflexible claw.

The slops pail disappeared into the corridor, and a new tin bucket came back. The soldier reached for his keys.

"Embassy," Spence said. "I have rights as a foreign citizen. I want to talk to a lawyer."

He moved toward the threshold of the cell, and the guard leveled his rifle at him. "*Asseyez-vous, monsieur.*" He gestured for Spence to sit and reached in his pocket for the keys.

"Why am I being kept here?" Spence raised his voice. "I want to see someone who speaks English. Hello." He shouted. "Hello!"

The guard swung the metal door shut, and Spence heard the bolt of the locks being shot home, then the footsteps and the rattling slops pail moved off down the corridor.

At night there came again the distant sound of car horns from the other side of the prison. Twice he saw the marigold flashes of fireworks in the night sky above the paddy fields. It was less than a week till the elections. He wondered if Velo-André knew he was here.

Spence returned to the low wooden bed. A cockroach crunched under his foot. Up here on the country's central plateau it was cold at night, but the ragged blankets they had given him smelled so unsavory that he preferred to try to sleep without them. He shifted on the loose canvas of the bed, trying to find a comfortable spot between the wooden struts.

Spence closed his eyes, but sleep would not come. It was impossible. He got up, picked up his walking stick, and hobbled backward and forward in the darkened cell, trying to exhaust himself. He walked four paces, then turned with his shoulder against the wall, then walked four paces back. Four then four, four then four. Moonlight shone through the high, narrow window and threw his shadow onto the metal door.

They wouldn't shoot him, he reasoned. They couldn't shoot a foreign citizen. Not around election time. But then the embassy had no idea he was in the country. And the few people, like Hanssen, who did know he was there could easily be persuaded that he had left. He wondered now if he should have gone to the authorities in Morondava, or tried to contact the international press from there. In his rush to get back to the capital, he had inadvertently played into his opponents' hands.

Four then four, four then four. His good leg was beginning to tire, and he lowered himself onto the wooden bed again. The car horns had stopped now, and the city was inaudible. A cicada on the warm stone outside his cell kept up its shrill alarm for a few more minutes, then fell silent.

Spence stretched out and lay shivering in the darkness. From somewhere far along the corridor he thought he heard the cell door of a fellow prisoner open, and the low murmur of a voice. Spence concentrated, straining his senses to pick up the sound. It hovered, tantalizingly, on the very limits of his hearing. For a moment it had sounded like someone speaking English.

The voice fell silent, then began speaking again.

"Bless you and keep you . . . "

Spence knew he hadn't imagined that. The person was speaking English. More—he recognized the voice. Spence struggled up from his bed. There was no support on the wall to grip, and he had to roll onto the floor, then lever himself to his feet. He hopped to the metal door and began banging on its pitted surface.

"Father Mitchell. Father Mitchell. Are you there? Hello. It's me—Spence. From Morondava."

There was no hatchway in the door. Spence dropped to his knees, put his cheek to the rough, dusty surface of the cement floor, and yelled through the gap underneath it. Then waited, breathing heavily in the pungent, musty darkness.

An insect scuttled across the floor of his cell. Even with his ear turned to the corridor he could hear nothing now.

The Lear Jet came in low over the capital of Madagascar, banking into line on the western approach, headlights blazing. It landed at the far end of the runway, where the MiG jets sat with tarpaulins over their engines, then it taxied back to the hangars. The logo on the door read, NORCO OIL.

Outside the hangars, a dark blue Range Rover pulled up, and Charles Hunter stepped inside. "You've got a new car."

"This? No, I've always had this," its occupant said in the darkness. "I use it for unofficial business."

Charles Hunter settled back as the big car rolled past the front of the airport building, turning down the long, gentle incline to the paddy fields and the outskirts of the town.

"Good flight?"

"Passable. Where's Spence?"

"Safe. We locked him up."

"Thank God for that."

The Range Rover cruised on, past a village band practicing for the election celebrations, past a row of wooden kiosks illuminated by neon tubes. "So what's the quickest way to get rid of him?"

"Get rid of him?" Istasse hitched up the sleeve of his jacket and wound his watch. The Range Rover skipped a pothole. He turned, and the neon light from the shops opposite caught his face. "I don't think I can do that, Charles."

The car headlights picked out a donkey in the middle of the road. The driver swerved and sounded his horn.

Hunter said, "Do you have an alternative suggestion?"

"He's a foreign national. Officially he's in prison for employing people without a work permit. He's committed no crime against the state. Certainly nothing that qualifies for the death sentence."

"Istasse, I don't think you quite understand. This fellow knows everything. He knows we sabotaged that plane. He knows we—"

"We?"

Hunter fell silent for a moment and ran a finger under the collar of his shirt. "He knows your accident investigators lost the evidence," he said carefully.

"They didn't lose it. I'm sure they could still find it somewhere."

"Claude, I'm not sure what I'm hearing here. What are you saying to me?"

"I am telling you. No—I am reminding you, Charles, that this was never a political conspiracy. The state never knew about it, and the agents of the state were never involved. I've always been quite clear about that. Now I'm prepared to keep Spence out of the way until you plan what you're going to do with him."

"You mean till after the elections."

"But I have not and will not be involved in the..." He searched for a word. "The covert aspects of this arrangement."

Hunter smiled without humor. He brushed the blond hair back from his forehead. It was clear now why Istasse had collected him in an unmarked car rather than the government limousine he was used to, and why this conversation was taking place in transit rather than at Istasse's home.

"You're dropping me in it?"

"No," Istasse said. "I am merely maintaining my position."

Hunter felt his anger building. He cracked his knuckles.

Outside, some charcoal sellers walked in front of them, black sacks balanced on their heads.

"Tell me," Hunter said at last, "why do I have the feeling that I've been doing all your dirty work for you?"

Istasse was unrepentant. "You've been doing your own dirty work, Charles. However much I might have benefited."

"We had an arrangement."

"We had an understanding," Istasse said. "It's quite a different thing."

Hunter studied a fingernail. He had hit it with a hammer while fixing some shelves at home, and the upper half had turned purple. His instinct now was to reach across and grab Istasse by the lapels; instead he ran his thumb over the irregular surface of the fingernail, then pressed it quite deliberately until he could no longer tolerate the pain.

Istasse said, "I was talking to an old girlfriend of mine a few weeks ago. Madame Peyrame from Morondava. Perhaps you met her once. She was comparing the art of seduction to the art of politics. Implying more than you say. Of that, I accept, I may have been guilty."

"You realize"—Hunter's voice was level—"that if I go under, I could easily take you with me."

"I doubt it," Istasse said. "What would you say? That I asked you to withhold the oil find from Velo-André? I'll say that you were merely waiting for a more reliable administration to come into power and that I knew nothing of your designs—which is more or less the truth, isn't it? I don't know about the West, but over here people are still inclined to think the worst of multinationals, so in the final analysis I've probably got more credibility than you have. Actually you're probably worrying unnecessarily. Mr. Spence has nowhere to go. I heard that back in Canada he is wanted on a murder charge."

"They dropped it. The hospital had his blood group from the injury to his leg. It didn't match the killer's."

"In that case," Istasse said, "it seems you're the only person with a grudge against him."

Hunter reached in his pocket and pulled out a gilt-edged card. It was the official invitation to Istasse's election-day banquet. He tore it in half and put it in the ashtray. It was the kind of gesture to which only a beaten man would resort, but then they both knew he was in a no-win position. According to the *Economist Intelligence Monthly,* the Madagascar election result was now virtually a foregone conclusion. At this late stage, if Hunter suddenly pulled out, Istasse could sell his oil concessions to one of a dozen other companies. Hunter's only chance of doing business, as Istasse well knew, was to continue to shoulder the responsibility himself. Whatever that entailed.

"So where would I find Spence now?" he asked.

Up ahead, the high walls of the state prison towered above them. Istasse nodded toward it as they rolled past. "Visiting hours are three till six."

Hunter got out at the Colbert Hotel. The Hilton was more modern, but the Colbert had more style. Also there was less chance that there he would run into any of his former business associates.

In his room he took a shower, then put on one of the hotel's bathrobes and sat on the balcony, looking out over the dimly lit town, the floodlit palace, and the oil lanterns moving like fireflies around the lake.

He had trusted Istasse. He had allowed himself to trust Istasse, and Istasse had exploited it. In Istasse's position Hunter would probably have done the same thing. Implying more than you say. Heckterman was the master of that. Hunter was quite adept at it himself.

Now he had a problem. He knew what the solution was, and all he had to decide was whether the risk was worth the gain.

Charles Hunter was not dissatisfied with his lot in life. As chief executive of Norco U.K. he presently wielded more power than ever before in the forty-seven years of his life, but it was nothing compared with the power he might enjoy as head of

Norco. Moreover, with the preferential share options that went with the presidency, the fortunes of the company would become his own personal fortunes. If, as he planned, Norco could be transformed from a minor player to one of the major international oil companies, Hunter would be not just one of the richest but also one of the most powerful men in the world.

This was the big game. This was Heckterman's kind of game: playing the faultless company man on the surface and swimming with the sharks after dark.

If he succeeded, no one would know. Very few people would even suspect. Robert Heckterman would guess. He had more or less guessed already. And if Hunter reeled in the Madagascar job, it would all be his—the presidency, the money, the power, the celebrity. It was all there. Twinkling. Just out of reach, like the city below him. And the price, the price Istasse had set, the price Istasse knew he could not resist, was a single killing.

Hunter walked into his room. He unlocked his slim case and took out the gun that lay between the pressed shirts. He felt its weight, smelled the clean oiled metal, balanced it in his hand. Outside, the city lights beckoned.

They had taken Spence's watch when he arrived, but from the height of the sun above the paddy fields, Spence judged it to be about eleven A.M. when he heard the keys outside the door.

The door swung partly open and jammed on the concrete floor.

"Father Mitchell."

Spence struggled to his feet and clutched the old missionary's hands. "Mitchell. Mitchell." He felt weak with gratitude. Behind them, in the darkened corridor outside, he could see the guard holding his rifle. "I figured you hadn't heard me."

Father Mitchell looked embarrassed by the warmth of the reception.

"Oh, yes. It just took awhile to get them to admit that you were up here. Sit down. Sit down." He turned to the guard.

"Une chaise, s'il vous plaît." Then he stood, waiting for the cha...
to arrive.

The missionary was wearing a cream-colored cassock, belted at the waist. There was a Bible in his hand under the capacious sleeves. The guard came in with a folding chair, and Mitchell sat on it.

"What are you doing here, anyway?" Spence asked. "Hanssen told me you were working for the government."

"The Assemblée Nationale. Yes, well, that's why I left Morondava." Mitchell leaned forward with the Bible on his lap, the blue from the window reflecting in his spectacles. "But I'm doing this as well now. Actually," he said, pulling on his nose and laughing, "you see, Perpetude was right in a way."

"Right about what?"

"Oh, she said I wouldn't enjoy doing nothing but committee work up here. Religious committees. The abstraction of an abstraction. She said I'd miss the practical side of my work in Morondava. You know—like being able to commission a new roof for the church or repainting the refectory. She always maintained that we undervalue these things."

"Have you seen her recently?"

"Perpetude? No. I got a card from her. She's in France."

"Is she coming back?"

"Oh, yes. She will always come back, Perpetude. She has such conviction. It's shaming, really. Anyway, that's why I'm here. Um. Being practical."

"Doing what?"

"This. Prison visiting. For just now anyway. To be frank, I've half decided to go back to Morondava. They never found a replacement, so I've reapplied for my own job there. Strange, isn't it? How you don't really recognize happiness till you lose it. Anyway I hear you've had a spot of bother."

Spence laughed. "You can say that again."

"Still, it's not all that serious. I'm sure you'll get off with a fine."

"A fine for what?"

"This work-permit business. They don't seem to be all that worried about you."

"Father Mitchell, they haven't told you half of it. There's oil in Morondava. Norco found oil in Morondava. I went back there, and we redrilled the well. They already killed the last drilling crew to keep it secret."

"Who did?"

"I've no idea. Could just be Norco. Could be political as well. They arrested me as soon as I stepped off the plane here. They didn't say anything about work permits."

"Oh, my." Father Mitchell took off his hat and fanned himself. His mottled brow was furrowed with concern. "Are you sure about this?"

"You think I'd make it up? Ask Hanssen. He should be up in the capital any time. You can go down to Morondava. Go down to the rig. There's a lake of oil there."

"My goodness." Father Mitchell looked behind him at the guard standing in the shadows of the corridor. "Well, um. My goodness. What do you think I should do?"

"First thing get a message out of here. Get word to the embassy. Get word to Velo-André. Once someone else knows I'm here, they can't kill me."

"Oh, come on now, I'm sure they wouldn't...Ha... They wouldn't do anything as drastic as that."

"You don't know half of it, Father Mitchell. They already sent a hit man after me once."

"A hit man." Father Mitchell scanned Spence's face for signs of madness. The guard walked into the cell and tapped his watch.

"*C'est fini,*" he said.

"*J'arrive, j'arrive.*" Father Mitchell stood up, fumbling for the pocket of his cassock, getting his bony hands caught in the folds of the sleeves. He finally found a notebook and a pencil. "You'd better give me your passport number." The guard took the notebook from him and wagged a finger.

"*Interdit,*" he said. He was already taking the missionary's chair out into the corridor.

"Just go to the embassy," Spence said. "Go to Velo-André, Minister for Mineral Resources. Velo knows I'm here. Talk to him directly. Don't leave a message. You have to talk to him directly."

"Of course. Of course I will." The missionary picked up his skirts and sidled out through the door. "I'll be back," he said, then the guard dragged the door over the concrete floor and slammed it shut behind him.

Chapter 33

The afternoon dragged on with no sign of Mitchell. A tiny procession of ants made their way under the door and diagonally across the floor of his cell, negotiating the contours of the crumbling cement. They picked up the bread crumbs that had fallen from his lunch plate and filed back under the door with them. Spence watched the sun slide down below the bottom right-hand corner of his window frame. Night fell. There was silence outside and silence in the corridor beyond his cell.

Outside, the searchlights illuminated the shards of glass on the top of the perimeter wall. The cicada near his window began its perpetual alarm. A winged beetle blundered around the walls of his cell, then found its way out through the window. Spence slept.

He was woken by a key turning in the lock.

"Father Mitchell?"

An armed guard stood outside. "*Venez,*" he said.

"What? Me? Come?"

The guard handed him his walking stick.

"Father Mitchell sent you? Minister?"

"*Oui, Minister,*" the guard said.

Spence laced his shoes and followed. The corridors were

of stained and cracking concrete, illuminated by naked bulbs, with rusting metal doors cemented into the wall.

They descended two floors on the metal staircases. From somewhere he could hear a prisoner shouting and beating on his door with a tin cup. They descended another floor, through two sets of ancient padlocked gates, then a third, more modern set with an electric locking system.

He came out into a high entrance hall, painted green with a noisy fan on the ceiling. A woman and two children sat on one of the wooden benches. They had the look of people who were accustomed to waiting. By the door an old man was stretched out asleep. There was a desk along one wall with a metal grille across it. The area of wooden desks and typewriters beyond it was abandoned but for a uniformed desk sergeant with luxuriant sideburns who passed Spence an envelope containing his wallet, watch, gold ring, and some loose change.

There were no forms to sign. At the far end of the entrance hall his guard unlocked the heavy embossed door. Spence could see a courtyard beyond, and beyond that the lights of traffic.

"Father Mitchell?" he asked, pointing outside.

The desk sergeant nodded.

"Velo-André?"

The desk sergeant nodded again and waved a hand toward the open doorway. The guard with the rifle had already lost interest; he was standing in a corner by the faded anti-AIDS poster, sharing a cigarette with a friend.

In the street outside there was an old black Peugeot parked with two wheels on the curb. Spence climbed into the front seat. The door catch and window mechanism on his side were damaged, so his door had to be closed from the outside. The chauffeur got in again, and they set off across town.

They had been gone for five minutes when an attaché rang from the Canadian embassy to be told that Mr. Spence had already been released on bail by a friend.

★   ★   ★

Along Soarana the poor were already bedding down under the iron arches of the railway station like so many pods of vanilla.

"Are we almost there?"

"Almost."

They had turned off the main road several streets back and were now negotiating a series of back streets. By the lights of paraffin lamps he saw a pig rooting in the gutter, a nursing mother, a wooden barricade around a hole in the road. Washing hung on a tree. A woman in a black brassière stood in a doorway.

"What do you call this district?"

"Ampefiloha."

For some reason it sounded familiar. The car turned one final corner, lurched over one more pothole, then stopped. The driver got out and opened Spence's door for him.

"Is this the place?"

The driver nodded.

Spence stepped out into the warm, pungent night.

"Which house?"

The driver turned to the lane beside them and made a gesture with his chin.

"Up there?"

"Yes."

"You wait here."

"Okay."

Spence began walking up the lane. It rose in shallow steps to a small, cobbled square. Behind him, beyond the car, he could see an orange light and hear what might have been a political broadcast transmitted over a cheap transistor radio. In front of him there was silence and darkness.

He could now see into the square. There was a tree at its center. Under the tree a man in a light suit was sitting on a bench.

"Father Mitchell? Velo?"

There was no reply. Spence took two more steps forward,

his cane tapped on the worn cobbles. "Velo?" he said again, and the man rose to his feet, taking his hand from inside his jacket.

"Hello, Spence," he said in perfect English as the moonlight shone across his face, and Spence recognized the features of Charles Hunter.

Spence took in the short, bulky gun in Hunter's right hand and remembered a time, months ago, when, lying at the foot of the V-door with the sky spiraling around him, he had believed himself to be on the threshold of death. Then as now he felt no fear and no sadness, only anger; that finally it should come to this, that he hadn't foreseen it, that everything would be finished so soon.

Hunter looked pale and dark-jowled, as though he were still suffering the combined effects of anxiety and jet lag. But now he smiled.

"I was worried for a while that you wouldn't come."

Spence turned and looked down the lane. The car was blocking its far end. Against the reflection of the moon on its side windows, Spence saw the reflection of Hunter's driver.

Spence said, "What do you want to talk about?"

"I don't want to talk," Hunter told him. "I just want to get rid of you. I thought I could rely on our friend Kirk, but it seems that in murder, as in everything else, if you want it done properly, you have to do it yourself."

"Killing me isn't going to solve anything, Hunter. There's oil down there, I've got my proof now."

"You don't have anything, Spence. That oil belongs to Norco. I plan to see that we keep it."

"Velo-André will back me up. As soon as he realizes I'm missing, he'll send a team of people down there to investigate."

"I'm afraid your friend Velo is busy trying to keep his political chin above water. He doesn't have time to look up old friends."

"I'm telling you, Hunter: everyone in Morondava knows there's oil there now. You just need to fly over that rig and you can see an inch of it floating on the mud pits." Spence wet his lips. His eyes were on the shadowed face, but all his attention was focused on Hunter's trigger finger. "A week from now the whole country's going to know about it."

"A week from now I don't give a damn who knows, Spence. Why do you think we kept the rig here?"

"You've done a deal with the opposition government."

"There." Hunter laughed without mirth. "You're using your brain now. Maybe you should have done some of that before we got started on this pantomime."

"You found oil, but you didn't get on with Velo's government."

"Do you blame me? You think I'm going to drop the biggest find this side of the Gulf into the hands of some Marxist who would nationalize as soon as we're producing? Now that he's on the skids, we can get a deal going with Istasse and exploit it properly."

"Assuming Istasse wins the election."

"He will. That oil find at Mansalava is the one thing that could have saved this government's bacon."

"So you killed all these people just to keep a secret?"

Hunter nodded.

In the half-light Spence scrutinized Hunter's face for any sign of guilt and saw none. He shook his head.

"We see things differently, Spence. You've spent your life grubbing around in the mud, drilling holes in the ground. There's a lot of people think that's what the oil industry consists of, but it's not. Oil isn't just the black stuff you get on your hands. Oil is energy. Oil is power. Look what it did for the Arabs. If you've got oil, you've got fate by the throat. You control the future of the world. The way Velo-André sees it, it's jobs for half a million paddy farmers, but it's a lot more than that. If this country becomes a major industrial power, it controls the whole of the Indian Ocean. Where else is there: Mauritius, Mozambique, the Seychelles . . . We're talking about commanding a quarter of the Southern Hemisphere. You think that's not worth the lives of sixteen men?"

Spence shook his head. "I don't see how it's anything to do with you, Hunter. You're like me, you're here to do a job. You don't have to rule the world."

"Somebody has to."

"Do they?"

Hunter raised the gun. Spence tensed. The hand that gripped his walking stick was slippery with sweat. There was nowhere to run to. Why was Hunter waiting? Was he deliberately prolonging Spence's agony? Was he gathering courage, or was it just the bullish English compulsion to prove himself right?

"I'll tell you this," Spence said. "I don't care who controls the world energy market. I don't even believe it matters. But you killed my friend, and I care about that. I would have stopped chasing you except that you had his wife killed too."

"Well, hopefully now my problems will be over," said Hunter amicably. Again there was no flicker of guilt. Spence wondered, irrelevantly, if Hunter was mad or just incapable of understanding life on anything other than the grand scale.

Spence said, "You can't shoot me here."

"Why not?"

"It's the middle of the town. It's too conspicuous."

"Actually it's the one place a shooting wouldn't be noticed. We're in the red-light district. White men get mugged here every day. If it happens anywhere else, there's a full-scale investigation, but this is no-man's land."

That's where he'd heard of Ampefiloha—it was the district where the American had lost his wallet and then his trousers. Ampefiloha was where Hanssen came on his trips to the capital, visiting his "little honies." Spence looked around the chipped walls and crumbling balconies. There was a joke about the man who dies in a whorehouse, but he couldn't remember it.

A second passed. If he rushed toward Hunter, it would only bring his death a moment sooner, and now every sliver of time seemed precious to him. He waited for the explosion, wondered what it would feel like and how long it would take him to die.

"Spence."

Someone had called his name. Spence roused himself as if from a dream. Hunter's concentration wavered, and Spence came forward, bringing his stick down hard on Hunter's wrist. The voice called his name again, but Spence had hurled himself into Hunter, knocking him over the wooden bench. He turned and looked desperately for the gun. Hunter's driver was running up the lane toward him. Someone was approaching from a lighted doorway. The revolver was nowhere to be seen. Then Hunter caught him behind the knees, and Spence crashed to the ground.

Falling, he saw the gun lying on a flagstone at the edge of the open sewer. Hunter saw it at the same time, and they reached it together. As they struggled, hand over hand, a third body launched himself on top of them both.

"Break it up. What the fuck's happening?"

"Hanssen!"

"Let go," said Morgan Hanssen. "I've got his neck."

Spence panted. "Get away. There's a gun."

"What gun?"

Hunter was lying on top of him. Spence could feel the cold metal between them. He had no idea if he was holding the handle or the barrel. Hanssen was behind Hunter, trying to haul him off, and now Hunter's driver appeared behind Hanssen. They began to separate. Spence could feel his fingers being prized from the gun, then there was an explosion between them that kicked Spence out of the melee and flung him across the cobbles. The deafening blast echoed around the square. Lying, gasping for air and looking at the sky, Spence felt his abdomen with his scorched hand. His shirt felt warm and mushy. Panicking, he tore at the fabric, prodding at the skin beneath. There was no wound. The night was full of voices. Hunter's driver was running back down the lane toward his car. Hanssen sat on the cobbles with his legs apart and an expression of dazed incredulity on his face. Spence looked around for Hunter and found him, kneeling, ghostly pale, contemplating the ragged hole in his own belly. As the crowd of underdressed women gathered around him, he keeled over, still staring blankly across the square, one hand trailing in the gutter.

Chapter 34

Spence sat under the front awning of the Centre Culturel et Sportif. Below him the tennis balls were bounding backward and forward across the nets. From the direction of the town came the sound of music and political invective, both given the same nasal monotony by cheap loudspeakers, both diminished and attenuated by the morning heat. He'd been coming here for the past three days, escorted at a respectful distance to and from the Hilton by a pair of uniformed policemen. They were standing by the gates now, sharing a cigarette. Spence saw them straighten as Velo-André came through, carrying a briefcase and walking, as he always did these days, as fast as his short legs would permit.

He smiled as he drew closer and sat down, breathing and perspiring.

"Steady on, Velo, you'll give yourself a heart attack."

"Ha. Then maybe Dr. David will prescribe me some repose." Velo-André took off his jacket and hung it on the back of the chair.

"Coca désinfecté?" Spence asked as the waiter approached.

"No, thank you," said Velo-André. "Committee meeting in fifteen minutes. I have not so much time. Listen. You were correct. There is oil in Mansalava."

"So our problems are over."

Velo-André smiled. "Your problems are over, my friend. My own problems have just commenced. *Regarde*." He took a newspaper from his briefcase and spread it on the table in front of them. On the front page was a grainy photograph of Istasse shaking hands with Charles Hunter. Beside it was a more recent photo of the incumbent president, Rakoutouson, in full regalia.

"What does it say?" Spence asked.

Velo-André brushed a fly away from his face. "It says that General Istasse, this fellow here, has deliberately misled the Alliance Centrale and is not fit to govern. It tells that he is being asked to stand down from office."

"I would have thought you'd be pleased at that."

Velo-André regarded the tennis players with envy. "Not so much," he said. "I was almost looking forward to being voted out. So much responsibility."

"You could resign."

"No, that would not be proper. The public now has trust in me. I must support the president. He needs loyal men around him."

There was a silence but for the birds twittering and the distant loudspeakers. Spence looked up and found Velo-André watching him intently. "Have you thought about staying here to work for us?"

"Yeah, I've thought about it, Velo, but I'm afraid my answer's still the same."

"Even for some months?" Velo-André asked.

Spence smiled. "That's just the problem," he said. "I'm scared that if I went down to Morondava, I'd never leave. I'd end up like Morgan Hanssen, growing old under a palm tree."

"There are worse ways to live."

"I guess," said Spence.

"Well, if ever you change your mind . . . "

"Sure, Velo, I'll let you know."

"In that case I will say farewell." Velo-André glanced at his watch and began buckling his briefcase. "During these days my time is not my own, but if you call, my driver will take you to the airport and assist with your departure."

"Really, I can manage, Velo. If you just tell the police that I'm free to leave the country, I'll be more than grateful."

"It is I who am more than grateful."

Spence stood, and the African gripped his hand. "I pray that you will change your mind."

"Don't say that," said Spence. "This place makes me superstitious."

At the driveway to Claude Istasse's house the electric security gates were locked. When Perpetude stepped down from the taxi, one of the armed paratroopers came across to challenge her.

She asked the taxi to wait, but the paratrooper told it to drive on. As a compromise the taxi driver rolled on another twenty yards and parked in the shade of the tamarind trees, nervously watching in his wing mirror as Perpetude remonstrated with the soldiers.

Finally one of the uniformed men went to talk into the intercom at the gate. Perpetude stood apart from the small knot of journalists, on the far side of the road, waiting for a response. It was hot out of the shade. She had arrived that morning from Paris and was still wearing the pleated skirt she'd worn for the journey.

After a while the guard signaled her across the road. They checked her bag before they allowed her through the gates. "Just a formality," he told her. For the moment Claude Istasse had many enemies.

She had never met Mimi before, but the woman matched quite well with her mental image of Istasse's wife—classic Western good looks, Parisian clothes, blond hair worn back from her face and held in place with her sunglasses. She was wearing a loose white shirt and holding a pen.

Perpetude introduced herself.

"Yes, I've heard about you. Claude's in the garden." They

walked through the house, which Mimi Istasse had designed herself. By daylight Perpetude was able to appreciate its refinement, but there was something about the spacious marble-clad interior that, like Istasse's wife, looked rather overplanned.

Istasse was sitting by the white wrought-iron table with a stack of papers in front of him. Topmost was the center spread from *Time* magazine, which Perpetude had read on the plane—there were large color photos of Hunter and Istasse and a smaller black-and-white insert of Velo-André.

Istasse looked up as she approached. There was no need to explain. He smiled philosophically.

"Would you like a drink?" his wife asked.

"Thank you, I'm not staying. I just came because the phone was off."

Mimi offered her a seat.

Istasse flicked a page of the article. "You know I had nothing to do with this." He was referring to the plane crash.

"I know. I didn't come to accuse you, Claude." She smiled. "You have enough people doing that already."

He looked relieved by her trust in him. He was taking things better than she had imagined. "You said something, Perpetude, last time we met. You said, 'Why spoil it all by running for president?'"

"You might run again."

He shook his head.

"Come on, Claude. In a couple of years this will all have blown over. You're young still. There aren't many men of your quality in Madagascar. Maybe this had to happen to you."

"Is that what you came here to tell me?"

"No. I came here to ask you where Spence is. The police are all full of self-importance. They say he's under their protection."

"Well, as far as I know, he's been staying in the Hilton." Claude Istasse looked at the date on his Rolex. "Actually I heard he was leaving today. Probably the three-thirty flight." There was a hint of triumph in his voice when he added, "You've just missed him."

Perpetude checked her own watch. She had seen the out-going plane at the airport when she arrived. Maybe its departure would be delayed. She stood up abruptly, pushing back the metal chair, not quite managing to conceal her anxiety.

"I'll, um . . . good-bye," she said. "I have to go."

Istasse smiled slowly. "Tell me, Perpetude, was there something between you and him?"

"We were friends. Will you say good-bye to Mimi for me?"

"Friends."

"I just want to see him before he goes," she said.

"You've forgotten your bag."

Clause Istasse held it out to her. When she took the strap, he held on for a moment longer than necessary. Long enough to grab her full attention.

"I could have had him killed, you know. That was my big mistake. Not having him killed."

Perpetude looked him in the eye, looked straight through the statesman's eyes, to the uncertain, impressionable student revolutionary who still lived behind them. "That was what you did right, Claude. Remember that. If there's any hope for this country, that was what you did right."

Then she ran away from him, through the open-plan dining room, toward the back door, her heels clattering on the pink marble floor.

Istasse lived on the opposite side of town from the airport. It took fifteen minutes to drive to the center of Antananarivo. Then the tunnel under the palace was blocked, and they had to take a detour around the lake. The center of the town was full of people. It seemed as though all the students who had once demonstrated against Rakoutouson were now demonstrating against the oil company, Norco.

In front of the medical school they got snared in another

demonstration. Students banged on the roof of the taxi, fire-crackers exploded on the pavements. The air was full of stream-ers and confetti. Hemmed in on all sides, the taxi crawled along at the same speed as the procession. Perpetude knew that if she left the taxi here, she would never find another one. It was another ten minutes before they reached the far side of the lake.

The Zuma was closed to traffic, blocking the road to the airport. Perpetude looked at her watch. It was already past the plane's departure time. She paid off the taxi and ran through the main square on foot.

The Friday market was still in progress—a forest of square umbrellas. Perpetude hurried through them, past a man selling lottery tickets, an old woman peddling her basket of scrawny ducks. Her heart was beating like a schoolgirl's. Children ran behind her, laughing, asking for money.

Her own breathless desperation astonished her. Why was she hurrying? Why did she want so badly to see him? Till now she would have said she had erased Spence from her mind. Her feet slipped on a piece of discarded mango peel, and she regained her balance. A Frenchman tipped his hat at her. The prostitutes clicked their tongues. She was running through the tourist end of the market now, past the stalls that sold trinkets, pressed flowers, and pictures assembled from dead butterflies. She ran past tables of tortoiseshell and embroidery, crocodile skin and crystals. Her heart pounded, her breasts hurt from running. She checked her watch again. If the plane had taken off, she would have heard it. Surely she would have heard it. A taxi hooted at her from the far side of the road, and she ran toward it.

Spence stood with Morgan Hanssen, dwarfed by the tall win-dows, on the gallery above the main hall. The 747 was parked so close that they could see the tiny figures of the captain and the copilot checking instruments in the cockpit. Hanssen drained his beer and looked down into the departure lounge. "You'd better go now," he said. "They yoost about ready to run."

Spence put his glass on the floor and led the way back down the steps. They fought through the press of travelers in the main lobby to the customs barrier.

"Well, Morgan," he said, "I guess this is where I thank you for saving my life."

"Yoost as long as you do something with it," said Hanssen. "Maybe when you get to my age you'll realize how stupid you was to leave this place."

"Maybe I will. Maybe I'll see you then."

"I hope not. You can't have this much fun and live past eighty. Here, don't forget your bag. Whaddaya want me to tell Pappatoot?"

"I wrote her a letter. Tell her . . . no, don't tell her anything. I guess I said it all." Spence picked up the carryall at his feet and walked through the opening in the barrier.

They searched his baggage, stamped his passport, tore his boarding pass, and ejected him onto the warm runway. The shrill noise of the engines filled the air. Forty yards away, at the foot of the gangway, an air hostess checked the time. Spence stopped halfway to the aircraft and looked back. Hanssen had returned to the gallery that ran across the central window. He was leaning on the rail and waving.

A woman had joined him.

Spence stopped and squinted into the reflections from the glass. It wasn't Perpetude. It couldn't be. He waved and called her name, but she couldn't hear him. The air hostess was beckoning him toward the gangway. Spence turned back and hurried toward the airport building.

"I've forgotten something," he told the girl at the door to the departure lounge.

"The plane is leaving."

"I'll only be five minutes."

"The plane is leaving now. Your baggage is on board."

"I don't have any baggage."

At the customs barrier a policeman barred his way.

"You must go back. The plane is departing."

"I must talk to someone."

"No time to talk, the plane is departing now."

"Just three minutes."

The policeman stepped aside, and a perfectly accented Frenchman carrying a walkie-talkie said, "Excuse me, to whom do you wish to talk?"

"*C'est moi qu'il cherche,*" said a dark voice. On the other side of the barrier stood Perpetude Peyrame. She looked flushed and beautiful, breathless and disheveled.

"Hello, Spence," she said.

Spence felt his heart turn over. "How did you get here?"

"I arrived today. The embassy said you were leaving."

The airport official began to interrupt her in French, but she held Spence in her eyes.

Spence said, "You were in France. I didn't know how to reach you."

"I know."

The airport official talked into his walkie-talkie and put his hand on Spence's shoulder.

"You must go," said Madame Peyrame. "Or they will close the doors."

If anything, she was more beautiful than he remembered her. She reached across the barrier to hold his hand. Her touch was like electricity, and when his hand closed around hers, he was unable to let go.

Spence pushed aside the barrier. He took her in his arms, and the crowd closed around them like the sea.

"Perpetude."

"Go," she said gently. "You must run."

"Forget it," Spence said.

"What?"

"We're going back to Morondava."

She laughed incredulously, then saw he was serious about

staying and pressed her head into the hollow of his neck.

Looking back, he saw the airport official make the most celebrated of all French gestures: raise his shoulders and lift his hands in the air. Then he, too, was lost from sight behind the people. Spence dropped his walking stick and picked up his carryall. Arm in arm, he and Perpetude made their way toward the door.